MORE THAN GOLD

Morgan wore her leotard and tights. She could explain she was heading for the gym to practice when she saw him. Jack gave her no need to explain. Neither of them spoke a word.

He walked directly to her, his gait easy, unhurried, his weight balanced. She had to look up as he approached. Morgan watched him, a dark Poseidon, a devil-God rising from the sea, advancing toward her, the light of the water in his eyes. Her heart beat so hard she was sure he could see her chest moving. Yet they continued to stare, one at the other.

He stopped in front of her. Too close. He breathed hard from physical exertion. Morgan felt the same although she had done none of the work that he'd performed while she watched his efforts.

Her eyes rose to Jack's. Gone was the coldness she'd always seen there. Gone was the hostility that normally greeted her when she found herself in his line of vision. His eyes were liquid, large brown circles that spoke to her without language, without tongue or teeth or movement. She heard his mind, his heart, his need for her already knew the words.

BOOK YOUR PLACE ON OUR WEBSITE AND MAKE THE ARABESQUE ROMANCE CONNECTION!

We've created a customized website just for our very special Arabesque readers, where you can get the inside scoop on everything that's going on with Arabesque romance novels.

When you come online, you'll have the exciting opportunity to:

- View covers of upcoming books

- Learn about our future publishing schedule (listed by publication month and author)

- Find out when your favorite authors will be visiting a city near you

- Search for and order backlist books

- Check out author bios and background information

- Send e-mail to your favorite authors

- Join us in weekly chats with authors, readers and other guests

- Get writing guidelines

- AND MUCH MORE!

Visit our website at
http://www.arabesquebooks.com

MORE THAN GOLD

SHIRLEY HAILSTOCK

ARABESQUE

BET BOOKS

BET Publications, LLC
www.bet.com
www.arabesquebooks.com

ARABESQUE BOOKS are published by

BET Publications, LLC
c/o BET BOOKS
One BET Plaza
1900 W Place NE
Washington, D.C. 20018-1211

All Kensington Titles, Imprints, and Distributed Lines are available at special quantity discounts for bulk purchases for sales promotions, premiums, fund-raising, educational, or institutional use. Special book excerpts or customized printings can also be created to fit specific needs. For details, write or phone the office of the Kensington special sales manager: Kensington Publishing Corp., 850 Third Avenue, New York, NY 10022, attn: Special Sales Department, Phone: 1-800-221-2647

First Printing: October, 2000

10 9 8 7 6 5 4 3 2 1
Printed in the United States of America

To my sister Loretta Hailstock who had a dream and fought to win it despite overwhelming odds.

ACKNOWLEDGMENTS

To my son, Christopher D. Coles, III, Regional Gymnastics Champion from New Jersey, who helped with a lot of the technical information on gymnastics exercises, routines, and skills.

Jon Schafer of the Schafer's School of Gymnastics in Lawrenceville, New Jersey, for his help and expertise in providing years of training and practical experience with gymnastics students. Both my son and daughter were students at his school and I was a student in the adult gymnastics program for six years.

Brian Welch, of Clay, West Virginia, who provided details of the city of Clay where the fictitious school of gymnastics is set.

Matt Ferrell of the United States Olympic Committee, who provided information regarding athletes traveling in foreign countries.

Gwynne Forster, fellow author and friend, who has traveled widely for the United Nations and lived and worked with the Korean people. She provided insight into customs and traditions.

PROLOGUE

Brian Ashleigh stared at the screen in the small, plushly appointed room. He sat in a great chair of soft rose velvet. It had wide arms, and both the seat and back moved to slightly recline for additional comfort. The room was a small auditorium that could seat fifty people, but only he and four other men occupied the space. Three of them sat on the first row, separated by a seat between them. One man sat in the center of the rows of seats and the fifth man sat alone on the last row, away from the group. It was his nature. He worked alone and didn't approve of this plan. The child on the screen was only a few years younger than one of Brian's daughters.

Dressed in a white leotard, she stood poised on the uneven parallel bars, her body leaning forward, her hands reaching for the next bar as she began another of several routines he'd watched more than once. At nineteen she was America's sweetheart. The darling of an age of satellite television, palm-size video machines and music that made his eardrums split. She was beautiful, golden brown with long hair she'd tied into a ponytail. It bounced as she went from routine to routine, swinging sideways as it and her body seemingly floated on air from one release move to another. Brian had been an athlete in his youth. His sport had been basketball. He'd played in high school and college, before it was necessary to be six foot seven to even be considered for anything more than the bowling league.

He knew the drill of hours of practice, the bandaged knees, muscle spasms and exhaustion that every athlete was committed to in their quest to stand in the spotlight. Morgan Kirkwood had spent most of her young life in pursuit of that goal. This would be her chance, that moment in time that she'd worked toward. She had everything going for her: a past she'd overcome, her luck at finding the right venue and having it recognized. At nineteen she'd lived more, seen more, experienced more than most adults. She'd spent hours honing her muscles, refining her routine, working toward a goal that could only shine on one person in the world.

And he was going to ask her to give it up.

His eyes followed her across the film. She moved to a large clear area covered with blue carpet designed for floor exercises. Music began, an upbeat peppy song. She was poised, confident, ready. She wore a smile on her face that showed no fear and no cares beyond her routine. Stopping in a corner, she started the first run, crossing the blue expanse of rug with an easy rhythm that almost made her routine appear effortless. Then she did the unexpected and did it well, so well he wasn't sure he'd even seen it. He watched her leap into the air, defying gravity, drawing her arms close to her body and making several turns and twists that had technical names like layout and double axial, but he couldn't remember which one went with which move, before her feet touched the ground with the sureness of a billy goat on a familiar mountain. No one in the room moved or spoke. Morgan Kirkwood had them spellbound. Brian was sure they were holding their breaths, just as he was doing, just as America did each time this leggy child came to the center of the arena.

She hadn't been slated to succeed at anything, not gymnastics, not even at life. She'd spent her early years on the streets, homeless, fending for herself, eating garbage and fighting to survive, trusting no hand that reached for her. Hands could look benevolent but turn quickly to swat her aside like an unwanted fly. Brian's heart tightened for this child. The woman who'd seen her on a playground and recognized her potential had been her caseworker and eventual parent. She'd convinced Morgan to take lessons at a local gymnastics school and Brian had no doubt it had changed her life. He felt like a dog asking her to give up what she'd worked for her entire young life. But he had no choice.

She was due to go in a few months. Seoul, South Korea. The Olympics. Morgan would go and the United States would watch their televisions for the two-week period when it looked like all was right with the world. To the average Joe, the world stopped and paid attention to the ministry of athletes, giving them the role of ambassadors of good will. Yet for Brian it was a much bleaker period. It was the time of terrorists and fools. It brought out the worst of the worst in the effort to disrupt, disturb, maim and kill. He was glad the event would not be on American soil.

The film was more than half an hour long. Morgan went through her routines over and over. Several different days and outfits passed through the magic of video. Brian looked at her face. He liked to see people, wanted to read through the outside and see if the inner soul was good or bad. He'd been successful in most of his character calls, and looking at Morgan he could see her youth, her idealism, her complete blindness to the things he'd seen in his own lifetime. Yet he was about to ask her to join him in one of the worst. He needed her to save the United States from embarrassment on a worldwide scale. He needed her to attend the Olympics, and while she was there he needed her to steal. Break into a heavily guarded prison and return with a man, an intelligence agent, who held secrets that had lain dormant since World War II.

In exchange for this little package, which could get her caught or killed if she was lucky, he'd grant her a wish, but only one and only within reason. *He* defined reason and he offered the wish.

"Shall we watch it again?" Jacob Winston sat on his right. Jacob was in charge of the witness protection program and Morgan Kirkwood might well meet with him in the coming months. It was why he'd asked Jacob to attend. Along with him had come Brian's friend, Clarence Christopher, Director of the FBI.

"I've seen enough," Brian said. "Send it to my office."

Brian spoke into a phone connecting him to the projectionist in the glass booth behind them.

Replacing the phone in its cradle, he stood up. The four other men looked at him. "What do you think?" the youngest one asked, the man sitting on the farthest row, apart from the group, his face hidden in shadow. He was a loner, Brian knew, and he also knew what the man thought of the mission and the inclusion of Morgan Kirkwood as part of the plan. He disapproved of every aspect that involved the girl.

Jack Temple was a young, educated black man who'd joined the police academy, but had been recruited for work with the Central Intelligence Agency. Jack left his position and came forward, walking down the steps to the floor of the auditorium with unhurried steps.

"I'm against this," he said and not for the first time. "We'll get her killed or she'll get us killed."

"She'll be trained as best we can. She'll be a rookie, but everyone was a rookie once," Brian told him.

"She's not a rookie," he said. "She's less than a rookie. She's a goddamn civilian."

"Jack, she was *your* idea," Forrest Washington, Jack's immediate boss, pointed out.

"*She* wasn't my idea. I wanted an agent, not a child."

"Child? She's not that much younger than you," Brian said.

"You grow up fast in this business," Jack replied.

"She will," Brian told him.

She would have no choice. Jack looked young to Brian, although he was twenty-five. Brian was nearing twice his age and he would be sending him and that nineteen-year-old child on a job to save face for the United States, its president and the country at large. Neither of them would ever be able to speak of it.

Jack stood face to face with him, although a head taller, and Brian made a decision he'd known he'd have to make even before seeing the film.

"It's time," he sighed. "See if she'll do it."

CHAPTER 1

Twelve Years Later

Morgan Kirkwood hadn't made her bed over a warm grate in some filthy alley in the southeast section of Washington, D.C., for nearly twenty years. She'd replaced shoes made of torn newspaper soles and discarded rags with designer suits, handmade boots and satin bedsheets, but her sense of danger, the need for self-preservation, piqued her senses the moment she stepped from the oven heat of the garage to the air-cooled comfort of her kitchen.

Someone was here.

She could feel him. A man. She didn't smell a male scent or the faint odor of sweat. Not even a cologne betrayed his presence. It was the air that had changed. It hadn't been stirred like a morning cup of coffee or hastily rushed through by an aerobic exerciser. Whoever was here had passed through it with ease, barely moving, seeking, but not with stealth, more with purpose. Morgan had schooled herself to be aware. Living on the streets of D.C. had given her a course in survival, in being prepared for anything at any time. She thought she'd forgotten it, but her senses were alive, and adrenaline pumped into her blood. Her mind sharpened as she thought of what was at hand that she could use as a weapon. Internal radar scoped the space, trying to hone in on the hiding place of her assailant. She didn't sense more than one.

He could be a robber, someone looking to feed a habit, someone she walked in on, but Morgan knew better. Whoever was here was looking for her. He'd been coming for twelve years. Finally they'd connected.

Tonight one of them would die.

Morgan put her purse on the counter and stepped out of her heels. The kitchen tiles were cool to her stockinged feet. Her clothes were a disadvantage, but she couldn't do anything about them. She'd been to dinner with friends and wore a straight dress with short sleeves and high heels. The dress had no pockets and she'd like to keep the car keys, but the dress had no place to put them. She was going to need her hands. As her mind probed the space around her, hunting for the hiding place of her killer, she removed money and her drivers license and, along with the keys, stuffed them inside her bra.

The kitchen had a pantry, but she didn't feel him in there. The space was small and crowded with canned vegetables, flour, sugar, bottles of maple syrup and other nonperishable foods. The dining room and living room were both accessible from the kitchen. Neither room had any hiding places that didn't involve furniture. There was a hall closet near the front entrance. Like most people living in development housing they entered through the garage. Morgan's house wasn't in a development. It was set apart, far into the woods, alone, deserted and, now she felt, vulnerable, but the garage was connected to the house by a short hallway. The front door was only opened for guests and to let the air in on warm, breezy days. It was much too hot today. Every house would have its air conditioner running, and the neighbors would be too preoccupied with the noise of life to notice anything different even if they could see Morgan's house.

Taking a knife from the kitchen rack, she noticed all of them were present and accounted for. The killer must have his own weapon. Of course he would, she thought, nearly laughing at her own stupidity. He hadn't picked up anything or moved anything. Every piece of furniture was in the exact place. Every dish, every pot was exactly where she'd left it.

But he was here.

She knew he would come, knew someone would. First Austin Fisk, reporter for that rag the *St. Louis Star,* begins poking into her past, calling for interviews and following her around. Then the mysterious feeling she was being watched by someone other than Fisk. He was too much an in-your-face reporter for covert action, but she could feel it. All the time. No matter if she went to the mailbox or drove into St. Louis to meet friends, there was that feeling of being under surveillance. She could see nothing, no matter how often she looked over her shoulder or glanced in the rearview mirror, only the feeling remained. There was no visible evidence of anything, but she knew someone was there.

Morgan moved through the space of her kitchen like a thief. She didn't want to be surprised. Her eyes shifted from side to side, taking in the entire room and all its crevices. Her heartbeat accelerated, pounded in her chest and her ears, and she consciously willed it to slow down. She needed all her wits, all her thought processes to be at their best if she was to survive.

He would know she was in the house. She'd disabled the alarm when she came in and he would have heard that. Somehow he'd gotten past the code that she'd programmed into the system. Morgan knew that wouldn't be hard to do. This was a good system, but it wasn't foolproof, especially for the kind of person they would send after her. What she had was worth a good price. The killer would be experienced, paid well and ready for anything.

Morgan had to be ready too. She circled around the living room, checked behind every piece of furniture and almost convinced herself she was being paranoid. She went to the stairs. She wouldn't go up. There was no way out if she went to any of the bedrooms. There were four bedrooms. He could be in any of them. While she checked one he could surprise her from behind. If necessary she'd go back the way she'd come.

Suddenly she saw something. A shadow. She whirled around. Nothing. Had she really seen it? Morgan was sure of her mind. If she saw a shadow, it was there. She moved toward the area.

Slowly, her shoeless feet making no noise on the tiled entryway, she got to the stairs, looking right and left. Nothing.

Suddenly, he was behind her. A hand came over her mouth, cutting her scream. A gloved hand that tasted like engine oil clamped her mouth closed and prevented her from making a sound. She tried to scream, but he pulled her head back, wrenching her neck to the point of pain. His free arm grabbed the hand holding the knife and pulled it backward until the pain in her arm forced her to drop her only weapon. Then he circled her waist and his leg spread between hers and wrapped candy-cane style around one of hers. This kept her from kicking. If she tried to lift a foot she'd lose her balance and fall. Still she fought, using whatever appendage she had free, arms, hands, her body, her head. She tried to butt him, but he moved, anticipating her blow.

Morgan fought with every ounce of the twelve-year-old street waif who learned to withstand the dangers of being alone and female. She concentrated her energy, winding it into whatever move she made, concentrating her entire weight into the blow she intended to deliver. He outwitted her at every turn. But he relaxed the hold on her mouth. Taking advantage of it, she bit down on the hand in her mouth. Her killer screamed, but held fast to her, dashing her hope of escaping his hold. He kicked her leg out, too far for her to remain upright. They both went down to the bare floor. She scrambled, trying to get away, but he was larger, faster, stronger. He grabbed her about the shoulders and flipped her over, pinning her to the floor.

Morgan's hands were free and she pounded at the shoulders and head of the killer. He grabbed her hands and pinned them above her on either side of her head.

"Morgan, stop it!"

She looked at him.

"Not you," she said, and renewed her struggles.

"Stop it or I'll kiss you."

Every nerve in her body froze.

"That's better." For a moment he still held her, but then he sat back and moved away from her. Morgan was surprised. Why hadn't he killed her? She was surprised to find it was him.

Jack Temple.

She'd hoped whoever came would be someone she'd never seen before. To be killed by someone she knew, someone she'd met. She couldn't call him a friend. They'd been a part of the same team once and when they parted, Morgan never expected to see him again. And now he was here.

Here for her.

She had to get away. Morgan inched away from him. He wasn't looking at her, but resting his head on his drawn-up knees. He looked winded. Maybe she could use that, but she had to act now. Morgan would have to pass him to get to the front door, and it was locked. Her only option was to go through the garage or one of the windows. She had an escape route, but she couldn't use it with him running behind her.

In a split second Morgan sprang to her feet and darted for the kitchen and the garage door. She wouldn't have time to open the door and take the car. Her best bet was to get out the side door and run into the woods. It was only fifty feet to the trees. Hopefully she could get there before he shot her in the back. She couldn't go toward a neighbor. She didn't know if he'd be willing to kill more than one person, but she wasn't going to take the chance. And her nearest neighbor was miles away.

Jack came after her. She heard him, but refused to turn around and look over her shoulder. He was a big man. She'd known his strength twelve years before when they were in South Korea together; she as a contestant in the Olympics and he as one of the coaches for the United States swim team.

Her stocking feet slipped on the permanently waxed kitchen tiles. Jack was on her in an instant. They crashed to the floor. She took his weight on her side. Again he flipped her over.

"What is wrong with you?"

"Just kill me now and get it over with," she hissed. She was breathing hard, her voice holding more bravado than she felt. How would he kill her? Strangle her? A bullet? The knife she'd lost the battle to hold onto? She could feel a heavy object pressing against her through his coat.

"Kill you?" He looked at her with piercing eyes that bore through her, but gave nothing away as to his intentions. She saw cold-bloodedness in them. "You think I'm here to kill you?"

"Yes, I do." Her chin shot out without her even thinking about it. She'd learned it in her youth. *Never back down. Never show fear.* And that gesture came back to her now. "Why else would you come?"

He got to his feet, pulling her with him. Morgan immediately looked for other methods of escape. He was stronger than she was, taller, maybe even faster, but she wouldn't let his advantages be disadvantages for her. She'd try anyway.

"I'm here because you called."

"I never called you."

"You called Jacob Winston."

Jacob Winston was the director of the witness protection program. She wasn't in the program, but if anything ever happened to her, she was to contact him.

How could he know that? "I never called anyone by that name." She hedged, buying herself time.

The look he gave her told her he knew she was lying.

"Look, we need to talk."

He released her and stepped back. Morgan didn't know if he'd let her walk away if she tried, but his distance seemed to ask for her trust. She wouldn't give it, not yet. He could be anyone and he still could be here to kill her, but he had given her the proper buzz word. *Jacob Winston.* She hadn't called Jacob, but she had contacted him, by a secure electronic mail transmission. Her name hadn't been disclosed, only a code she thought she'd forgotten. It, too, had come to her mind as quickly as her street tactics had returned. She could personally attest to the will to stay alive now. Her message gave details of Fisk's efforts to interview her. She'd also mentioned her sense of being watched. That had been two days ago. She hadn't heard from Jacob.

"Let's go someplace else," Jack suggested.

Getting out of the house was a good idea. She was alone with him here and he could certainly overpower her, as he'd demonstrated twice. Going someplace very public would be a wise move. Before she could reply, the doorbell rang. Morgan froze for a moment as if another killer had already appeared.

"Are you expecting anyone?"

She shook her head. Frightened, Morgan's hand came up as if to catch hold of something or someone for support. Jack cautioned her, pulling a gun from under his jacket. She'd known it was there. She'd felt it while he had her pinned to the kitchen floor. Noticing her hanging hand, she dropped it to her side. Jack motioned for her to go to the door. She picked up the knife that had been her weapon against him and went toward the portal. He took up a blend-into-the-wall position which would have been laughable if she wasn't already geared up to be frightened to death. Morgan peered through the curtain and saw her friend, Michelle O'Banyon, standing alone on the porch. She relaxed. Her whole body went limp and she grabbed the doorknob tighter than she would have if her adrenaline wasn't working overtime.

"It's all right," she said to Jack as she pulled the door open. "Michelle, what are you doing here?"

Michelle pulled the screen open. "I can't come in, Morgan. I'm in a real hurry," she said in a rush. "I have to get to the train station, but since I was passing and I've been carrying this bowl around in my car for a week, I thought I'd drop it off."

Michelle hated being indebted to anyone, even if it was for a bowl containing potato salad which Morgan had taken to a backyard barbecue and left. She offered the package to Morgan, who realized she was still holding the knife. Both of them looked at the gleaming blade at the same time. Morgan offered a weak smile. She was glad she hadn't actually cut Jack with it.

"I was cooking," she explained.

She moved sideways to place it on the small table next to the door where sat a vase of fresh flowers. Morgan changed them once a week. She loved the smell of them. This week it was roses. She'd had carnations last week and an exotic bird of paradise spray the week before. She laid down the knife and turned back to Michelle. The knife fell off the table and clattered to the floor. Morgan instinctively turned and in that split second the explosion sounded.

Morgan turned in time to see Michelle blown inward through the door. Blood splattered across the room. Morgan straightened, a look of amazement on her face. Michelle's body was flung through the foyer. She slammed into the wall and hung there, suspended like a slack puppet for a moment before sliding to the floor. Morgan's heart hammered as she realized Michelle was dead. She started for her. Jack sprang from his hiding place, tackling her, bringing her down to the floor and covering her with his body. Shots rang out, showering the house from the outside. Windows exploded, spraying glass over the room. The vase on the table was hit. She felt a shard pierce her bare arm. The walls above her were riddled with bullets. She could hear bullets crashing through the windows of her living room, knew the splattered whisper of them finding solace in the books that lined one wall of that room.

Morgan cowered under Jack. Clenching her teeth together, she dug her fingers into his arms, holding him as her protector. The gunfire seemed to grow faster and louder. Outside it sounded like there must be an army using its entire arsenal against them. When would they stop? How many were there? Morgan couldn't wait.

"We have to get out of here," Jack shouted in her ear. "We'll go to the garage and take your car—"

His sentence was cut off by a huge explosion coming from the garage. Morgan knew her car had just been vaporized. There would be no escaping using it.

"Follow me," she told him. "I have a way."

"You're not going to try the back door?"

"No," she said, throwing him a look that would have stopped any street thug.

Morgan crawled on her belly as if she were a seasoned soldier. Jack followed her. Outside he'd made out four men, but there could be more. From the artillery they were throwing at the house, he knew it was only a matter of time before they came inside. There were four entrances, including the garage entryway and the sliding glass door off the great room in the back. He'd made sure they were all locked, but none of them would stand up to bullets. The glass doors and windows were definitely a weak point. He had to believe there were people in the back waiting for them to come through one of the doors.

Morgan went toward the kitchen. She opened a door which

led to the cellar. He'd explored it earlier. She had a gym down there, hidden, concealed. He'd found the entrance that opened by using a code on a security panel. He didn't know how she got it built under a house this size and this old. But the normal basement, which must have been of standard height, had been lowered to a cavernous size where she could tumble and jump up and down on trampolines and parallel bars. There was no musty smell, only the latent odor of chalk she used to coat her hands and maintain a tight and dry grip on the equipment. Jack hadn't seen any exits on that level. On the level above it were only windows. The old double-door entry had been cemented over.

"There's a way out down here?" He grabbed her shoulder, stopping her on the steps.

"Yes." She didn't provide any more information, only continued to run down the stairs as fast as she could. Jack followed. He knew she could lie. She could run cons, pick pockets, steal into and out of places without being noticed. She could throw a knife with an accuracy rate of a thousandth of an inch to the mark. Thankfully, he'd reached her before she had a chance to use her knife-throwing talents on him. He remembered her file, the things she'd done to survive before she was adopted, before she found her place in the gymnastics arena. She could be leading him to his death, but he didn't think so. The bullets were real. She knew that. And he had no choice.

Morgan punched in the code with a speed that said she could do it in her sleep. Then she pulled the door open and they began their descent into her private gym. The door closed behind them. This was her *alone* place. No one knew of this room, or she wouldn't conceal it so carefully. Jack wanted to take a moment to question her about this space, but his mind was on escape. If they got out of here, he could ask about it later.

Down they went. Down a long set of stairs that wove back and forth, flight by flight. Although he had found no exit when he'd checked this two-hundred-foot room, not on the flooring under the apparatus or through any of the exterior walls, he knew it was here. She'd concealed it well and he thanked her for it now. Above his head the shooting stopped, but he could feel, not hear, but know the silent footfalls of the intruders.

"They're in the house," he whispered.

"How good are you at gymnastics?" she asked.

Jack was thrown by the question, but answered it the only way he knew how. "I can hold my own."

"I hope that's good enough."

He had the feeling she knew he was lying. They passed beams and uneven bars, trampolines, a pit filled with foam rubber cubes over which a single wooden bar hung. In front of them was a wall of mirrors and nothing else. Jack didn't think they could walk through the mirrors, but it looked as if there was nowhere else for them to go. Without his seeing her do anything, a panel opened electronically in the ceiling. It was next to a light at the far end of the gym. When the panel opened a rope lowered to about twelve feet off the floor. Morgan jumped onto the beam as if walking on a four-inch-wide pedestal four feet off the floor was part of her natural state. She negotiated its length without a waver of imbalance, her feet as sure as if she were walking on flat ground. At the end of the beam she leapt two feet straight up and grabbed the hanging rope. With grace as elegant as any athlete in competition and without using her legs for support, she pulled her weight up hand over hand and swung her lithe body through the opening.

"Come on," she said, looking back at him. "They're going to find this door any minute now."

Jack didn't have time to hesitate. Climbing the rope wasn't a problem. He could do that, though not as gracefully as she had. He needed to use his legs. Getting up on a four-inch piece of wood with a padded covering to grab the rope was something else. He made it on the second try. He didn't need to jump far to grasp the rope. Once he reached it, he was up and through the hole in the ceiling in no time.

"How do we close this?"

Morgan did nothing more than touch herself. She had no remote unit, keycard or any other device that he could see, yet the rope and panel started its movement back to the original place. If he hadn't found this opening, he was confident the people shooting at them wouldn't find it either. Even if they did, could they reach it? Jack breathed a sigh of relief. They were safe for the time being. All they had to do was be quiet and wait out the time.

Once the panel closed the space was pitch black. Like being in a darkroom, no light escaped into this area. He had no idea of the dimensions. Was it large enough for him to stand up or was it a crawl space? The air here was stale, musty, feeling as if no one lived here or wanted to live here. He could still smell the chalk, but it was old, like going into a school when they were tearing it down and the bricks and mortar that held the building together had settled into screaming memory of the thousands of voices that once shared the space.

"Give me your hand," Morgan whispered.

He reached toward her voice in the dark. It was the kind of voice that should be heard in the dark: low, rich, seductive, sexy. His hand brushed her waist. She found it and moved it away from her body but kept hold of him. She stood. Feeling the pressure of her hand pulling at him, he stood too.

"Don't let go," she whispered, and she started to walk.

"We aren't going to wait here?"

"Now that they've found me, they're not going to leave until they find where we're hiding. We have to go."

She pulled on his hand and he started to move.

"How big is this . . . place?" he asked, spreading his free arm out to ward off whatever was denied his eyes and to try and maintain his balance in total darkness.

"You don't have to worry about bumping into anything."

That wasn't his concern. The two of them walked. She led and he followed. About thirty seconds after they started in the pitch darkness, she switched on a flashlight. Jack noticed there were no cobwebs. The place wasn't a room but a long narrow corridor with paneled walls and light sconces. Before climbing through the ceiling tile they'd already come to the end of the building. They must be outside of the house by now.

"How far does this go?" Jack asked after they'd walked another three minutes.

"It will end soon."

It did. The paneling ended at another wall. Jack trusted her when she said there was an exit. At the wall was a heavy door which swung open easily, as if its hinges were oiled regularly. Again this one required an electronic code for access. They went through it and into a tunnel. Morgan turned and reset the code then closed the door. It not only had an electronic lock, but she bolted it with three primitive slats of wood that fell neatly into wooden place holders. Anyone trying to get through it would be greatly hampered even if they tried to blast through it with gunfire. She'd thought of everything.

And that made him uncomfortable.

If she'd put this much thought into an escape plan, someone must really be after her. Why? He hadn't gotten that information. He'd wanted to talk to her, but there hadn't been time. Before they got to say anything the bullets had started flying.

After the door was secure she pulled a backpack from a concealed shelf.

"Turn around," she ordered.

"What?"

"I never expected anyone to be with me. I have to change clothes. So turn around or I'll switch this light off and you'll lose your equilibrium and fall over."

"Wouldn't you like me to unzip you?" he asked playfully.

"Funny," she replied with a look made grotesque by the single beam of light in the vast darkness.

Jack smiled, then turned around. He could hear her taking her dress off. The familiar sound of a zipper being pulled down made him think of things he had no time for now, like how she'd felt lying under him on the floor before the melee started. He could see a shadow thrown against the wall. She pulled something over her head. He had a mental picture of her without that black dress and his body suddenly tightened. He heard the thunk of something falling and her quickly scooping it up.

"A lot of planning went into this," Jack said to get his mind off his thoughts.

"Didn't you think I was up to it?" she quipped.

"That's not it," he replied. That was exactly it, but he wasn't about to admit it. "It's just for someone who's such an upstanding citizen, this is not the usual finished room."

"You can turn around now."

She was wearing black jeans and a black T-shirt. Her hair

was completely off her face, pulled into a ponytail that fell over her shoulder as she leaned forward tying black sneakers. He was suddenly reminded of the nineteen-year-old he'd seen on a strip of film twelve years ago.

"I thought you said you knew all about me." She started walking again. "Didn't you learn *all* my talents?"

Jack ignored the barb. "Where is this leading?"

"To the outside."

The ground under them changed from flat to a smooth incline. Its steepness rose sharply until Jack had to practically crawl. There was no paneling here. He was in a tunnel with corrugated metal cylinders angling toward some unknown area. It was cold but dry. He could smell the earth, not the sweet smell of freshly turned or freshly planted ground, but the dank, mildewy odor of dirt. Morgan stretched the distance between them without seeming to notice. Then they reached a ladder embedded in a cement wall. Immediately she started to climb. Without hesitation, Jack followed. At the top, she pushed at a grate, using all her strength. It opened and Jack could see the sky above them, clear and starry. Fresh air rushed in with the scent of night on it. He breathed in deeply.

Morgan took no time to look at the sky or the stars. She came out of the hole in the ground, and as soon as he cleared it, she slammed the grate back in place and concealed it with the ground vegetation.

Jack looked around the area. They were in the woods. The road was visible about fifty feet ahead of them. Crickets and cicadas vied for dominance in the normal night.

"Where are we?" he asked.

"Still in the line of fire."

CHAPTER 2

Jack followed her line of sight. The headlights of two cars came along the trees. They drove slowly and sprayed a search-light into the woods. They were obviously looking for someone and Jack knew he and Morgan were the prime suspects.

"Climb the tree," he commanded. She didn't question his authority, but started up the trunk. Jack followed her. They'd just made it into the leaves when the light swept the trunk. Jack stopped her. They settled in the arms of two branches, her body pressed into his, and waited, peering through the leaves, neither saying a word.

The cars rolled by slowly, continuing to search as they moved down the road. Jack and Morgan remained hidden in the branches, rigidly alert. When the car went around the curve in the road, Morgan relaxed against Jack. He felt the tension in her body leave it. He slipped his arms around her, securing her to his chest. He told himself it was to keep her from falling, but Jack knew he wanted to hold her. It had been twelve years since he'd had his arms around her. He thought he could forget her, but throughout his career she'd made several appearances in faraway places during long nights and in his dreams. She hadn't known it and she never would. He could keep her safe, but that's all he could do.

Jack looked through the branches, after the car. It was no longer visible. He waited, turning to look in the other direction, wondering if there were more vehicles. From the gunfire that slammed into the house, there had to be more than two cars. Jack had counted more than seven handguns, an equal number of rifles, more assault weapons than should be on the streets of a major city, let alone a small community like St. Charles, Missouri. The noise from the rapidly firing guns muffled the other machinery. He couldn't make out how many other types there were. Who were they? What did they want?

Morgan moved suddenly. She inched away from him to begin her descent to the ground.

"Not yet," he said, restraining her. Moments later a pickup truck sped past them. In its wake, it bent the branches of nearby bushes to the ground. Before they could snap back, another car came behind it, barreling forward with the same intense speed. Morgan shrank back against Jack. Her arms tightened around his waist. She lay her head pressed against his shoulder.

Ten minutes later they were still holding each other. Jack felt it was safe to move.

"We should get going," he said.

They climbed down without a word. Morgan struck out immediately in the direction the trucks had gone.

"Where are you going?"

"I have a car," she told him. "I'm going to get it."

Jack's car was back at her house. He hadn't parked in front of the house. The car was several hundred feet from the entrance to her driveway. He'd walked the remaining distance. It was a cautionary action. Jack had been part of the CIA too long to get caught with his pants down, but today seemed a blunder he hadn't been prepared for. Thankfully, Morgan had an escape plan. Jack admitted he was impressed with Morgan. Few women he'd known would even have an escape plan, or the presence of mind to keep their heads in the wake of certain death. Jack had thought of Morgan as the vulnerable nineteen-year-old who needed looking after, but she proved him wrong and he admired her for it.

"How far is this car?"

"About a mile from here." She walked with purpose, the backpack not slowing her gait one bit. Jack matched her stride.

She left the road where the cars had been and continued her trek through the woods.

It was totally dark and only his keen night vision and training made it easy for him to see where he was going.

"Why don't you tell me what's going on?" Jack asked.

"Didn't Jacob fill you in?"

"He had no time."

"Why not? I sent the message two days ago."

He grabbed her arm and pulled her to a halt. "I only found out today."

Her eyes changed. They were barely visible in the darkness, but he saw the difference before she moved her gaze to his hand. He let her go. He had the feeling she knew he'd rushed to her side, but then he dropped the idea. She couldn't know. They hadn't seen each other for twelve years. She remembered him from the Olympics, but she had no knowledge that he'd come here as soon as he discovered she could be in danger.

"Twelve years ago I didn't just go to the Olympics." She started walking again. "I helped the government get a man out of a South Korean prison."

Jack knew this. He'd been part of the mission. In fact, her actions had been the direct result of his own idea, one he no longer regretted, but had from the very first thought should have been used only as a final solution.

"Now someone is trying to kill me."

"Twelve years is a long time. Why did they wait until now?"

"I don't know. Olympic fever. Maybe they didn't know where I was. Maybe something has happened to trigger this action." She glanced at him, never breaking her stride. "I only know they started playing that tape and Austin Fisk showed up."

"Fisk."

"You know him?"

Jack's instinct was to deny it. He denied everything. It was ingrained in him. If he were ever captured in a foreign country, he was to deny knowledge of anything except his cover. The problem here was he had no cover and he felt more and more vulnerable the longer he stayed in Morgan Kirkwood's presence.

"I know of him. We've never met."

"But . . ." she prompted.

"But he's tenacious, not likely to let a fish go once he's got it on the hook."

"And he's trying to hook me."

The ground they were covering flattened out and Morgan increased her pace. He checked her breathing, but she looked as if this were a country stroll on a pleasant Sunday afternoon. Finally they came to a fence. Without hesitation she scaled the twelve feet to the top and used her backpack to cover the circular barbed wire. Jack noticed the small black and white sign stating U.S. GOVERNMENT PROPERTY. DO NOT ENTER. Morgan didn't appear to see the sign, but somehow Jack knew she knew it was there. He followed her over in the same manner and they continued through the nearly complete blackness.

"We're not going to be suddenly surrounded by men in green fatigues with rifles at the ready, are we?"

Morgan actually smiled. It was the first time he'd seen her do that.

"What is this place?"

"It's an abandoned research base. No one's been here since the Vietnam War ended back in the seventies."

"No one but you?"

She didn't answer. She didn't have to. She'd come straight here without a path or a road. She'd made her way to this place as if from memory. Finally they stopped at a wreck of a building. It was an old barracks and looked as if it were set at the edge of the woods. Any paint that had been on the outside of the wash-worn wooden structure had long since been beaten off by wind and rain. Weeds had grown into vines and trees, snaking in and out of broken windows and doors as if they were giant reptiles taking back from the world what it had stolen from them. The entry door lay close to the ground, hooked onto a rusty hinge by nothing but the grace of God.

Morgan marched straight for the place. She pushed her wiry frame under and over branches, easily going toward her purpose.

"This is where you have a car?" Jack asked, ducking so the swinging branch missed him.

She didn't answer, only continued toward a more dilapidated structure behind the barracks. This one was a corrugated metal building that looked like a huge tube of which half was above the ground. They were usually used as temporary buildings, but with the military anything temporary took decades to replace.

Inside there was little light, but this fact did not deter Morgan Kirkwood. Her actions made Jack think she possessed some kind of internal radar that guided her in this dark space. Her feet never faltered as she went from task to task. The cavernous room looked to have once held bunks. Jack remembered his own time in the service, the bed he occupied with a chest at the foot. It held all his worldly possessions and they could acquire nothing that would not fit in that three-square-foot space.

"Brace yourself, Mr. Temple. There's going to be an explosion."

Jack checked the window. He crossed the room, skirting the dirt and dust that had taken up residence in the abandoned metal container, to where she stood. Morgan opened a concealed panel in the wall and pulled something out.

"What is that?"

"A remote control." It was a black rectangle, the size of a cellular phone. She pushed the only button on it, a white disk the size of a dime. Jack heard nothing. "It'll take ten minutes," she said. Then she replaced the control in its hiding place and concealed the panel. Nothing looked disturbed when she finished.

Without another word, she started walking again.

"Just a minute." He stopped her. "Isn't it time we developed a game plan?"

"I have a plan," she informed him in a voice that said *don't push me.*

She went through the doorway back into the night. Stepping as sure-footed as if she were walking on smooth concrete, she traversed the yard in front of them. Jack ran to catch up with her.

He grabbed her arm and brought her around to look at him. "You want to clue me in? It seems we're in this together, whether that pleases you or not."

"It does not."

Jack took a deep breath. Why had he come here? At least he knew how she felt about him. Despite the way she'd relaxed against him in the tree not half an hour ago, she didn't want him around. Jack admitted he wasn't used to this kind of reception. Women were usually glad to see him. But not this one.

"Morgan, I know you're scared. I know these things have never happened to you before, but we're going to have to work together if we're to survive this. It's not over."

"I know that." Her teeth were set and she spoke through them. "It's why I'm getting this car and getting out of here."

She turned to walk away, but again he stopped her.

"Where are you going then?"

"I have a place."

"Where?"

She clamped her mouth closed. She wasn't going to tell him. It made sense. He even admired her for her caution. Anyone who could set up an escape plan as intricately executed as she had would be smart enough only to tell someone she trusted implicitly where she was going. And she didn't trust him. He had the idea that she trusted no one. Good, he thought.

He followed her when she started walking again. They went to another abandoned building. Just as she reached the door, the explosion happened. Jack instinctively grabbed her and pushed her to the ground. He rolled over, coming to his knees, all the while keeping her with him. The sky behind them was bright orange. Jack expected the people trying to kill them to come through one of the buildings.

"It's the house," Morgan explained.

"What?"

"The explosion."

"You blew up your house?"

"To smithereens," she said dryly. "Now, there's no trace of me. Nothing to be found. I'm completely invisible."

Invisible. That was the perfect word to describe her. Since she was born, practically no one had thought twice about her. A waif on the streets, unwanted, unseen by finely dressed strangers who'd deny she even existed, to be swatted away like some insect. She loved her house, the friends she'd made in the last twelve years. She'd been cautious, disguising herself with the skillful use of makeup to keep people from recognizing her as the skinny teenager crushing roses to her chest as she sang *The Star Spangled Banner* in front of a stadium of spectators and millions of television viewers.

Morgan walked fast enough for it to be an exercise program. She often rushed when she thought of her life on the streets, as if she could outrun the memory of that time. No matter how fast she walked or ran the memories stayed with her.

And not only those of being on the streets. There was Jack. And that kiss. She thought she was over him, but how could she be over something that never had a beginning? And without a beginning, there could be no middle, no end. That's where she and Jack stood, strung up in some nether region where life didn't exist, where love didn't exist, but where Jack had kissed her, where there was the promise of something, but before she could define it, it ended. Yet Morgan would take its memory to her grave. When Jack threatened to kiss her at the house, every nerve ending in her body reacted to the memory of that one, long ago time when the two of them shared a small piece of heaven that would be forever trapped in some untouchable cavern where unrealized dreams are stored.

She arrived at the building where the car was hidden. Pushing aside her thoughts, she suddenly wanted to get away fast. Time seemed important. She didn't have the feeling that anyone would discover them if they stayed here, but she wanted to be away. She knew it was her thoughts egging her on, her memories she wanted to distance herself from, even though logic told her she could never get away from them.

The entire place looked abandoned. The army left nearly thirty years ago, closing the base and leaving it like an obnoxious relative. The sense of decayed life hung over the place, giving it the look and feel of a graveyard at midnight. Light and air seemed to enter a building and hang there, trapped and stale, as lost as the past.

Morgan shivered as she wedged herself through the door of

the hangar. The cavernous building was dark inside. She coughed at the dry air.

"Wait here," she told Jack. He caught her arm as she started to walk away.

"We should stick together."

"There is only room for one of us where I'm going."

Pulling her arm free, she left him, disappearing through a door at the far end of the room. In minutes the wall which had been in place for the past twelve years slid away as if it were highly oiled and maintained. The car rose on the elevated platform and she started the engine.

Jack faced her in the headlights. He squinted, covering his eyes, and started toward the car.

"Let me drive." He opened the driver's side door.

"No," she said.

"You're in no condition."

"I'm driving," she stated, and she reached for the door. Jack held it, stepping between her and the door.

"I'm not moving," she said slowly. "If you don't get out of the way I'll leave you here."

For a long moment they stared at each other. Two lions ready to spring, growling, snarling animals with equal strength and equal stubbornness, vying for domination.

"Jack, you showed up today out of the blue. I don't know if you're on my side or here to kill me. You saved my life tonight and for that I am grateful, but I set this plan up years ago and I'm going to carry it out. Now get in the car or get out of the way."

He hesitated only a moment before going around to the passenger side. Morgan took off as soon as he pulled his lean body into the seat. She didn't wait for him to put on a seat belt or even close the passenger door. The dust cloud behind the car couldn't be helped. As she went through the electronic gate, she hoped the dust would settle enough to cover the tracks, but if it didn't there was nothing she could do about it, and she vowed to worry about only the things over which she had control.

And that brought her to the man sitting next to her. He intrigued her, even aroused her, but she had no idea why he was here, and that scared her. She'd met Jack in the airport just before they boarded the plane to Seoul. They were both going to the Olympics, she to compete with the gymnastics team and he as one of the swim team coaches. She remembered seeing him at Dulles International just outside Washington, D.C. His eyes seemed to seek her out. She shivered the moment they made contact. He held her gaze for only a moment before dropping it to return to his own team. Afterward he appeared to go out of his way to ignore her. At least until that last night. The night of the final competition. The night she'd stolen into a foreign prison, nearly lost her life, raced like fire to return to the arena and take her place on the balance beam and then to end the night with tears in her eyes and Jack Temple's arms around her.

Jack stared at the road ahead. Frequently he glanced at the speedometer, expecting Morgan to use the car to relieve her tension. She held it to the posted limit, going not a single mile over the legal speed. Jack took a moment to review the car. He'd been disappointed when he saw the monster vehicle she'd appeared with. They needed something low and sleek, something that could hold the road and become one with it. If they needed its power, he wanted to make sure it was there.

He could hear the purr of the engine. It told him that this car was as finely tuned and carefully maintained as the escape route the two of them had taken to get out of the house. It was unpretentious, but not the one he would have chosen for an escape.

He just wondered where they were escaping to. They were heading east on Route 70. It told him nothing since this route could take them anyplace between St. Charles, Missouri, and the Atlantic Ocean.

"Morgan," he spoke her name softly. He felt she was concentrating so intently that any sudden noise would shatter her ability to control the car. "Where are we going?"

She didn't answer right away. Jack began to feel she hadn't heard him when she spoke. "Don't worry. I know the way."

She switched on the radio to a country music station and went back to her driving in silence.

Jack wondered about her. What had happened to her in the past twelve years? How had she lived? The house they'd left in the quiet wooded area was beautiful, with furnishings and paintings, although he'd seen none of her trophies or ribbons, cups or medallions he knew she owned. On her way to the Olympics, she'd picked up a double score of awards. She dressed well and had many friends. She hadn't married or even been engaged, but she was a beautiful, desirable woman.

Morgan continued to drive. The night disappeared hour by hour. They hadn't stopped for gas or food or to use a bathroom. Jack kept tabs on her reactions, making sure she was alert. He had no complaints about how she handled the car. She drove the way she'd done everything since he'd met her, efficiently, competently, as if she knew what she wanted and how to get it. She and the car merged into one. The road made up the third part of the strange trio. She drove as if this were part of her daily commute, that she had been over this surface day in and day out, that she and the bumps, holes, smooth edges, ragged surfaces knew each other intimately and swayed and moved to avoid any inconvenience.

While Jack wasn't concerned about Morgan's driving, he was, however, concerned about her. She was burying her feelings, swallowing them inside and using the car as a transfer device. He wasn't sure she knew she was doing it. From the profile he'd read he knew she'd been very shrewd as a child. Spending years alone on the street had taught her to hide her feelings, to keep them inside and never allow anyone to see what she felt. The car was a safe haven for those feelings. What she couldn't talk to him about, what she knew needed an outlet, she gave it through the car, but it was a controlled giving. She looked as if she were on automatic, like she'd set the car to drive itself and turned on her own personal cruise control to keep from feeling anything.

Jack knew better. There was at least one time when she didn't keep her feelings to herself. She'd poured them out with long heart-rending tears while he held her in his arms. He wanted her to trust him enough to do it again. He wanted her to tell him what she felt. Despite her facade of strength and ability, she probably hadn't done anything like trust another human being in twelve years, maybe longer. He'd been there for her before. It was important that he be there again. He'd helped her through it before.

Helping her again was why he'd come this time.

"That was a pretty amazing house," Jack began. "I suppose the options we walked through won't be found registered at the city building department."

For a long moment Morgan remained quiet. Jack didn't think she'd talk to him at all.

"Come on, Morgan. I'm on your side. I haven't asked anything about why you had a secret escape route or a car, with an engine that purrs like a kitten, hidden in an abandoned military base. The least you could do is talk to me."

"Why are you here?" She broke her self-imposed silence with a voice so low he had to strain to hear it.

"I don't know. I was hoping you'd tell me that."

"I don't need your help and I don't want it. So if it's all the same to you, I'll let you out at the nearest town and be on my way."

Jack sighed. He wasn't used to people not wanting his help. Often when he got to someone, they were willing to follow him, assuming he knew how to keep them safe. He wasn't sure about Morgan. He had no idea how much trouble she was in.

"Morgan, can we start over?"

She took her eyes off the road and looked at him for as long as she could before returning her attention to the road. "I don't think so," she said.

"Morgan—"

"I didn't build the gym myself," she started speaking at the same time as he did. Jack allowed her to finish. "Before the Army base closed, the commander had it built as a gym for his children. He had the foundation dug and moved the house to sit over it. Once the base closed the house was vacant for years. I got it because of . . . connections." She didn't explain any further. "So you are correct, Jack. It won't be found on any building department's plans."

"What about the escape tunnel? Did he build that too?"

"That was mine."

"You did that?"

"Don't look so surprised. I am capable of many things."

"It's not that. It's why?"

"Why did I think I needed one?" she asked. "I suppose that's a moot point now. I needed it, it was there."

"And the explosives?"

"I wasn't sure that would work." She almost smiled. "I found an old manual at the base one night. It wasn't about making bombs. I found that information on the Internet. The manual was about the techniques of disarming bombs."

"Why would you want to bomb your own house?"

"I didn't hurt anyone," she rushed to say. "That's why it was ten minutes after I set the timer. I left a recording warning anyone inside they had ten minutes to get out before the house was blown up."

She hadn't answered his question. "But it was your home." Jack couldn't imagine leaving a place he'd lived in for twelve years by destroying it on purpose.

Morgan took her time answering. "I didn't want to leave anything around that would help someone find me."

Jack thought she'd chosen her words very carefully. He wondered if she was telling the truth. Why wouldn't she want any trace of herself left? He thought about the house she'd lived in. It was beautifully decorated, but impersonal. Morgan lived there, yet the only room that he could say he felt her a part of was the gym. She might walk through the other rooms, but her presence was invisible, everywhere except that chalk-filled air of the underground gym.

"What's this all about, Morgan?"

He couldn't have shut her up more quickly if he'd put duct tape over her mouth. And he could think of something else he'd like to put over her mouth. It wasn't tape.

Jack wondered what she was thinking. It had been twelve years since they'd last seen each other. He thought that was enough time, but it was wiped away in one tumble to the floor

of her hallway. He'd seen her struggling under him and he
wanted to kiss her.

She wanted to be unseen, unknown and untraceable.

At daylight Morgan pulled off the main road and zigzagged
through a series of secondary roads until she finally reached a
narrow strip of blacktop that seemed to be swallowed by trees
and bushes. The blacktop faded into a pothole-ridden, broken
road and then dropped all pretense of being paved. The car's
suspension system barely registered a change. Jack wondered
exactly what was under the hood of this nondescript vehicle.
Certainly more than he had initially given it credit for, but
Morgan had planned carefully, and this car was no less outfitted
than that tunnel above her gymnasium.

"Can you tell me where we're going now?" He spoke for
the first time in hours. His throat was dry and his knees cramped
from sitting in one position for so long.

Morgan swung the car sharply around a bend and a house
came into view. The road changed from packed earth to gravel.
The house wasn't what he'd envisioned. With all the trees
around them he expected a log cabin or some hidden away
building with crumbling walls and in serious need of a paint
job. What he saw was a sprawling three-story mansion with
high white columns and a veranda and balcony that appeared
to run the full circumference of the building. In front of it was
a large man-made lake. They drove around it, along an oval
driveway outlined with deep red stones that led up to the wide
porch and double front doors.

Morgan stopped the car and got out. Placing her hands on
her lower back, she arched it, then raised her hands to the sky
and stretched. She gave a reviving cry, reminiscent of the first
stretch of the morning. Hours of sitting had taken a toll on her
too. She rotated her shoulders. Then, pulling the backpack from
the car, she started for the house.

"Do you own this house?"

"No."

"Are you sure we'll be safe here? I didn't see any gates
around it."

She continued walking. "I've only been here once."

"You seemed to know exactly how to get here."

"I know a lot of things."

Jack let that go. He needed to determine their immediate safety before delving into her education, street or otherwise.

"Who owns the house?" he asked.

"It belongs to a friend of mine. I have permission to use it anytime I want." She opened the screen door and punched a memorized code into an electronic lock. Morgan's world seemed to be populated with electronic locks, gates and doors.

And now assassins.

Jack didn't doubt the people after Morgan weren't amateurs. They knew who she was and exactly where to find her. The fact that she was so well-prepared for them is a story he wanted to hear.

"This friend of yours," Jack spoke. "Is he here?"

"No."

"How do you know he won't decide to come up for the weekend?"

"Because we left *her* splattered all over my foyer."

Jack was smacked by the cryptic comment. He knew Morgan was hurting inside and trying to deal with it. There wasn't time for grieving, not even time to do the right thing for a life that was so suddenly ended. He understood her grief. He'd seen it before, even experienced it himself when he lost a friend during a raid in Lebanon. He had seven men to think about. He couldn't stop when one of them went down. But Remy hadn't been shot. He'd been caught, not killed. At least not right away.

"There's a bathroom down that hall and several others upstairs."

"Morgan?" She hadn't stopped moving since she got out of the car. She walked quickly from room to room on the first level. Another familiar action for someone grieving and trying not to let anyone else know. He went to her and took her arms. He turned her to face him. "How do you feel?"

"I'm fine." She tried to pull away, but he tightened his hold. She winced, but he knew he wasn't holding her too tight. He loosened his hold anyway.

"You're not fine. You're remembering. You're no longer

driving. Your concentration isn't on anything and that leaves you time to remember. Tell me. Don't go through it alone. You don't have to.''

She looked at him then. Eyes that had been avoiding his shifted to stare straight at him. Her brown irises were huge and bright. Then she slapped his hands away.

"I said I was fine." She stepped away as if she were back on the streets, scared, alone and fending for herself. "There is food in the refrigerator and plenty of entertainment if you want it. If you're tired, there are eight bedrooms on the second floor. I'll be in the last one on the right. You can use any of the others."

She disappeared, leaving him alone.

Morgan needed some down time. Her nerves pulsated fire. Red and raw, they spewed flames, licking at the backs of her eyes, until she wanted to scream. Her eyes were blurry from the intense pain in her head. The headache had begun last night, but she'd staved if off while she drove, wishing she had her medication handy, but knowing it had gone up in flames with the house on Wild Meadow Lane. She had a small bottle in the first-aid chest, but that was in the trunk. The road had been practically empty for most of the drive. She didn't have the beams of other cars' headlights stabbing her with illumination, and the steering wheel acted as an anchor, keeping her sane.

Her kind of life didn't come without a physical manifestation of the abnormalcy that was all but tattooed on her forehead. What a normal life was like she had no clue. She'd traded the streets for what she thought should be normal. It had the promise of normalcy, but it had been temporary, only letting her glimpse the good life. She could be part of it for a price and that price was time. For a short period she could live like the rest of the world, but then she would trade one set of circumstances for another. Some people tried to cope by disappearing into bottles of Jack Daniels or pints of Boone's Farm Apple Wine, an elixir so cheap it burned through tissue on the way to the stomach. Others escaped the world through slow forms of suicide like crack, heroin or one of the psychotropic drugs with long names and short initials. With her it was stress-induced migraines. She wasn't sure her own methods of coping weren't as potentially dangerous and suicidal as daily doses of cyanide.

The headaches began the winter after she'd moved to St. Charles. At first she thought they were normal headaches, but their constancy made her realize headaches were generally symptoms of some other physical problem, and that her body was telegraphing her a message so loud she couldn't ignore it. Morgan visited her doctor for a complete physical. It rendered nothing organically wrong with her. The doctor determined, from her description of head-exploding, light-sensitive pain, that she suffered from migraines. Morgan understood the stress and worked to provide physical outlets for it. The first was an exercise program that resulted in her building the escape tunnel. She hadn't begun thinking of it, but later thought her headaches would be less frequent if she knew she could hide or escape the house if someone came looking for her. For a while this had helped and she felt better, slept better. Then Austin Fisk entered the picture with his constant questions and implicit threats of bringing the world to her door. The headaches returned with a vengeance so forceful they could rival any switchblade stab.

And now Jack.

She could do nothing with Jack around. He threw her equilibrium off big time. In this state she was too aware of him as a man. She could use his arms around her, protecting her, for the moment keeping her fears at bay. But that was a door she could not open. Not now, at least. Maybe not ever. She still hadn't come to terms with his presence. Why did he show up now? Although he'd saved her from exposing herself too soon when they were in the tree, he could still be her assassin.

She went to the bedroom and closed the door. Pulling the drapes shut, the soft green tones of the guest room disappeared, and the furniture melted into shrouded shadows. The darkness eased the throbbing pain somewhat. Closing her eyes, Morgan massaged her temples a moment, then went to the bathroom in search of aspirin. She thought of Michelle lying back in her house. It was doubtful anyone would find anything of her after the explosion. Poor Michelle, who never hurt anyone, and never had a headache judging from the contents of this medicine cabinet. Closing the mirrored door, she went back into the bedroom and lay across the bed.

It was too far to go back to the car for the medicine. Sleep would have to do.

Jack didn't pursue Morgan. He understood what she was going through, and even though she didn't have to go through it alone, she was insistent on not allowing him to help her. Jack didn't know if he blamed her. He'd come to see her because he'd been there when her message came through. Jacob Winston was his friend and they were meeting for lunch. Her message interrupted their departure and Jack told Jacob he'd check it out. He wasn't authorized to work in the United States. His area of concentration was overseas, the Middle East and Asian countries, oil-producing areas and places where nuclear weapons could become an immediate threat. After the Soviet Union collapsed and each of the states became its own country, the threat increased with bureaucracy in chaos. There was little or no accounting for medical research, viruses and super-viruses, or weapons of mass destruction. Paperwork and missiles fell through cracks as wide as superhighways. Some of them found their way to Middle Eastern countries and that's where he came in. With his coloring and ability for language, he was less likely to stand out than some of his contemporaries.

Jack surveyed the house as he thought of his job then and now. The downstairs was clean of bugs and the kitchen was fully stocked with food. Both the refrigerator and freezer were filled to capacity. The cabinets bulged with every type of dry goods. He wondered if Morgan was telling the truth. She said she'd only been here once, but she moved through the house as if she were a swimmer moving through water.

Jack checked the locks downstairs on the doors and windows before going upstairs. Bedroom by bedroom he checked them for anything out of the ordinary. They were all clean. At last he got to the door where Morgan told him she was going. He knocked lightly. She didn't answer. Gently he turned the knob and opened the door. The room was in complete darkness. She lay across the bed, asleep. Her feet dangled over the side and she still wore the tennis shoes she'd had on for more than twelve hours.

She couldn't sleep that way. Jack knew she was exhausted, but her feet would swell and she wouldn't be able to walk. He went in and closed the door to keep the light out. The room suddenly seemed much longer than it had when he looked inside. He felt as if he were intruding on her. Feelings toward her made him warm and he felt himself becoming aroused. She looked so peaceful in sleep. When she was awake she was always on guard. He'd seen it twelve years ago and he saw it yesterday when she came into her house. Sleep was her only refuge, the only time she could let her guard down, drop all the masks she held firmly in place, the barriers that kept the world away from her, kept her safe from needing another person. There was only one time he knew of her need, of the fire she kept encased inside her. He remembered it still, as if it had happened yesterday and not twelve years ago.

He'd kissed her. A kiss that moved him, changed him so he never forgot it, but also scared him so badly he could only turn and leave. He walked away from her, but he wanted to run. She'd altered his reality, jolted it as surely as if she'd taken a tire iron and beat him about the head. And there was nothing he could do but stand and accept the pain.

Jack took Morgan's legs and lifted them onto the spread. He unlaced one shoe and eased it off. She sat up.

"What . . ." Her eyes were wide and afraid.

"Shhh," he said, reaching out and pushing her down. "Go back to sleep. I'm here."

She lay down and closed her eyes. Jack stared for a moment. He'd never seen anyone as beautiful as Morgan Kirkwood. Even at nineteen when he'd viewed her on the film in the CIA headquarters building, she was the most beautiful woman he'd ever seen and she was barely more than a child. She was still as beautiful, but no longer a child. She was a woman and he couldn't help being aware of it. Jack stood there for another moment before forcing himself back to his task. Quickly he removed her other shoe and pulled a light blanket over her.

The air conditioning had been turned on and he didn't want her to get cold.

He looked down at her, wanting to kiss her forehead, wanting to curl her body into his and hold her, the way he'd held her in the tree, but he couldn't trust himself to stop there. He brushed his knuckles down her face and left the room.

The door clicked quietly closed.

Morgan Kirkwood opened her eyes. She raised her hand to her cheek and slowly caressed it against her skin.

CHAPTER 3

Outside a perfect May morning was in the making. Jack walked into the backyard noticing the area had both advantages and disadvantages. The house sat alone in the middle of a manicured yard. The landscaper had probably been paid well to clear the land and form a sloping emerald green lawn that extended from the house to the trees at its perimeter. Square-cut hedges dressed the outside of the house, broken here and there for massive flowering plants, roses, philodendron, forsythia, a holly bush whose bright red berries would contrast the snow in winter, and the ever-present bougainvillea, which must be law for every landscape architect since it appeared in most yards in the eastern United States.

The perimeter of the property was ringed by oak and syca-more trees. The trees prevented anyone from surprising them, but conversely they had three hundred feet of open space before the trees would provide cover for escape should it be necessary. The front of the house also had the reflecting pool. Jack found pumping equipment and a fireman's hose. This far from another house or any other form of civilization, the house had its own water supply in case of fire. It also had its own emergency generator. Michelle O'Banyon must have been very well-to-do. Jack wondered about caretakers. Someone had to keep the lawn cut and the refrigerator stocked. He wondered about the road too. It was hidden from a casual driver and far enough back that when it became nearly impassable, any normal driver would assume they'd made the wrong turn and go back. It was good for hiding, Jack thought.

Morgan had to feel comfortable to come here. He turned to look at the upstairs windows. Her room faced the open yard where he stood. The closed drapes indicated her sleeping quarters. He thought of her lying up there, oblivious to the danger they'd gone through, and he knew there was more ahead of them.

The shot that took out her friend, Michelle, had been a Meier RD-12, a gun that shoots a spray of bullets in the form of a circle. The impact is enough to cut through bone and tissue surrounding the heart and fling it against the wall ahead of the body. The average hit man was a sharpshooter, whose weapon was as personal to him as his fingerprints. Their choice of firearm was something small, easy to carry, easy to dispose of if necessary. The bullets that had killed Michelle O'Banyon came from a weapon he knew. It was stock-in-trade for his profession, military, deadly and identifiable to terrorists.

Jack turned back, continuing his surveillance of the area. When he reached the trees he estimated the distance to the house at three hundred feet, the length of a football field or three Olympic-size swimming pools. Leaning against a tree, he pulled his cellular phone from his pants pocket. The small, government-issued instrument was state-of-the-art. As thick as a Hershey candy bar, it contained all the internal technology to reach any other phone or communication device on the planet. He flipped it open to palm size and tapped out the memorized code onto the flat keypad, then pressed his thumb to the identification pad and spoke into the speaker. Through a massive amount of secure computer code, his verified signal uplinked to a military satellite thousands of miles above the earth and bounced his scrambled voice code back to a specific secure phone in FBI headquarters only eight hundred miles from his present location.

"What the hell is going on there?" Jacob Winston, director of the witness protection program sounded angry. Jack knew an LCD panel lit up in Jacob's office revealing Jack's location and identity. Before Jacob even lifted the receiver he knew who was on the phone. "I've got reports of Morgan Kirkwood's house exploding, gunfire exchanged and one dead body. What happened?"

"I'd like an answer to that question myself," Jack replied. "I'd only arrived on the scene when the light show began."

"Is she safe?"

"For the time being. We escaped the house before she blew it up."

"She blew it up?"

"There isn't time to explain everything that happened, but she's an amazing woman, Jacob. She had a planned escape route you'd have to see to believe." He hoped his voice didn't reveal his emotions. He'd never had a problem doing it before, but whenever he thought of Morgan Kirkwood, any rules of keeping himself separated from the situation evaporated like ice on a griddle at five hundred degrees. "We drove all night to our present location." Jack was careful to keep names out of the conversation. The line was secure as far as he knew, but no system was foolproof. Jacob knew where they were and he'd been identified by both voice and thumbprint before the phone at FBI headquarters on Pennsylvania Avenue in the nation's capital had even rung. Jacob could locate him by the signal from his cell phone if he needed an exact location.

"Is she safe?"

"Not in the long run. Twenty-four hours at best."

"You're there to make sure she's all right." Jacob appeared to be giving him orders. "I'll send enforcements. Can you hold?"

"I'm not authorized."

"I'll clear it."

"Copy," Jack said. "I'll still need to check in," he paused. "I need to know the situation."

"She hasn't told you?"

"She's got a problem with trust. One I believe is validly supported by circumstances of the past." Jack didn't have to tell Jacob of Morgan's Korean operation which had gone horribly wrong. He already knew most of the details. "She thought I was here to kill her and I'm not sure she doesn't still think that."

He stopped short of accusations, but knew Jacob understood the implication. "Do you have anything?"

"Nothing," Jacob said. "Other than her message about her suspicions, we can only assume it has something to do with her past. That's your ballpark."

He and Morgan had been together on one mission, twelve years ago. What could that mean now? "I'll check into it."

"We'll talk later," Jacob said, indicating there was more on the table than could be communicated over satellite links despite the security measures in place. "Sit tight, we're on our way."

The phone went dead. Jack checked the state of the drapes on Morgan's windows. Nothing had changed. He hoped she was still sleeping. It was nearly time for him to sleep too, but he had one more phone call to make.

Brian Ashleigh headed the Central Intelligence Agency. He was a great guy, a hands-off manager to his direct reports. Jack didn't report to him. He reported directly to Forrest Washington, director of antiterrorist activities in the Far East. Forrest gave his agents in the field the freedom to act. He realized the agents had to have the latitude to make decisions on their own. There was no book of rules to follow for the situations a field agent could face. It was instinct, experience and intuition that was the guidebook.

But Forrest was away on vacation and Jack had to call the director in his stead. The problem was, Jack shouldn't be here at all. He had no rights and no protection under the law other than that of a private citizen. This was not his pool or even his neighborhood. He had no authority here. The fact that Morgan Kirkwood's life was tied to his presence and ability to protect her, or that she'd once been pivotal to a successful CIA operation, meant nothing to Brian Ashleigh. She was no longer active. She'd performed one operation and had been duly retired.

When this call was verified and his identity confirmed, Ashleigh would burn his ass over the satellite-linked carpet.

Where was Jack? Morgan's first thought when she woke was of the man who might be here to harm her. She checked the clock. It was afternoon. She'd been asleep for hours. Her headache was gone and she felt better. Not rested, but better. She hadn't felt rested in years. After yesterday it seemed like a lifetime. And she was hungry.

Pushing back the blanket Jack had thrown over her, she got out of bed and folded it neatly. She didn't know which of the rooms he'd chosen to sleep in, but the house had presence to it, a stillness that said nothing was moving and no one was about. No smells came from the kitchen, no coffee or television playing to disturb the rhythm of air currents. Morgan had made a study of air in the house she'd occupied. She knew any changes due to barometric pressure or the presence of living human beings. This house wasn't her domain, but she could feel the quiet. Jack was here, but he was asleep, not moving, not disturbing the air.

Morgan wanted to look for him, peep into each of the bedrooms and see if he was comfortable, see if the chiseled features in his face changed to the little boy face she imagined it could be. Jack's features were hard. She wondered what he did to keep his face so stern and serious. Through the long night of driving, his face had remained still, unchanging, immobile. At the beginning he'd sneaked glances at her, but after a while his stare was trained on the road ahead of them. She wondered at the practice it must take for him to put total concentration into a task. He probably had the same technique when he slept, but she wouldn't know that since she wouldn't look for him.

The kitchen was stocked to the rafters. She'd known it would be. Michelle had told her there was plenty of food, and Morgan didn't expect any less than she saw. She knew Michelle had grown up poor, dirt poor. She'd come from the mountains of Tennessee, from a large family, where money was short and mouths long. For years she didn't wear shoes, didn't go to school, didn't eat and didn't see any future greater than the one in front of her face. She'd told Morgan this during her first Ladies Auxiliary Annual Tea Party. The kind of place where the society of the town congregates to socialize and plan. Michelle had pulled herself up from the uneducated muddy streets and changed her life, but her kitchen was always packed with food as if she were afraid she'd have to return to that life of hunger. Morgan understood her. They both had the same kinds of backgrounds. Morgan's had been a fight for existence and Michelle's a struggle to survive. They came from the same cloth and believed in the same things. Except for Jack they would have died on the same day. A tear slipped into the corner of Morgan's eye and she wiped it away.

Jack had already eaten. There were dishes in the drainer that had been washed and stored. Morgan knew he had to be as hungry as she was, but her migraine superseded her need for food.

Quickly she scanned the contents of the freezer. Thoughts of broiled steak and baked potatoes dripping with raw butter, lumped high with gobs of sour cream wafted through her mind and made her mouth water. Only there were no potatoes to bake. She could bake pork roast and couple it with warm applesauce and gravy-laden mashed potatoes from a box. There was frozen shrimp and lumpfish, a tray of baked lasagna she could cut and microwave. And for Michelle's efforts at dieting, there were packaged dinners from Weight Watchers, The Budget Gourmet and Lean Line. While Morgan would love to have a decent meal, the preparation time was too long. Her headache could return if she didn't fill her stomach soon. She wondered what Jack had eaten as she pulled the lasagna tray from the freezer.

As the microwave sent radiation at a frequency of 2,450 MHz into the molecules of her food, causing them to move rapidly and generate enough heat to cook it in a few minutes, she stared through the kitchen window. The glass structure composed the entire wall, broken only by the huge wooden frames that sectioned it into six panes and separated the outdoors from the inside. Without the frames, the double layer of tempered glass would appear invisible. Without adornment, the window's giant panes were nearly as large as she was tall. The lawn on the other side was bright green and healthy, but Morgan's mind saw a cool pool of water and a man swimming in it.

Jack's strokes were strong and rapid. His shoulders rotated through the liquid, propelling him forward toward his goal of the pool's end. Back and forth he swam, switching direction with only a mere disturbance of water. He fascinated her and she found it difficult to look anyplace else while he swam. But Jack Temple had been a coach, not even a competitor. He had been within the age range, no more than twenty-five she estimated. Competition wouldn't be a problem for him. She wanted to ask him why he was coaching and not competing, but he stayed away from her. His body radiated a don't-come-near-me message. Consequently, she gravitated toward him, but kept her distance, usually observing his personal practice sessions from the far end of the audience section or through the glass observation room.

She usually left before he completed his routine. Morgan had watched him enough to know the length of time he took before returning to the residence village and his team.

Except for that one night.

Maybe she had the next day's mission on her mind or her own final competition had driven her to the pool. Whatever the reason, she overstayed her timing and Jack came out of the water to find her, the only spectator, in the stands.

Morgan's heart hammered in her chest. They'd spoken to each other once, on the plane when they'd both headed to their seats at the same time and the plane hit an air pocket, causing them to collide. His hands caught her arms and she looked into his eyes. She couldn't move, couldn't speak. Now she felt the same way watching him come toward her. She stood, wanting to run, feeling the need to escape. He was dangerous. She knew dangerous men, could recognize them in a snap. Jack was deadly. She should run from him, stand clear whenever he was around. Yet he attracted her like morning attracts the sunrise. She couldn't keep her eyes off him. Danger poured from him like the water rolling off his shoulders and chest. It shimmered down his athletic legs, glistening like rivers of black gold.

Morgan stood up and moved to the floor. Her gym bag hung on her shoulder. Her brain told her to leave. Her preservation depended on her getting out of the room, but her feet took root in the cement flooring. Jack's eyes pierced through her, holding her in place. Morgan couldn't have moved if she'd wanted to. Her feet had nothing to do with her former street mentality. She wasn't trying to protect her turf or stand up to the neighborhood bully. There was something about Jack that drew her. It was visceral, mysterious, magical even. She had no explanation. It was as if they had to be together, but coming together would mean fire and perishing. There was no way to stop it. It was destined. She could only stand and wait, watch while doom reached out for her. She would embrace it, knowing it was forbidden, that nothing good could come from it, but helpless to do anything to change the forces that had already been set in motion.

Morgan wore her leotard and tights. She could explain she was heading for the gym to practice when she saw him. Jack gave her no need to explain. Neither of them spoke a word.

He walked directly to her, his gait easy, unhurried, his weight balanced. She had to look up as he approached. Morgan watched him, a dark Poseidon, a devil-God rising from the sea, advancing toward her, the light of the water in his eyes. Her heart beat so hard she was sure he could see her chest moving. Yet they continued to stare, one at the other. The room about them shrank, bringing the humid air closer and making it hard to breathe. Heat escalated, growing hot enough to boil the pool water.

He stopped in front of her. Too close. He breathed hard from physical exertion. Morgan felt the same although she had done none of the work that he'd performed while she watched his efforts. His body heat grew, enveloping her in its flames. She could almost see the red-gold color of the encompassing wave as they teased her with their all-consuming power.

Her eyes rose to Jack's. Gone was the coldness she'd always seen there. Gone was the hostility that normally greeted her when she found herself in his line of vision. His eyes were liquid, large brown circles that spoke to her without language, without tongue or teeth or movement. She heard his mind, his heart, his need for her already knew the words.

His short hair glistened with pool water, bright, caught by the ceiling lamps that bathed him in a soft gold glow. Morgan watched a drop of water roll over the curve of his ear. It caught the lobe and hung there like a star, its light captured and sparkling bright. More drops joined it until the tiny weight became too heavy and burst in an exciting explosion.

Morgan gasped. Jack's hands reached for her waist, aligned

their bodies, engulfing them in the dual heat of furnace-hot generators. Her gaze came back to his. For a moment she saw a question in the depths of his eyes. Then his head dipped and his mouth captured hers in a searing kiss. An ageless, timeless communication of man to woman. A fire-hot, molten revival of life. A circling, waving tsunami of need pouring from one to the other and back in a ceaseless wave of desire, passion, rapture.

Morgan had secretly dreamed of him. She'd imagined this kiss in the darkness of her bedroom, never thinking it would ever be a reality. He lifted his head to reposition his mouth over hers. Morgan grabbed his arms to keep from falling and Jack's arms embraced her, deepening the kiss. She melted into him, her arms encircling his neck, his arms caressing her back.

Jack's hands moved to her hair, combing upward from her neck over her crown, anchoring her to him in a frontal full nelson.

His mouth grazed hers, like a burning prairie fire, dry and coarse, and moving out of control, pushed along by the wind. Morgan tumbled like the brush into him. Going up on her toes she made room for Jack to pull her closer as if he were the fire and she the lifegiving air it fed on. Long ancestral caravans of relatives rushed into Morgan. A sweeping panorama of her own female ancestry rushed in a ghostly progression, making her realize the force from which she'd come, the women who'd slaved and toiled to bring her here to this life and this man. A desert of hope in a sprawling mirage of spewing fountains.

They hung like that, supporting legs and arms and torsos. Bobbing heads switched positions like the ticks of a clock. They dodged, danced and connected. Two complementing souls finding each other over a planet full of people, knew their joy, the wonder of being alive, the height of a thousand yesterdays and the singularity of one frozen moment in time.

Jack broke contact just as he'd begun it. He shifted Morgan's head to his shoulder, letting her rest there while they both hungered for air and each other. Nothing so cataclysmic had ever happened to her before. There were no words to describe it, not now, not in the past, the present or the future. Only the perfect tandem communication between two souls.

Then Jack released her. He stepped back, their personal space still twined, their auras mixed, their heat comingled. Morgan felt the connection between them, as strong as iron chains, bonding them together as invisible as a breeze. His eyes were hot on her, so hot that had she not already been contained inside a form of skin, she would have flowed across the floor like the puddles of water about them.

Emotion didn't cross his face, but his eyes changed from loving and wanting to questioning, confusing, and finally regretting. Then the shutters closed over his face as surely as if he'd donned a mask. Morgan felt a coldness pass between them as if she stood in the path of a cold, frigid wind. Then Jack turned and walked away.

The gym bag on her shoulder dropped to the wet floor. Droplets of water rained upward, splashing against her legs and soaking into her stockings. A moment later her knees lost their power to keep her upright. She sank to the tiled flooring, oblivious of her tights, unconcerned about the bones in her knees, uncaring of the potential for hazardous injury to future competitions. All she understood was that something special, unique and wonderful had been offered to her, but like everything else in her life, it had been jerked away almost before she could touch it.

The sound of a mixer jolted Morgan back to the kitchen. She whipped around looking for the source of the noise. Her gaze darted from one appliance to another, but there was no mixer. Nothing moved. The counter was nearly free of all electronic devices used to make work in the kitchen a marvel of efficiency and time-saving convenience. Yet the sound continued. A wisp of movement caught Morgan's eye.

She turned toward it, forgetting the pool scene which had played out so many years ago, to find the subject of her thought leaning against the doorjamb. It had been twelve years, twelve years of nights since she'd seen him. Long, restless, unfulfilled nights, when she could capture an image as fleeting as stardust.

Now there he stood—solid, comfortable, commanding and sexy as a soft night with a moon on the rise. Then the fog surrounding her brain lifted. It wasn't a mixer she heard. It was the sound of giant rotors beating the air.

A helicopter!

They'd been found. But how?

Jack came through the door.

She glanced over her shoulder. The window suddenly made her feel exposed, vulnerable. "Who did you call?" she demanded.

"It's all right. They're here to rescue us."

Jack headed toward the back door.

Morgan grabbed his arm, stopping him. She listened to the sound. He'd think she was crazy if she told him she could hear the type of helicopter it was. She'd spent a lot of time listening, training. Every morning and each evening the traffic control helicopters flew over the major arteries leading to downtown St. Louis. She also knew the sound of commercial helicopters. She'd once dated a helicopter pilot and he'd taught her how to tell the difference. He wanted her to be able to distinguish his approach from the traffic control system. Morgan admitted she wanted to learn. Anything that might help save her life in some future time, she took advantage of. This might just be the time.

She gestured toward the window. The sound was high. "Who did you call?" she asked again.

"Jacob Winston."

Jack pulled himself free and headed again for the door. She listened intently. Morgan didn't know a military helicopter. She could only tell that this one sounded heavy. Its beat through the air had a slower rhythm than the commercial ones. She didn't know what that meant, but instinctively she understood there was a danger present.

She turned as Jack reached the door. Through the windows she saw the helicopter. Its dark hulk lined up with the huge wall that provided beauty and light, but no protection. In a second she was after Jack.

"Jack, no!" She lunged across the room, slamming into Jack as bullets shattered the window. Glass spewed across the kitchen with hurricane force. She and Jack crashed into the wall of the small enclosure and sank to the floor. Their arms caught together as they crammed into the tiny space, each one trying to protect the other.

"Got any ideas how we get out of this?" he whispered in an ironic form of humor as the bullets stopped shattering everything around them.

"No," she said flatly. Her hands moved quickly over him, frisking him in their awkward position on the floor. She found what she appeared to be looking for. Reaching inside his pocket she pulled the cell phone out and smashed it against the wall next to Jack's head. He reached past her trying to halt her attack on the device, but in his position he was no match for her determination. The phone fell in pieces which Morgan picked up and pulverized until the electronic enemy could no longer hurt her.

"That was our only link with help."

"Well it wasn't working properly if this is the help it summoned."

"Follow me and stay down." He crouched into a crawling position and led her up the back stairs. Thank goodness Michelle's "cabin" was no cabin. Bullets plummeted the house. They ran through the upstairs toward the front of the house. Abruptly Jack stopped and looked at the ceiling. Morgan followed his gaze.

"It's moving," she said, tracing the path of the helicopter above their heads.

He didn't speak, but pulled her faster. They ran down the front stairs and to the cellar door. Jack went into the darkness. Morgan wondered what he was doing, but she didn't take time to ask. She followed him. As if he'd been here before, he went straight to a panel and flipped several switches. Then they started back to the cellar stairs. The sound of bullets became louder the closer they got to the top. Jack stopped before barreling through the door.

"We've got to get outside," he whispered. Morgan thought he talked more to himself than to her.

"The helicopter is out there."

"I know," he answered. "We better hope there is only one of them."

"What are we going to do?"

"Bring it down."

The idea had come to him in a flash and he wasn't at all sure it would work, but he'd been in tight situations before and knew he had to work with whatever tools presented themselves. In this case the tool was water.

"I want you to stay here."

"No!"

"I don't have time to argue with you."

"Then don't. I'm not staying here. You might need me."

"You don't even know what I'm going to do."

"I don't care. Whatever it is you could only have thought of it in the last two minutes, so it can't be that well thought out. I'm not staying here, so stop wasting time."

"I knew you'd be trouble the moment I saw you," he muttered. "Stick close and keep your head down."

At the side door Jack listened until they knew the helicopter was at the back of the house. Cautiously he looked out. Grabbing her hand he quickly pulled her through the door and to the fire hose he'd discovered earlier.

He pulled hose from the circular frame that held it neatly out of the way. He touched the water pipe and could feel the pressure there.

"Unroll this," he told her, indicating the tan-colored hosing. "Keep doing it until it's all off the frame. At my signal turn on the water." Again he touched the knob which when opened would force water through the tubing.

Jack took the end of the hose and started toward the back of the house. He stopped at the edge and looked for the helicopter. The range of the hose was designed for the height of the house. Jack glanced at the roof above him to gauge the distance. The helicopter had been low enough to spray the kitchen with bullets. He only hoped when it came back around, it was low enough for the water to impact it.

He listened as the sound grew louder, coming toward him.

The direction was right. His heart pounded. He was only going to get one chance. Looking back, he saw Morgan. She had nearly unrolled all the hose. He thought of her standing on her beam so many years ago. He'd put her in danger that day and he'd done it again today. She only had him, even if she didn't realize it yet.

Turning his attention to the task, he spotted the helicopter the moment it swung around the house. Like a giant bug the cabin came into view, its windows smoky gray to prevent glare. Jack knew he would be in plain view, and the guns mounted on the sides of the aircraft would have a perfect target in his jean-clad body.

Jack readied the hose. He lifted his hand and held it in the air. The helicopter flew slowly, its rotors whipping the air, sucking the air upward, creating clouds of dust. Jack thanked the dust for the camouflage it afforded him. He was banking on human nature. It was natural to jump, react in some way, to the sudden splash of a blinding wall of rainwater heaved up by one car and hitting the windshield of another. This was his intention. He had surprise on his side. He hoped he also had perfect aim.

Quickly he dropped his hand, then grabbed the hose in a photographer's stance. Water started through the spiral of hose Morgan had unleashed. He felt it blow through the fabric hose as it swelled and hardened the hose about his feet and legs. A light second later it gushed through the spout like a thrusting geyser. Pointing the hose at the juncture just under the beaters, Jack aimed the extension. The helicopter swayed to the side as the g-force connected with its mark. Jack took a step forward, spraying water over the windshield. Then he found the opening in the side and water gushed into the cabin, surprising the pilot. The man fought the flow, letting go of the stick in an attempt to plug the hole and move away from the impact. The helicopter became a huge, uncontrolled, metal weight with no method of remaining airborne. The big-nosed craft pointed downward. The tail rotor spun the machine around backward.

Jack worked with it, keeping the water flowing, moving as the craft moved to keep the water going inside and disorienting the pilot. Since the craft was low to the ground when it came around the house, it had little recovery distance or time for the pilot to grab the stick and pull the helicopter out of danger. It struck the ground in a labyrinth of snarling metal and shattering glass.

Morgan turned the water off at Jack's command and came running in his direction. Jack held onto the hose in case he had to use it. The pilot lay forward in his seat, restrained only by the shoulder harness required of all pilots in flight. Morgan stopped at Jack's arm. Her hand found his instinctively. He dropped the hose and squeezed her fingers, barely conscious of the action. They both looked at the mass of white metal stained with green grass and dirt, its rotor blades pitched into the ground like huge steel knives. The engine hissed and ticked. A white smoke came from a closed panel near the top.

"Is he dead?" she asked.

Jack didn't answer. He started forward. Morgan followed, still holding his hand.

He stopped at the entrance to the craft. The door had been ripped from its mooring and lay several feet from the mangled mess. Blood drained from the head of the helicopter's only occupant. Jack didn't think he was dead. He took a step forward and realized Morgan still held his hand.

"What are you doing?" she asked.

"I'm going to get him out of there."

"Do you think that's a good idea? It might explode."

"If it didn't do it on impact, it's not likely to happen now."

He dropped Morgan's hand and went toward the man in the seat. "If there's anything in the house you want, get it now and go to the car."

"Why?"

"He isn't alone." Jack indicated the unconscious man. "The minute he doesn't answer the radio signal with his source, there will be others."

Morgan took a step back. She hugged herself and looked around as if afraid she'd find someone behind her.

"Go!" he shouted. "Meet me at the car in *one* minute. Not a second longer."

CHAPTER 4

Jack hated this job. He couldn't pinpoint the exact moment when he'd become dissatisfied with what he did. Maybe he had always been dissatisfied. The world sat on the brink of destruction and often he was the linchpin holding the two sides together. He knew it would always be that way. That there were younger men, more idealistic, men who hadn't been beaten by their lifestyle, ready to take his place. He wanted out and he was going to get it. It should have been easy. He should be sitting at his house in Montana with his feet up, smelling the crisp air and enjoying the mountains that were both majestic and imposing, where the likelihood of terrorists coming across them was small. That hadn't happened. The decision had been taken from him when he'd gone to Jacob's office for a leisurely lunch and ended up here, on this road in broad daylight, heading east with no apparent destination in mind, but with unknown assailants behind them and not a clue as to why.

He wished he hadn't come here, that he hadn't had the misfortune to be in Jacob's office when the message appeared on his screen. Jacob hadn't shared it with him. His friend had only canceled lunch. Urgent business was the excuse, but the look he'd thrown at Jack said the message somehow concerned him. Intuitively he knew that. Curiously, he rushed to see the screen. Jacob cleared it, but not before the name Morgan Kirkwood jumped off the monitor like a bridge to his past.

Jack was planning to resign. It was his reason for being in Washington. He'd told Jacob first. Jacob was his friend, the closest thing to a friend he had or dared have in his line of work. Jack planned to formally present his resignation after lunch, but that hadn't happened. Abruptly he changed his mind when he realized Morgan was involved. Badgering Jacob was useless. The only thing he learned was that the former Olympic champion lived in Missouri and that she had never, in the past twelve years, left a message for anyone in the bureau.

Something had to be wrong. Jack knew it on more than one level. First, that Morgan had called for help and secondly that Jacob immediately reacted to her name after a twelve-year silence. Something had to be seriously wrong. Jack felt responsible. Morgan Kirkwood had begun to turn her life around. She was on her way to being a normal working American. Then he'd come into her life, without her knowledge, and changed all that. It was his fault. She would never have been in this situation, whatever it was, if he hadn't given his plan to the powers that be. But he had. And he couldn't undo it.

So he'd volunteered to check out the situation and get back to Jacob if there was the tiniest bit of trouble. What he'd seen couldn't be considered tiny: one murder, an explosion, a daring escape, a drive through the night to a hidden house in the woods and a helicopter fight with a fire hose. Jack didn't know what had sparked any of this, but he was going to find out, and he was going to find out now.

He swung the car into a rest stop and cruised into the farthest parking space. It was afternoon, but only a few cars were parked in the spaces. No one was around them. He got out of the car and went around to Morgan's side. He opened the door and pulled her out of the seat.

"We need to talk," he said by way of explanation.

Instead of going toward the building, he headed for the wooded area in the back. Several empty picnic tables dotted the landscape. He dropped her hand when they were well away from the parking area and the small building where weary travelers stopped to use restrooms, check maps and load up on junk food before returning to their cars, vans and trucks and heading again for distant destinations.

Morgan looked tired and scared, and although she fought hard not to let it show, Jack could see it. He gritted his teeth and forced himself to not turn away. He didn't want to see her looking like this. If he let his emotions get in the way he'd put off asking his questions. "I want to know what is going on," he started.

"I don't know."

"Someone is trying to kill you and you have no clue why?" There was more anger in his voice than he intended.

"I think I said that."

"Why did you contact Jacob?"

"Just how do you know Jacob?" she countered. Jack was wondering when she was going to put the fact that he knew the director of the witness protection program together with his presence.

"My acquaintance with him is not the question. What is the reason you called him?"

She folded her arms under her breasts and closed her mouth. Jack looked at her. He needed to change his tactics. Threatening her wasn't what he had in mind. He needed to make her talk. Even if she didn't want to. There was one way he had of making her talk. He'd discovered it in Korea when she came off that gym floor after her final competitive rotation. He took a step closer to her. Immediately her arms went to her sides, her hands curled into fists. She stepped back, but Jack saw her body harden. Every line of her being went on the attack.

Morgan knew the look in his eyes when he'd stepped forward. She'd seen it only once before, but it was unmistakable. Jack was going to kiss her. She turned around. "I'm going to the car," she threw at him as she started to leave. He caught her arm and spun her around.

"Not yet. I want to know what's going on."

"Give me one good reason why I should tell you anything?" She snatched her arm free.

"Because I just saved your pretty little ass—"

"Which wouldn't have been in danger if *you* hadn't called Washington," she interrupted.

Jack took a deep breath and let it out. "You're right."

She blinked at his words. She hadn't expected him to agree with her. Her stare had to be evidence of that, but she was right. Although she couldn't believe Jacob Winston had anything to do with their situation, someone else did. For a moment she thought it might be Jack, but he'd saved her more than once.

"I came here to check out the situation."

"Well, so far you're not doing a very good job."

Jack grabbed Morgan's upper arms and pushed her against the trunk of a tree. The rough surface dug into her back. The action surprised her but she revealed little to let him know.

"Stop it!" he shouted, his face only a couple of inches from hers. "I'm sick and tired of you complaining about everything. I know you're scared. Fear is natural and I won't think less of you if you show it, but stop this clawing at me. We're in this together."

Morgan raised defiant eyes to him. She wanted to cry, but she wouldn't. She was scared, yet her eyes were dry. She hadn't been this scared since she was in Seoul, hanging from the top of a prison wall with one hand, nothing beneath her but useless air.

Jack looked back at her, giving nothing away. He was as hard as the bark digging into her back and she knew he was right. She had been clawing at him. Ever since he'd shown up in her house, she'd been trying to hide how she felt, falling into old habits, attacking before she could be attacked.

She held his gaze, knowing he wouldn't back down. She understood this was a crossroad. This was the moment where she either trusted him or she would have to survive alone.

She stared into the phantom depths of his eyes, looking for a sign, something to guide her, but with Jack there was nothing. He only gave away what he wanted other people to see, and he wanted her to see nothing. She dropped her head. She lifted her hands, placed them at his waist and stepped into his space. Her forehead touched his chest and rested there. She felt him stiffen. She knew her action surprised him. It was uncharacteristic for her too, but she needed the contact and somehow with Jack it seemed all right. Her arms circled his body as she took comfort from the liaison. Jack held himself still while she lay against him. After a while his arms came around her and he cradled her closer. She held onto him, trying not to think, not to read anything more into his arms than comfort.

He was a cold man. The one who had kissed her so passionately and then walked away as if she were just another part of the water, and he was a rock over which she passed, had his arms around her. Her impact on him was the same as a single drop of water passing over the sheer cliffs of a stone mountain.

Yet Morgan heard his heart beating. The rhythm was fast, faster than she thought it ought to be for a man of stone.

Jack should let her go. His arms shouldn't be around her. She felt too good and she smelled like soap, a lemon concoction of some type. He didn't like flavored scents. They gave away too much. He was used to finding people by scent as well as cunning. He never wore cologne, used only basic soap, unscented deodorants, detergents and shaving creams. You could hide a body, suspend yourself on closet shelves or in the branches of trees, but you couldn't prevent fragrance from giving away position. Yet he didn't mind it on her. He liked knowing her scent, knowing how the perfume touched her skin, mixed with her special chemistry to produce that combination that was favorable to his taste. He wanted to move his nose closer to her, inhale the fragrance, feel the warmth of her skin against his mouth.

He didn't dare. What he was doing was already too close for comfort. His body knew it and soon she would too. With an effort greater than any man should be asked to put forth, Jack pushed her away and stepped back.

"Thanks, Jack," Morgan said. She looked him straight in the eye. "I didn't mean to make you the object of my anger. I'm not used to having anyone . . ." She trailed off. She wasn't used to having people help her, having people looking out for her. Jack knew her history. She was a loner. In that they were alike. He didn't often have anyone at his back either.

"We're in this together," he told her. "I'm here to help you. I'll keep you safe."

At least he'd try. He looked in her eyes, hoping for trust, or to find the worry he'd seen since their reunion two days ago gone, but it was there. She trusted him, he could tell that, but she was still worried. The look nearly undid him. He turned away. It was that or kiss her.

"We need a plan," he said a moment later when he felt in control enough that he wouldn't act on his instincts.

"I agree," she said.

"First I need to know what we're up against."

Jack looked at Morgan carefully. He wanted to see her reaction to the request. Each time he'd mentioned her running she'd evaded the question. He wanted to see what she did now. He wanted to know if she was about to tell him the truth or if she was about to lie.

It was textbook. He'd learned the technique early during his days of training. Eyes to the right, accessing the creative. A quick intake of breath. All she had to do was begin with "to tell you the truth," to complete the total picture. She was going to lie.

"I honestly don't know," she told him. Not the first-order phrase, but the second. She knew something, but she wasn't about to give him the benefit of her knowledge. Now he wished he had kissed her. He knew how to seduce a woman, use his own sexuality to get her to tell him what he wanted to know. He'd done it before, not often, but when necessary he'd used whatever methods were at hand.

Why hadn't he done it with her? Why hadn't he seduced her to gain her trust, her will to give him everything he wanted? He knew why. She wasn't the usual victim. He had feelings for her. And he'd kissed her once. He knew what that had done to him then, and if he tried it again he wasn't sure if he could remember his purpose or if the same thing would happen to him now that had happened before. He'd lost himself in his need for her. Lost so much of himself that he had to walk away without an explanation, stay away for years, lying to himself that she was only a job and he didn't want her in his life. Yet at the first mention of her name he was on a plane, breaking into her house and holding her in his arms.

"Do you have a plan?" She interrupted his thoughts.

"Twelve years ago we were in Seoul together." Jack had

to play a card she didn't know he held. He needed her to tell him the truth. This time he'd get it by giving her a bit of himself. Hopefully, she would do the same.

"Yes," she replied.

"You broke a man out of prison."

"Excuse me," she said with only a slight hesitation. She was better than he thought she'd be. He'd seen her in action before, but he thought he could surprise her. Instead she played her own hand. "I was in Seoul for one reason."

"To break Hart Lewiston out of jail, steal some vital documents and turn them both over to CIA agents who would get him out of Korea." This time he did see the surprise on her face. "Then you were to compete in the Olympics. You weren't expected to win the gold medal."

Morgan turned away from him. She grabbed ahold of the tree he'd pushed her against for support. He could see by her head and shoulders she was putting his presence in Korea twelve years ago together. He hadn't been a mere coach of the swim team. He'd been a CIA operative there to make sure she succeeded. Or what? What if she hadn't succeeded? Was he there to also make sure she wasn't captured? That she wasn't left behind in a condition to talk, to tell anyone what she knew, what her mission had been?

"Who are you?"

"I'm your protector."

"In Seoul . . ."

"There and then."

"Now?"

"Now I'm here to find out who is trying to kill you," he paused. "And why."

Morgan looked up at him, her heart in her eyes. She didn't try to conceal her feelings or her doubt.

"Protector, Morgan." His voice was low, sensual and inviting. She felt it almost with a tangible quality as if he'd woven the words and draped them over her shoulders. "I never had a wish or an order for anything other than that. I would never do anything but keep you safe."

He took her arm and led her to the picnic table. She sat on the table with her feet on the bench. For a while neither of them spoke, then Morgan linked her hands and looked at the trees along the back of the picnic area. "I didn't intend to sing," she began. "There was so much going on, in my head and in the arena. The arena looked like a wave of color, people screaming and cheering. I tried to find someone I knew in the crowd, but there was no one and everyone. People smiled at me, shouted my name, waved American flags." She paused. "I was so glad I was an American. I could go home, back to a place where life on the streets was better than life in that hole. I could return to a place where I'd never have to remember the prison I'd seen, the horribly emaciated men with things growing off their bodies that shouldn't be there, people without teeth and with blood crusted in places where they should have faces. When the music began I don't know what happened. My chest filled with a fear I'd never known, not when I was on the prison ledge and not when I was running through the streets. I didn't understand any of it. Then I heard the music. I remembered insignificant things like being in grammar school in a play we did. It taught us to learn the anthem. And the voice came. At first I didn't even know it was mine. I thought it was all inside my head until the crowd went wild. Everyone was on their feet and I didn't know why. I thought the prison guards had come or the police and they were heading for me. I thought of running, hiding, doing anything to get out of the limelight, but it wasn't to be. Coming down from that center block threw me into a horde of reporters, coaches, well-wishers. They herded me away to an interview room. Everyone wanted to know how I felt. What made me sing. I was used to thinking fast, coming up with lies to get out of any situation, but I was in over my head and I had no place to go."

She stopped, remembering what came next. She was coming apart. Every question someone asked took a huge effort to answer. She looked for help. He was in the room, against the back wall. Jack stared directly at her. Her eyes darted toward him. He nodded only slightly, but it was enough to give her an anchor. She took a deep breath and got back on track. She answered questions, coming up with lies to support her when needed. Thankfully most of the time she could answer with the truth. She called on her teammates, sitting next to her, giving them most of the credit, saying she only did what they had all come to Seoul to do—win! It was the truth for her team, but for her it was a lie.

She smiled at the cameras, held her hands up clasped in the hands of other team members, but she was crumbling inside. Her eyes were bright and she blinked rapidly to hold back the tears. She needed to get out of the room. The air was heavy and she felt it pressing against her. When her coach finally called an end to the interview, she left at the back of the line. Midway down the hall a hand came out and clapped over her mouth. Another went around her waist and she was dragged backward into a dark closet.

"It's me. Jack." He spoke in the darkness and her struggles stopped. She recognized his voice although they'd exchanged no more than a dozen words in their entire time together. He turned her into his arms. "Let it out," he whispered. "We're alone." Morgan clung to him as if he were her lifeline. Tears she couldn't stop poured from her eyes, wetting his shirt and soaking through to the dark skin beneath it. She cried for everything in her life, her mother, her stepmother, the man in the prison, her team, her lies, even the bullies she'd fought with on the streets. She didn't know how long she stood there, enfolded in Jack's arms, drawing his strength or why no one came looking for her. She only remembered cradling herself against his strong body, feeling his soft kiss on her hair and forgetting everything and everyone else in the world.

For a while, after she stopped speaking, Jack didn't say anything. They sat in silence looking at the trees. The answers weren't out there. Only the two people sitting here, not looking at each other, had the answers. He noticed she stopped without mentioning the two of them. He wondered if she was thinking about it. He wondered what she felt in that closet when she cried on his shoulder. He thought of it more often than he cared to admit. Holding her, letting her cry against him, being there when she needed someone. He often wondered in the intervening years who it was she needed, who was the man whose shoulder she used to tell her joys and sorrows. But he'd always cut the thought and think of something else. It made him angry to think of her with another man. He knew there had been others.

It was an irrational anger. She wasn't his. They weren't lovers. They were barely friends. More like two people who'd met due to circumstance. It bothered him that she thought he'd returned as her assassin. He'd never hurt her. He couldn't.

"Tell me about the escape." Jack pulled his thoughts away from the past, his voice gruffer than he intended. She tied him in knots and it showed.

"It was supposed to be easy. I'd studied the floor plans, knew every detail down to the last window."

"I don't mean that part."

"You already know that part, right?"

He nodded. He knew the details of what went down. He wanted to know what else she had taken or what she knew, what would cause someone to try to kill her twelve years later.

"What did you leave Seoul with?"

"The clothes on my back and a gold medal."

"And that's all?"

"That's all."

She didn't hesitate. This was a sign of the truth, but she was lying. She was good. She'd had plenty of practice at survival training on the streets and he'd seen it firsthand.

"What about information?"

"The clothes on my back," she repeated succinctly as if she were speaking to a retarded child.

Jack stood up and faced her. Morgan stared at her hands. He said nothing until she looked at him. When she did he placed his hands on the tabletop on either side of her, trapping her within his space.

"If you only left with the items you mentioned, why was your house rigged with explosives? Why did you have an escape plan in place? Why were you so prepared for something to happen, so much so that you'd practiced it until you could do it in your sleep? You had a car waiting, one that could hold its own against a military humvee. And I'm not going to even mention the access to a closed military base. Why had every contingency been planned with unerring detail if all you left Korea with were the clothes on your back and a gold medal?''

Jack's face was close enough to hers for him to see the pores in her skin and the tiny dark specks across her nose, but her eyes were steady and calm, cold even.

"I was a girl scout," she answered, her voice holding as much ice as the coldness in her eyes. "Always be prepared."

"You were never a girl scout. You were a streetwise kid on the fast track to jail or a nameless bullet from a drive-by shooting until your social worker adopted you and channeled that idle energy onto a beam and a bar.''

Morgan pushed his hands away from her sides. Jack took a step back. "You think you know me, don't you? You don't know the half of it. Where did you grow up, in some pretty little house with a picket fence, or in a shore town where the tourists come each summer and where you can always find a girl on the beach?" She took a long breath. "Well life isn't like that for all of us."

"No, it's not. And you don't have to tell me I don't know you. I know everything."

"You wish you did."

"I know everything about you. I probably know more about you than your own parents. After you left Seoul you spent a brief time in D.C., being debriefed I'd guess. Then you moved to St. Charles and virtually disappeared. You never changed your name, but it's not that unusual. There's no man in your life now. You have plenty of friends, women friends, but you're not gay. The last man you had a sexual relationship with was named Orren Sheridan. You went out with him for six months, had sex two to three times a week and always ate ice cream afterward. You gained eight pounds during that interlude. Lost ten when it was over. Would you like me to tell you the color and flavor condom he preferred?''

Morgan leapt off the table and turned her back to Jack. Rage boiled inside her like a nuclear reactor on full, gathering strength as its core went from superheated to rocketing meltdown. A dark river of fury hidden in her core, down under her soul, a muddy bed of anger that ran red and flashed through layers of logic and restraint, erupted with orgasmic force. Morgan found this mountain inside herself. A deep, wide vessel, molten, bubbly, white-hot with a hunger that fed through her organs as it fought with little or no resistance to get to the surface.

Her eyes burned and blood poured into her face, searing her with its heat. She knew it had to be a dark countenance of horror displayed there. She felt invaded, exposed, naked. Jack had ripped away everything she held closed up in her heart, stripping her of the carefully constructed camouflage, leaving her bare for the world to see and gawk at, held up to the multitudes to be criticized and stoned. She hated him for it, but she couldn't deny it.

There was something she could do, however. She turned back to face Jack. She could prove to him and to herself that she wasn't that streetwise nobody, because that nobody would have retaliated with her fists, that nobody would have extracted a pound of flesh for the insult. And Jack deserved to be hit, flattened, but she had choices. Her adoptive mother had told her that. Whatever she was, whatever decisions she made, were one of a set of choices. She wouldn't deny that it would feel especially good to ram her fist down Jack's throat, but she would make the civilized choice.

She turned and walked away.

"Damn!" Jack kicked the ground. What was it about her that got his juices working? They couldn't have a decent conversation without it escalating to the ground zero point of a nuclear explosion. Jack sat on the table, his feet in the same position as Morgan's had been. He needed to calm down before returning to the car. He rested his elbows on his knees and closed his eyes.

Morgan's face rose in his mind, not the face of the woman in the car, the one who hated him, but the nineteen-year-old in Korea. The woman who had come to the practice pool and knotted his stomach into Gordian knots. He'd created this monster and *he* had to get it under control, but first he had to get himself under control. He had emotions. He'd tried to hide

them, had done so successfully for the past twelve years, but
Morgan had the ability to unravel him with no more than a
look. He couldn't blame her if she hated him for the rest of
his life. He hadn't intended to blurt that part out about Orren
Sheridan. He hadn't intended to betray anything he knew, but
he couldn't keep it in. She got to the core of him, made him
angry. She didn't do what he expected and while one part of
him admired her for it, the other wanted her to conform. But
if she conformed, she wouldn't be the same person.

This had to be the contradiction his father had told him about.
He could use some advice now. Since he'd set foot on U.S.
soil, nothing had worked as he expected it would. He hadn't
resigned. He was in the middle of nowhere with a woman he
couldn't get a straight answer out of and he still didn't know
what was going on. Each time he asked her a question his mind
either went south or he stumbled over their past. If only he
could tell her the truth.

Jack stood and turned toward the car. Morgan sat in the
passenger seat, her back straight enough to contain fused verte-
brae. She stared straight ahead. He climbed into the driver's
seat. For a moment they sat in silence, looking at the same
scenery, but somehow he knew her mind wasn't on grass and
trees.

"I apologize," he said. "I never meant to say that."

"It's all right," Morgan answered, her voice flat, unemotional. "You shouldn't even know the things you know."

"It seems we're making a really bad start here. We can't
start over."

"Yeah, too many bullets flying through the air."

Jack laughed. He wasn't sure if she meant to be funny, but
he wanted to lighten the air in the car, which had taken on the
solidity of raw honey. He glanced at her and hoped to see a
slight smile, even the shadow of one would be welcome, but
she still sat rock-solid straight and stared through the glass.

"Morgan, I need to know what is going on. I can't help you
if you won't tell me the truth."

"The truth!" she burst out, swiveling in her seat to look at
him. "What about telling me the truth? What about leveling
with me? For the past twelve years you've been privileged to

my life, every aspect of my life, and why? I'm a nobody. Yet you and God knows who else can diagram my life like it was a complex sentence.''

"Not totally," he contradicted her, using a calm voice, when he again wanted to grab her and make her understand the life he thought so much about was in danger. But he'd hurt her emotions, not just hurt them, trampled over them, riding rough-shod like some cowboy outlaw. She wasn't one of the scum of the earth he was used to dealing with, and he wasn't immune to her.

He touched her hand. She pulled it away. "Morgan, I'm concerned about you." She looked at him then. "Why is some-one trying to kill you?"

"I don't know." Her answer seemed serious, honest. Jack decided not to push her. She had something or she knew some-thing. He had to give her time to trust him enough to want to tell him the truth. He only hoped whoever was trying to kill her would wait that long, however long that turned out to be.

"All right." He changed the subject. "We have to ditch this car."

"Why? It's faster than anything we could rent or steal."

"It's been made. That guy in the helicopter had plenty of time to get the make, model and color, not to mention the license tag number."

"He'll get nowhere with that."

She surprised him again. She'd taken extreme precautions to make sure she could survive. From the looks of her plans, she expected to be alone, dependent on no one and nothing but her own resourcefulness. Suddenly he felt sad. He knew what her life had been like on the streets and since, but it was a paper life, unreal, a dossier to be computer tagged and filed, read by privileged eyes only. What had it done to the person sitting beside him?

"Morgan, you're not alone this time. I'm here." His fingers stroked the back of her hand. A few seconds later his fingers closed around her hand. Her thumb moved across his palm. The gesture was small, only a mere brush of her finger, but for Morgan it was a step the size of the Grand Canyon. She didn't work in a team. She trusted no one and relied on no one. She was a loner, just as he was. Even her choice of sport, gymnastics, was a solitary event. There were six women on the United States team, and while they could only win the gold medal for their country based on the combined scores of the group, the individual performance was the rate at which they were judged. Yet simply running her thumb over his hand, wrapping five long slender fingers around that of another human being, was like a scream. And he was here to make sure that scream was heard.

CHAPTER 5

Janine Acres sat at a table in the bar in the Continental terminal of Atlanta International Airport sipping a margarita. She'd had it shaken and salt generously applied to the lip of the glass. For an airport bartender, used to adding water to scotch or tonic to gin, the man made a masterpiece of a margarita. Janine loved them, but rarely drank any. They killed too many brain cells, and she often needed all her brain cells to cope with training the future gymnasts of the world.

She smiled at the thought. This was what she and Allie had joked about doing when they trained together. They were going to become coaches and have a school that turned out only Olympic-class gymnasts.

Janine checked her watch. Where was Allie? Alicia Tremaine. On the team she had been Jan and Alicia was Allie. Life hadn't quite given them their dreams, but it hadn't squashed them either. Not like they were doing to Morgan Kirkwood.

Janine owned and directed a gymnastics school and camp in Clay, West Virginia. When Allie finished competitive gymnastics, she landed a job commentating on sports on a major cable station. Since then she'd gone on to acting and now starred in a major television sitcom. That's what probably held her up, Janine thought. It was hard enough to reach her by phone. You had to go through a ton of secretaries and assistants before getting to her, then she had so little time to talk. But when Janine mentioned the news report on Morgan, the two agreed to meet.

As Janine checked her watch for the third time, Allie appeared in the doorway. Who would have thought that skinny kid, who tried to hide in the doorway of the gymnastics class, would become the head-turner of stage, screen and television? Janine watched her approach, noting the men at the bar swiveling around with interest as she passed them. Allie seemed not to notice them as she scanned the area. Janine stood up as her friend approached. They hugged, covering the years of absence that kept them apart.

"I ordered you a drink. I hope it isn't too watery," Janine said.

"I guess that's my cue to apologize for being late," Allie said, slipping into her chair. "I apologize."

Janine suddenly smiled. "Allie, you're going to be late for your own funeral."

The tension that Janine felt somehow eased. She licked the salt rim and took a drink. Allie swished the straw in her scotch.

"How have you been?" Allie began.

"Fine. The school is going well. I have more students than I can handle."

"And you love it."

Janine grinned. "I admit it. I do." Then she turned serious. "You know Morgan loaned me the money to begin the school. She even donated some of the equipment. I still have it. I don't know how it would ever have gotten off the ground without her."

"I didn't know that. What happened to the endorsement money you received?"

"Spent."

"Janine, you spent it all? On what?"

Janine wasn't that proud of her past. "Parties, high living, family." She frowned. "Suddenly I was no longer young, no longer a darling, endorsements went to someone else. I spent like there was no tomorrow and then it *was* tomorrow. The only person who knew was Morgan. She came through with the loan and the school was born."

"Morgan was always friendly." The sarcasm wasn't lost on

Janine. Morgan was anything *but* friendly. She was cautious, staying by herself, waiting, hanging back, looking to see when someone would spring at her.

"I've been thinking about that recently," Janine said.

"What? How friendly Morgan was?"

"Remember that last six months, before we left for Korea? Morgan became a different person."

"It was the pressure. She wanted to win and she wasn't the favorite. We all knew it. And our coach kept harping on it during every practice session." Allie took a sip of drink.

"That was only psychological pressure. He thought she'd work harder. She was exactly that kind of person. Tell her she can't do something and she'll find a way."

"She sure did," Allie confirmed. "It surprised the hell out of me when she went through that routine on the beam. I'd never seen anything like that before."

"She did pull a big rabbit out of her hat that night." Jan hesitated. "But before that, during the training, I thought her nerves were on edge too, but I don't think so anymore."

"Why?" Allie asked. "What's happened?"

Jan wasn't sure she knew if anything had happened. In fact she felt pretty stupid right now for her intuition. It wasn't like her to get on a plane and fly three hours for a meeting. "It's probably nothing more than coincidence, but after I heard that news report about her house exploding and no mention of her, I started thinking."

"She couldn't have been there. There was only the mention of one body and that wasn't Morgan's."

"Then where is she and why hasn't she contacted her friends?"

"Janine, when was the last time Morgan contacted you?" She waited a second, but the question was rhetorical. Morgan hadn't contacted any of them since she got off the plane from Seoul twelve years ago. Even when she donated the money and equipment for Janine's school, she only came once in person. All the other transactions were between their two lawyers. At the time, Janine thought it was to save emotion between the two of them. Morgan knew Jan was the sappy one. Morgan didn't like to show emotion. Standing on that pedestal with the tears and *The Star Spangled Banner* playing had probably been the pouring out of years of pent-up passion. Her body was so full of holding it in that if she hadn't done something, she would have exploded. Morgan's life had been hard and she didn't trust people, but if she could help a friend, she would. Jan knew the Olympic team was Morgan's family.

"Did Morgan ever say anything to you?" Jan asked.

"About what?"

"About what was going on in Seoul?"

"You mean with that swim coach? God, he was good-looking." Allie smacked her lips together as if she were appreciating fine food. "What was his name?" She stared across the room, concentrating. "Something Jack or Jack something, I can't remember, but Morgan said nothing about him. Not a word."

"I don't mean the coach. I mean anything about anything?" Allie shook her head. "Did she say something to you?"

"She mentioned only once that she didn't think she would die a normal death."

Allie put her drink down and leaned forward. "What does that mean?" she asked slowly.

"I don't know. She wouldn't explain after she said it. In fact, she laughed it off, but you know Morgan. She was always so serious about everything. I let it go, but now I wish I hadn't."

"Do you think we should go to St. Charles and talk to the local authorities?"

"It sounds melodramatic, Allie. I know that, but I'm afraid something might have happened to her."

Country music poured from the radio, twangy voices that Morgan had grown to appreciate, detailed lovers losing each other, other women trying to take your man or gossip in the town that would bring you down, and women vowing to stand by her man. Morgan heard the messages and understood. She'd been all those women and knew all the men. Now more than ever she understood the stories these miniseries told in three-minute bytes. She knew why she'd taken to them, drowned in the sorrow that each of the women felt when the man she loved turned and walked away or put his arm around the blonde and strutted off with a backward glance that said, *you lose*.

Jack drove in silence for some time. Morgan felt as if the air had been damped down. She wouldn't go so far as to say cleansed, but she wasn't angry anymore. She wondered about Jack. What had his hand on hers meant? Where was this going, not just the car, although she had no idea where he was heading either, but so far the direction was all right. She wondered where this entire episode would lead them. Would they survive it? She had to admit she was glad to have someone with her.

She'd imagined running before. She knew it would come to this one day, but all her planning had been for one. She never expected any allies, certainly not the one man who had occupied space in her closed heart for the past twelve years.

Unbidden, her mind returned to the past. She thought of him—at the end of the gymnastics arena. Back in a time, a history they couldn't relive, couldn't change.

Morgan stood six feet back from the springboard. Her heart hammered in her chest. Everything about her was wrong. She was too nervous, her hands were sweaty, her breath came too fast and she was too aware of the activity in the room. This was her final competition. It was now or never, she thought. This was the moment she had worked for her entire life, yet her mind was blank. Where were the words she was going to tell herself at this moment, where were the song lyrics, the inspirational refrain that had been part of the opening night ceremonies and was threaded throughout the last several days as a reminder and inspiration for the years of training that had brought the athletes to this moment? Where were her affirmations? Even a mantra would be welcome at this point. Yet she was numb. There was nothing there except the memory of the last hour clogging her brain, memory of an exercise gone wrong. What would the director say when he heard the details of her failure? She didn't know and didn't care.

No one expected her to win here anyway. They'd told her that to her face. She looked at the scoreboard. She needed to be perfect to win. Why was she even here, even trying? No one was perfect and they all knew it.

The short distance to the beam looked like a mile. The

springboard only a square in the vastness of the enveloping cavern. The beam only a ribbon in a sea of blue foam. She took a deep breath and looked at the crowd. The seats were full, everyone moving, talking, looking at her. Then they too began to recede. They blurred into a multicolored collage, moving away from her as if she'd been drugged. Their sound went with them, reducing in volume until all she heard was a soft rush of a wave coming ashore.

She wasn't the favorite in this event. If she lost no one would think anything of it. And after what she'd done tonight in the prison, it was all she could do to remember her routine. Morgan closed her eyes and raised herself to her toes. Then she came down again on her heels. She opened her eyes and found Jack Temple in her direct line of sight. He stood against the far wall, looking her directly in the eye. She was sure his mouth curved into a slight smile and that he nodded at her. His strength gave her motivation. She took that strength, latched onto it, made him her focus. Going up on her toes again she started her run. She reached the carpeted springboard. Both feet hit the end at the same time. Using her body weight, Morgan propelled her long frame into the air. Everything slowed down. She could see every move, feel everything around her, as if she were in a dream, one in which she was both spectator and participant. She was aware of her hair, her ponytail flying about her head, the air in the room pressing against her, the feel of her leotard against her skin. She swirled around as if she were performing a synchronized water dance. Tucking her arms close to her body, she completed her mount to the four-inch, fabric-covered beam with a full-twisting front flip. Her feet connected with the apparatus with the precision of a diamond needle cutting through metal. Her knees and ankles locked and she stood straight and tall to the one man whose eyes she could see. The rest of the sixty thousand people could have been at home with the millions of spectators around the globe watching this performance. The only one whose approval she sought as she stood upon the four-inch structure was Jack Temple.

Her routine continued in the same manner as her mount: slowed down, allowing her to see clearly every twist and turn. Jack looked on as she went through the splits, the handstands, the tumbles, with flawless accuracy. She could hear the pounding of her feet and hands as they made contact, see the small puffs of dust form clouds as she went from one effortless exercise to the next. Then the dismount loomed before her. It was the most difficult part of the routine.

Height was the key. Standing at the far end of the beam, she began the three-step run and bent her knees, then stretched— and reached for the ceiling, clawing as much air as she could reduce to physical possession. Climbing into the fluid medium she tucked her body into a ball, tumbled head over heels twice, then extended herself into a straight missile, locking her elbows in and twisting her entire frame into a full layout before hitting the impact-absorbent floor as if her feet had just found the opposite magnetic pole and once set could not be dislodged without a searing force. Her arms rose into the air saluting the judge and the crowd.

For a moment the entire arena was silent. She looked around. The audience swirled like a blurred photograph. Then thunder struck, a deafening force that broke the calm and clamored to the top of the building, threatening to tear the domed roof from its hinges. She could hear her name chanted and the scores went up on the lighted board. She watched the tens come up one by one. Each of the judges had rated her the same.

She looked for Jack Temple at his post by the wall. He hadn't moved. This time, instead of a nod he saluted her win. A moment later she was attacked by her congratulating team members and sight of Jack was lost.

She wondered about him now. Glancing sideways, he still drove without a word, but apparently with a mission. In Korea she didn't think he knew how much his presence had done for her routine, but now she wasn't so sure. He said he knew everything about her. Did that include her psychological makeup? Could he read her mind, her thoughts? Did he know what she needed, and had he stood against that wall for moral support or to send her signals that the worst was over, nothing else mattered? She'd done her job.

Hart Lewiston was on a transport plane with a full medical setup on his way to a military base in California. Only a few people knew a woman, a mere child with fantastic agility, had been instrumental in getting him out of the prison, and none of them could put the name of Morgan Kirkwood with that black-clad figure who could skirt the building ledge with the same nerve-racking calm of a high-wire acrobat.

At least no one Morgan knew.

Backwater towns are the worst places to hide. Small villages and hamlets have too many prying eyes and too many curiosity seekers. They needed a large city, a place where people were more apt to be concerned about their own lives than what was going on next door, a place where there were many transients and no one asked questions or remembered faces. And Jack needed to make another phone call.

Since they'd left the house in Illinois they'd been traveling east. A green reflective sign pointing toward Indianapolis loomed ahead. Jack pulled off the road at the first exit ramp and headed toward downtown. They needed to get rid of the car, but they couldn't pull into a hotel without one.

"Where are you going?" Morgan spoke for the first time in hours, it seemed.

"I have a plan," he told her. "There's a field office here. I can get us some help."

"No!" Her eyes shifted to him and he saw fear there.

"What are you afraid of?"

"I don't know these people. Who are they and why are you willing to trust them to help us?"

"Morgan, they're operatives of the United States government. It's their job."

"I've been in this place before. Operatives of the United States approached me. Riddled me with lies and half truths and got me involved in an operation where I was expendable. I didn't like it then and I won't walk back into that kind of situation again."

"It's not your call." His voice was hard. He forced it to be that way. He really wanted to reassure her. He understood her fear. He'd had the same feelings in the past, but he knew this was the best course of action. It was regulation, by the book. Jack wasn't often a rulebook player. He found rules restricting, and they often needed to be revised for the jungle, the desert, the terrorists after him and the powers trying to make it his last day on earth. This had to be different. This was Indiana, not Iran.

Jack had been the reason Morgan got into this, but he didn't have full authority on his side. He only knew part of the story at the time and she could have lost her young life. Thank God she hadn't. He didn't know if he could have lived with himself if anything worse had happened that night.

"We need help, Morgan." His voice was softer this time. "Backup. Other agents to escort us back to D.C. I promise you everything will be fine."

She hesitated, obviously not trusting him. She had been on her own so long, fending for herself, never really allowing anyone to get close to her, get near enough to trust. Why should she trust him, especially if she knew she was here because of an offhand comment he'd made in a conference room twelve years ago.

"Morgan, you're going to have to trust someone. I promise I'll take care of you."

She sat back. "You already said it wasn't my call."

She lapsed into silence and Jack took it as consent. He continued toward town, but wasn't going to drive directly to the field headquarters. He knew better than to trust out of hand too. He'd call first, set something up. He had a friend in the Indianapolis office. Maybe he could even get a call into Jacob, find out if anything further had developed as to what the real reason was that Morgan Kirkwood had been put on a hit list. Who was trying to kill her?

And why?

The main street into the center of Indianapolis was a corridor of insurance companies. Few people expected anything else in Indiana except the 500, a wide track for race cars to circle. Most have probably forgotten that Michael Jackson and his entire family were born in Gary, or that all the music and video clubs have a warehouse address in Terre Haute. Indiana is only the way to get someplace else. Jack admitted he considered it that way too. He wasn't here to stay. It was a way station on his trip to the capital. He only hoped whoever was after them didn't realize they would stop here. At least not until they had vacated the place and had a clear and definite idea of what the next move should be.

He hated working without a plan, even if it was one he made up minute by minute. The problem was he didn't know the problem and that made it impossible to solve.

The air in the conference room on the fifth floor of FBI headquarters was thick with concern. The newspaper accounts of Morgan Kirkwood's house exploding made front-page news in St. Charles, but was buried on page three of the *Post-Dispatch*. Jacob could thank a quick-thinking agent working at the paper who reported a gas leak as the cause. The official report revealed a dangerous explosive and a timing device as the real cause.

"Where are they?" Forrest Washington had cut his vacation short when word reached him that Jack Temple was under fire in the Midwest. Jacob knew the man was concerned about Jack. Their relationship to each other was the same as Jacob's to Clarence Christopher, the director of the FBI. They bonded, became more than friends—they were family.

"Jack called three nights ago. Since then there's been no word," Jacob replied.

"We can't reach him either. Apparently, his phone has been deactivated. We did find a known member of the Korean mob at the out-of-the-way house of the dead woman in St. Charles. What's the connection?"

Clarence Christopher sat forward. It wasn't often the two major arms of the government's law and order forces intersected and Morgan Kirkwood didn't appear important enough to be the catalyst for this high-level meeting. Unfortunately, Jack Temple had stumbled into something and Morgan was the pointman.

"You tell us," Christopher said. "We inherited the Kirkwood woman and were given only part of the story. Don't bother to deny it." He stopped Brian Ashleigh with a wave of his hand. Both Jacob and Clarence knew how agencies worked. They didn't reveal anything that wasn't necessary. So the file

Christopher had read on Ms. Kirkwood gave her background and a few details of the one and only sanction she'd been party to. What Ashleigh had in his protected files was the rest of her story.

Washington slid a manila envelope across the polished surface of the conference room table. "This is the whole of it," he said. Jacob opened it, finding a CD and some papers inside.

"The CD is a video history of her. The notes tell you everything we know."

Christopher raised a silver eyebrow.

"Everything," Washington repeated.

Jacob knew of her involvement in freeing Hart Lewiston from the Korean prison during the '88 Olympics. Twelve years had passed without a sound from her and now the Koreans were after her. It didn't make sense and Jacob liked things to add up.

"Lewiston is a U.S. senator, a presidential candidate. Does he have anything to do with this?"

"We've checked him out," Ashleigh admitted. "He's as clean as snow."

"What about the Koreans?"

"We can't find a connection."

"Revenge?"

"After twelve years?"

"It's a matter of honor. They probably know she helped free Lewiston and she beat their number one champion out of a gold medal."

"Makes no sense," Jacob replied. "The same people aren't in power any longer."

"What about those that are?"

Just how much money did Jack have on his person? Morgan thought of this when he left to ditch the car. She wanted that car. It had taken a fair amount of time to restore it to peak performance. That car could outrun any police vehicle between here and New York. It served them three days. It did seem longer. She couldn't believe he'd only shown up in her life three days ago. It felt like they'd been running forever.

Morgan looked around at the room. It was standard Holiday Inn fare, clean, bright and with a view of the pool below. She thought he'd pick an out-of-the-way motel, something cheap and not the kind of place you'd expect to find a CIA operative and a fugitive from a twelve-year-old Olympic competition. Again she wondered about the cost and how Jack was paying for it. He wouldn't be stupid enough to use a charge card, she hoped. If he had, someone would surely have traced them by now. She whipped around, looking at all the windows and doors, suddenly feeling vulnerable. Paranoia would invade her mind soon. She needed to talk to him, to find out what he planned, but they didn't communicate well. She'd learned that twelve years ago by a practice pool. And from three days alone in the car with him.

Morgan was alone and hungry. She had plenty to survive on for a while. She didn't know how long. Her plan, if she ever needed one, was to abandon the house and make her way to Washington, D.C. in the car. There she would contact Jacob Winston and turn herself in. She'd met him once and she trusted him. He was a fair man, tall, serious with blue eyes, and she felt he genuinely cared about her. If he suggested she go deeper into the program, she would do it. Now she didn't know. She hadn't expected to have anyone with her. She never expected to see Jack after they returned from Seoul. She never expected to have him look at her and find her body tingling with unfulfilled longing.

Jack was a problem.

She had to get away from him. Now was the perfect time, before he got back from wherever he'd gone to dispose of her car. He worked for the CIA, she thought. He was the professional here. He could take care of himself. So why was she hesitating? She never hesitated before. She always knew exactly what she wanted and how to get it. She'd often had to fight for it, and she'd taken her share of the knocks, but she could take care of herself. Jack was a hindrance. She needed to be alone, running by herself, taking care of herself.

She swung around, searching for her backpack. Loading it over her shoulder, she checked the room for anything else she might need, then went toward the door. With her hand around the knob she stopped. Should she leave him a note? He could return and think she'd been kidnapped by the people looking for her.

Grabbing a piece of paper and pen from the desk, she wrote quickly, but did not write a note for Jack. She scribbled the hotel phone number on a scrap of paper and pushed it into her pocket. She would call him in a few minutes and tell him she was all right. She wouldn't wait for him to talk. She wanted to hear his voice one more time, but would not give him time to talk her out of her decision.

Morgan opened the door and peered into the long hallway. The carpet, a maroon pattern that gave with her step, stretched the length to the elevator. Lights at regular intervals bled overlapping pools on the floor and walls. Morgan looked for the stairs. That exit should be better. The elevator was a trap, a tiny room, with no escape. When it opened she would be prey to anyone on the other side of the sliding doors.

Someone like Jack.

Or worse.

She left the room and closed the door. Ten feet away, in the opposite direction, a red exit light hung over a door marked "stairway." She headed for it. The door's weight, designed to provide protection from fire, gave as she pushed it open and turned to softly close it. Inside, the walls were white. Huge pipes six inches in diameter ran up the wall behind the door.

Morgan turned, took a step and walked directly into Jack. She would have fallen if his hands hadn't come out and grabbed her.

"Where do you think you're going?" He squeezed her hard against him. She didn't struggle because she knew it was useless. She was caught. His eyes were angry. She'd seen anger before and it didn't frighten her.

"Let go of me." She pushed back, needing space and air. He surprised her by being there, but being shackled to his body was too close for comfort. This was another reason she needed to get away from him. She wasn't the same woman when he was close, and she couldn't drag him into the mess she'd made of her own life. Even if he was better trained than she was.

Even if he could save her life. She could get him killed and she wasn't willing to let that happen.

She might have known he'd take the stairs instead of the elevator. Didn't everything about him tell her he'd take the stairs even if it were thirty flights? His body was muscular and hard. She'd been pressed against it more than once and she knew the contours of his chest and arms.

"I'm getting out of here," she hissed, more angry with her own reactions than with his unannounced presence.

"So you can get killed?"

"I won't get killed. I've been on my own forever," she threw at him. "In the first place, my plan didn't include you. So leave me alone. I don't need you. Whatever I have to do I can do without your help."

Jack stared at her without a word. It went on long enough to make Morgan uncomfortable. Suddenly he hauled the door open and pulled her through it. In seconds they were back in the hotel room staring each other down like two gunfighters in the middle of town at high noon.

"Prove it," Jack challenged, anger so tightly wound he felt he'd snap any second now. She blinked her eyes as if she were confused. "Prove you don't need me around and I'm out of here." Jack grabbed her wrists. She gasped and he nearly let go. "I haven't done a tenth of what I can, but you don't need me. Show me how you don't need me." He noticed the way her breasts rose and fell under the light fabric.

Morgan stepped forward, pushing her hips against him. Her mouth clamped on his. He didn't pull away. Her tongue dove into his mouth. She used her mouth as the only weapon available to her. Moving her head, she repositioned her mouth, taking more of him as he joined her in the kiss. Her hips rubbed suggestively against his lower body. She could feel his arousal. She raised one leg, wrapping it around one of his and shifting up and down, feeling the heat and the hardened bulge in his pants. As expected he released her wrists. She felt his arms circle her waist and begin to pull her closer. At that moment she jerked her leg and pulled him off balance. Together they went down. At the same moment they hit the floor Morgan rolled away. With the speed of lightning she grabbed his arm and twisted it behind him in a way that forced immobility.

She looked at him for a few seconds, breathing hard. "This is what I could do to get out of that," she said. Holding his arm only long enough to make her point, she dropped it and went to her bedroom.

Jack collapsed with the slamming of the bedroom door. In all his years no one, *no one* had ever gotten to him the way she did. And a woman! He didn't mean to belittle women. They could be as tough as men. He'd run up against his share of them. This one he should be able to overpower with a nod, and she'd taken him down, reduced him to nothing more than a weak mass of need. And she'd been so cool about it. So calculating. Unemotional.

Damn, he cursed, she was getting to him.

Morgan opened the door to the bedroom half an hour later. Her face was clean of makeup and her hair was loose about her shoulders. She'd brushed it straight. It fell to her shoulders then curved slightly upward on the ends. A tease, Jack thought. He wondered if she'd done that to entice him. If so, it worked. He wanted to slip his hands in the soft mass, bring it to his nose and inhale the clean flowery smell of her shampoo. And he didn't want to stop there.

Jack planned to leave as soon as it was dark. Morgan had foiled his plans more than once, but today she'd proved he couldn't leave her alone, he couldn't trust her not to get herself killed. It would be better if he could. He'd like to walk away. He'd like to forget everything and just go, but he couldn't. It wasn't in him. Maybe the idea of quitting wasn't part of his future. He hadn't started out to find trouble, but it had found him and there was no way he could leave Morgan to fend for herself. No matter how much she thought she could handle it.

Or how much she set off his hormones.

He needed to call Forrest Washington and find out what, if anything, had turned up. When he ditched the car he hadn't had time. He thought he needed to get back to the hotel and as it turned out, he did. He even ordered room service so he wouldn't have to leave the woman he was now sworn to protect.

"I'm sorry," she said, standing in the doorway. "That was unfair of me. I should never have done it."

"It was effective," Jack said.

"It's not like I do this all the time," she replied angrily.

Before Jack could answer, there was a knock on the door.

"Room service," he explained as he went to it. He put his hand on his pistol and looked through the peephole. He opened the door and the waiter set up the food on the dual desk-table. It was small and they would have to sit close if they were to eat together. Jack paid the waiter in cash and moments later they sat across from each other.

"Do you trust me enough to tell me the truth?"

"I have told you the truth." Her voice was a little higher than usual but she controlled it. "I don't know anything more."

"What about Korea? What happened there?"

Morgan stuffed a small red potato in her mouth and chewed. She didn't look at him, yet Jack stared at her as he waited. She took her time. She wanted to tell him. He could almost taste it. She wanted someone she could talk to, tell about that night.

Jack had been there. He knew some of what she could tell him, but not all. He didn't have a clue why someone would wait twelve years to come after her. He wouldn't rush her, wouldn't push her into doing or saying anything. She would tell him. He knew ways to get her to talk. He could force her to tell him what he wanted to know, but he wanted her to tell him on her own. He wanted her to want his help. He wanted her to need him. He knew she would do it, but she would only trust him in her own time.

"I won a gold medal," she finally said.

Jack linked his fingers and rested his forehead against them. Morgan had disappeared into the bedroom right after she ate. He could hear the water running in the shower. There was no window in the bathroom and they were on the ninth floor. There was a window in the bedroom, but he didn't think she'd want to die scaling the side of the building trying to get away from him. This was not the prison. There was no ledge, no intricate ironwork for her to grab hold of. Between her room and the ground was only the brick face of the building, no place to get a foothold for anything greater than a spider, and while she might be able to dismount from a beam and stick to the floor, she wouldn't be able to use any of those skills from this location. The door was her only means of escape and she'd have to pass him to reach it.

What was he going to do? Short of tying her to the bed, he needed her cooperation. In order to save her life, he needed her to want his help. Why wouldn't she? She couldn't still think he meant to harm her. He could never do anything like that.

Jack knew ways to get information. He was adept at torture. He could pry anything out of anyone. He knew ways to make a man talk, cry, beg, call for his God, his king, even his mother, but Morgan he couldn't touch, couldn't reach. She was too smart not to understand the danger she was in. If he left her, she'd be dead before the sun set. She was good. He gave her credit for planning and executing the plan, but he didn't know how she would act on the spot. Could she use what was available? Did she understand how people thought, acted, their natural instincts? He didn't know and he wasn't willing to test it with her life. She would have to put up with him, like it or not.

Why was she as tight-lipped as a crab clamped onto a finger? There had to be a reason, something important, something she was protecting more than her own life. Jack wondered what it could be. He knew everything about her. Things the CIA didn't know he knew. He'd seen her file, read it completely and remembered every detail. There was no one she'd ever had a lasting relationship with and no unaccounted-for time periods. But Morgan was proving a master at many crafts. Deception could be one of them. There could be pieces missing from a written report. Something that wasn't in her file. It had been twelve years since she moved to Missouri. What could it be? Jack stopped. What or *who?*

Then the thought hit him. He needed to ask her a question and he needed the element of surprise. Jack wanted to be sure he saw her reaction before she had time to conceal it. Seconds if he was lucky.

Leaving the area that connected the two bedrooms, Jack went through the opening and straight to the bathroom. The water could no longer be heard falling into the tub. Jack didn't care if she was in the tub or standing naked in front of it. He opened the door. Morgan stood there, her body wrapped in a fluffy white towel. Jack didn't give himself time to think. He went through the mist and stood in front of her. He thought to grab her arms, but didn't want to touch her. He wanted an answer and he didn't know what he'd say or do if he touched that dark, wet skin.

"Do you have a child?" he demanded.

"Sure," she said without the slightest hesitation. "Triplets."

It told Jack nothing. Her eyes hadn't changed in the instant, but then she looked down. A moment later she turned to leave. His hands came out to detain her. She pushed at his arms. Instinct made him resist.

"Let go of me," she said, not bothering to conceal the anger in her voice.

He didn't.

"Just who do you think you are, anyway?"

"You want to know who I am? I'm your worst nightmare, Morgan Kirkwood. I'm that bad boy you've been warned about. The one with the leather jacket and bulging muscles. The one whose jeans are too tight, who wears T-shirts with cigarettes rolled up in the short sleeve of one arm, the one who's comfortable on any street corner and can deal with the crap no matter what it is. I know where the drugs are sold, have been sold and are going to be sold. Hell, I may have even used a few. Anything you want, I can get it. If you need medicine in the middle of the night or want someone knocked off, I'm your man." He hit himself in the chest.

"I'm no valley girl," she countered. "I could have any bad boy I wanted, good guy too."

"But the good ones don't fascinate you. And I fascinate you, don't I, Morgan? I make your mouth dry when you see me. Your body tingles and gets tight in all the right places. Life flows between your legs and your body goes all hot, but you like it, don't you? You like that feeling. It tells you you're alive. You want me, want me to touch you.''

He took her chin in his hand. ''Like you did that other bad boy. It's there, Morgan. It shows in your face, in the slant of your body. You wanted him, just like you want me. You might have put on airs, denied it to your friends, but you wanted him. You wanted to be pushed up against the lockers and kissed. You wanted all your giggling girlfriends to see it, so you could reign supreme in that small universe. But if he says anything to you, if I say anything, you use that razor-sharp tongue of yours to cut me to shreds, put me in my place, while all along, all I need to do is stand close to you, breathe the same air, let you smell the danger in me and you'll melt like a soft marshmallow.''

Jack took her mouth then without resistance. He pulled her against him, unmindful of the damp towel that separated him from her hot skin. She was soft and smelled of soap and hot water and something that could only be defined as her own personal perfume. The combination of it sent his senses reeling and his purpose with it. He knew in seconds he shouldn't have touched her. He'd kick himself later, but now his arms encircled her and she moved her arms around his neck. Her body was soft and warm and it seemed to wrap around his with precision.

Jack was supposed to teach her a lesson. He was supposed to maintain control, but it snapped within microseconds of her action. It had been years, twelve long years, since he'd held her in his arms, since he'd kissed her, twelve years of dreaming and waking to find himself holding empty air. He wouldn't forgo the pleasure now. It was more than pleasure. It was paradise. She was real, alive and in his arms. Her mouth was hot and her body was soft in places he'd forgotten existed. Jack was lost and he didn't care. His tongue swept past her lips to taste her, devour her, drink her in as surely as if she were a twelve-year-old vintage. He wanted her badly and his mouth told her that, savagely taking what she had to give. He crushed her to him, lifting her off the floor and pushing her against the wall, driving his body into hers.

It wasn't enough. He wanted to make love to her. He wanted to lose himself in her warmth, tearing the towel away from her and gazing on the golden glint that covered her skin from neck to toe. He wanted them safe in bed and he wanted to make every one of her dreams a possibility, each of her fantasies a reality. With her this close, with him inhaling the soft perfume of her skin, he knew everything he'd dreamed could come true. He understood fantasies and he was intimately acquainted with reality. What he held in his arms was real. She was heaven or at least as close to it as he'd ever come.

The moment he touched her he knew he was lost. If she'd fought, pushed him away, it would have been better than this torture he knew couldn't continue. He lifted his head at the thought and buried it in her neck, kissing her skin, sampling the soft texture of smooth velvet. Her arms tightened around his neck and he squeezed her and his eyes shut. He kept them that way for a moment. He needed another second to hold her. Then it was time to destroy both their worlds.

"That's it, Morgan," he whispered, his voice filled with emotion. "I'm your bad boy. The kiss is over. Your arms released." He pulled her arms away from him. "It's customary to run your hands down the bad boy's rock-hard chest." He demonstrated using her hands. "You like it, don't you? All bad boys have rock-hard chests. It's the law. And then it's time for the bad boy to move on, Morgan.

"To the next one, and the next one, and the next . . ."

Morgan didn't know how it happened. She heard his voice, heard the soft words. They had been sweet, mesmerizing, sexual. They pushed all the right buttons, turned her on. Then they changed. The softness remained but the words hardened. No longer did the letters have curved edges. They weren't rounded and comfortable, falling on her ears like sweet caresses. These words had metal spikes, long and ugly, protruding like daggers even through their whispering delicacy. They were nailed into Morgan's mind. The pain hit her like lightning striking. Then her hand was curling, turning from a long slender appendage that had dropped to her side into a tight fist. Her entire body tensed, then without volition, without thought, with nothing behind it but the brute force of an outcast teenager and all the shoulder she could muster, her arm swung out and she slapped him. The noise resounded about the room with the strength of a sonic boom.

They were both surprised. Morgan had never slapped anyone. She'd been in fights as a teenager, many of them, staking her claim, showing bullies they couldn't run roughshod over her, proving time and again that she was tough enough to make it on the mean streets of Washington, D.C., but until today, until this moment, until Jack, she had never slapped anyone. She considered it the ultimate insult.

Jack's hands came up to grab her, but he stopped himself. Murder surged into his eyes, black chips of obsidian, but it couldn't hold water if he saw what must be reflected in her own eyes. For a moment they held each other's gazes, poised like two mountain lions ready to battle over turf ownership. Then Jack stepped back from her as if he needed distance to keep himself in check. Morgan didn't move. She didn't back down. She never backed down.

"And the next one," Jack said. "And the next one."

Jack turned his back and left her. He closed the bathroom door. Morgan slipped down the wall until she was sitting on the floor. Her head fell forward and tears seeped from her eyes. He'd done what no other man had ever been able to do. He'd stripped her of everything. How appropriate it was for her to have on no clothes. He hadn't left her anything. He knew everything about her now. Her weaknesses. How much his presence destroyed her ability to think straight. How if he came close to her she was no more than a roman candle ready to explode. And explode she would.

Morgan pounded the floor in anger, but there was nothing she could do except hurt her hands. She knew how she felt about Jack. She hadn't thought he knew until a few moments ago when he burst into the bathroom and kissed her. She couldn't call what he'd done a kiss. He sapped her of life, removed the carefully constructed wall she'd lived behind almost all of her life. He'd shattered the glass, melted the invisible structure in the heat of the unleashed fire that should have burned the small bathroom and the two of them to cinders. But Fate wasn't that kind. She had never been kind to Morgan.

Fate had always been the ghost who stepped in to kill her dreams. It had taken her best friend, Jean, from her, but brought her foster mother, Sharon. Then it had taken Sharon and given her the Olympic chance, a carrot she didn't recognize for what it was. Her chance at the top of the world would be marred by a small matter of breaking into a foreign jail and living, but not to tell about it.

She forgot about Fate. It abandoned her for long periods. Then it came back just when Morgan thought she was off screwing up someone else's life. She should have remembered Fate never completely abandons her. She came back when Jack appeared and now she had left again, giving her another opportunity to face him and see the scorn in his eyes.

CHAPTER 6

"The plan was to get Hart Lewiston out of jail," Morgan began as if she were answering Jack's question from dinner. She wouldn't acknowledge anything that had happened in the bathroom. Nothing had happened there, she told herself. She stood in the doorway, dressed all in black, the same as she'd been the night she got Hart Lewiston out of the jail. Jack turned to look at her, but didn't move from his seat at the bar. She came into the room. She didn't sit or go near him. She needed space, the entire floor, the entire state. She paced around before continuing.

"I had memorized the floor plan. I knew the layout, all the exits, the doors, cells, guard rooms, bathrooms, warden offices, laundry. I knew the exercise yard, the intake pipes, water pipes, heating ducts. I'd memorized everything about that prison from the barbed wire fencing to the width of the ledge surrounding the roof. I'd practiced getting in and out of it. A special setting had been set up just for me. It was designed to help familiarize me with the layout. I'd practiced a special routine in daylight, twilight and darkness. I could do it under a full moon, in dense fog, or rain, or sleet. I could do it barefoot or with cramps in my toes. Nothing had been left to chance. Regardless of time of day or weather conditions, I was prepared. Everything was under control."

Jack knew everything she told him, but he didn't want to interrupt her.

"Then it happened." She turned to look at him. He sat still, frozen almost, as if moving, breathing, the tiniest twitch of a finger would break her fragile connection between time-present and time-past and she'd decide not to continue.

Morgan, however, had no intention of stopping. That night had been burned into her brain like some cerebral video disk that played for an audience of one.

"The building was built of red brick, old brick. It must have been there for centuries. The stone was rough to the touch and hard to get a foothold on. Much of it crumbled when I touched it. Putting weight on it, even my 103 pounds of muscle, was enough to make the walls turn to dust. It's a wonder a strong wind didn't topple the structure in on itself."

"But you got inside," Jack prompted. His voice was low, without emotion or inflection. This was a story she'd waited twelve years to tell. And she was telling it to him.

"I climbed the wall, imagining it to be the rock wall in the special gym. My feet slipped more times than I expected. It took longer to do the Spiderman act and then the timing was thrown off."

Morgan sat down on the sofa. She stared into the past. She no longer saw Jack, although she was aware of his presence. She was always aware of his being there. She wanted to reach across the table and take his hand, make him again the anchor that kept her grounded on the earth. But she remained where she was and Jack stayed in his position.

Her heart pounded in her chest. It had done that on the final night of the competition. When she should have been in the arena, waiting her turn or resting with her team members, she was scaling bricks that needed pointing. At the top she found the entrance, a small window. The grate on it was old, rusted and no longer fit into the base of the cemented window frame. As expected the grate was loose and she easily pushed it aside. The room was empty. Her heart slowed as she felt this job might go as planned. She should never have allowed that thought to enter her brain, for nothing afterward would follow the plan.

"Morgan."

She'd stopped talking. Her memory was replaying the night, but Jack wanted the details. "I got into the building through a window near the roof. He wasn't in his cell. It was on the top floor at the edge of the hall near the tiny room the window led into. The cell was empty."

The place smelled of human waste, sweat and hopelessness, like something had died there long ago and the walls held onto the odor of decay and rot as a warning to all who came after. She fought to keep from coughing. Even now, half a world away from that place, Morgan wanted to cough.

"No guards patrolled the classic row upon row of iron-barred cells. The lighting was dark and I couldn't see into the other cells." She could hear the murmur of collective pain. It covered centuries of life and death and despair, day after day of relentless boredom. Boredom that became agony. If you've never heard it, it's difficult to explain, so she didn't try to tell Jack what it sounded like. There were no words to describe it. It had to be experienced, and Morgan knew she'd never want to sentence anyone to that kind of torture.

"I started down the rows, keeping my breath controlled, not wanting any of the prisoners to see me, call out and alert a guard. But it was already too late. The guards knew I was there. The prison had an electronic surveillance system. No one told me."

"They didn't know," Jack supplied.

"I found Hart Lewiston. He was in the cell near the end of the row. The lock mechanism was exactly as I'd been told. I opened it with the key I'd been given. Hart had been drugged. I thought he was asleep, but I couldn't wake him."

This is when fear first set in. Morgan knew she wasn't going to be able to complete the assignment. She wasn't even sure she could get out without being killed. Her hair had been pulled up and confined with pins. On her head was a black skullcap, matching the black body suit she wore as camouflage for the night and muted light of the halls.

Her face, already dark by natural selection, was painted with a black, odorless grease. She was designed to blend into the walls, no more noticeable than a shadow.

Morgan was going to have to carry Hart back to the room

in which she'd entered. She grabbed his arm. It was cold and hard.

"At that moment I knew he was dead."

"Who was dead?"

"Lewiston. The man in the bed had been dead a long time. His body had begun to harden."

"Morgan, you're not making sense. Hart Lewiston is alive. You got him out of the prison."

"I was going to try to carry him back," she continued as if she hadn't heard him. "But the man was dead. It was all going to be for nothing. I was going to die for a man who was already dead. They knew. The Koreans knew. Someone talked, told them, set me up."

She stood up then, hugging herself, holding her arms around herself as if she would spill out.

"I turned to run. All I could think of was the tiny window in the small room, getting back to it, getting to the roof. The helicopter was to meet us there, me and Hart Lewiston. It would take us to safety. But I knew as I rushed down that hall that there would be no helicopter when I got there. Nothing would wait for me except the thin, dimensionless air. I would be stranded, alone, unprotected, huddling in darkness until they found me. Still I raced to it. It was my only hope and I streaked toward it.

"Suddenly, someone stepped out in front of me. He grabbed me. I struggled, went to scream. He clamped a hand over my mouth. He wore a uniform. I couldn't see his face, but I could feel the buttons pressing into the tight skin of the jumpsuit I wore. He whispered in my ear for me to be quiet. I was too frightened to do anything else. I kept thinking, this is it. This is where I die. After surviving the streets of D.C., facing down bullies, drug dealers and pimps, after scavenging in garbage cans for enough food to survive on, after coming all the way to Korea and getting so close to the goal I'd worked my entire life to attain, I was going to die in a dark prison twenty-five thousand miles from home."

"Morgan." Jack came up behind her. "You're all right. You aren't in Korea now. This is only a memory. It can't hurt you."

Morgan knew he thought she was reliving the experience,

not just telling him what happened. She was. She was back in the prison, twelve years earlier, twelve years younger, with twelve years' less experience. She was nineteen years old, more afraid than she'd ever been facing down a knife on a corner in the murder capital of the world.

" 'What you're looking for is in there,' he said. 'You've got three minutes.' He slapped an envelope into my hand and released me. I went to the door he pointed toward and found a man lying on a bed. He'd been beaten. Blood crusted on his face and legs. His clothes were torn and ragged and he looked older than time. His hair was matted and thin and his skin had a gray tinge in the weak light. I didn't even try to get him to walk. I stuffed the envelope in my suit and grabbed his arm and heaved his weight over my shoulder."

"What happened to the guard?"

"I don't know. He wasn't there when I looked in the hall again. The other prisoners woke and started making noise. I didn't stop to find out why. I headed for the little room. The hall looked a mile away. The weight on my shoulder wasn't that heavy, but it slowed me down. Suddenly bright lights flared and sirens went off. Guards burst through a door at the end of the hall, cutting off my escape route. I immediately changed direction and headed for the other end. There was a door that would lead to the roof. I needed to get there. That's where the helicopter was to pick us up. So far I hadn't heard it. I wouldn't let myself think it wasn't coming. I had to be positive. So I willed it to be there. All I had to do was reach it. The noise of the guards' feet sounded fast. Lewiston grew heavier, but I kept going. A bullet whizzed past my left ear. I didn't know what it was. I just thought this was a lesson they hadn't taught me. They'd given me sharpshooting and hand-to-hand combat training, but they'd fallen short in the area of bullets coming close to the body. I shifted Lewiston, but kept going. My one thought was reaching that door. Lewiston was dead weight, holding me back, and for all I knew he could already be dead."

A second bullet hit the wall next to her. Concrete chips flew into her face. She didn't bother trying to brush them away. She pushed at the door, praying it wasn't locked. It wasn't. It should have been. She thanked whoever had been there for her. Maybe the helicopter would be on the roof when she got there. If she got there.

She swung through the door, reversed and swung the lock into place. It wasn't a fancy lock. In fact, it was medieval. The prison didn't call for sturdy locks anywhere but on the cells. This was a simple board that folded down into a wooden slot, like the locks on western movie forts. She remembered the Indians always broke through those doors, and she understood her time was growing shorter and shorter.

"You got him out." Jack interrupted her thoughts. She turned to him and nodded. Then she continued her story.

"We made it to the roof with only a bullet in Lewiston's sleeve. One grazed my arm, but only burned the fabric of my suit. I didn't even know it until I was changing clothes much later and discovered the hole and a small drop of blood. There was no helicopter. I listened but could hear nothing other than the guards behind me."

"How did you get down?"

She turned and stared at him. "Don't you get it, Jack? We weren't supposed to get down. I was sent there to cause an escape attempt. We were both supposed to be killed."

"You don't know that."

"Don't I?" Her gaze never wavered. She knew it as sure as she knew her name. "I was there. There was no escape route. Hart wasn't where he was supposed to be. The guards were coming from both directions. There was no helicopter. The man was practically dead and I had to carry him. If ever a setup was designed for failure, this was it."

She stopped and took a deep breath. Her heart hammered in her chest.

"Morgan, they would never have let you die in there. They'd have gotten you out."

"Jack, you're a smart man. Look at who I was. I had nothing, no parents, no one concerned about me. I'd been on the streets, a vagrant, someone lost in the system, non-productive, hard-core unemployed. All the labels fit me. And they had a man in a foreign jail who had secrets in his head. They needed to get him out or kill him. If one or both of us died in the process, the mission would be accomplished. It didn't matter the outcome. If he got out, that would make them heroes on a world-wide scale. If he died, he'd be one of the honored dead. No one would ever know my involvement. I was expendable."

"If what you say is true, why didn't they just have the guard kill Lewiston? You said there were already dead men there. What would another dead body mean?"

"That would mean someone at the prison was playing his hand. It would look better if an escape attempt took place. Then he could be shot while attempting to leave. And what would a nobody from the streets of D.C. mean? The government would deny everything."

"But you're here now."

"That is true."

"How did you get off the roof?" He went back to the Korean story.

"I used the rope." She stopped to focus it in her mind. "I don't know where it came from. I'm sure it hadn't been there long. It was already set up. It looked like something used in a circus. It was stretched taut and there was a roller or pulley-type mechanism that I could hold onto and slide to the ground."

Jack frowned.

"I think the guard, the man who caught me, was an agent. He set the rope up. It was a special kind of cord, probably nylon, the kind circus acts use. It stretched from the roof to a point outside the prison fence. At first I didn't know what to do with it. The guards were getting closer. I couldn't scale it hand over hand to the ground. There wasn't time to harness Lewiston and send him alone, then go after him. And I didn't know who would be on the other end. Lewiston couldn't have weighed more than ninety pounds. I slipped the harness over him and jumped into it with him. The guards broke through to the roof just as I started the flight downward."

Morgan was fully in the present now. She no longer felt as if she were on the roof of the prison in the dark of night with bullets that could pierce her body and cut her life short.

"I knew we were going to fall hard. It hadn't rained in the week I'd been in Seoul. The ground would be hard, packed. We'd be lucky if we were killed. If we only broke our legs the prison guards would be on us in seconds." Her voice was flatter now. "Lights were flashing and sirens sounded loud and close. Just before we reached the ground, the agent I'd made contact with earlier broke our fall. As he cut the harness, separating Lewiston from me, two cars came from nowhere. A man, whose face I couldn't see, jumped out of one of them and took Lewiston. He got into one car while I was pushed into the second one. It couldn't have been more than fifteen seconds from the time we got to the ground until we were speeding away from the prison."

Morgan finished. She felt drained, tired, in need of sleep. She slipped into a chair and hung her head. It had been so long ago, yet it had been yesterday. She'd never ended that night. She still lived it over and over in her dreams and in her fear of someone coming to take back what she had.

For a long time neither of them spoke. Morgan didn't have the energy to wonder what he was thinking, what he thought of her story. Did he believe her? She didn't think so. Jack was one of them. He worked with the kind of men who'd sent her into that prison, that valley of death, and who never thought she would emerge.

"It's funny," she laughed without humor.

"What?" he asked.

"The very men who sent me to that prison are the ones I'm running to now for help."

He didn't say anything in reply.

"Am I going to survive, Jack? Or is this another staged play that has only one inevitable end?"

Jack stood up and came to her. He took her arm, pulling her up from the chair with ease. Silently he led her to her bedroom. Morgan was suddenly tired. She sat on the bed while he went to the bathroom. She heard the water running. He came back with a glass of water. Morgan drank greedily as if she needed to replenish the liquid in her body from her feet up, as if she'd expended all the energy to run the prison hall, scale the stairs and slide down the rope to the ground.

"Lie back," Jack said, taking the empty glass.

She obeyed. "Do you know who he was, Jack?"

"Who?"

"The other man. The guard who set up the rope?"

Jack shook his head. "You should rest now." He turned to leave.

"Who was the other man, Jack?"

He stopped and looked at her.

"The man who cut me out of the harness. The one who took Hart Lewiston and was so careful to keep his face hidden. Was that you, Jack?"

He stared at her for a long time. She didn't think he'd tell her. She could see the man's shadow in her mind, but not clearly enough to put form to it. Yet there was a familiarity about him, some non-visible imprint that told her she knew him on some level.

Morgan had never thought about that man until tonight. He'd simply been a savior, a nameless agent there to get her and Lewiston to safety as fast as possible. Hart Lewiston needed to go to an airstrip to get him out of the country. She, on the other hand, had a date with a crowd in the Olympic Pavilion. The two cars separated and Morgan didn't dwell on anything else about him except her report which later told her he was safely away from Korean soil.

"It was you, wasn't it, Jack?" she asked again.

"Yes," he whispered and closed the door.

Jack went straight to the minibar and broke the seal. He grabbed a one-shot bottle of Johnnie Walker Red and upended it. It was an incredible story. If Jack hadn't been there for part of it, he might not believe it. He felt sick. Had they really done what Morgan believed? Had they set her up to fail? And had he been an unwitting party to the deception? If she hadn't come out of that prison he was there to get her out. If she were killed trying to get Lewiston out he wouldn't have been able to get in.

The lights and sirens had his heart in his mouth when they suddenly lit up the prison yard and surrounding area. It was then he saw the rope. He didn't know how it had come to be there, and it wasn't until Morgan was swinging her legs over the fence that he understood its reason.

The plan was for Morgan to get to the roof and the helicopter

would pick them up and take them to a point between the arena
and the airport. Morgan would be taken off the helicopter and
Lewiston would be taken to a ship offshore. She would go back
to the arena and complete her competition.

Jack assumed something had happened to the helicopter. It
wasn't unusual for things to change during an operation. When
the lights came on and the sirens sounded, guns would have
been trained on the sky. Landing a helicopter would have been
suicide. The rope and the cars were backup.

Now he wondered. Morgan had to be wrong. If she had been
found in the prison, even if she and Lewiston had been dead,
it would have been a serious embarrassment to the United
States.

He shook his head. She had to be wrong, but somewhere in
Jack's gut he knew part of her story was the truth.

CHAPTER 7

The bed was comfortable, a peach-colored comforter over standard white sheets, covering a firm mattress, but Morgan couldn't find a place which complemented her body. She'd turned over more than once, punching the pillows up then flopping down on them. It wasn't her body, however, that was the problem. It was her mind. It was active, too active and that was affecting her ability to find comfort.

She'd told her story to Jack. Almost all of it. There were two items she left out. The ring. And the papers. A gold ring with a heavy crest and some papers written in Korean. It was what they were after. What they wanted and were willing to kill her and anyone in her path to get. They'd already killed one person trying to get to her. Would they get to Jack? The thought almost cramped her stomach. She doubled up, folding her arms over her abdomen and drawing her knees to her chest. She'd lived all these years remembering him, thinking of him swimming in some pool. She'd relived his kiss, fantasized his arms around her countless times, but she'd never put him in her nightmare of escape. This had been a solitary run, one in which she alone made her way to safety. And now she had his safety on her mind.

She flipped over again. Opening her eyes, she saw the bathroom in the darkened room. That was why she couldn't sleep. What happened there. What she refused to admit or discuss with Jack. It was on her mind. *He* was on her mind, keeping her awake. Jack had kissed her, devastated her with his mouth. That was going through her mind, repeating over and over to the rapid beating of her heart. He'd been right about her, pegged her as surely as if she were a child caught stealing.

He was the bad boy of her mind, but she was the bad girl too. What set her apart was she looked like the debutante. Her adoptive mother had worked hard to smooth some of her rough edges, teaching her manners and how to choose the right clothes, taking her to ballets and concerts at the Kennedy Center. And she was the phenom of the school too. She'd racked up trophies for gymnastics since she started in the sport at thirteen.

Everything was going for her, popularity, good grades, friends, a loving mother, but she was attracted to the dangerous guys, the hard bodies who were often in trouble and whom she could deal with on their level, yet she shied away from them, thinking that life on the street would rear up and snatch her back to it.

Jack was like the bad boys. He was the ultimate dangerous one because he had her heart. He'd discovered her secret attraction for him in Seoul and he'd tried to use that against her tonight. And she had been powerless to stop him. She wanted to kiss him. She wanted it from the moment she discovered it was him pinning her to the floor of her hallway. She watched him, stared at him when he wasn't looking, just as she'd done to the guys in her school. She only looked at them when they weren't looking at her. She rarely initiated conversation when they were near, and often refused dates when asked.

And Jack was the epitome of the bad boy, all of them rolled into one. But with him she couldn't refuse. She couldn't not talk to him. She couldn't not remember his kiss—either the one in Seoul or the one in the bathroom.

Morgan sat up and pushed her feet to the floor. Why had he shown up right now? She'd planned to escape on her own if the need arose. She would get to Washington, contact Jacob Winston as she'd been instructed and take matters from there. She could have done it too. She was sure she would have made it, but now she had no car and she had Jack. They, whoever they were, had to know he was with her. After the helicopter, there was no doubt that someone would have gone over the house and found some clue to his identity. He'd already called Washington and that had resulted in them coming close to being killed. Jack's quick thinking had saved them. But if Jack had never shown up, where would she be now? He'd known to keep silent and stay put when they were in the tree and he'd saved her at her house and at Michelle's "cabin" in the woods. She never would have thought of the water hose.

Morgan stared at the rumpled bed. She gave up trying to get to sleep. She wished they'd taken an efficiency. She'd have a kitchen and she could cook something. She liked to cook, but they were on the ninth floor of a hotel. She could do nothing except return to the living room and confront Jack.

". . . we don't believe she's dead and we're going to find her." Morgan stopped in her tracks when she saw Jan. The face of Janine Acres, her former teammate, filled the television screen. "Morgan is a very self-sufficient woman. Since the police admit they haven't found a body we can only assume she wasn't in the house and that she's somewhere alone." This came from Alicia Tremaine. Morgan hadn't seen Allie in years. She hadn't changed. She was still beautiful and poised and in control. She played the same kind of character on her television program. Morgan stiffened when the film of herself came on the screen. It was the same clip they used of her every time the Olympics came around. There she stood, twelve years earlier, wearing a red, white and blue leotard, crushing roses to her chest, tears spilling down her face like Niagara Falls as she sang *The Star Spangled Banner*.

"What are they doing?" Morgan whispered to herself. She took a step toward the television as if she could stop the action. Jack turned to look at her. "No," she said, the sound coming from low in her throat. "They don't understand."

She went to Jack. "You've got to do something. They don't know what they're doing."

"What's wrong?" he asked.

"They'll be killed. Anyone that has anything to do with me, they won't hesitate to kill them. They haven't an inkling of what's headed their way." She stared at Jack, pleading with him. She needed his help. He could do something, call someone, get help for Janine and Alicia. "We have to go back there," she said, more to herself than Jack. "We have to find them and let them know I'm alive. They have to stop looking for me."

Jacob heard his wife, Marianne, laughing. He stared through the window, watching her and his three-year-old daughter, Krysta, splashing in the pool outside their Rock Creek Park home. For a moment he thought of joining them. The cool water would be refreshing on his skin. His heart swelled when he looked at Marianne and grew even larger when Krysta was included in the picture.

Jacob had met Marianne because of his job as director of the witness protection program, and he often thought with a smile of how much he had changed since she became part of his life. And how protecting one woman had led to such happiness for him.

He could always look at the tangible Marianne and see the intangible need to help someone else. He supposed that was one of the reasons Morgan Kirkwood intrigued him. Jacob had left the file Forrest Washington had given him in his office, but he'd brought the CD home.

Returning to his computer, which was constantly on, he reviewed the CD of Morgan Kirkwood's early life for the third time that day. There was nothing confidential about the contents. The paperwork, back in his office, detailed her interview and training with the CIA prior to the Korean Olympics. It gave in-depth information on her biological parents, her life on the street, her adoption, her adoptive mother's death from cancer, and Morgan's career as a gymnast.

The CD played, showing him a younger version of the woman whose older face he'd seen from a photo in the file in his office. There was little here for anyone to see. Morgan Kirkwood's early life through some photos of her in detention centers, her adoption proceedings which had been filmed as a matter of court record, several practice sessions in various gyms with different outfits and different degrees of skills, and her performance at the Seoul Olympics. The CD moved onto Morgan with a tearstained face, holding her roses as she sang. Like everyone else in America, Jacob remembered this moment. In the following interviews when she looked afraid and alone, she never answered the question of why she sang, more than to say she thought it seemed appropriate.

He wondered whether Brian Ashleigh and Forrest Washington had held out on them again. Finding Morgan Kirkwood was not Jacob's responsibility, just as protecting her wasn't Jack's. Jacob dealt with people in the program, not finding missing persons, but she had raised the consciousness levels of someone extremely high up in the system. His director, Christopher, had said it. She was too small a person to concern people like Brian Ashleigh, yet he'd come personally to a meeting about her. That intrigued Jacob, but he was finding reviewing her life a waste of time. There was definitely something missing that made Morgan Kirkwood important.

Jacob read between the lines. At the level Morgan Kirkwood sat, she must be unfurling some extremely high feathers. She'd been home from Seoul for twelve years. She'd lived a normal, unassuming life. Then suddenly Olympic fever hits the country and her life is in danger.

What was the link? Whose buttons did Morgan Kirkwood push? Who was pushing back? And with a deadly force.

Krysta's voice, high and laughing, pierced the silence, and Jacob knew she was coming in from the water. In a moment, Marianne would appear and tell him it was time to get away from his job. She never asked him who he was working with or what was going on. She'd been part of the program and understood the confidential nature of what he did. This CD was part of every public television system in the U.S. He'd seen it over and over on the news since Morgan's home exploded, and no sign of her had been found since. But Jacob knew she was alive. Somewhere between St. Charles and Washington, D.C., she was with his friend, Jack Temple. They were together and in danger.

"Daddy, I went swimming." Krysta bounded into his office and ran to him. Her three-year-old voice couldn't say "swimming" correctly, but Jacob understood her. She climbed into his arms, her swimsuit and body wet from the pool. He ignored the water and pulled her onto his lap.

"How far did you swim?"

"As far as Mommy. All the way to the other side." She pointed toward the window. Jacob swung around in the chair and looked over his shoulder.

"That's wonderful." He kissed her wet hair.

"Who is that?" Krysta asked, switching her attention with lightning speed the way children often do.

"One of America's heroes," he answered, knowing any explanation would be too much for her to understand.

Marianne came in then. "Krysta, you're wetting your daddy."

Krysta looked at her mother as if nothing was wrong. Jacob glanced at his wife and his heartbeat thumped. He thought after five years of marriage her presence wouldn't affect him so strongly, but he was wrong. He hoped the urge to make love to her never went away. Even when they were in their nineties he wanted to look at her and feel this sudden quickening of his heart.

"Come on, it's time to get dressed." Krysta jumped down and ran toward Marianne's outstretched hand. Marianne looked over her daughter at him. "It's time you closed up shop."

"Closed up shop," the little girl repeated. They turned to leave. At the door Krysta turned back. "Daddy, can I be a hero?"

Jacob smiled. "Of course you can."

"Do I get a ring, too?"

"If you want one." Jacob didn't understand the reference, but appeased her anyway.

"And flowers?"

"All heroes get flowers."

They left the room and Jacob reached forward to terminate the program. His hand stopped in mid-air.

Jack hung the phone up. Morgan looked at him, more nervous than she could remember being since she stopped competing. The garish light of a convenience store on some back highway not far from Indianapolis washed Jack's features into craggy shadows that made him look more dangerous than she knew him to be.

He had led her from the hotel to a black Jeep Cherokee and driven until the density of the city population gave way to suburban developments and then to rural farmland.

"They'll be safe," he told her.

"How do you know?"

"Because I trust the people I just talked to," he snapped. She watched his shoulders drop and knew he regretted it. In a calmer voice, he said, "They'll find them and keep them safe."

"Maybe I should try one more time." Morgan moved toward the phone, but Jack's hand on her arm stopped her.

"You've tried, Morgan. She isn't answering that cell phone and you already said it's been years since you dialed it. You don't even know the number is still hers. People change plans all the time."

Morgan felt defeated, beaten, helpless. She could accomplish nothing, help no one, not even herself, and it was her fault her friends could die. She should have known. They'd made a pact. It sounded silly now to think about it. She hadn't given it a thought until she saw Jan and Allie on the television screen. They had been so young. She was eighteen. Her mother had died only two weeks before and Jan and Allie came to her, both of them fifteen, taking her with them, back to their families, so she wouldn't be alone. They had vowed that summer that they would be friends forever. If any of them needed the others, they would come. All they had to do was call.

Jan and Allie stood by that vow, like musketeers taking up the banner of truth, and it was Morgan's fault that she had not held up her end. That they would look for her, after so many years of silence, was something outside of her realm of belief. No one ever looked for her, except her mom. No matter how many years had passed Morgan still thought of herself as alone in the world. For a small space of time, while her adoptive mother lived, Morgan had been part of something, a family, friends, her gymnastics partners, but when her mom died, everything went with her.

"Trust me, Morgan." Jack broke into her thoughts. She

squinted at him in the harsh light. His face was set, still deeply detailed by the bulbs that had mosquitoes creating a glow about them. Every once in a while she'd hear the sizzle of a bug light. At the moment nothing passed between them except the grotesque sound.

Morgan realized she did trust him. She'd hardly trusted anyone in her entire life. She could count the people on three fingers whom she'd be willing to let into her life. No wonder she didn't recognize the feeling when it came. But it was there for Jack. She'd trusted him since they left her house. He'd do what he said and she wasn't going to have to pay for it. He wasn't going to come by later with something she had to do to pay up for the deed. Jan and Allie would be safe because Jack was a man of his word. Jan and Allie could be trusted to keep the vow. Morgan felt ashamed of how well she had kept it.

Senator Hart Lewiston sat quietly in his campaign office. Huge reproductions of his face graced the walls. Bumper stickers, posters, buttons with LEWISTON FOR PRESIDENT were scattered about. A computer sat on his desk and a television in the corner. It was switched on, but he'd muted the sound. Outside the glass-enclosed office, phones rang, people scuttled around, the place was a battle zone of activity. For a moment he could just watch. He hadn't had a moment to himself since months before he officially threw his hat in the ring. From that point on it had been at least one event every day, some days more than one. He'd talked to labor and industry, visited college campuses, whistle-stopped across the heartland, shaken hands with the old in nursing homes and lifted children into his arms in kindergartens. He was tired and ready for the end. But he had months ahead of him before the election.

It hadn't been an easy road for Hart. Unlike his wife, he hadn't grown up having all his needs fulfilled. He never wanted for food or clothes, but his family couldn't afford the latest fad clothes or the newest electronic toys. Yet he grew up happy. His father had been a country lawyer and Hart idolized him, expecting to follow in his footsteps. When he thought of his life, he never chose public office as a goal. Then his father was made a judge and their lives took a different course.

Hart went to law school as expected, but after graduation he clerked for a judge in D.C. before taking a job in the Central Intelligence Agency. The CIA made all the difference, sending him to foreign countries on covert missions. It took him to Seoul, where he was caught and sent to prison. Hart hung his head, remembering the nightmare of his time there. Sweat popped out on his brow. His breath came in gasps. His heart beat faster. He stopped the thoughts. He wouldn't let them return. The nightmares were over. The panic attacks were in the past. He wouldn't go through those memories again.

Elliott Irons, his campaign manager, came through the door. Hart sat back, silently thanking the younger man for coming in and jerking him out of a dream that could occur whether he was asleep or awake. Elliott was forty-seven, but looked twenty years younger. He had a full head of blond hair, stood six feet tall, had been married to the same woman since the day he graduated from Harvard Law School, and believed in all the ideals of America. How he got into politics, Hart would never understand. He came from a family of politicians, but Elliott wasn't made in the same mold.

His family was a strain of men with so many skeletons in their closets that to go to the can they had to negotiate for toilet paper. Elliott's grandfather had been governor of California during the 1930s. He'd left a colorful legacy including some scandalous activities involving land deals and the Hollywood movie machine. Elliott's aunt had caused a major scandal in the political arena when she was discovered with a high-ranking official of a foreign government in a state of total undress. His father was a senator, serving on some of the same committees as Hart, and Hart had to constantly keep him from dipping into the till. Yet these people had produced Elliott, a trustworthy young man with boundless amounts of energy. And Hart would trust Elliott with his life.

"I had a great idea this morning."

Hart wondered if Elliott ever slept. Or did he dream of campaign strategies during periods when he should rest.

"Have you been watching the news?"

Hart nodded, glancing at the television with its mime figures. It was his duty to follow the news, listen to what everyone was saying. Often he used opinions for his benefit.

"Did you hear they haven't found any trace of that gymnastics champion?"

Again he nodded. This time his entire body tensed, but Hart was too good at hiding his feelings to let anything his campaign manager and friend said show on his outward countenance.

"She was in Korea at the same time you were in prison there. I thought we could pull this into the limelight somehow. Perhaps showing footage of her in the full arena during the Olympics and couple that with a reenactment of the daring escape you made the night the Americans took first place in that competition. It will tear America's heart out."

Elliott paced the room like some Hollywood film mogul with a new idea.

"I prefer to forget that ordeal," Hart said.

"Hart, it's perfect." Elliott sat down in a chair in front of Hart's desk. "Right now Olympic fever is sweeping the country. This campaign and those athletes vie nightly for the first and second spots on the news. When that girl went missing it would be the perfect combination. We could increase our percentage poll by at least a point."

"We don't need a point, Elliott. We've got enough votes now to swing the election. As long as I don't do something rash like rob a bank or go on national television airing dirty laundry, I'll be president-elect come November."

Elliott stood up again. "It never hurts to play it safe."

"Elliott, when it comes to political candidates, the public has a thin layer of trust. Either they believe in them or they don't. In our recent past they've had plenty of reason to distrust the lot of us. It won't keep them from voting, even if they have to choose the lesser of two evils. I think we have plenty going for us right now. We don't want to kill our own campaign with distrust."

"What do you mean? Look at the polls. If the election were held today, you'd win in a landslide."

"And I'd have you to thank for it." Elliott didn't often need stroking to know he was a force in this campaign, but Hart understood that Elliott was a push-forward manager. He never looked back and he never stopped. He wanted to keep going forever forward until the race was won. Hart often thought Elliott would have been a great coach for some sports team. They'd been friends a long time and Elliott's enthusiasm for winning had never wavered.

"We've got commercials running every hour," Hart explained. "Billboards crisscross the country, bus and subway advertising in all the major cities, speaking engagements so close together that any deviation in time schedule could collapse the entire structure. People can't turn around without tripping over something with my face on it. It's getting to the saturation point. Soon they'll notice that line they've drawn. The one that will make them question the reality of the campaign promise."

"Hart, you believe in everything we've said."

Hart nodded. "I do. But I'm not John Q. Public. The man on the street when inundated with information will often begin to question it. I'm saying we need to keep doing what we're doing, but adding a commercial that correlates me with Morgan Kirkwood may not be the best idea."

"It would be wonderful. And don't worry about the public. They believe what we tell them to believe. The good thing is it's all true."

Elliott left him a moment later, when one of the campaign workers knocked lightly on the door and whispered that he had a problem. Elliott was right on top of it. He would handle it, solve it and go on to the next item that cropped up. Hart was privileged to have him in his camp. He was an idea man, a visionary, a take-charge guy and a strong supporter.

As activity on the outer side of his door escalated to a new level of frenzy, Hart pulled a phone from his inner pocket and dialed. He didn't want to use the one on the desk.

"Is it done?" he asked without acknowledging either his or the receiver's identity. A second later he disconnected the call, returned the phone to his pocket and observed Elliott speaking into a phone in the center of the room.

Elliot's idea wasn't without merit. The use of Morgan Kirkwood's footage might add a few points to the polls, but it would bring him back to a time in his life that he didn't want to revisit.

Morgan sat in the Jeep next to Jack. They hadn't talked much since leaving the convenience store. Morgan had her own thoughts to contend with. She wasn't comfortable with the trust factor, but she wasn't uncomfortable with it either. She knew Jack's orders would be followed. His voice on the phone had been no-nonsense. She could imagine people flying through doors and tires squealing as they jumped into cars and peeled rubber to get to Jan and Allie. She was still a little nervous for them. She wouldn't be completely comfortable until she knew they were safe.

Jack had talked of other things while he spoke into the phone. He hadn't mentioned the name of the person he spoke to, but she had listened to the one-sided conversation. Other than the safety of her friends, Jack had spoken about a meeting. They were on their way to it now. Morgan had to trust that if he could help Jan and Allie, he could also get her to safety.

She glanced at Jack. He didn't talk much, but she guessed in his line of work silence was a matter of course. His profile in the dark was strong, and Morgan admitted he looked better now than he had twelve years ago. She wondered if he still swam as often as he did when she first knew him. He had to be doing some exercise because when he'd kissed her she felt every inch of his body. It was just as hard as it had been in Seoul. His face had changed though. He's lost an almost indefinable quality of . . . freedom was the only word she could use to describe it. He had more character lines in his features and he moved with an air of command, but he moved inside an invisible box. One that said, *don't touch me*.

Morgan felt a little sad. He reflected her own life. Both of them had been changed by that trip to Seoul. Somehow she knew it had begun there. When Jack entered a room, people noticed. They instinctively moved aside as he passed, sensing both the danger he radiated and the aloofness that set him apart.

Morgan knew these traits could also be a powerful aphrodisiac. It drew her to him. Without volition, her thoughts returned to the hotel bathroom and Jack's mouth crushing hers. Quickly she dashed thoughts going in that direction, but not fast enough to keep her body from flashing hot.

"Why did you decide to do this kind of work?" Morgan asked the first question that came to her addled mind.

"Tired of your own company?"

"A little," she admitted.

"You don't decide this," Jack answered. "You get recruited."

"Who recruited you?"

His head slowly turned and he looked at her with piercing eyes. She could even see them in the half-light of the Jeep's cabin. She knew he wouldn't answer.

"How long have you been at it?"

"Too long."

"Well, you must be very good."

"I thought you said I wasn't doing a very good job of protecting you."

She dropped her eyes a moment. "I've changed my mind." She looked up, but his expression was closed. "If you hadn't been with me I'd be dead by now. And I wouldn't have known what to do about Jan and Allie."

Jack swallowed. She noticed it, but that was the only change in him. She wondered if her life mattered to him or if she was only a job. He hadn't said it in words, and his actions in the hotel room resulted from anger and frustration at her withholding information from him. She could be misinterpreting his feelings, making things up in her own mind. Was she making too much of a simple kiss? The problem was, it wasn't simple. It was devastating. She couldn't forget it and at every turn it popped to the front of her mind, derailing her thoughts and making her intensely interested in knowing more about Jack. Maybe she was only a job. If he weren't here with her he'd be someplace with someone else. The thought made her heart tighten a little and set her teeth on edge.

"Have you protected a lot of people?" she asked.

"Some," he said, volunteering nothing.

"Women?"

Again he let his gaze travel to her. This time slowly as if

he had all the time in the world. Morgan held her breath. She
wanted him to deny it, lie to her.

"Some," he said.

"Did any of them die," she hesitated, "while . . ."

"You're not going to die, Morgan. I'll make sure of that."

"You can't know that. We don't know what those people
are thinking, how they found us the last time, how long it will
be before they come again."

"I know my job. I do it well. There's nobody better that can
do what I do." His voice had no vanity in it, no brashness or
bragging. He spoke as if it were fact.

"Are you saying you're the best?"

"I'm alive," he answered.

Morgan shivered at the coldness in the statement. Jack was
a force unto himself. A lone ranger. He worked with no one
and relied on no one. He said it in every breath. He didn't need
anyone and didn't want anyone. No attachments was his policy.
The aura about him spoke it as loudly as cheap perfume.

Jack understood why we study history. The past never really
goes away. It waits for you, waits until some point in the future
when you least expect it to screw up your life. Then, there it
is—ready or not. Without warning, it imposes itself, returns,
forces you to face it, recognize it, and act, without the power
of veto. Jack's past was here. It had to be dealt with. Sitting
next to him, as they sped along the dark road in the middle of
the night, on their way to a rendezvous point in western Ohio,
was Morgan Kirkwood—his past.

It began on a night not unlike this one. He was driving
back to the residence hall after a practice meet. He'd dropped
off several team members who'd ridden with him and was
alone in his car. He smiled to himself, as he'd done then. The
team had won. They were all elated, high on adrenaline and
looking forward to conquering the next meet. Strange, Jack
thought, how youth hadn't prepared him for the future. It had
just happened. How could he have known, on that other night
as he raced through the darkness, that he'd end up here? That
the road to here wasn't a straight line. It went up hills and into

valleys, around back roads and across superhighways. It took him past farmhouses, grass huts, into bug-infested jungles and through homes that cost more than the entire treasury of some countries.

What he'd told Morgan was true, although he'd glossed over the worst of it. He had been the bad boy type, but when it came to being bad, he'd done the worst. But not here, he'd done it in the name of the law, under the protection of the United States government, going into places the government couldn't go and doing jobs he couldn't speak of, jobs that had few or no records and dealing with people who had no names or faces. He hung alone, worked alone and all problems were his to identify, postulate and execute. His means were his own concern. He answered to no one.

And he'd been selected for his career because of a swimming meet. He didn't know who had been at that meet, but someone had seen him and recognized something in him. The man who actually approached came during his time at Olympic training camp. He'd simply given him a card with an address on it. No explanation, just a comment, "Twenty hundred hours, tonight. Speak to no one. Come alone."

He looked back now, not understanding how he could have been so naive. He thought it was some kind of invitation, that there was an initiation ceremony or even a hazing, like they did in college for fraternity pledges or some ritual for newcomers to the camp. The party he expected to attend turned out to be dinner and a long conversation with a man from the CIA, who offered him a job. The man told him they'd been watching him for some time, that he had all the qualities they looked for in good agents: physical ability, intelligence, aptitude and teamwork. They also needed someone who could swim.

Jack remembered returning to his room that night. No thought of practicing or where he was entered his mind. He only thought how weird the night had turned out and how strange everything had sounded, yet he had no doubt that the man he'd had dinner with was serious. He reviewed his own situation, his sisters, his parents, the loving home in which he'd grown up, how his parents struggled to give their children anything they needed, but not everything they wanted.

Jack thought eventually to follow in his father's footsteps and become a pharmacist. Today, after all he'd been through, all he'd done and seen, he couldn't imagine himself in a white coat filling prescriptions or even going so high as to becoming a doctor. What he looked forward to now, before he'd become immersed in Morgan Kirkwood's life, was going to Montana, fixing up his home, putting down roots. He might even get married and have children. His parents would like that.

Glancing at Morgan, he wondered what she wanted to do.

"When we get out of this . . ." he started, deliberately saying when and not if, ". . . what do you plan to do?"

"I don't know. Some part of me never thought it would come to this. The other part never thought about anything after getting to Washington."

"You'll be all right when we get there. Jacob is a good man. He'll protect you."

"You and he are good friends."

"We've spent some time together. I was best man at his wedding five years ago. He's got a kid now."

"Boy or girl?"

"Girl. Krysta. I've never seen her."

"Have you ever been married, Jack?"

He shook his head. He'd never even come close. His work didn't allow for relationships. Jack had met many women, most of whom had been hiding something or were part of some plot that involved the United States and its allies. He'd known they were agents. Morgan was the only one who touched him with her innocence. When she carried Hart Lewiston out of that prison and within the hour stood in front of the world, albeit with tears streaming over her face, as if she was strong enough to withstand the demons from hell, Jack had been more than over the edge. She was the only woman he'd ever come close to falling in love with and since then he'd hardened his heart to anything and anyone else.

Only when he'd seen Morgan and held her in his arms did all that hardness break as surely as a quarry stone is reduced to gravel.

"I've never been married either. Marriage was one of those things that wasn't one of my goals."

"I thought it was a goal of all American women."

"Only those that live the American dream."

Jack understood the way she said it that she felt the dream wasn't within her grasp.

"One more point," she went on. She turned in her seat to look at him. "Just for your information, I've also never had an abortion or been pregnant."

"I apologize for that." He'd been so angry when he found her trying to run away. He wanted to know who she was trying to protect. He still thought there was something or someone. "Your actions are the same as a person trying to protect someone. I thought I could get you to tell me who, and that would make my job easier."

He remembered his method. It probably wasn't the best, but he'd had little control when her saw her. Her skin, dark and slick with water, the smell of the soap and the way her face looked all clean and fresh and softened in the mist of the small room. Her hair was off her face and her eyes were huge and melting. He'd have to be a dead man not to respond to having her so close and wanting for twelve years to fulfill his fantasies.

"The only person I'm trying to protect is myself," she paused. Then in a lower voice, she said, "I wouldn't want you to get hurt either."

"Thank you," Jack said. "We're going to make it."

She reached over and placed her hand over his. Jack grabbed it and squeezed. For a moment they sat like that, the car silent except for the noise of the road and the wind and the singing of his heart.

Morgan heard it first. The sun had risen an hour ago, bringing the day into full light. Traffic hadn't picked up much. Three miles back the road split into two ribbons with a dense crop of trees separating them. Along the opposite side was a long-running bank of trees. They tunneled through them. Trapped. The place was perfect for an ambush and it seemed Jack had driven them straight into it. If someone wanted to lead them in only one direction or to kill them, this was a perfect setting.

"It's back."

"Yep," Jack agreed. "And we're sitting ducks."

Morgan craned her neck, looking out the front windshield, then the side windows trying to see the helicopter she could hear. "I don't see it."

"It's directly over us."

"What do we do?"

Jack didn't get to answer. A shell exploded in front of the Jeep. A flash of red fire and black smoke cut their ability to see. Morgan grabbed the chair arms and gulped air as the force of the blast pushed her against the upholstery. Jack fought the four-wheel drive vehicle, trying to keep control, maneuver around the pothole created by the explosion, and stay on the road. The Jeep fishtailed wildly as if it wanted to follow the laws of physics while its driver tried valiantly to break them. Gravel and twigs spit out from under the tires like shrapnel as they crunched onto the shoulder. Jack cut the steering wheel sharply and re-established the Jeep on the road.

"Why aren't there any other cars?" Morgan finally whispered. "Someone had to hear that explosion."

Jack accelerated. "It's my guess that somewhere ahead and behind us are road closed signs. It's a classic ambush technique. They let us pass through, then close the road at two ends."

Morgan narrowed her eyes, looking through the side window on Jack's side of the Jeep. The crop of trees was dense, but there were places she could see through to the other road. It was clear of cars and a cornfield ran along the road. It was only late May and the corn wasn't very high. It looked more like pineapple plants than corn stalks.

Another explosion hit the ground. Jack swerved, guessing right as a chunk of the ground scooped out like a moon cleaving from the ground and hurtled leftward.

Bullets rat-tatted against the ground around them. One hit the side of the Jeep and shattered a back window. Morgan screamed as she grabbed her head and leaned forward. Glass exploded inward.

"We're going to have to get out of the car." The odds of a bullet or something worse hitting a major system and the Jeep turning into a giant toaster were escalating. "When I stop, get out as fast as you can and go into the woods."

Morgan grabbed her backpack and slipped it on. She rolled the window down as Jack swerved right and left. Another shell exploded. Jack plowed into the trees and came to a stop. Morgan forced the door open and rolled out, Jack right behind her. She started running.

Low-hanging branches slapped him in the face. Morgan didn't stop going even though the branches must be hitting her too. Jack couldn't tell how far it was to the other end, but if the people chasing them were smart, and he knew they were, the other side was no sanctuary.

"Morgan, stop," he shouted. She slowed and turned. He grabbed her arm and pulled her to the ground. Together they listened for the helicopter.

Morgan looked up. "Do you think they can see us?"

"No, but I don't think it's safe—" He stopped, listening. The bird was overhead. He followed the sound with his eyes. It was flying away from them back toward the road.

Jack thought about their options. They could go back to the road and get the Jeep, but they would only have the road to drive on and he wasn't sure they could make it. Even the four wheel drive couldn't get through trees this dense. If they kept going forward, there was no telling what was ahead of them. He could almost guarantee they'd find men with guns trained on them. If they went sideways, the same fate awaited them.

Suddenly a powerful explosion shattered the air. Jack instinctively covered Morgan, pushing her to the ground. A second thunderous blast convulsed the air.

"The Jeep is no longer a means of escape," he explained when she looked at him.

Morgan's hand squeezed his arm. She faced the opposite direction, away from the road. "I hear voices."

Jack heard them too. "We have to go or they'll find us."

Pulling Morgan behind him, he ran straight ahead, parallel to the road. He wanted to come out ahead of the Jeep. About fifty yards later, he turned and headed toward the road. They had one chance. They'd have to get back to the road, cross it and hide in the trees on the divider median. If no cars were coming along the other side of the road, the median was their only refuge since the cornfield hadn't grown tall enough to hide them. It might not save them, but it would buy them some time.

He stopped suddenly. Morgan ran into him, but he kept them balanced. He placed his finger to his lips to keep her quiet. Then he listened again for voices. He could hear tree branches and leaves being beaten aside. They were gaining on them. He wondered what happened to the helicopter. He no longer heard the sound of the rotor blades. It could have left, but he doubted it. Jack hated being blind to all the possibilities of failure. And he didn't like surprises. But they had no choice but to keep going forward.

He signaled Morgan to follow him. They made it to the edge of the trees. They were ahead of the Jeep. The chopper sat on the blacktop, facing the burning hunk of metal, big and imposing and as nonchalant as if it knew there was nothing to worry about. Jack smiled. This was at least a bit of luck.

"Stay here," Jack told Morgan.

She grabbed his arm. "What are you going to do?"

"I'm going to get us a ride."

Morgan looked back toward the charred Jeep they'd traveled in and then at the helicopter sitting as new and polished as the day it left the hangar. "How?"

"I'm going to steal it."

"Jack, there's someone in that helicopter."

"I know." He patted her arm. "Trust me."

He left her, crouching close to the ground and moving like a sand crab. The pilot in the helicopter wasn't looking his way. He was facing the opposite direction, and unlike road vehicles, helicopters had no need for outside mirrors. Unless the pilot turned around, he'd never see Jack.

And Jack was counting on that.

Morgan watched with her heart in her mouth. The voices behind her were getting closer. She hid behind a tree, but kept Jack in sight. She was going to have to move soon or die right here. Jack was still hugging the ground and the man in the helicopter cabin glanced every so often toward the trees. Morgan's heart thumped in her chest. She prayed to herself, asking

God, once her only friend, to please keep him safe and let his plan work.

Jack scuttled along until he would be in the line of the pilot's vision should the man turn his head. Jack waited. Morgan calculated the rhythm of the pilot's movements. It was basic human nature. People moved repetitiously, especially when they were waiting. Unconsciously they created a method of doing something. In this case, for the pilot, it was glancing at the crop of trees. He did it in forty-second intervals. Just sitting made active people bored. She thought the pilot was either bored or keyed up. He'd been throwing bombs, shooting at the Jeep and hanging over the field trying to do aerial reconnaissance. She was sure it took adrenaline to kill people. He was probably on his way down now. She hoped Jack knew that and that Jack was also reading his rhythms.

The pilot glanced at the trees, then turned back. He looked down and bit a fingernail. Jack moved then, skirting behind the helicopter and stopping on the balls of his feet. He waited a while, longer than Morgan thought she could stand. Her heart was in her mouth and the sounds behind her, sounds that meant instant death, were closer. She froze, her heart thumping in her throat. She wasn't even sure she could move when it was time. Then Jack disappeared. She could only see his feet.

Morgan prayed again. The sound behind her grew louder. They were close, too close. In a moment they would be on her. She had to move. She looked back. Jack's feet had disappeared. Her glance flew to the pilot. He was gone too. Then a body fell onto the ground. It was on the opposite side of the helicopter. She couldn't see who it was and she couldn't wait any longer. Jumping up, she rushed for the helicopter, going toward the side where the pilot had been. Whatever was about to happen would be done now. Maybe if he had knocked Jack down, she could surprise him and give Jack enough time to recover. Before she reached the door, Jack jumped in the pilot's seat. Morgan's heart burst and her step faltered. A second later a man broke through the perimeter of the trees. Morgan felt him more than saw him. He shouted for her to stop. Her feet took off and she ran for the cabin door. He shot at her. The bullet came close. Too close. The sound took her back to the prison, and the fear of being killed welled up inside her like a monstrous weight that slowed her ability to lift her feet and run. She trained her gaze on the helicopter, making it her goal, and continued as fast as the nightmare would allow her. Another bullet came close enough to her feet to spike the ground, shattering the blacktop into pieces of tar as dangerous as an exploding grenade. A clump of pavement hit her leg. She stumbled at the impact, fighting to maintain balance. She kept going, her eyes still trained on the helicopter. She couldn't stop. She was too afraid. She felt the burning gravel raining against her pants legs.

Jack swung the door open. She jumped into the passenger seat and he took off. Shots rang out as they ascended straight up. Jack worked the controls, expertly getting them away from the bullets that sounded more like popping corn than the elements of death. Morgan strapped herself in, then hunched in the seat, expecting one of the pellets to burn through the cushioning and into her back any second now. It took moments, but felt like hours, before they were out of range.

"They can't hit us now."

She let out a breath and slumped forward, closing her eyes and trying desperately to abate the fear that lodged in every cell of her body.

"Are you all right?" Jack asked.

She looked at him. "I'm fine," she panted, completely out of breath. She'd never been so scared before in her life. "My leg burns a little." She reached down. Her hand touched something wet. She pulled it back. Blood covered her palm.

"I've been shot."

CHAPTER 8

"Jan, will you stop that? It's getting on my nerves." Allie snapped at her friend. Allie sat on the bed in the two-room safe house playing solitaire. She was as bored and frustrated at being cooped up as Jan, but she was more used to waiting. Her profession often called for the hurry-up-and-wait method of working. Jan's however, was made up of constant activity. When Jan wasn't teaching, she was stretching or creating routines, going over the new or changed rules of the Olympic committee, doing books or ordering new equipment. Twenty-four hours a day her life was filled with activity.

"Stop doing what?"

"Pacing. That constant walking up and down. If you have to do it, go in the other room."

"I don't want to go in the other room. I don't want to talk to Agent Burton or Agent Tilden." She'd steadfastly refused to call them by their first names. "It's been two days. They virtually snatch us off the street, bring us here to the middle of nowhere, tell us Morgan is alive and that they're protecting us for our own good. Well I don't believe it for a second."

Allie got up and walked to the window. There were no bars on it, but they were so far away from anything that running was a useless endeavor. Allie hated being confined, but Jan was paranoid about it.

"Why don't we go for a walk or a run. We could both use the exercise."

"You know they'll follow us."

"Yes, but it will get us out of here." Allie hated rooms where the only place to sit was on the bed. She liked sleeping in beds, but sitting on them for long periods was uncomfortable.

She opened the door. The two men in the other room came instantly to their feet.

"We're going for a walk," she announced in her official actress playing goddess voice. Neither of them contradicted her. They reached for their jackets which covered the gun harnesses each of them wore. Jan and Allie both had on T-shirts and shorts, clothes from the suitcases the agents had acquired when they checked them out of their hotel rooms and, according to Jan, imprisoned them here.

The foursome left the building. It was a beautiful ranch house in the shade of huge trees. The air outside was warm and comfortable.

"Has there been anything more from Morgan?" Jan turned suddenly and spoke directly to Max Tilden.

"No, ma'am."

"When do you expect to hear something? I mean don't you agents have to check in regularly?"

"I can't say when we'll hear anything. And yes, we do check in regularly." His voice was startled and formal. Jan loved that she could get on their nerves. She was usually a very nice person, but they'd taken her freedom and she was irritated by it.

Jan cursed to herself and walked away. Agent Burton followed her. She took off in a jog. He had to run to keep up with her and Jan knew he looked silly jogging in a suit and tie.

"She isn't always like this," Allie explained. "She's just a little . . . concerned."

"I understand. Your friend is in good hands. Jack Temple is the best. He won't let anything happen to her."

Allie smiled quickly, using every ounce of her acting ability not to let on that the name set off church bells in her brain.

She turned to continue walking, and so Agent Burton didn't have a full view of her face.

Temple! That was his name. *Jack Temple!* She had once known a Jack Temple and so had Morgan. It couldn't be the same man. Morgan had been attracted to him, although she thought no one knew it. Allie and Jan knew it, but neither spoke of it to Morgan. They'd learned the boundaries of their friendship and unless Morgan brought up his name, neither Jan nor Allie would introduce it. Yet they had discussed him without Morgan. Allie shook her head. Jack Temple was a swim coach in Seoul and now he was an agent protecting Morgan.

This couldn't be the same guy. But suppose it was? A sneaky smile crossed her face and Allie took off jogging.

There is always more blood than the wound calls for, Jack told himself as he looked at the widening stain on Morgan's leg. She might only have been grazed, but she could have a hole in her leg. Jack's hand shook on the stick he held controlling the chopper. The bird dipped slightly before he compensated. He had to land.

Morgan suddenly unstrapped her belt. With bloody hands she pulled her shoes off and undid the zipper to her pants.

"What are you doing?" Jack shouted over the noise. Morgan hadn't put on her earphones. She lifted herself from the seat and started pulling at her jeans.

"Taking off my pants."

"Why?"

"I need something to stop the blood and I need to know how bad it is." She continued to struggle in the confined space. "God, it hurts." Morgan bit her bottom lip, holding herself still for a moment.

Jack tried to concentrate. "How much pain are you in?"

"It burns." She pulled the word out, making it two syllables.

Morgan peeled her jeans over lace panties. On the outside she might be all practical with black jeans and T-shirts, but underneath, hidden from everyone's view, burned the hot pink lace of the real Morgan. Jack turned his attention back to the operation of the whirlybird. Moments later he asked, "How are you?"

"I think it's only a flesh wound." She pulled her leg up, twisting it into a position that should have hurt, but he'd seen evidence of her flexibility before. He remembered her climbing both the rope in her basement and the tree not far from her house.

She went to press the denim into her leg. "Don't do that." Jack stopped her. "There's a first-aid kit somewhere." Morgan looked behind him and found it. She had to twist her body to reach it. Her breasts grazed his shoulder. Jack could have been an intake valve if the amount of air he took into his lungs was any evidence of the blatant desire that seized him when Morgan's body touched his. "You should find something in there to clean it with," he suggested, unable to keep from glancing at the long length of brown legs that stretched the small length of the cabin. She smelled wonderful and Jack took a breath trying to hold onto the soft scent. She took a sterile gauze from the white metal case and cleaned the wound. Accidentally she brushed it across her leg. Pain made her suck her teeth.

"What's wrong?" Jack asked. She could hear the concern in his voice.

"Nothing." She continued cleaning the wound until she could see the skin. It wasn't as bad as she thought. The bullet had ripped the skin, but it had not lodged in her leg. "I'll be all right," she said.

"It didn't penetrate."

"It's a flesh wound, but it stings like the devil."

"Wrap it with one of those gauze bandages and take a couple of the pain killers."

Morgan did as she was told, swallowing two of the pills without water. She put her bloodstained pants back on, strapped her belt and put on the earphones. The sound of the rotors was muffled and she could hear Jack clearly.

"This isn't the first time you've dealt with a gunshot wound, is it?"

She glanced at him, then went back to scanning the ground below them. "No," she said in monosyllable.

"Have you been shot before?"

"No. It was one of my friends." She hesitated. "I'd been on the streets a while when it happened. Before I learned not to make friends. You know people out there, but you don't know them. We have our own code, an etiquette of life without boundaries." She spoke as if she were still one of them. "If anyone comes looking for you, nobody knows your name and nobody has ever seen you before. If you get sick or hurt, we'll all pull together to do what we can, but when we see you again we won't even acknowledge familiarity. I had friends before this. We were the same, rejects of society, people no one wanted. Her name was Jean."

She stopped, remembering the young face of her friend. Often dirty, but always smiling, Jean should have been a nun or a nurse. All she wanted to do was help people. The fact that they would smack her aside didn't seem to penetrate her young mind.

"What happened to her?" Jack asked.

"She died." Morgan didn't want to remember the night Jean died. She didn't want to talk about it, but Jack pushed on.

"How did she die?"

"She went for a catsup."

"Wrong timing?" Jack understood.

"Wrong timing," she confirmed. "We hadn't had anything to eat the whole day. We were hungry and had gone out to scavenge garbage cans. It was dark and late and children our ages should have been home snug in their beds." She delivered the last line with sarcasm. "We came down an alley and saw a couple arguing on the street. The man held a McDonald's bag in his hand. The woman suddenly walked off and the man threw the bag down in anger. When he stalked off, we ran and grabbed the bag. It was full and something fell out before we got back. When we opened it we gorged ourselves fast, eating with both hands, stuffing food into our mouths. We ate like it was our last meal, and it was since we didn't know where the next one would come from."

Each time Jack thought of her eating other people's garbage, his heart hurt. How could anyone let a child stay on the street?

"When our stomachs were full we started to joke. Jean said

she wanted some catsup for her fries. We'd dropped it on the sidewalk as we ran away. She got up and shouted she'd go get it. I stayed where I was. A moment later I heard the shots. Someone screamed. I screamed. I got up and started running for the end of the alley. I got to the street. Jean hobbled toward me. She had a bullet in her leg. Blood ran into her shoes. She collapsed on me. I wanted to run for help, but she stopped me. I tore her clothes away, looking for the wound. The bullet had gone right through her leg. She refused to let me call the policemen who were arriving only a few yards away from us. She said they would send her home, call her father and he'd kill her or do something worse. So I tried to stop the bleeding.''

Jack noticed her chin trembling. He'd never seen her do that before. Even when he knew she was scared, she always held her emotions so tightly there was no outward show of what was going on inside her. She must have really loved Jean.

"I got her back to our place. That's what we called it, 'our place.' It was a bunch of rags we spread out each night and slept on in a back alley in Southeast." Morgan stopped, taking a long breath. Jack knew she was fighting emotion, but it wasn't evident in the voice that continued. "Jean was delirious for three days. I was so scared I didn't know what to do. She got worse and worse each day. Finally, I couldn't wait any longer. No matter how bad it was for her at home, I had to tell someone, get her some help." Morgan stopped and swallowed. "I left her, went to the social worker, Sharon Peters, who'd been nice to me. I told her about Jean. She came immediately, calling a doctor from her car and telling him to meet us at our place with an ambulance.''

Jack saw Morgan's eyes glistening, but there was no sign of tears in her voice.

"It was too late when we got back. Jean was already dead.''

Morgan remained quiet after she finished her story. She hadn't relived that story in decades. Yet she felt as if it was always with her, that just as easily she could have been the one to go for the catsup and end up dead in that dark alley with no one to care.

After Jean died, Morgan never lived on the streets again. Sharon Peters took her home with her and Morgan stayed there until Sharon died of cancer just before Morgan's eighteenth birthday.

At Jean's funeral her father stood by her casket and cried. He looked grieved and tired. Morgan should have felt sorry for him. What she felt was anger. People shook his hand and said kind words in soft tones. Morgan glared. She knew it was all an act. Behind closed doors, out of sight of the world, he'd abused his daughter. Jean hated him. She would rather die in a dirty alley, taking her chances on the mean streets and back alleys of a world that no child should ever see, than stay in his warm, comfortable home in Richmond, Virginia.

Sharon Peters had taken her to the funeral and afterward returned her to her own house. She bought her new clothes and let her sit for hours in a bathtub full of sweet-smelling bubbles. She'd fed her huge meals and given her pocket money. Morgan accepted it all, squirreling it away for the day when she was back on the streets.

Losing Jean had left Morgan feeling empty and guilty. She'd waited too long. She should have gone for help sooner. She shouldn't have taken Jean all the way back to their place. It was her fault. Sharon understood her feelings, even though Morgan hadn't said them out loud. Sharon spent time with her. She took days off from her job to make sure Morgan was all right. She hugged her a lot and told her stories. Morgan resisted her love. She tried to hold herself aloof, but Jean was gone and there was no one. With her defenses at a low point, she let it happen. She let Sharon take her into a kind of life that would never really be hers. People like her lived on the streets and it was only a matter of time before she would be back there.

But she let Sharon hug her and hold her and she let her guard down for a moment before she'd quickly pushed it back in place. She knew it was unwise to begin to like someone who wasn't part of her street world. Eventually, they would throw you back to the sea of the unwanted. But Morgan didn't run away from Sharon's house. She was scared. Sharon voiced her feelings for her.

She knew Morgan thought it could so easily have been her they buried instead of her friend. Then Sharon told her she would keep her safe, always protect her. She could live with her for as long as she liked, having food and a clean place to sleep. She could go to school and make friends. It was a foreign world, but one that Morgan longed for as much as she wanted to be one of the girls in the pretty jeans she'd seen in the torn newspapers she slept on in "her place."

She stayed and Sharon kept her word.

Jack should pity Morgan. Her life was so different from the way his had been. She'd had nothing, but somehow she didn't ask for pity. She accepted what had happened to her. She didn't wear it on her sleeve or force the world to pay for it. She accepted what she had to and went on.

He'd spent most of his adult life in jungles, serving the government, going where he was sent and doing his job with quiet and unobserved efficiency. But he had a choice. At any time he could have left the jungle and returned to his quiet suburban home. Morgan's jungle was without end.

Jack checked the fuel gauge. He needed to find a place to set down. They'd used this as long as they could. It wasn't like he could have it refueled and continue on. He checked the ground. The land below was green and hilly. He wondered where they were. Morgan had thrown his concentration out the window by just being close to him. She didn't have to do anything. When she undressed in the small area and he discovered there was nothing seriously wrong with her, his mind had gone straight to her shapely legs and not to the airspace in front of them.

The story of her friend had taken something out of her. Jack glanced to his side, checking to make sure she was all right. She looked tired. They needed to find a place for her to rest, although if he mentioned resting, she'd protest that she was fine and didn't need to rest.

He'd been flying low, but then radar didn't usually track helicopters anyway. But with all the navigational and computerized equipment onboard, not to mention the gunwales, this bird was strictly military. Yet it wasn't new. More like salvage, something the government moth-balled or sold. So why would a military aircraft from a foreign government be trying to kill an American gymnastics champion twelve years out of the field?

Jack thought Morgan was beginning to trust him. She'd told him more of her life than he figured she'd ever told anyone else, except maybe her adoptive mother. He was glad she told him. It made him understand her need to survive. Underlying everything about her, he could tell she thought her entire life was a temporary situation. That no matter the notoriety or how solid a place she stood, everything would be yanked from her and she'd be back on the streets. It had to be her greatest fear, that "place" where Jean died, where life was ignored by people who had adequate food and clothing and where no one wanted to acknowledge these were people.

Jack wanted to take her in his arms and let her know she would never be one of them again. She'd gotten out of that and there was nothing that could pull her back into it. But he knew you couldn't tell people these things. The fear was inside them, ingrained from the hard knocks of experience. *They* had to let it go like an unwanted emotion. It had to come from the inside. No one else could make it go away. But he'd be there—

He stopped.

He wasn't going to be there. When they got to Washington, when this was over, Morgan would get a new life. True, she would never have to worry about the basic necessities of life, but he wouldn't be part of her existence.

The thought sobered him, but couldn't keep the sharp pull that settled around his heart from tightening.

Morgan's leg smarted more than she thought it should for just a flesh wound. Jack had nearly lifted her out of the cockpit and she'd hobbled to the cave, refusing to let him carry her. He'd gathered some wood and dropped it in a pile before disappearing to hide the helicopter. She didn't ask how you hide a thirty-foot black bug, just as she hadn't asked him if he could fly it. There were certain things she just accepted that

Jack could do. She didn't know why, but her experience had shown her that there were times and people she had to take on faith. There weren't many of them, but Jack was one. Faith, she thought. He made her believe they could survive.

Morgan reached over and grabbed some of the wood. She may as well get a fire started. The cave was damp and dark and a fire would add both light and warmth. Plus it would give her something to do other than worry that Jack would get caught and leave her alone.

She steepled the wood over a base of twigs surrounded by small rocks she gathered inside the cave. Then she lit the twigs and the branches caught on. Morgan hugged herself, feeling as if the coldness was seeping inside her.

"How's your leg?" Jack returned, dropping another armful of wood onto the cave floor.

"It's fine," she lied. It still hurt. She should have taken a pain pill while he was gone. She hadn't thought of it. She'd been too busy worrying about him. If she reached for them now, he'd know she'd lied. "Where are we?" she asked instead of concentrating on her leg.

"I'm not sure. I think we're somewhere in southern Ohio. These hills are the outskirts of the Allegheny Mountains."

"Do you think we're safe here?"

"For the time being."

Morgan lifted her leg and bent her knee several times. Her leg had begun to stiffen and she wanted to keep it flexible.

Jack looked around. He grabbed her backpack and set it in front of her. "Take one of those migraine pills. It will help with the pain."

Morgan opened her bag and took out a bottle of aspirin. "This is better," she said. She swallowed two pills dry.

Jack sat down in front of her. He spread his hands toward the fire. "I'm going to have to go and find us some food and water soon and another form of transportation."

"I should wait here?" She attempted humor, but her voice came out strained.

Jack nodded.

Morgan knew she couldn't walk a long distance. Her leg hurt, but she wasn't an invalid. She would be fine in twenty-four hours, back to normal for sure in forty-eight, but right now she'd be an anchor around his neck. They wouldn't starve or dehydrate in that amount of time.

She knew Jack wanted to get in touch with Washington. He needed that more than he needed the food and water.

"How far do you think the nearest town is?"

"Ten miles, I'd say." He glanced in the direction she assumed he intended to go. "I saw one as we flew over. If I'm lucky I'll be able to hitch a ride."

She looked at Jack over the fire. It turned his face slightly red. "Thank you, Jack."

"For what?"

"For saving my life. For rescuing me. For helping me remember. I planned this escape alone, but I'm awfully glad you're here."

The urge to move next to Morgan and take her in his arms was so strong Jack had to summon superhuman strength to keep his place.

"It's a life worth saving." He thought to pass it off as a joke, but his words came out dead serious. His gaze stayed locked with hers for a long moment. She broke it first, dropping her gaze to the fire. "How'd you start the fire?" he asked.

"Old Indian trick. I used two rocks to create a spark."

He shouldn't be surprised at her resourcefulness. He'd seen it over and over. She, who'd left her house without even a lipstick, could survive in the wilderness with assassins on her trail.

Morgan reached into her backpack and held up a cigarette lighter and a book of matches.

He smiled and she did too. God, Jack thought, he was in love with her. He stood up. Her eyes followed him. They were hungry eyes. His had to look the same. He didn't even try to hide what he felt. He took a step toward her. She started to get up.

"Stay there," he said. "It's time I started for town." He walked toward the door of the cave. Morgan got up anyway.

Jack wanted to help her to her feet, but knew if he touched her he wouldn't, couldn't stop there.

"Are you sure you'll be fine?"

"Absolutely," she said with a forcefulness in her voice that told him she was capable of surviving on her own. Jack tried to read her voice to see if there were any telltale signs that she was putting on a front. She could be lying. She was good at it, but just as he wanted her to trust him, he had to trust her too. He knew with her leg she could run, but she couldn't get far.

Jack hesitated, giving her a long look. He wanted to kiss her and the look in her eyes told him she wanted it too. He stopped himself. There was no relationship for them. She was a job. He had to keep her safe until he could turn her over to another authority. Then she'd disappear behind a door and he would never see her again.

"You're sure?" Jack asked instead of moving toward her. She nodded.

"Stay near the fire. Once the sun goes down it will be cold in here." He reached inside his pocket and pulled out a small gun. "If anyone comes near you, use it."

She looked at it as if he were handing her a snake with its fangs open and ready to strike.

"Do I need to show you how to use it?"

She took the gun flat in her hands. "No," she said. "I know how to use it."

Jack could hear, in the words she didn't say, that there was a story in between her sentence. He didn't have time to pursue it. The place they were in was safe, but Jack needed to get in touch with Washington and he needed to find another form of transportation. He also knew Morgan. He couldn't get her to tell him a story she wasn't ready to tell. He had to wait until she felt it was time to reveal another part of herself, a time when she was ready to open a scab and let the sore bleed out.

Jack had walked only two miles before the Dodge Caravan slowed along the road and stopped near him. The interior light came on as he got inside the minivan. The sun and its red and gold rays fell behind the emerald green hills in the valley where he'd left Morgan. The cave would be pitch black now except for the small fire she'd made. Jack didn't like thinking of her alone there, but he had to do this.

"Good to see you again, Ben." Jack leaned over and shook hands. Ben Laurini retired from the CIA two years after Jack joined. He'd befriended Jack the first day Jack walked into the training facility, and on more than one occasion something Ben had taught him came back when Jack found himself cornered and facing some serious form of death or mutilation.

"It's been a while," Ben said. "Glad to see you though. I've been looking for you for a while. I got a call from Brian Ashleigh himself. He too thought you might be in the area."

Jack thought someone might have called him. Even retirement didn't really mean retired when a fellow agent was in trouble. Ben was that kind of guy. He'd taken retiring from the field hard, but adjusted at the training facility. When he moved into full retirement and returned to his native Ohio, he'd taken to life as if he savored every day the good Lord gave him.

"How's Olivia?"

"Olivia is fine. The kids and grandkids are all doing well." Ben got the small talk out of the way quickly. "Your sisters?"

"Everyone is fine." He grouped his four sisters and parents into one complete sentence.

"Did you find anything?" Jack asked the question both he and Ben knew he wanted answered. He'd called Ben when he went to the helicopter. Using the on-board radio, he checked to see if Ben was still using his short-wave radio. Thankfully, he was and Ben told him he'd already been contacted. Jack arranged to meet him.

"I only had a short time, but I found out Miss Kirkwood's gym partners are being held in a safe house. They are concerned about her. It might be a good idea if you let the young lady call them. And I'm sure the two agents protecting them would appreciate it too."

Ben reached in his pocket and pulled out a cell phone. "Remnant from a past life," he explained.

Jack took it. "Anything else?"

"The people on the highway were long gone before anyone could get to them."

"What about the helicopter? I have it hidden back near the cave. We should be able to find out something from it. It's definitely military."

"I've already made the calls. They'll get the bird tonight. By morning you'll know everything it knows."

Morgan shivered in the cave. The fire was too small to heat the cavernous area. It gave her rudimentary light, throwing vast, grotesque shadows against the jagged rock. She felt the darkness close in on her. Fear made her tremble.

Jack had been gone a long time. She wondered where he was and when he would return. Paranoia made her think he'd abandoned her. Like her mothers, both of them. They'd left her in the world to make her way.

She hobbled outside. Morgan hadn't practiced in days and she felt the need to move. Of course, running for her life, climbing trees, and into helicopters in motion, wasn't the same as cartwheels, swinging from uneven parallel bars or tumbling around a carpeted floor. With her leg cramping her ability, she concentrated on upper body exercises. She stood on her hands and balanced her weight above her head. Going up and coming down on her good leg worked fine for several minutes. Then inadvertently she fell on the bad leg. Biting her lower lip, she held the scream inside.

Getting up, she tried it again. She remembered her coach's words that she could do it if she put her mind to it and even if one part of her body was hurt, the other parts worked fine. But out here in the dark, where could she find something uneven or even parallel so she could try her routines? She had nothing. So she made do with handstands and floor stretches.

Usually her mind was totally absorbed in her exercise. She'd review the routine or recite affirmations, but now she thought of Jack. She couldn't help it. No matter what she tried, since he came back into her life she could think of nothing else, especially after he kissed her in the bathroom. Her mouth tingled when she thought of that. Her body had been hot and she could feel every inch of him pressing into her. He wanted her as much as she wanted him. She'd forgotten that in the light of what he said, but she knew Jack wasn't as immune to her as he pretended.

She even wondered if his reason for going into town was to give himself some time away from her. If they were leaving in the morning there was no need for him to go and get supplies. They could live one day without food. Her stomach growled at that moment reminding her she *was* hungry.

Morgan went on trying to do exercises, but with her mind on Jack she kept coming down on the wrong leg. Finally she gave up and sat down.

The sky was dark, light coming from a half moon and stars that rained overhead like tiny points of glitter spangled in the darkness. Many nights she'd spent this way, alone with only herself and the stars for company. She hadn't thought of anyone other than herself. Before she'd befriended Jean, her next meal was her only concern. Now she thought of a man—Jack.

Then Morgan did something she hadn't done since she was twelve years old. She lifted her head to the heavens and wished on a star.

Jack took a cart from the rows of interlocking metal carriages and headed for the produce section. Ben had left the van with him. He hadn't told Jack how he was getting home and Jack hadn't asked. Camping supplies filled most of the back cabin. The gear could act as a cover and be functional. Again he thought of Morgan in the cave. She could use the blankets that sat on the back seat.

Jack also stopped in a store to gather a few things Ben hadn't had time to gather. They needed real food. He'd found a tin of Olivia's coconut macaroons which Ben knew he was partial to. He'd buy a ready-made salad and a few non-perishable foods.

One wheel squeaked as he pushed the cart. He considered returning it for another, but stopped, refusing to break one of his own rules. Only travel the distance once, he'd told himself over the years. This was a get-in-and-get-out situation. He wasn't here to compare prices or socialize with a neighbor he hadn't seen in months, who happened to turn one end of an aisle as he turned the other. He was here to grab what they needed and return. If he was lucky no one would remember he'd ever been there.

Equally lucky for him, the store was one of those gargantuan places with aisle upon aisle carrying everything from what a person would need to diagnose most ailments to swimming pool supplies. Bananas and Mrs. Smith's Apple Pie could share space in the same grocery cart with a color television, a bottle of white wine, work boots and books. *Stop and Shop,* the outside sign had read. Jack saw it as a true definition of one-stop shopping.

Besides the salad in Jack's cart he added bottles of juice, water, some carrots, Parmelat milk, crackers, a pair of work pants for him and a T-shirt advertising the Cleveland Browns. He thought of getting a matching one for Morgan, but stemmed the idea as too suggestive of a relationship. Instead he got her a pair of long pants and a plain shirt. His eye for size was perfect, especially after his hands had sized her from neck to hips, but he picked up a sewing kit anyway, in case the fit needed adjustment. On his way to the cash register he threw a comb and brush combination in the basket and stopped in front of a wall of cosmetics. He selected a tube of lipstick. Women could exist without a lot of amenities and Morgan had yet to complain of their hardship, but makeup was one commodity that rivaled food as a basic necessity of life.

On the same shelf as the lipstick Jack knocked down a box hanging from a metal extension. He bent over and picked it up. About to return it to its place, he hesitated. The box contained condoms. Pictures of Morgan naked in the bathroom flooded his mind like a reel of film. He gripped the cart tighter and hesitated, staring at the box. He lifted his arm to replace it on its metal arm, then stopped. A second later he threw the box into the cart.

"What the hell?" he muttered. It was better to err on the side of safety.

Jack obeyed all the rules of the road on his drive back to Morgan. He couldn't explain his feelings at being separated from her. He thought of her constantly, wondering if she were all right. Grabbing the lipstick, he held it in his hand.

When he returned he parked the van and covered it with as many branches as he could find. Carrying the bag with their food, he could see no light coming from the cave as he approached it. The lipstick was still held in his hand. His heartbeat accelerated. Had she run away again? His legs unconsciously moved faster. He rushed toward the opening. He was sure the bullet wound would hurt her too much for her to run.

"Damn!" he cursed. She was probably lying when she said it hurt. She knew one of them was going to have to go for food. She planned this all along.

"Jack." He heard his named called and swung around. Morgan sat on the ground near the cave entrance.

"What are you doing out here?" he asked, relieved to discover she was still here and safe.

"It was too cold in there."

She'd pulled her hair loose and it fell about her shoulders. Her face was outlined in the darkness. He took a step closer. The night was dark but there were still shadows softening her face. Jack controlled the breath he let out. He had to stop himself from charging over and pulling her into his arms, burying his face in her hair and taking her mouth as if the two of them needed to share the same breath.

"I brought some blankets."

"In that bag?" she laughed, indicating the grocery bag he carried.

"This one contains food. Are you hungry?"

She stood up. Jack noticed she favored her bad leg. She came toward him.

"Famished," she said, but the look Jack saw had nothing to do with nutrition and everything to do with sex.

"This is a job, Morgan." Jack turned and put the bag down, then faced her. "It's not a romance." The words seemed flat. Who was he trying to convince? He'd bought condoms. He could feel the small box pressing against him through his pants leg.

"What makes you think I'd want a romance with you?"

Jack sighed, then walked toward her. He could see her reaction. She wanted to run faster than any jackrabbit he'd ever seen, but she was a fighter. She'd stand her ground for as long as there was breath in her body. Well, he'd show her how much breath he could steal.

"The way you look at me."

"And how is that?"

"Like your body is ovulating and I'm the last piece of chocolate candy on the planet."

CHAPTER 9

"I do not," Morgan protested, her voice shrill and high.

Jack took another step toward her and stopped. He'd seen her movement. It was slight but recognizable. He admitted she was good-looking, more than good-looking. At nineteen she'd been a budding beauty. Today, after running for her life, everything about her was alive and vibrant and eager for someone to hold her. He continued, walking all the way up to her until he was so close he could feel the fire between them. It was red and living, swirling, ready to consume, take the life out of them with its oxygen-eating force. Jack waited, saying nothing. He wanted her to look at him, lift her head and look into his eyes. He knew she'd do it, knew she couldn't help but do it. He was patient. His life was built on being patient. Finally, she raised her eyes and her head. He let the moment linger, looking at her, running his eyes over her features like a lover, ready to take what was his. Then he leaned closer. Neither his mouth nor his body touched any part of hers. There was nothing between them but want and need. She swayed forward. He watched her eyes close and her body begin to melt. Her arms came up to grab hold of something to prevent her from falling.

"You're a job, Morgan. This is not a romance," Jack said, knowing what her reaction would be.

He stepped back as her eyes flew open and she regained her balance. She glared at him through storm clouds of emotion, then stalked off into the darkness as much as her leg would let her stalk.

As the darkness swallowed her, Jack let his breath escape. God! To say she didn't have a stranglehold on him was like saying the blood in his veins was ice water. She positively drove him mad, but the only way the two of them would survive is if they never crossed the line. He'd tasted Armageddon more than once, but with Morgan there would be no reprieve. She was leaving when he got her to Washington. Jacob would give her a new identity and a new life. They would never see each other again. It was unfair to both of them to get involved, begin a relationship that had nowhere to go. It had been the pattern of her life. People leaving her. He didn't want her to think of him as one of the others, someone from her past who'd come and gone.

She'd be devastated and he'd—. Jack didn't want to think about what he'd be when this was over. He wanted her more than he'd ever wanted any woman. He'd come damn close to having her in that hotel bathroom. He'd wanted to ravish her then and that want hadn't diminished by a single iota. His only refuge was to keep his head and keep on his side of the line.

Morgan was past angry. She sat on the ground, hugging her knees to her chest and rocking back and forth. Jack brought out the tiger in her and he seemed to do it on purpose. Why had he intentionally begun a fight? She'd done nothing, but they couldn't be together without some strong emotion occupying the same room. Jack was determined to make that emotion anger. She wondered why.

Morgan checked the sky for a possible answer. Earlier she'd been wishing on a star, now she wanted to know why Jack—

She stopped.

"He's afraid," she said out loud. He was afraid of her. Why? Every time she got near him, he retreated.

Morgan didn't have time to discover the answer. Something dropped in her lap and she jumped. Jack stood outlined in the darkness three feet from where she sat.

"Morgan."

She looked at what he'd dropped. It was makeup, lipstick, a comb and brush.

"You thought about me," she said, not bothering to keep the incredulity out of her voice. It followed right in with the train of her thoughts. Jack never bothered with anyone, but when he went out he'd thought enough to bring her back lipstick and a comb.

"They were at the checkout stand," he covered, with a slight lift of his shoulder. She saw the movement in silhouette.

"Why are you afraid of me?" she asked, voicing the thoughts that were uppermost in her mind.

"Why do you think I am?" His question was asked slowly as if he were buying time, trying to figure her out. He didn't know her as well as he thought he did. Maybe he'd read her file. She didn't know what was in it, but she was sure it existed somewhere in the annals of the CIA.

Morgan got to her feet. She moved toward him slowly. Her leg hurt but it was secondary to her purpose now.

"You push me back each time you have to touch me and you take serious measures not to touch me."

"I don't want to complicate things."

"We're running for our lives, Jack. Things can't get more complicated than that."

He stared at her but didn't answer.

"If we get killed all complications end, so it can't be the threat to our lives you fear. Tell me what it is?"

Jack didn't move, but Morgan noticed his shoulders move slightly. "You know Jacob Winston?"

"Not personally. We've met once."

"When we get to D.C., what do you think will happen?"

Morgan looked away. She hadn't wanted to think about getting to D.C. She knew she and Jack would part there and while her life was on the line here, she was still with him.

"I hoped I'd be safe."

"How do you think that will happen?"

"I don't know. I guess I'd find out what the FBI was going to do."

"And if they could do nothing?"

"Why are you asking me all these questions?"

"Morgan, Jacob Winston is the director of the witness protection program. That's where you're going when I get you to Washington."

So it wasn't her. He was afraid of her leaving him. Could she be right?

"Then you're not as impervious to me as you claim," Morgan challenged. She started toward him.

"Back off, Morgan. You're way out of your depth here."

Morgan didn't back off. She couldn't say what pushed her. She was so tired of Jack acting like he ruled the world. Her world at least. He made the rules and she was expected to follow them. Well, she wouldn't this time. Something inside her wanted to know that he wasn't all stone and granite, that he was human. That his control could enter meltdown the way hers did.

Jack stared at her, his eyes hooded and as impossible to read as always, but this time Morgan didn't care. This time she was determined to have the upper hand. She went toward him. He didn't move back, but she saw him react as if he wanted to. As quickly as it happened it was gone. He was in control again. A fragile control and she knew it.

"Let's test my depth," she said. She grabbed the snap on his jeans, releasing it and the zipper in one smooth stroke. Her hands moved faster than he thought or he was more surprised than anything else when she plunged them inside his pants and surrounded him. He was already erect. She'd known it, but the proof gave her more confidence, more power.

Out of pure reaction and self-preservation, Jack's hands grabbed Morgan's shoulders, crushing them so tightly she should have screamed. She didn't even feel the pain.

"Morgan, stop!" His voice was a wail, like a wild, wounded animal. She ignored him, raking her long fingernails over the rigid length of him.

"Tell me," she whispered, keeping her voice intentionally controlled, intentionally low and seductive. "Tell me, Jack."

Jack's knees bent and his head fell on her shoulder. She supported his weight, continuing her torture. She knew he was human, knew he wanted her as much as she wanted him. He'd told himself he wasn't human for so long, he believed it. She

refused to let him continue to think like that. She'd force him
to know the truth, just as he'd forced her to see it.

His breath on her neck was hard and ragged and his hands
would probably leave bruises on her shoulders.

"Morgan, please stop." He pleaded with her.

"You don't want that, Jack," she told him, continuing that
seductively low voice, a whisper and a caress in one. "I know
what you want. You want me. You've wanted me since that
first day at Olympic training camp. I could see it in your eyes."

"You're wrong." His words were stretched apart like a
person who was learning to speak the language and struggling
to remember the right combination.

"I could see it in the way you looked at me when you didn't
think I noticed. You kept me in your sight as if we were would-
be lovers with business ahead of us."

"I did nothing . . . of the . . . kind." He faltered.

"Didn't you, Jack?"

"That's not the reason."

"If I'm wrong, Jack, if we have no unfinished business, why
don't you stop me?" She moved her head back, giving him
access to her neck. He groaned. "Why don't you pull my hands
away?" She'd worked his jeans and shorts down. Her hands
touched his hot skin, drawing circles over his buttocks, teasing
the skin as she brought her hands closer and closer together,
closer and closer to the sensitive point of his erection. "I'm
here, Jack." Her tongue licked his flame-incensed shoulder. "I
want you." She kissed his collarbone. "Take me, Jack. Take
me."

"You don't know what you're saying."

"I do." As harsh as his voice was, she kept hers velvet,
dark and caressing like a summer night.

His hands squeezed tighter on her shoulders. The pain registered and she winced. Quickly he released her and like lightning
grabbed her wrists and pulled her hands away from his body.

"You want me to make love to you," he stated. His eyes
bore into her like a drill. "It wouldn't be love, Morgan. It's
lust! Do you hear me? Pure and simple lust. And in its most
basic form."

She didn't have the use of her hands, but she had her body.

She moved into him, making contact. Her breasts hovered against his chest. She spread her legs and let his erection find its home. His groan was muffled but she heard it.

"I'm not in love with you," she lied. Then she raised her head until her mouth was only a kiss away from his.

Jack's body was a mass of connected coils, but he was down to a single thread holding it all together. Morgan frayed that thread until an electron microscope would be needed to see it, but it held. One more rub and it would snap. She wouldn't cut it. He had to do that. He had to be the one to make the final step. She wouldn't make it easy for him. She wouldn't back off, step away, give him the chance to fall back into that safe world where there was no feeling, no emotion, no love.

"Morgan," he groaned and yanked on the wrists he held, pulling her forward. His mouth slammed into hers, rough and hard. There was no softness in him. His tongue rushed into her mouth and his hands banded her to him. He took the kiss as if decades had passed since he'd kissed anyone. Everything about him said there was no escape for her. She'd asked for it and she was getting what she demanded.

His hands moved over her clothes, ripping them from her and raking over her skin like claws. She felt their roughness on her breasts and shoulders as her T-shirt and bra were replaced by large hands. His mouth left hers and traveled over her neck. His teeth scored her skin, punishing it as he went to her breasts. His teeth closed over her nipple and she cried out at the pleasure that fissured through her, spiraling inside her and settling between her legs.

Her hands held his head, keeping him there, allowing him to torture her as she had done him. She knew he was trying to prove himself right, that he wasn't making love to her. That this was lust, pure and simple, as he'd told her. Basic, he'd said. But she knew better. She knew nothing like this had ever happened to her before and the experience for him was new and wonderful and full of promise. But promises weren't something Jack understood or relied on. He couldn't give to another person. He had no practice in trusting another person and to completely lose control as he was doing was something he would want to stop. He would stop too. She wouldn't let him. Morgan clamped her arms around his neck and molded herself to him, sliding her injured leg up and down his, feeling his hardness against her increase, listening to the groans that passed from his mouth to hers.

Jack held her crushingly tight, bending her backward as his mouth devoured hers. On one leg, she clung to Jack to keep from falling. She set her leg on the ground oblivious to any pain. His hands moved all over her. Burning heat surrounded her. She could almost see it glow in the darkness.

Jack had to be out of his mind. There was nothing else to explain it. He should stop. Now! But he didn't want to. He'd dreamed about Morgan, awakened in frustrated sweats from the erotic fantasies he'd shared with her. Not one of them compared to what was happening to him now. No dream could match her softness, the way she felt in his arms, the way her smooth skin contrasted his rough hands, the way her soap smelled on clean skin.

He was lost, over the edge, unable to do anything more than dive into the pool she'd created, make her his, keep her close and love her. The time for turning back had passed. He had to keep going. His chance to keep control ended when Morgan unsnapped his jeans.

Jack's leg pushed her foot aside and he lowered her to the ground. Quickly he kicked his jeans away and pulled his shirt over his head. He removed her jeans and shirt without finesse, yanking the pink lace panties down and over her long legs, giving no reverence to her injured leg.

At the last minute, he grabbed his jeans and pulled a foiled condom from his pocket. He sheathed the latex over himself. Then he was on top of her, thrusting himself inside her. She would have screamed, but his mouth clamped to hers and he swallowed the sound.

Morgan thought she was lost when Jack had first kissed her, now she knew what he meant. He was a beast and she his willing victim. He held her arms above her head as he thrust stroke after stroke into her. She was helpless to stop the unleashed animal. And she gave what she got, lifting her hips and taking him further and further inside until she was sure the two of them would split into equal halves.

Morgan pushed him over, rolling on top of him. She took the role of aggressor, vowing not to let him think she wanted to turn their struggle to tenderness. Jack would expect tenderness. She wouldn't give it to him. She'd give him what he gave her and he'd love it. She lowered herself over him, then began her ride. She rode him long and hard, her body joining with his. His hands took her waist, guiding her, completing the dance they both wanted to go on and on. Her heart beat fast and she thought it would burst with the sensations that flowed through her. She'd known life before, known love before, but after tonight, after being with Jack, nothing would continue the same.

And she wouldn't want it any other way.

Jack hadn't been this close to tears since he was eight years old and lost his first swimming meet by mere seconds. He rolled away from Morgan the moment the explosion he knew was inevitable between them shattered the night and he calmed down enough to move. He wanted to get away from her. He didn't want to discuss what had just occurred between them. He didn't want to think about it. He didn't want to admit that it had touched him more than anything else that had occurred in the past thirty-seven years.

He sat with his back to her, his head in his hands. Behind him he could hear Morgan's soft hiccups as she tried to regain her breath. He didn't have much time. Two minutes, three at the most, before she turned to him, before she touched him. He didn't want her to touch him. That's how this had started. And it was his fault. He could have stopped it. Why hadn't he? Why did he let her put her hands on him? And why did he let it go on?

"Don't do it, Jack."

He heard her soft voice, the one that sounded like warm brandy on a cold winter night. The one that sent chills down his spine and wrapped his resolve around her finger.

"Don't crawl back into the shell. It's broken, shattered. There are too many pieces to put back together."

Jack swung around and stood up. He took her hands and pulled her to her feet.

"Get dressed," he said.

He pulled on his pants, not bothering with his shirt. When Morgan had on her T-shirt and was trying to put her leg in her pants without falling, he grabbed her sneakers and lifted her off the ground. He carried her back toward the cave. Her head fell on his shoulder. She was light. Much too light for the strength she'd shown today and too light for the weight she'd pulled from his shoulders. She didn't know she now carried it.

Nothing remained in the cave. Jack had cleared it earlier, moving everything Morgan had left there to the van before he went looking for her. He'd unrolled sleeping bags for them to sleep in, but now figured they'd only need one. He carried Morgan to the van.

"Where did this come from?" she asked as Jack set her on her feet.

"I'll explain it later," he said. He punched the security pad on the key and the back door unlocked. Pulling it open, Morgan looked inside. "You'll be warm tonight." Her head snapped around at him. "The sleeping bags." Still the look in her eyes seared through him, leaving him unable to look away. Morgan stepped in front of him. She was barefoot and wearing no pants. Jack looked at her upturned face. She was beautiful and no light complimented her more than the moonlight casting soft shadows across her skin. Hair, framing her face, turned silvery and he wanted to comb his fingers through the mane he knew was thick and soft to the touch. His breath became shallow. He controlled it with a practiced skill.

He liked the way she made him feel, but she was right, it also scared him. She had a power he'd never before felt, one that made him both strong and weak at the same time. It made him want to be with her, yet ready to run away. Want to protect her, yet afraid of the threat she presented to his heart.

Morgan still stared at him as if she were waiting for him to make a decision. Jack had no choice. He wanted her as much now as he had in the past, moments ago, ages ago, a lifetime ago. He leaned forward, removing the small space that separated them and pressed his mouth to hers. No part of her body touched him, only her mouth. Sensation ballooned inside him and the heat they seemed to generate like the beginnings of a nuclear explosion sprang up, surrounding them with its swirling heat.

Tenderly his mouth brushed over hers, seeking, testing, tasting what was his for the taking. But Jack wouldn't take. He wouldn't plunder. Morgan was strong, but she was also fragile. Contradictions raged through him as his tongue moved past her teeth and he drank of her well. Where had she been all his life? How could he know she existed in his world and not fight the forces keeping him from her? He wanted to grab and pull her against him, but he held back.

He raised his hands and touched her face, still keeping their bodies apart. The fire around them glowed red, taking the air between them and creating a vacuum that sought to pull them together like opposites attracting. Jack kept them in place, positioning his mouth over hers and accepting the slow torture that surrounded his heart like an emotional noose. He never knew his life was incomplete until this moment. With this woman he understood the forces of the universe. His previous experiences had lacked the understanding that she was where his life headed. That around this were an infinite number of circles, no beginning, no end, only the continual revolution that brought them together. Running away made no sense. He couldn't run from the emotion, from the torture, from the love.

Jack took the step then. His heart nearly burst as years of running away from her slammed into him like the ghost of himself finally meeting his own destiny. His hands moved to Morgan's waist and he pulled her against him. She wore only her shirt which hung to her thighs. He slipped his hands under it to feel her skin. It was hot and soft and he felt his hand melting into her. He groaned at the sensation that arrowed through him when her hands slowly ran up his chest and connected behind his neck.

Still he kept the pace slow, although the effort was herculean. She was a gymnast. Her body had been sculpted through exercises, shaped to give it the strength it needed to perform on the various pieces of equipment, but Jack didn't think of that. His only thought was of the way it fit into his, as if some divine hand had found the separate pieces of a mold and brought the two of them together to form a whole.

Jack felt whole, complete. He walked Morgan backward to the van. At the open door, he lifted his head and looked at her. Her face was soft, and a mini-smile lifted the corners of her mouth. Jack's heart constricted. She climbed into the van and lay on the sleeping bag. Jack followed her. It was darker inside since he'd parked it in a secluded area and concealed it with tree branches. He could still see Morgan. His eyes read every inch of her body. Everything about her was aerodynamically wrong for gymnastics. She was too tall, her breasts too large, but Jack loved the combination. It was perfect for him. Jack pushed her T-shirt up one inch at a time as he kissed the silky skin it uncovered. She was a wondrous map which he planned to explore. He heard her gasp when his mouth touched her. Her hands caught his shoulders and she tried to draw him upward. He wanted to go, wanted to delve into her, but he forced himself to savor the moment.

They'd been an explosion earlier tonight. He wanted to commit every moment to memory this time. He wanted to know the sweetness of the torture she went through, carry them both to the brink of madness before consummation. He only hoped he could do it. His own body was rock hard. Blood pulsed through him like an out-of-control cyclone. He ignored it as much as possible.

He pulled Morgan up and removed the T-shirt. She kissed his bare chest, running her hands slowly up his skin, leaving trails that could have been molten flame in her wake. Jack clamped down on a groan. Her hands came down. When she reached the top of his jeans, he knew their power, knew what would happen if she took him in those wickedly wonderful hands again.

He kissed her as they sat, his fingers exploring her back and taking pleasure as she arched toward him whenever he moved his hands over her. He spanned her small waist and moved upward to cup her breasts. She opened her legs then and moved to sit over him. No space separated them, not even the absent light could have sought space. The kiss went deeper as her mouth demanded more. He shifted from side to side, kissing her, tasting her, devouring her mouth like a long drink of cold water when the temperature soared over the ninety-degree mark. He wanted more and more of her. Kisses weren't enough.

Jack pressed her back and removed his jeans. He slipped one of the condoms over himself and joined with her. Jack heard her sigh of pleasure as he settled between her legs. *God! This is heaven,* he thought. Everything Jack had thought about taking his time was lost the moment his body connected to hers. Pure sensation, lust, wanting, need, love, took over and he could think of nothing other than the combined pleasure that two people could give each other. Not any two people, specifically Morgan Kirkwood and Jack Temple. Her body was made for his. His blood pounded and his heart beat and his senses told him she was different, more than any woman he'd ever slept with before. Making love was something that didn't happen often, and while he'd thought he'd made love before, nothing compared to the woman in his arms, in his bed and in his body. She'd insinuated herself inside him, stolen into his pores when he wasn't looking and taken up residence. She was here for the duration. There was no going back after this.

Morgan was the Rolls-Royce of his life and he thanked the heavens he'd found her. He called her name as a sudden rush like an approaching tsunami pounded within him. Lightning flashed inside his head and drove him like a madman. Her body accepted the force of his as the wave topped him and crashed. His release was like falling from an airplane. The ground rushed upward but the parachute saved him and gently set him on the ground.

Morgan's arms were his parachute. She hugged him, slipped her sensual hands over his heated skin, as she rained kisses over his face. Jack was as weak as a man recovering from a long illness, but he knew the Morgan sickness which had invaded his body was something that had no cure.

And he didn't want one.

The house glittered white in the sunshine. It was one of those monstrosities left over from the Jazz Age or some age that never seemed to fall completely out of style. The rich passed them around like Faberge eggs, changing the interior once a decade to make it seem as if it were part of the present. The place should have been demolished years ago and a shopping mall put up, but it had survived to be decorated according to the taste of its present owner, who favored a Far Eastern motif. All the windows and doors had been covered with opaque sliding panels. He always felt as if he were entering a tomb when the doors slid closed behind him.

There was practically no furniture in any of the downstairs rooms. Some of them had a couple of steps leading down to a floor of gravel, which was carefully raked for evenness. Trees of odd shapes grew inside and appeared green no matter what the time of year. It was as if the owner never wanted the outside world to touch him, so he built his own world within the walls. Never having been above the first floor, he wondered if there were beds or if some other unexpected forms were used there.

He stopped the car at the end of the driveway, which stretched three miles from the road to culminate in a circle around a fountain. Atop it stood golden dragons spouting water in the four directions. A long sigh escaped him as he got out of the car. He hated coming here.

He got out of his car in the circular driveway and looked at the sky. The day was clear, warm, a hint of the humidity that could descend on the place without warning was in the air, but he wasn't uncomfortable in his suit and tie. The water dragons spouted at the relentless sky, arcing rainbows in the light.

His steps were heavy approaching the door. He had bad news and he never knew how it would be received, but whether there was quiet or explosion, he knew underneath was a seething heart that had no compassion, no conscience. He had little either, but he did draw the line at cruelty to animals and children. He'd never be involved in any operation that preyed on the innocent and defenseless. Children should be protected and maybe they wouldn't grow up to be like him.

He rang the doorbell. It was immediately opened by a maid who said nothing. She admitted him and showed him to one of the downstairs rooms. He'd been in this one before. This one had a floor, instead of a rock garden.

"What do you mean they got away?" The old man received

the news badly. He slammed his fist down on the oriental antique desk. A jade pencil cup danced in a circle on the black polished surface and a carved-ivory-handled letter opener jumped out of its tray to lay flat on the wood. "She's an amateur."

"I doubt amateur is the word to apply to Ms. Kirkwood. She was ready for us. She'd planned her escape. Had a way out fully orchestrated and she executed it beautifully. Exactly like she did in that prison twelve years ago."

"Maybe," the other man said. He got up from his desk and came around to face his adversary. "What about the Indiana house and the highway? She couldn't have had a plan there."

"She had help there and the man she's with is no amateur."

He secretly admired Morgan Kirkwood. She was a fighter, determined to stay alive, and so far she was succeeding.

"Who is he?" the man demanded.

They didn't know, but he wouldn't admit that. "As far as we can tell he's an agent. What branch, what government, isn't clear. Ms. Kirkwood is as patriotic as they come. I'd say he's U.S. He could be a cop or military, even FBI. No one else could have pulled off his stunts without a high degree of skill, training and experience."

"I don't care who he is." The man's hands disappeared inside the huge sleeves of his robe. He wore these garments inside the house. During the rare times he left this house, he wore the standard suits of the western world. But inside this sanctuary, the outside world didn't exist until someone brought it in. Unfortunately, he was that messenger. His voice was low. He had to strain to hear him clearly. "I want them both found and then I never want anyone to hear from them again. Do I make myself clear?"

He nodded.

"Either she's dead or you are."

Nothing was more erotic than a woman sleeping, Jack thought as he watched Morgan. A long T-shirt, exposed legs, just the shadow of promise, revealing skin beneath the fabric.

Jack's body got hard.

The sun had risen, but Jack hadn't disturbed Morgan. He'd left her to go for a run, but returned to find her still asleep. Since then he could only sit and watch her. The covering over the windows he'd used to camouflage the van kept the inside dim. He reached over and smoothed the hair away from her face. She stirred, but didn't awaken. He let her sleep. They should leave soon, but he enjoyed looking at her. It had been too long since he'd simply looked at a woman. He'd known women who scrambled to get to other places and women who cooked breakfast in the morning. He'd known women on assignments, when time was of the essence, but he'd never run with a woman and he'd never felt the way he did with anyone except Morgan.

She appeared vulnerable in sleep, like a child needing protection. Jack was surprised by the swell to his heart when he thought of her.

She reached up and touched his face, smoothing her fingers between his eyes. "You're frowning," she said. Her voice was the morning-after-sex voice. It grabbed him and wove a spell that told him he wanted her again. "What were you thinking?"

Jack took her hand and kissed her fingertips. One finger slipped into his mouth and he sucked it. "I think you sleep beautifully," he answered.

Morgan smiled and raised herself up enough to slip her arm around his neck. Jack held her, closing his eyes. He drank in her scent, the smell of her hair, the warm cologne of her body, the lingering aftereffects of a sexual encounter. He wanted her, not just now, but for always. Yet he knew it couldn't be. Holding her a second longer and squeezing her to him, as if to imprint a memory he could take out and hold in the coming years, he pushed her back.

"We have to go soon. You must be hungry."

"Your hair's wet," she said.

"I found a stream about fifty yards from here. If you need some time alone it's over there." He pointed toward the front of the van.

Morgan left after pulling on her clothes. Jack got their food out from the previous night. He cleared the sleeping bags, feeling the warmth of Morgan's body in the blankets she'd left behind.

He wanted to hold onto it, keep it for the future, but it escaped like a soft wind. He set the salads out and pulled drinks from the cooler Ben had left for him. She was gone a long time. Jack was about to go after her when he glanced up and saw her returning. He stopped still, straightening from his task.

She walked slowly, coming toward him. Her leg must not have hurt much any longer, for her limp was less evident than it had been the previous night. For a moment everything slowed down and he watched openly as she approached. She mesmerized him. He couldn't move his gaze away, not even able to pretend he wasn't looking. He stared—outright. She smiled.

A single tube of lipstick and a comb and brush had transformed her from the country girl, all wheat and morning sunshine, into a glowing, raving beauty. Her eyes seemed brighter, larger. Her mouth wore the dark color and her face radiated an inner glow. He wanted to go to her, take her into his arms and make love to her again. The night had been more than he'd imagined life offered. The two of them had scaled mountains, soared into the heavens beyond the moon until they entered that incorporeal area where time and space ceased existence, where only the few and the very rare are ever allowed. Yet with her, with Morgan Kirkwood, he'd found it. Together, they had crossed over the line, past the spot marked with the X and discovered something so beautiful that defining it wasn't necessary for the two of them. They'd experienced it and to recall it they only need touch or feel or think.

Jack kept watching her walk toward him. Her arms swung slowly forward and back at her sides. Her head moved and her hair swung about her face like a focus ring that kept him trained on that one area of the landscape. He knew never again would he be able to look at that place where they'd gone as a couple, a unit, a set, two lovers alone. Without her he could never go there again and the urge to experience it over and over was towering. He wanted her with him every day, every step of the way, for always.

At that moment Jack knew he was in love with Morgan. She complemented him, brought out qualities that were more than a job, even one where he cared about the principles behind it. She showed him lands he'd never expected to see, took him

An important message from the ARABESQUE Editor

Dear Arabesque Reader,

Because you've chosen to read one of our Arabesque romance novels, we'd like to say "thank you"! And, as a special way to thank you, we've selected four more of the books you love so well to send you for FREE!

Please enjoy them with our compliments, and thank you for continuing to enjoy Arabesque...the soul of romance.

Karen Thomas
Senior Editor,
Arabesque Romance Novels

Check out our website at
www.arabesquebooks.com

SPECIAL OFFER!
4 FREE BOOKS

ARABESQUE ®

A PRODUCT OF

BET BOOKS

3 QUICK STEPS
TO RECEIVE YOUR "THANK YOU" GIFT
FROM THE EDITOR

Send this card back and you'll receive 4 FREE Arabesque
novels! The introductory shipment of 4 Arabesque novels – a
$23.96 value – is yours absolutely FREE!

There's no catch. You're under no obligation to buy anything.
You'll receive your introductory shipment of 4 Arabesque
novels absolutely FREE (plus $1.50 to offset the costs of
shipping & handling). And you don't have to make any
minimum number of purchases—not even one!

We hope that after receiving your books you'll want to
remain an Arabesque subscriber. But the choice is yours to
continue or cancel, anytime at all! So why not take us up on
our invitation to receive 4 Arabesque Romance Novels, with
no risk of any kind. You'll be glad you did!

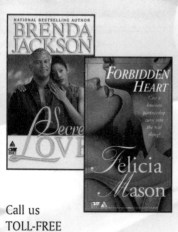

Call us
TOLL-FREE
at 1-888-345-BOOK

THE EDITOR'S "THANK YOU" GIFT INCLUDES:

- 4 books absolutely FREE (plus $1.50 for shipping and handling)
- A FREE newsletter, *Arabesque Romance News*, filled with author interviews, book previews, special offers, and more!
- No risks or obligations. You're free to cancel whenever you wish... with no questions asked.

BOOK CERTIFICATE

Yes! Please send me 4 FREE Arabesque novels (plus $1.50 for shipping & handling). I understand I am under no obligation to purchase any books, as explained on the back of this card.

Name _____

Address _____ Apt. _____

City _____ State _____ Zip _____

Telephone ( ) _____

Signature _____

Offer limited to one per household and not valid to current subscribers. All orders subject to approval. Terms, offer, & price subject to change. Offer valid only in the U.S.

AN100A

Thank you!

Accepting the four introductory books for FREE (plus $1.50 to offset the cost of shipping & handling) places you under no obligation to buy anything. You may keep the books and return the shipping statement marked "cancelled". If you do not cancel, about a month later we will send 4 additional Arabesque novels, and you will be billed the preferred subscriber's price of just $4.00 per title. That's $16.00 for all 4 books for a savings of 33% off the cover price. You may cancel at any time, but if you choose to continue, every month we'll send you 4 more books, which you may either purchase at the preferred discount price. . . or return to us and cancel your subscription.

THE ARABESQUE ROMANCE CLUB: HERE'S HOW IT WORKS

PLACE
STAMP
HERE

heart&soul's got it all!

Motivation, Inspiration, Exhilaration!
FREE ISSUE RESERVATION CARD

YES! Please send my FREE issue of HEART & SOUL right away and enter my one-year subscription. My special price for 5 more issues (6 in all) is only $10.00. I'll save 44% off the newsstand rate. If I decide that HEART & SOUL is not for me, I'll write "cancel" on the invoice, return it, and owe nothing. The FREE issue will be mine to keep.

Name _____ _____
        (First)   (Last)

Address _____ Apt.#_____

City _____ State _____ Zip _____   MABR

Please allow 6-8 weeks for receipt of first issue. In Canada: CDN $19.97 (includes GST). Payment in U.S. currency must accompany all Canadian orders. Basic subscription rate: 1 year (6 issues) $16.97.

BUSINESS REPLY MAIL

FIRST-CLASS MAIL   PERMIT NO. 272   RED OAK, IA

POSTAGE WILL BE PAID BY ADDRESSEE

heart&soul

P O BOX 7423
RED OAK IA 51591-2423

to heavenly mountains he didn't know could be viewed by mortal man. He wanted her again, wanted that feeling again, that ultimate trip, a journey that could only be made with her.

Nearly incapable of speech when she stood in front of him, he couldn't resist the urge to touch her. His hands brushed her arms lightly and he stepped close enough that she had to look up at him. He leaned toward her gently, holding himself in the greatest check he'd ever done. Then he kissed her, tenderly, cradling her in his arms as if she were a work of art so fine and so delicate that it required the greatest care.

Jack wanted her again, wanted to make love. He knew tomorrow was their enemy and that time for them had become finite. He crushed her against him, feeling the blood in his body rioting through his system, knowing the imprint of her smaller frame outlined against his.

He was only a thread away from undressing her when he heard her stomach growl. The sound was like a huge hammer striking a boulder. He couldn't remember the last time she ate and he knew her migraines would return if she didn't get some food. With an effort greater than the forces needed to pull down a mountain, he slid his mouth from hers, but kept her in his arms for just a little longer. He inhaled her scent, knowing that even if he were blind he'd be able to pick her out of a crowd by the distinctive fragrance that spoke her name. It was as identifiable as fingerprints. Slowly he pulled back, letting his hands run down her arms to her hands. He held them a moment and smiled, then stepped back, allowing the space between to calm his chiming nerves.

He reached into the van and picked up the plastic containers of food. She curled her feet under her as she leaned against the van wall and took the salad they'd left untouched the night before. Jack went to the small cookstove and poured two styrofoam cups of coffee. Giving her one, he sat opposite her with his own meal. The dressing had made the lettuce soggy, but they ate it anyway. Morgan drank deeply of the juice and coffee. Jack carefully opened a single packet of sugar and dumped it into his cup. Then he slipped the torn-off top into the bottom and dropped both into a small plastic bag. Morgan watched him. He didn't meet her eyes, because he didn't want her to see what was in his.

"Jack, where were you born?" Morgan asked as she finished her salad and set the plastic container aside.

It wasn't the first time Jack had heard the question, and it usually came from a woman. The planted story Jack usually told sprang quickly to his memory. He had an alias, many of them, and reading the situation or direct orders usually told him which one to use. Morgan wasn't an order and she'd proved beyond a shadow of a doubt that she wasn't *just a job*.

He couldn't give her the company line and he couldn't wave her off with one of his fabricated aliases. All that remained was the truth. She deserved that. She'd had so many lies in her life. He couldn't heap another one on the tottering pile.

"Lexington, Kentucky," he answered with the truth.

"We're not that far from Kentucky. Do your parents still live there?"

He nodded. "My dad retired last year. He was a pharmacist."

"And your mom?"

"She's a lawyer. She still practices, but only takes cases that interest her."

Morgan smiled. "That's wonderful. I thought about that once."

"Being a lawyer?"

She shrugged. "Being helpful," she paused. "What about brothers? Sisters? Do you have any?"

"Four sisters. They're all married with children."

"That's nice." This time her smile had sadness to it. "You must have wonderful holiday reunions."

Jack only nodded. For reasons he knew would conjure up her own poor memories of holidays, he refrained from giving her details of the Christmases he'd spent with his family or the seven nights of Kwanzaa celebrations, the summer picnics or family ski trips. Jack's life of late had been all jungle and farce. He'd forgotten the happy times, put them away to deal with day-to-day needs, but they were there, waiting behind a door he only need open to remember and relive.

Morgan's doors to the past were locked, entombing memories she fought to hide. He doubted any of them would make her smile.

"Tell me about Jack?" Morgan broke into her thoughts.

"What?"

She looked up. Her brown eyes were huge and filled with wonder.

"You know everything about me. I only know that you exercise, eat salads instead of junk food, neatly tuck the torn-off tops of sugar packets inside the bottoms before throwing them away." She glanced at the sugar packet. His eyes followed her lead. "I know"—she hesitated suggestively—"almost nothing else." Stretching her leg toward him, she ran her toe up his leg. "So tell me about Jack."

Jack hesitated. He couldn't help it. It was both habit and ingrained teaching. He didn't talk about himself. Often he turned the conversation around to gain information from the other person, but today he was going to tell Morgan what she wanted to know.

"My childhood was normal. I did all the things children do, summer camp, winter sports, braces on my teeth, extremely shy of girls."

Morgan laughed. She turned on her side and rested her head on her hand. Jack liked the way her hair fell around her face. She looked as if she were a child and he was telling her a fascinating story.

"Our family gatherings were always happy," he continued. "We get together during the holidays and I attend when I can."

"How did you become interested in swimming?"

"When I was eight my parents put a pool in our yard and I spent all my free time in it. I joined the swim team in high school and chose my university because it had a first-class team. While in college I was asked to join the Olympic team."

"As a coach?"

He shook his head. "As a competitor." He looked at her wide wonderful eyes. He wondered why he'd never noticed how expressive they were.

"I would have been in high school then," Morgan added.

"I turned it down."

"You did!" She nearly sat up.

"Not immediately. I went to the training camp." He told

her the story of his experience at the camp. And his fateful dinner with his recruiter. "They offered me a job."

"But you were only in college," she protested.

"I remained in college, but I turned down going to the Olympics." Jack had always wondered what he would have done if he'd made the other decision. During lonely nights in the jungles or while hiding in the hot sands of some foreign country, he had thoughts of how different his life might be if he'd turned down the CIA and gone on to try for the gold medal.

Morgan, ironically, had made the same decision. She'd done exactly what he did, but her choice took her to the limelight, center stage of the world. Not only did she complete her mission, however bad the circumstances, but she went on to show the world that she was champion material. Jack admired her for that. Even the tears she cried when it was over didn't take away from the strength of purpose she needed to do what she had done. He wasn't sure his masculine and supposed greater physical strength could have matched hers if he'd been in the same position.

"When I graduated I went to work for the police department in Chicago. That's where I met Jacob Winston."

"Did he recruit you?"

"Jacob works for the FBI. He didn't recruit me. He left Chicago for Washington a few months after I joined the force. We had become friends and have stayed that way." Jack didn't elaborate on who had actually approached him. It was a story he didn't tell. Not even his family knew how he'd gone from police officer to Middle East expert. Somehow he wanted Morgan to know the truth.

"I'd stayed with the department two years. The city changed drastically in some areas. A huge number of Koreans escaping oppression in their own country settled in an area called Little Korea. It was my beat. I picked up the language enough to communicate with the locals. Then people started dying in that area. A serial killer targeted Koreans. The city was in an uproar to find the killer. Factions split along racial lines and the newspapers were increasing circulation with stories on the ineptitude of the police force or its lack of concern due to racial lines."

"I remember that," Morgan said. "It was my first year in college. There was a Chinese student in my dormitory. She did some modeling to pay her tuition. So many people mistook her for Korean. They asked her a lot of embarrassingly racist questions.''

"I was assigned to the detective in charge because of my knowledge of the language and my friendship with some of the people. We found the killer, the husband of one of the victims. He was trying to cover up the death of his wife by killing other innocent people.''

"How did that get you into the CIA?''

"Shortly after the trial ended I took a few days off. I went up into Michigan. I was to meet some friends and we were going skiing. Instead of meeting them, a man named Brian Ashleigh was waiting for me at the cabin we'd rented. He laid out the plan for me to join a special forces group of the CIA and I've been there ever since. When Brian moved I moved. He's the director now. I still work for him, although indirectly. I report to Forrest Washington, director of anti-terrorist activities in the Middle East.''

"How did you end up a swim coach?''

"It was a cover. They assigned me because of my former status and because I'd been tapped by the Olympic team, although I'd turned it down. If you failed to get Hart out, we were your backup. We were going in even if we had to storm the place.''

"The information he had must have been sterling for so much effort to go into his rescue.''

Jack knew no one had ever told her the complete truth of what Hart actually had in his head. Jack couldn't tell her now either. It was still classified information.

"It was,'' he said, without committing anything.

"I guess it's lucky we got him out. Look at where he is now.''

Brian Ashleigh stared at footage he'd seen hundreds of times. He didn't see the need to go over it again, but Jacob had been excited when he called. Brian leaned back in the rose velvet chair at CIA headquarters. His eyes were heavy and he wanted to go home, but he watched the flickering image of Morgan Kirkwood singing the national anthem.

"I don't see anything I haven't seen before, Jacob.'' He

rubbed his eyes. "I can watch this on the nightly news. I don't need to use this room to see it."

"That's right, Brian. We've seen it so much we don't see what's there. Look at her hands."

The film started again. Brian stared at the screen. Morgan went through the routine prior to her last one. It was on the floor. She moved quickly and competently. Brian knew this routine well enough to perform it himself, but he gave it his undivided attention, taking special note of her hands. When she finished the minute-and-a-half exercise summary and raised her hands to salute the judge, there was nothing special about them. They had a little chalk on the palms, but nothing extra. No cuts or bruises. Then the film moved to her last routine. She ran toward the beam and did the now-famous somersault with her special precision landing onto the apparatus. Since that time every gymnast in the world tried to duplicate this one action.

Brian leaned forward, studying her hands with new resolve. Something about her right hand was different, but she kept moving it. Then the routine ended. The sound of the crowd exploded in the room, but Brian could clearly see she wore a ring. The spliced film went on to the singing sequence. Morgan clutched the roses to her breasts as she sang. Tears flowed down her cheeks. Brian recognized the photo that had made worldwide news. Only this time he could clearly see the ring on Morgan Kirkwood's finger, an addition that had not been there during the floor exercise, but had appeared for her next routine.

"That's got to be it," Brian stated aloud, coming out of his chair as if the small auditorium had just been filled with flying bullets. "I want that segment of the film blown up in detail."

"I've already had that done," Jacob told him. "The ring is that of a Korean emperor. If it's not a reproduction, it's extremely expensive and no one in Korea would have given it up voluntarily. According to the report I've received, the ring was lost. The president gave it to his wife on their marriage. It's assumed the ring was stolen."

"How did Ms. Kirkwood come to have it?"

"I don't know."

"She didn't have it going into the prison," Brian said. "Directly after getting Lewiston out she was taken back to the hall. She had to have gotten it somewhere between the two. The only stop she made was at the prison."

"Why would such an item be in the prison?"

"I guess that's the next question in the riddle."

"Riddle?"

"Brian, why is Morgan Kirkwood such an important person?"

"She isn't."

Jacob stretched his long legs out in front of him and, resting his elbows on the chair arms, threaded his fingers together. "I sat in a conference room with the two top people responsible for defending the laws of the United States, discussing a woman who shouldn't have as much clout as that kind of meeting would require. Now who is she?"

Brian glanced at the control room and both he and Jacob left. They didn't speak on the way to Brian's office. Inside, Brian closed the door. Both men sat in front of the desk.

"We thought we had everything under control before we sent Ms. Kirkwood into the prison. In truth, nothing went right from the moment she entered the facility. The blueprints we'd received had never been updated. New walls existed that weren't in the plans. Surveillance equipment had been installed that was unknown to us. She went in blind."

"I'm sure that kind of thing has happened before. It doesn't make her a top priority for two phases of law enforcement twelve years after the fact," Jacob commented.

Brian sighed. He knew Jacob was thorough and that he was extremely perceptive. He'd often wanted him on his team, but Jacob's allegiance to his job and to Clarence Christopher were deeply rooted.

"She's the granddaughter of a very powerful man," Ashleigh said.

"I thought the report says she has no family. That she was adopted as a homeless child."

"It does," Brian admitted. "We didn't find out until she was well into her training."

"Does she know?"

Brian shook his head. "Neither does her grandfather, but we have to keep her safe nevertheless"

Brian wondered if Jacob was quick enough to know that protecting her under the auspices of the CIA meant under orders to do so.

"How come her mother never told her?" Jacob asked.

"We don't know. She was left alone as a child. She could have been too young to remember. When she came to work for us she was a legal adult."

Jacob nodded.

"Who's her grandfather?"

Brian wasn't required to reveal that. It wasn't germane to finding her or to keeping her safe. Her grandfather's ignorance of her existence and Ms. Kirkwood's ignorance negated any reason to reveal the association. But Jacob had come to him with the ring. It was the only link they had and it gave him more information than they'd received since Jack disappeared in St. Louis.

"Supreme Court Justice, the Honorable Judge Angus Lewiston."

"Hart Lewiston's father! Morgan Kirkwood had gone into a prison and saved the life of her own uncle and neither of them knew it?"

"Hart Lewiston is not her uncle," Ashleigh corrected.

"He's her father?" Jacob's face showed more surprise than Brian Ashleigh had ever seen him display.

"If Hart Lewiston wins the election, Morgan Kirkwood becomes the First Daughter."

CHAPTER 10

Ohio Route 821 intersected Interstate 77 at Exit 6. Jack brought the van to a stop at the highway entrance. He waited longer than necessary at the road sign. Morgan expected him to consult the cache of maps he'd stored in the pocket next to the driver's door. She heard no paper rattling and Jack made no move either. She looked right and left before turning to face him, a questioning frown on her face.

"What's wrong?" she asked.

"South leads to Kentucky and my parents in Lexington. East leads to Clarksburg, West Virginia, the closest FBI office." Morgan was reluctant to go to the FBI. Instinct told her something was wrong. The road between here and there had few places to hide. If they got into trouble there would be nowhere to go. On the other hand she didn't want to do anything that might put his parents in jeopardy. Morgan knew Jack had never laid his problems at their door.

"Which way are we going?"

Jack hugged his arms around the steering wheel and looked her way. "It's your call."

Morgan's lips turned up in the corners, but she didn't say anything. She looked at the road, first left, then right. Jack had once told her she had no say in what he decided.

She wanted to choose Lexington. She would have if their lives were normal. If they were two lovers sightseeing in mountainous beauty she would love to meet his family. She wanted to see his parents, see if she could see Jack in their faces. She wanted to meet his sisters and their children, but this wasn't a normal situation. They weren't vacationers out for a good time.

"West Virginia," she said after a moment.

Jack made no protest, no comment on her decision. He headed up the entry ramp. Pulling into the light flow of traffic, he turned the radio on. Static poured out loudly. Turning the volume lower he pressed the Scan key. The first station the electronic device found was a country station. Bonnie Raitt's whiskey-hoarse voice sang "Something To Talk About." Morgan usually sang along, even going so far as to dance around her kitchen when this song played. Today she sat still.

She sat with her private thoughts for a long time. Jack was quiet too. Morgan wondered what he was thinking. After last night when the two of them had made love with such abandon, she wondered if he regretted it now. When she got to the FBI what would happen? She knew she couldn't say she wanted to go to Kentucky. She wanted to go to the ends of the earth as long as the two of them could go there together.

"Who's going to meet us at the FBI?" she suddenly blurted out.

"Brian Ashleigh and Jacob Winston."

"Have you talked to them?" She swallowed hard as if the office were only a mile away and they'd be parting within the hour.

"No," he said.

How could they have shared last night and he turn her over today as if she were some rag doll? Didn't last night mean anything, or this morning? He was there when she opened her eyes and she had the feeling he'd been watching her for some time. Her hair was still wet from the pond she'd used to wash up. The water was cold to touch, but she submerged her body in it. She needed to defuse the temperature gauge that Jack had the ability to elevate. The pond was clear and beautiful and she suddenly wanted a bath.

She felt great when she returned to the van, and the way Jack had looked at her, she thought they were on the right road. That the two of them would have a future together. It had been a long time since she thought of a future, and in her circumstances it was almost laughable to think that the two of them could have anything together.

"Jack, take the next exit." Morgan sat forward suddenly and pointed.

"What?" His foot was already on the brake and the van was slowing.

"Go toward Belpre."

"Why?"

"We can take Route 14 from there."

"Where does that lead?"

The green and white sign said they were one mile from the exit.

"We're going to get the ring," Morgan told him. "It's what you've wanted all along. I gave them everything else, told them about everything I saw and did. The ring is the only thing I held back. It's what I took from the Korean jail. The one piece I never gave to the CIA."

Jack took the exit when it came up. He turned the van south and drove until he saw the junction for Route 14.

"The town is called Clay," she informed him. "It's small and sits near the Elk River."

"This is where you hid the ring?"

"It's where it's hidden. I was wearing it during the final rotation of the competition. During the interviews I kept my hands under the desk."

When she saw reruns of that film she looked nervous. Of course she was nervous, and it hid the fact that she was hiding her hands.

"I thought you'd never been in this part of the country."

"Why would you think that?"

"The way you act. The way you look at it."

"I've been a lot of places," she told him. Morgan understood what he meant. It was the wonder element. She'd seen it on her own face and that of other competitors when they went to competitions and then got to see cities they hadn't been to before. It was the wide-eyed wonder look. Morgan knew she had it. The land was beautiful and the moonlight last night had been breathtaking. She couldn't help seeing beauty in the things around her, and Jack was a contributor to that beauty. Her eyes were open a little wider today and she looked at the world as birds flying in the sky and corn waving along the road. It wasn't just scenery blurring past them, life moving at the speed of light, it was specific. She wanted to see every blade of grass and listen to the cry of the birds performing their own acrobatics.

"I've been to Clay once. I only stayed for one night."

Jack rubbed the back of his neck as if he were tired and stretching the muscles there. "I'm not even going to try to figure this out. Why don't you just tell me the story."

"The women on the news, Jan and Allie."

Jack nodded. "I remember them."

"Jan owns a gymnastics school and camp in Clay. The ring is hidden there."

"Tell me what's so important about this ring?"

"I think it belongs to the president of Korea."

Janine Acres kicked the door closed. She had a large glass of her own personal recipe for pineapple surprise in each hand. The drink consisted of blended pineapple juice, ginger ale, a banana and coconut. Allie lounged in one of Jan's leotards on the floor in the gym. Both of them had completed the exercise program Jan often required of her students.

Jan sat cross-legged on the blue carpet and handed a glass to Allie, who sat up and sipped it through the long red straw Jan had added to the pastel yellow liquid.

"What is this?" she asked.

"Something that's good to the taste and good for you."

Allie took a long swig. "This is positively sinful. I'm not even going to think about how many calories are in this."

"You haven't gained a pound in decades."

"Due to hours of hard work." She frowned. "Did you think to give our two friends one of these?"

"I did not." Jan sipped from her glass. "After they held us for days."

"They let you come home or I should say James Burton let you come home."

"He followed right along with us," Jan reminded her. "And if you haven't noticed he's keeping us under house arrest."

"We must not be in much danger," Allie surmised. "He'd never have let us come here if it would put the school in danger."

"Well, more than one parent has noticed the presence of two strangers. This is a small town."

Allie's smile was wide. "You think the parents have noticed that you're attracted to Agent James Burton?"

Jan stopped still, holding her glass out for a moment as if she were about to drink from it. Then she dropped her hand and the glass to the floor and leaned toward her friend.

"I, attracted to that big—"

"Tall, strong, good-looking, unmarried man who fits the right age, height, weight and personality profile," Allie interrupted her. "You better believe I do. He's attracted to you too."

"Allie, you've been reading too many of your own scripts. This is not a television program or the movies."

"It's also not a script. If it were, there would be much more action. And you'd have already slept with him."

"Allie!"

"Oh, don't go acting as if you've never thought of the idea or that your morals are as Victorian as the last century's. I've seen you looking at him when you didn't think I noticed. The lust in your eyes is true. I'm surprised you didn't spontaneously combust there on the spot."

"You are out of your tree."

"And when you tripped over that rock while we were out jogging," she went on as if Jan had said nothing. "I thought our dear agent was going to pick you up and carry you off right then and there."

"Allie, you're dreaming. The man no more notices me than he realizes he wears the same three ties over and over. And can we change the subject?"

Allie didn't say anything. She looked about the gym, leaving Jan to her own thoughts. Jan admitted to herself that she did think of Jim Burton. She didn't know her face showed how much she was attracted to him, but he rubbed her in all the wrong places and sometimes she wanted to scream at him. There were equal times she wanted him to take her in his arms.

"How many kids do you have working out here?" Allie asked.

Grateful for the distraction and glad to be on safer ground, Jan told her about the school. "I have a manager who runs the regular school. There are about two hundred kids going through each week. The team school has eighteen dedicated young women and seven young men. In the summer about two thousand campers go through here."

"Wow, Jan, I'm impressed. I had no idea you were doing all this."

"That's because you've only come to visit once in ten years."

"You could visit me too."

"I could if I could get through that wall of secretaries, assistants, script people, best boys, producers, actors, grips—"

"Stop," she laughed. "I get the picture."

"Truly, Allie. We should keep in touch."

"We will," she agreed. "All this equipment looks fairly new."

"Most of it is."

"You said Morgan sent you equipment when you first started."

Jan pointed to the trampoline at the end of the room. "She sent the tramp, the vault, those two beams and various mats. When she visited the one and only time she was here she brought the beams herself. With what she sent me I had enough to open the doors."

Allie set her glass on the floor a distance away from both of them. She uncoiled her legs, leaned back and rolled over in the graceful manner Jan tried to instill in her female students. Lying flat on her stomach, close enough to whisper to Jan, she said, "Look over there." She indicated the double glass doors that led into the cavernous room. The only natural light that filtered into the gym came from those doors. Blocking what little there was with his huge frame stood Jim Burton.

Allie waved him in.

Jan's heart thudded. "Don't do that," she said anxiously, but Allie continued to wave.

He opened the door, holding it that way with his foot. Both women stared. He was looking somewhere else, not at them, not even inside the gym, but at something that was outside. Jan's anxiety was replaced with fear. Had someone come? Did they really need protection? But Jim didn't appear afraid. He hadn't said anything and he wasn't going for the gun she knew he carried. She'd seen it on occasion, and once when they'd both come around the same corner from opposite directions she'd walked into him. Using her hands to keep from falling, she'd grabbed for him and found the hard outline of the gun.

"Jim?" Allie sat up. "What's wrong?"

He didn't have time to answer before two people came through the door—Morgan Kirkwood and Jack Temple.

Astonishment showed vividly on the faces of her two friends. Morgan greeted them with a huge smile. She didn't know how much she missed them until this moment. Neither Jan nor Allie moved from their places on the floor. Morgan looked about the room, taking in the placement of equipment, looking over the expanse of floor as if it were a blue sea.

The thought came to Morgan at the same time her feet began to move. The uneven bars were directly in front of her. She grabbed the lower bar, swung her legs into a kip and piked to roll under the bar and come up on the wood at thigh level. For a moment she remained poised there, her chalkless hands aligned with her shoulders, gripping the bar, elbows locked in place, her weight supported on her legs and hands. She leaned forward, overbalancing until her body's center of gravity propelled her forward. Going over the bar she executed a perfect circle, keeping her entire body as straight as a ruler. She did it two more times, then, with feet and hands on the same bar and her body bent in half, she executed the circle again, coming out of it and flying through the short distance to grip the higher bar. Here she swung, piking her body and pulling her long legs up so they missed the lower bar. She did a half-giant, standing for several seconds completely straight, but upside-down as she reversed direction and swung the other way. Two giants later, another reversal and preparation for the dismount. She swung forward, her hands letting go of the bar, tucking her body and doing a half-twist, then a tumble before straightening and sticking to the padded floor.

Without volition her hands reached for the ceiling. Her training was ingrained. Ending with a salute was what she'd learned to do. For a moment no one said anything. Morgan couldn't see Jack or the other agent who stood in the doorway. Jan's mouth dropped open and Allie's eyes widened into an incredulous stare.

Then both of them were on their feet and the three women ran toward each other. They collided in a bear hug that sent the three of them tumbling onto the floor.

"I can't believe you can still do that," Allie said. "This near-thirty-year-old would be out of commission for days if I tried that maneuver."

Morgan laughed. "Mine might be too." She'd forgotten about the bullet wound to her leg. The leg was better. She barely limped much, but sticking to the floor forced her to lift that leg in an unintentional Kerri Strug maneuver. "How are you two?"

"Fine," Jan said. "We were so worried about you. No calls in months and then out of the blue that story on the news."

"I never thought you would take off for St. Charles looking for me. Who did you think you were?" She swung her gaze from one to the other. "Sherlock Holmes?"

"We're your friends, Morgan." Allie's voice was a sharp reprimand. She stood, affronted. "We made a pact. What did you think we'd do?"

Morgan didn't think they'd remember the pact. Her heart filled when Allie made the statement. After twelve years there were people who cared about her.

"I'm glad you're all right," Allie said, lowering her voice. Morgan remembered Allie's methods. She only used the gruff, I-don't-care voice when she was really scared. It was Morgan's guess that Allie had been hiding her feelings from everyone, even Jan.

"Ladies, I hate to interrupt . . ." Jack began.

Morgan was instantly on her feet. She went to Jack, unable to avoid the limp, and pulled him forward. "Guys, I want you to meet—"

"Jack Temple," Allie completed the introduction without surprise. She and Jan stood. Allie offered her hand and Jack shook it. "We were in Korea together."

"I remember," Jack said. He looked at Jan. "Both of you."

"Nice to see you again," Jan offered.

"This is wonderful," Allie said. "We'll order some junk food and revisit old times. Like we used to do. We'll even invite Agents Burton and Tilden to join us." She threw Jan a glance, but the other woman ignored her.

"I'm afraid we'll have to postpone that," Jack said.

Morgan suddenly remembered their purpose for being there.

"Is something wrong?" Jan asked. She took a step forward. "You're limping," Jan noticed.

"There's no danger," Jack said at the same time.

"Jan, don't worry. The school is fine," Morgan told her. "I need to get something and then we have to go."

"Get what?" Allie asked.

"It's better if you don't know," Jack answered before Morgan could tell them the truth.

"Don't know what?" Jan asked, a hand coming to her throat. Morgan recognized the nervous gesture.

"Jan, I have to get something I left here," Morgan appealed to her.

"What did you leave?" Allie asked.

"You don't have to say it like I left a ticking bomb." Allie could always get her anger up. "I left nothing dangerous, but I need to get it and then we have to go."

"Why are you limping?" Allie demanded.

"Allie, don't," Morgan warned. "I wouldn't have come here if I'd had any other choice."

"Have you seen a doctor. You know how a simple—" she started the memorized speech.

"She's all right," Jack said. His voice was calm and had a calming effect on the room, which seemed to be spinning out of control. "Morgan hurt her leg when she was trying to get through a door. She's had medical attention." He didn't tell them he was the medic. "All she needs now is to let it heal. Jumping off those bars wasn't the best thing she could do for her leg, but could anyone ever talk her into anything that was good for her?"

Her friends looked at each other and then at her. She knew they were silently agreeing with Jack. He'd manipulated them and they didn't know it. He'd taken the heat out of their discussion and told them only a portion of the truth.

"There's a doctor who comes to the camp every day. He'll be here tomorrow. You can have him look at it." Jan wanted assurance. Morgan nearly smiled. It had been years, but they were all the same.

"Where are you going from here?" Allie asked.

Morgan felt Jack's hand on her shoulder before she said anything. She looked up at him, knowing she couldn't tell them the truth. It was better if they didn't know. "Washington, D.C.," she said finally. It was the original destination, but she knew as soon as they had the ring, they wouldn't even leave the state of West Virginia. The FBI office was only ninety miles away in Clarksburg. That's where they were headed.

Morgan had spent her life lying. She'd lied to everyone from the crooks on the streets to the federal government. She'd lied to Jack when they'd started their run. Lying to the two women in the world who'd been her true friends, who'd staked their lives on helping her, even if they didn't know it, made her feel as if her heart were bleeding.

She was never going to see them again. Once she did get to Washington, she'd be relocated, put safely somewhere without friends and without anyone who knew her from the past. She hadn't been a good friend. She'd let the years separate them. Now that she knew this was possibly the last time they would be together, she wanted to stay. She wanted to spend the night, the week, a month, talking to them. She wanted to learn everything about them, about the years that stood between their last meeting and this one. But Jack had spoken. She knew he was right. They had to leave. There was danger.

"I already found the ring," Jan interrupted her thoughts.

Jan's words stopped everything. Even the pain sliding up

her calf seemed to halt. Morgan stared at her, trying to think of something to say. "What?" she asked without emphasis.

"A few years ago we expanded the gym. All the equipment was moved for renovation and to put down the new carpet. I suppose years of pounding on the beam dislodged the package inside."

Morgan's throat dried and speech was cut off.

"I heard the rattle and thought something might be wrong with the apparatus. I thought the metal was bent and it could be a future hazard."

Jan always put safety first. She would check the equipment several times to make sure it was properly set up before allowing anyone to use it.

"One night after everyone was gone I decided to find out what caused the noise. I found the hidden package."

"Where is it now?" Jack asked.

She moved her gaze to Jack. "In a safe place." She looked back at Morgan. Her eyes were piercing, but Morgan saw hurt in them too. "I knew you didn't just give me the equipment because I wanted to start a school."

"I did." Morgan contradicted her with the absolute truth.

"It was convenient too." She said it as a challenge, almost defying Morgan to disagree with her.

"It was convenient." Morgan dropped her gaze to the floor. "I needed to make sure it was safe and I couldn't keep it in St. Charles."

"Jan, you knew Morgan would come here," Allie spoke up. "This is why you insisted the FBI agents bring us here. It had nothing to do with you needing to run the camp."

Jan didn't answer. No one in the room expected her to.

"Where is the package now?" Jack asked. Morgan could feel the insistence in him.

"We can't get it tonight. It's in a safety deposit box at the bank. I have a full camp turnover starting at six A.M. I'll be up to my ears in work. I can't possibly get there tomorrow."

Morgan could feel Jack's defeat. He didn't want to stay here. She shouldn't either. She told her friends there was no danger, but there was danger. She was uncertain how much of it existed.

Jack, she knew, had assessed the situation. Unfortunately, there was little he could do about it.

"I guess that means you're stuck here until Monday morning," Allie stated the obvious. "Now we can call for the junk food."

"Does he ever sleep?" Allie asked, nodding toward the man in the garden below the bedroom Jan had assigned Morgan. The two women stood on the balcony overlooking the vast grounds.

"I don't think so," Morgan said. Jack prowled the property, checking to make sure everything was secure. Morgan felt safe around him. "This place is gorgeous." Morgan hoped to change the subject. "Jan has turned it into something to be proud of." They had left the school, which was in town, and come to the camp only a few miles away. The school was first-class and the camp was internationally known. Set picturesquely in the hills near Clay, there was a park nearby and plenty of wooded areas, giving the camp a country club look which parents would enjoy, but which also made the kids feel comfortable. The gyms, pools and cabins were well-lighted and airy, with equipment that sparkled due to a constantly on-call maintenance staff. Morgan wouldn't mind practicing here herself. Every summer the top athletes in gymnastics spent part of their time here, meeting with campers and helping out with training. "Remember when we used to go to places like this?"

"Yeah," Allie nodded. "After the Korean games I signed more and smiled for more photos with kids and their parents than I did helping out with skills." She smiled and sat down in one of the balcony chairs.

"I think I would have liked teaching." She stopped, unwilling to bring up things that could never happen. "There was this one kid at a camp in Pennsylvania. His mouth dropped open when he saw me and—"

"He's the one, isn't he, Morgan?" Allie interrupted her story, bringing the discussion back to Jack. Morgan didn't need to ask who the "he" was she referred to. Allie had been dividing her glances between them since they arrived. "There hasn't been anyone serious since Korea, has there?"

Allie had a facade to her, a hidden personality inside an invisible casing. She didn't often let you see the real Alicia Tremaine. Morgan supposed that was why she liked her. She reminded her so much of herself. It also made her a good actress. She could hide inside that wall and only show the public what they wanted to see. But just as she would hide herself, her ability to see through another person was uncanny.

"I didn't quite think it showed so clearly." She hadn't seen Allie in years except on the movie screen. Yet in a matter of a couple of hours, Morgan's life was an open book.

"It's only apparent to people who can see," she said. "I doubt he even knows you're in love with him."

It was on the tip of her tongue to deny she was in love with Jack, but at the last second she bit the comment and held it inside. Morgan moved from the balcony railing and took the chair opposite one of the only two friends she had in the world. Jack was no longer in sight below her.

"We knew all about you going to watch him swim when we were in Korea." Morgan's eyes widened in surprise. Allie went on. "I wanted to taunt you with it, but Jan wouldn't let me."

"Jan knew too."

"Of course we knew. We lived with you, knew when something piqued your interest, and each time someone mentioned Jack Temple's name you would tense up, or try not to. We were girls back then, still in high school most of us. Our entire world, excluding the gym, revolved around boys. But somehow you were older. Jan and I wanted to be just like you."

"You're kidding." Morgan never thought anyone would want to be like her. She had nothing. They had everything.

"You were so poised and so serious and knew what you wanted, and God you were good. I'm sure it wasn't only us. We didn't know how much Jack meant to you."

"Allie, it's so complicated and I can't explain it. Until a few days ago I hadn't seen Jack in twelve years. And in a another few days, a week at the most, I'll never see him again."

"Why? You're not leaving the planet are you?"
"Something like that."

Hart Lewiston switched the green-shaded banker's light on his desk off and leaned back in the chair. Moonlight streamed in the windows, casting shadows over the richly appointed furnishings. Tears rolled down his face. The folder in front of him could no longer be seen, but he didn't need to see it to know its contents. Every word, every photograph had been printed on his memory as if some microscopic-sized Michelangelo was inside his head chiseling them in place.

Disaster had struck. It waited thirty-one years to flare up and shoot him down. He'd been a prisoner in a foreign jail. He'd been tortured, starved, drugged, beaten to within inches of his life, yet nothing could be more devastating than the unsolicited information that lay before him in an innocuous manila folder. He had a child. A daughter. A fully grown woman he didn't know existed until thirty minutes ago.

Tears rolled to the corners of his mouth. Hart tasted the salt as he wiped them away with the back of his hand. He and Carla had never had children. They'd been married for twenty-three years. Since his child was eight years old. Images of family holidays, picnics, school functions when he was eight years old floated through his mind. He saw himself dressed as a dinosaur for Halloween and opening brightly colored Christmas presents.

Hart wanted to think of what he could do to rectify the situation. Someone undoubtedly knew of the child's existence or this folder wouldn't have been sent to him by special messenger. And to his home when he was sure to be here. Campaigning took him on the road ninety-eight percent of the time. Yet this folder had come tonight, after Carla had retired and he'd planned to follow her. Whoever sent it knew his schedule.

He tried to think clearly, but it was made difficult by the image of the nineteen-year-old girl with a bouquet of roses crushed to her breast, on his mind. Hart recognized her at once, and then when he saw the photo of her mother, he knew without the shadow of a doubt that his past had returned to bite him. He should call someone.

But who?

Elliott Irons would have a coronary when he found out. What about his father, a Supreme Court justice, or Carla, sleeping soundly in their bed only a floor away from the turmoil boiling inside him. She was not the one to call, although he wished she were. He should be thinking of his campaign, his bid to be the next president, what this knowledge if given to the press would do to his ratings in the polls. Would America stand behind him when they became aware of his daughter and her life?

Morgan Kirkwood, born to Rose Kirkwood and Hart Lewiston at Temple University Medical Center in Philadelphia, PA. Hart repeated the words he'd read on paper in his mind. A copy of her birth certificate was enclosed, along with adoption papers and birth certificate when Sharon Peters adopted her. An account of her life on the streets and her exploits at the Olympics in Korea, even her part in saving his life, were all there. In five neatly printed pages, the entire focus of his being had altered.

Did she know? He wondered. Had she known he was her father all these years and hated him with every bit of her being? Did she dislike and distrust him so much she wouldn't even appeal to him when she was living on the streets and he was comfortably ensconced in the lap of luxury? He felt like an unfit father. Even in these surroundings, where Carla had worked with decorators for months to find just the right fabric for curtains and just the right furniture for the rooms, he felt like a failure. He should have known. He should have found Rose. The furniture in this office alone could probably have paid for his daughter's entire career of gymnastics lessons.

Hart reached for the phone and punched in the numbers he didn't need light to distinguish. He checked the clock but couldn't see it in the darkness. Switching the light back on, the dial desk read 3:39 A.M. He had to find her. He needed advice on what to do and what was about to happen. Whoever sent him this material didn't do it to keep him informed. They wanted something. Hart needed to think clearly and act.

He was going to have to tell Elliott. His campaign manager deserved to hear about this before it made front-page news. And Carla. Little did she know that her night would be disturbed with news that would blindside her.

An alert voice answered the phone. Hart knew the man on the other end had been asleep, but he was used to being aroused in the middle of the night. Disaster seemed to happen after dark and the director of the FBI was a man who dealt with disaster.

"Clarence, this is Hart. We need to meet."

CHAPTER 11

Jack stood rock still in the darkness. He blended with the trees, becoming part of the landscape, unseen and unnoticed. Yet he could hear and smell everything around him, the crickets, cicadas, mosquitoes, the pine trees, forsythia bushes, the scented soap Morgan wore. She was behind him, quiet, trying to do what he did, but she was an amateur. Her perfumed body announced her presence long before she actually got to the place she stood.

He waited for her to make a move, for her to make it known she was behind him. Minutes went by without a sound. She was good at patience and good at keeping quiet. If it weren't for the fragrance, he wasn't sure he could tell she was standing there. He estimated she was about ten feet from him, behind a bush to his left. The wind, a gentle breeze, filled the night with smells; the trees, moist earth, clear air also brought hers to him.

Then a hand touched his right shoulder. Right not left, his mind whirled. Morgan was on the right. Instinct made him go for protection. He grabbed the hand, twisting the arm and turning at the same time. He found his gun in his hand without conscious thought. Brushing the feet from his assailant, they both went down. He brought the gun up to the assailant's head and then the knowledge that the body he landed on wasn't hard and unyielding, but soft and female, penetrated his consciousness.

"Damn it, Morgan, don't ever do that again." He shouted at her. "What are you doing here?"

She was paralyzed with fear. Her body was taut and her breath came in gasps. Jack removed the gun from her head and rolled away from her. He sat up, reholstered his gun and stood. Morgan still lay on the ground away from him. She'd turned her back to him. Jack could see her shoulders moving as she tried to compose her fear into something manageable. He let her do it alone. He knew she wouldn't want his help just yet. He faced the trees so when she finally turned, she wouldn't know he'd seen her.

Jack heard her get up. He turned back.

"I'm sorry," he apologized. "I knew you were behind me, but I didn't know you were that close. When you touched me I thought it was someone else."

"It's all right," she said. Jack knew it wasn't all right. He'd scared her more than she'd ever been scared.

Jack took a step forward. Morgan raised her hand, palm outward. He stopped.

"I—I need some time alone," she said. She turned toward the house.

"Morgan," Jack called. She turned back.

"Is this what you do, Jack? Is this how you live? Thinking everyone is out to do you harm, and you're ready to kill."

She left him, walking fast and determined. He was here to protect her. Why didn't she see that? Jack felt his gun under his arm. It was part of his body and had been there since he'd started working this job. But it scared Morgan. More than that he'd pointed it at her, although that was enough for the normal person. He'd begun to think of Morgan as more than normal. Guns had been pointed at her before. She hadn't told him, but he knew it. He knew how she reacted when she saw it the first time and how she'd reacted a moment ago. He just didn't know why.

Jack tried to go back to his observation of the perimeter of the camp, but Morgan intruded on his thoughts. Looking over his shoulder for the fifth time, he saw no light coming from her room, but the downstairs lights blazed brightly through the windows. She could be in one of the downstairs rooms talking to either Allie or Jan. They were a close group and hadn't seen each other in years. Jack knew where he should be. He should be with her. But she'd said she needed time.

Abandoning his post, he went toward the house. Convention dropped from his shoulders on his way. He didn't know who he would pass if he went through the house, so he decided not to do it. He stood under the balcony and, bending his knees, jumped up and caught the bottom of the supported platform. Pulling himself up by the strength of his arms, he raised his head up above the floor. He saw the carved slats of the railing support. Gritting his teeth, he grabbed the post with one hand, snaking it through the opening and getting a grip that withstood his hanging weight. Repeating the action with the other hand, he pulled himself up and then over the protection rail.

The glass doors leading to her bedroom were closed to the night air. Jack wanted to stalk directly through them, but he stopped, remembering he'd already frightened her once tonight. Barging in like Rambo would gain him nothing. He stopped and peered through the sheer curtains. She lay face down on the bed, fully clothed. Jack opened the door quietly and went inside. He smelled the soap scent.

He removed his gun and laid it on the dresser near the door. He went to the bed and knelt beside her. "Morgan," he whispered.

She jerked toward him. He thought he'd find tears in her eyes, but they were dry. Her hair fell past her shoulders and obscured part of her face. She looked alone, vulnerable. For a second they stared at each other, then she swung around and threw herself into his arms. Jack gathered her to him, helpless to do anything but hold her close. He pulled her onto the floor, wrapping his arms around her soft body and feeling the weakness that invaded his being whenever he held her. He concealed his face in hair that hinted of fresh lemons and thanked God she'd forgiven him.

Jack had never thought much about needing forgiveness, but he really wanted to be in her good graces. He sat back on the floor and kept her in his arms. He didn't want to move. He'd be content to hold her this way for eternity.

But they didn't have eternity. If they lived through the next seventy-two hours, it would be a miracle.

The air in the room was thick enough to cut with a knife, although no one was saying anything. What Hart had said had them all silent. Elliott Irons stood at the window overlooking Pennsylvania Avenue, raking his fingers through his hair. If the guy lived to be fifty, it would be only by the grace of God. Carla sulked in a corner, tears running like Niagara Falls since he woke her more than an hour ago. Clarence Christopher, sitting behind his desk, was the only other person who appeared to keep his wits. He was also the only one not personally involved with Hart, the only one with nothing to lose when this news broke.

PRESIDENTIAL CANDIDATE HIDES OUT-OF-WEDLOCK DAUGHTER FOR THIRTY YEARS. He could see the headline now, seventy-point type, like they used to announce the end of World War II. Vietnam and Desert Storm didn't get nearly the coverage as WWII, but none of them would hold a candle to this coup. The opposition would make sure of it.

"Is this everything?" Clarence looked over his reading glasses.

"It's all that came," Hart said, dropping into one of the chairs in front of the desk. "Clarence, I didn't know."

"Are you saying this is all true?"

He nodded. "I remember Rose Kirkwood. I met her before Carla." He glanced at his wife. She gave him a withering look through her tearstained face. "We were young. She worked for the State Department, the Office of Protocol. Our projects threw us together a lot. We started to rely on each other, back each other up, even do research to help the other." He paused a moment. "I don't remember when our relationship changed. . . . I suppose that trip to Paris played a big part."

Hart didn't elaborate on what had happened in Paris. It started with water. His shower didn't work and they had to appear at a state function, a command performance. It was Bastille Day, a big event in France. Hart was too young and too nervous to appear late by waiting for the hotel to repair his shower. He went across the hall to Rose's room and asked to use hers. It was so innocent, the beginning. Then again it wasn't. He'd felt differently about Rose for months. He'd made himself close to her, positioning himself at her side whenever he could, attending the same meetings, same parties, dancing with her so he was able to hold her in his arms.

Then Paris happened.

He'd gone into the bathroom. It was like walking into a room intense with her presence. He drank it in as if he were some mythical god and the airborne elixir would restore his strength. He could still remember the smell, apricot.

He would have survived the room, his secret intact, but the door behind him opened. He turned. She held a huge towel in her hands, outstretching it like an offering. "You'll need a clean towel," she said. Hart couldn't speak. Her eyes told him everything he needed to know. He couldn't stop himself from going to her, kissing her, making love to her, forgetting everything he'd told himself about a relationship between them.

And they were late for the dinner.

"She changed after that trip." Hart began again. "I thought she'd found someone else, that she regretted what had happened between us, that our races made a difference. I didn't see much of her after we returned, never alone, only able to talk to her during a meeting. Then one day she didn't come to work. A week went by and when I asked I was told she'd resigned without notice." Hart remembered the hurt that sliced through him when he overheard the news. No one told him directly. He'd come in to get coffee and someone else had remarked that she'd resigned. "I went to her apartment, but she was gone. She'd moved and no one knew where she went."

He leaned forward, picking up the photo of Rose as he remembered her, darkly beautiful, her hair up in an array of curls, except for the bangs that reached arched eyebrows over hugely expressive eyes and a smile that crushed his heart. The accompanying photo of his daughter had those same eyes.

"Clarence, I need to find her. Call it a favor. This is a town built on favors. I need to know where she is."

"No!" Carla Lewiston's voice cracked in the room. "Hart, we can't let this get out. Whoever they are, pay them, do whatever they want. This could ruin us."

Hart stood and turned toward his wife. Elliott also faced her. "We can't keep this a secret."

"It's been kept a secret for more than thirty years. She's dead, Hart. Dead! Why do we need to bring her back to life?"

Anger fissured through him. Hart stopped himself from moving toward her. He knew if he got close enough Carla would see a side of him he wasn't sure he even knew was there.

"Hart, she's making sense," Elliott agreed. "We need to deny everything if this comes out."

"I've denied her her entire life."

"Hart, you don't even know that she's alive," Carla argued. "That explosion was total. She could have been blown into so many parts no one could identify her. And if she did survive, she's an adult. She's not a child who needs your guidance. Walking into her life now could ruin her too."

Hart weighed her comments. He stared at the woman he thought he loved. They had never wanted children, never thought of having them or discussed the possibility. They simply never needed to. Now he knew he had a child. She was grown, had been for some time, living, making decisions. She was old enough to have children of her own. She could have made him a grandfather and he'd never know. Suddenly it was important.

"I don't know if I can explain this to you." He swung his glance between his wife and his campaign manager. "This is important to me. *She* is important to me. I can't explain why. I didn't know about her, never knew what happened to Rose until earlier tonight. But we produced a child and regardless of that child's age, she exists and she deserves to know who she is. I deserve the right to meet her and explain, answer questions and ask some of my own. She could hate me, resent me for upsetting her world and even her life." He glanced at his wife, acknowledging that she could be right. "But whatever the consequences, I need to know."

"This could cost you the election, Hart," Elliott spoke with authority. "The black vote would die, southern whites evaporate like water dropped on a hot stove." He ticked each group off on his fingers. "The opposition would crucify you. We'll be lucky to have more than our own votes come election day."

"Elliott, I think you're wrong. We're going to lose votes, there's no doubt about that, but we have to do something and we've only got a few hours to make a decision on what that will be."

Hart took a deep breath. His heart was pounding and he didn't especially like what would happen to his career. He'd worked hard to get where he was and it probably looked like he was throwing his chances away, but he wouldn't back down.

"Clarence, will you help me?"

"Hart, can't we wait until after the election?" Elliott asked.

"He's right, Hart. You're vying for the highest office in this country, the most powerful position in the free world. News that you have an illegitimate child will make headlines in every newspaper in America. To discover she's a former Olympic champion will further scar you. Your opposition will paint you as an adulterer, an unfit father, a philanderer, any label they can think of. They'll make Carla a martyr for sticking by you, if she chooses to do so. If not, they'll champion her for getting away from a man who would abandon his child. This is a no-win situation."

"The people who sent me this"—he reached for the folder— "did it for a reason. They aren't going to wait for the results of the election." He turned back to his campaign manager. "And, Elliott, there are some things more important than elections."

Clarence Christopher agreed to help Hart Lewiston find his daughter. The trio had left his office only moments ago. He gave them enough time to get down the elevator and exit the building. He could have told Hart immediately where his daughter was. He withheld the information because of Hart's wife and his campaign manager. Hart was a friend and he'd be a good president if he got elected, and until a few moments ago Clarence knew no reason why he wouldn't win the election. Hart trusted his campaign manager and he'd been married more than twenty years. But Clarence exercised caution. And he needed to pass this tidbit on to Brian Ashleigh.

It was almost six o'clock in the morning. The sun had been up for an hour, but he knew Brian Ashleigh would be in his office. A widower, Brian had no ties to keep him at home. He lived and breathed his job.

"Ashleigh," he identified himself into the phone.

"Good morning, Brian," Clarence said. He didn't identify himself. "I think it's time we had another talk."

"What's happened?"

"Hart Lewiston just left my office. He's calling a press conference this morning to acknowledge his daughter."

"Daughter?" Brian said, but Clarence heard the muffled curse in the background.

"I'm sure it's no surprise to you who his daughter is."

"How'd he find out?" Brian didn't deny that Clarence had good information.

"Someone sent him a file. It's complete, comes with photos and text. I have it on my desk."

Saturday was a big day at the camp. Students left and arrived on that day, departures after breakfast, arrivals after lunch. More than 150 campers traded places on Saturdays with the maintenance crews working doubly fast to get the cabins ready for the next group.

Jan and Allie were busy registering and being useful. Agents Burton and Tilden, whom she'd met the night before, were apparently doing what agents do. Jack was gone when she woke up, but left instructions that her face was too well-known for her to help. Someone was bound to recognize her.

She stayed in her room, watching old movies on television, while everyone else did something useful. Even Allie, whose face was much more recognizable than her own, was directing traffic, showing people where to park and answering questions. Morgan could hear the shout of recognition whenever anyone put her face with her name. She looked through the balcony window. Allie wore a bright red and white full-body gymnastics suit that looked as if she'd had it painted onto that perfect body.

The way she looked, Morgan was surprised Jan let her direct traffic. She could cause an accident more than prevent one.

Turning away, she looked at the bed. It reminded her of Jack. The gun had scared her, frightened her because of what Jack did, the danger he put himself in to save someone else. He was here to protect her the same as he'd done more times than she knew. The enormity of him dying while trying to protect someone else hit her harder than the fact that he'd held a gun to her head.

When he came to her, all she could think of was losing him. That sometime in the next few days he could be killed trying to keep her alive. She wanted to tell him how frightened it made her, but she didn't. She kissed him and everything seemed to focus. He knew how she felt. He knew she was afraid. He knew she loved him and that her heart was involved in every thought she had about him.

They made love on the floor where they sat. Jack was barely able to undress her before their need to be together had them trembling. It was fast, fiery bright and as explosive as nitro. She burst over the edge with him, falling at G forces greater than she'd known. Then together they floated back to earth, back to the bedroom floor where their legs were entwined with each other's and their discarded clothes.

Morgan fell asleep in Jack's arms. She remembered a floating feeling later as he lifted her to the bed and the added warmth of his body as she hugged it to her and went into a dreamland where she and Jack lived blissfully.

In the morning he was gone. Allie brought her breakfast and orders that she was to remain where she was. "Or there'll be hell to pay," Allie added her own quote.

She felt trapped, although getting out of the room and to the ground by means other than the door was a snap. Jack's reasons were sound, even if his delivery method was rough. She'd been with him a while and understood the danger. Allie hadn't had anyone shooting at her, and despite the special effects on the screen, she'd never run through a copse of trees with guys with guns behind her or had a bullet graze her leg.

Morgan crossed the room again to look through the window. The bedroom was spacious, appointed in a feminine pink with green accents. The carpet was a deep green that reminded her of a forest, while the walls were painted apple green. The comforter on the bed was done in pink and the accent pillows a deeper shade of the same color. Morgan passed the sitting area where she'd watch TV. There was a writing desk with a computer and a phone. Morgan had no one to write or call and nothing to access on the computer. All she'd done since she showered and dressed this morning was walk back and forth to the window. It was nearly two o'clock. The arriving campers had shown up in force right after lunch and were just now beginning to thin out. Morgan wished she could go to one of the gyms and practice, but they would be filled with parents looking around or new campers checking out their surroundings. The last movie she had any interest in went off an hour ago and soap operas weren't something she'd ever watched. The news wouldn't be on for a few hours. She didn't know if she wanted to see it. It was full of her and what had happened. No one knew, and in the past few days, they'd made up things to fill airtime left over from the coming Olympics in St. Louis or the presidential campaign.

She turned the television back on and started flipping through the stations. Maybe she'd watch something on the Discovery Channel or relive some war on the History Channel.

There was a short knock on the door and she heard Jack's voice. Dropping the remote control, she ran to the door and pulled it inward.

"Hi," she smiled.

He came in, closing the door behind him. She went into his arms and kissed him. At that moment she felt something was wrong. Behind her the television droned on with the news. She hadn't intended to stop at the news.

"What's wrong?"

Jack crossed behind her and picked up the remote. "In a surprise move . . ." He switched the TV off as the newsman began another story.

"Jack?" He wasn't looking at her. He flipped the remote over and over in his hand. Something was wrong.

"What happened?"

"There was a press conference this morning in Washington. It involved you."

"Me! How? Did someone come forward about the helicopter?"

"This is separate from that."

Morgan went to the sitting area. She walked around him and stood directly in front. "Give it to me straight."

"Your biological father came forward this morning to acknowledge you. He's trying to find you."

"I don't understand."

"The newscast didn't tell everything, but he's sure you're his daughter."

"Jack, who is it?"

"The last man on earth you'd expect," he said, turning around and pointing the remote at the television. The screen came on instantly.

". . . this news only came to his attention recently." The story started in the middle. Morgan looked at the photo in the corner. Hart Lewiston smiled his campaign smile from the right side of the screen. "More on this as details become known." The camera shifted to another angle and the anchorman faced the new camera. "We'll have the complete report later in this broadcast."

The newscaster went on to her story. She looked at Jack, whose face was quizzical. "What?" she asked. She went back to the television listening intently, but there was nothing new there. "Jack—"

It hit her then. Her head whipped back and forth between the television and Jack. "Hart Lewiston?"

Jack didn't reply.

"Jack, Hart Lewiston is not my father. The man's trying to get elected. This has to be a scam. Somehow he's trying to get sympathy for his campaign by coupling himself with me."

"I called Washington."

"Did you talk to Hart Lewiston?"

"I talked to Brian Ashleigh and Forrest Washington. They told me the whole story."

Morgan's anger got the better of her. "Why didn't they tell me? Why didn't you tell me you were going to do it? Shouldn't

I have anything to say about my own life? Jack, you can't believe this." She threw her hands in the air. "I can't believe it. What on earth does he have to gain by dropping a story like this? He could lose the election."

"Exactly," Jack agreed, his voice low. "Which is why it seems he must be telling the truth. Why else would someone in his political place commit this kind of suicide?"

"I don't know."

The door burst open and Jan and Allie almost fell inside. "Morgan, are you watching the news?" They stopped when they saw the look on her face.

"It's a lie," she stated. "It's got to be a lie."

"Morgan, I thought you'd be a Hart Lewiston supporter," Jan said. "He represents all the things you used to say you'd want in a candidate."

"I am a supporter. I plan to vote for him." The implication of his action hit her then. She turned to Jack, grasping his arms. "Jack, he'll be a target. You've got to stop this."

"I thought there was no danger." Jan took a step forward.

Morgan looked at the floor, then up at her friend. "The idea, Jan, was to come and go quickly. I never thought you'd find the package and move it. There is danger. Someone is trying to kill me, but you knew that. I never wanted to or expected to spend the night here. I'll understand if you want us to go."

"Don't bother," Jan said. "I'll only worry about you somewhere else. At least here I know where you are."

"What about the school? There are hundreds of kids here."

"I've got it covered." Jack addressed the point. Jan trained her gaze on Jack. "Agents Tilden and Burton and I have been scouting the place. If anything happens, one of us will be on top of it."

"I believe you," Jan said. "I have the children of several hundred families at this camp. I can't risk any of them."

"I promise you we'll be gone minutes after the bank opens on Monday. We can't go before that."

"We're in danger too, aren't we?" Allie asked a question, but everyone could hear the statement in it. "Whoever is looking for Morgan knows about us. We were on television. Then the two agents showed up and kept us locked away for two days before bringing us here. This is a control. You expect something might happen?''

''It might. The people after Morgan want what she has, not particularly her, but I have no doubt they'll kill her to get it.''

''Why didn't they try to kill me?'' Jan asked.

''They may not know you have anything. If they do, you may have saved yourself by putting the package in the bank,'' Jack answered.

''I don't understand,'' Jan said.

''If anything happens to you, your safety deposit box will be frozen. It could only be opened in front of a U.S. Marshal. Everything inside would be scrutinized. Something these people couldn't afford.''

''What happens now?'' Allie asked.

''We stick with the plan. On Monday, Morgan and I leave. Agents Burton and Tilden will stay a while longer. Within a couple of days everything should be back to normal.''

''You make it sound like we have a cold and it'll go away in a day or two.''

''I don't mean to trivialize it. There is a real danger.'' Allie moved closer to Jan. ''At the moment I think we're safe. I promise if anything changes, we'll get out of here.''

Jan nodded.

''Jan, I think we should leave now,'' Morgan suggested. ''We can go to a hotel or sleep in the van.''

''No,'' Jan vetoed the idea. ''Sticking together is safer for us all.''

''Morgan, what about the news?'' Allie asked.

''It's got to be a lie. Some stunt Hart Lewiston is foisting on the American public.''

''Why?''

''I haven't a clue, but he can't know what he's brought down on himself by this announcement.''

The camp was buttoned down. Everyone was safe, asleep and accounted for. Jan, tired from her day of campers and worry, retired early. Only Allie and Morgan remained awake. They were in the beam gym. Morgan wore a leotard much like the one Allie had worn earlier in the day. Hers was just as tight, and where Allie's was red, hers was white. It had a blue slash of color that anchored at her shoulders, slicing across her chest to the left and down her back to the right like a long scarf.

She did a back handspring using both hands, then a second one with no hands. Coming up, she pirouetted on the beam to face the other direction. Doing a couple of dance steps, she reached the other end of the beam, pirouetted again and started a run to dismount.

"You've been at that for over an hour. It's time you took a break," Allie said.

Morgan's leg was back to normal. She barely felt a twinge of pain. She'd put herself through a long routine, making sure there were no after-effects of the grazing.

Concentrating wasn't something she could do tonight. Morgan had fallen off the beam more times than she'd been on it. She found it difficult to focus her mind. Could it really be true? Was Hart Lewiston her real father? She'd watched the news all day, since Jack and Allie and Jan had come into the bedroom and told her about the press conference. She didn't understand it and she wanted to understand. Part of her kept trying to see the logic, the reason. It was insanity. Morgan squeezed her eyes shut.

She tried to remember her past. All the nights she'd lain on the dirty ground in the back of some warehouse or on the grate of a subway, she'd wanted to forget. Now she tried desperately to remember what her mother had said about her father.

It was too fuzzy. She couldn't remember anything, but she was sure she'd never said anything about his being a politician or even someone who had plans for public office. Morgan picked at places in her brain she'd shut down years ago, trying to remember if her mother had sat forward in interest at a television program or when the news came on where she might have seen a photo of him. Did she ever stop what she was doing and stare at the screen with a familiar expression, a knowing glance, a wondrous expression?

Never. Morgan answered her own question. Her mother had given nothing away. Nothing that would lead Morgan to think that Hart Lewiston and she had anything in common, much less the sharing of blood.

The gym had mirrors covering one entire wall. Morgan jumped off the beam, but instead of going to where Allie practiced, she walked to the mirrors, looking, staring, observing every detail of her face. She got close to the glass, nose to nose. She tried to pull an image of Hart Lewiston into view, compare it with her own. She could see nothing of herself that was him. Her cheeks were high and highly colored. She blamed it on the beam routine, but she knew it wasn't only the exercise. Her hair was dark brown, while his was blond. Her eyes were almond-shaped, while his were more round. One by one she compared the mental images of the two of them. Her assessment ended without giving her a single indicator that would lead her to conclude that she and presidential candidate, Senator Hart Lewiston, were connected in any way. Yet he obviously thought so.

Why? she wondered. He had nothing to gain and plenty to lose. Why would he do this? Why would he call a press conference to acknowledge her? She was thirty-one years old. She didn't need a father at this late date. Someone else must have found out. That could be the only reason. If he'd remained quiet all these years then the decision to go public five months before the election had to have a catalyst somewhere else.

"Morgan, my muscles are absolutely screaming."

Morgan suddenly remembered she wasn't alone in the gym. Allie was behind her. She'd been running routines on the beam across from hers. When Morgan turned she was breathing hard and resting her head on her arms, which were on the beam.

Grabbing her towel and wiping her face, Morgan went to the back of the gym and pulled two bottles of water from the refrigerator. She sat down next to Allie, who was no longer leaning against the apparatus. She'd transferred to the floor, crossing her long legs Indian style. Morgan joined her, lifting her water bottle and drinking. The water refreshed her.

"Did you get it out of your system?" Allie asked after taking a drink from her own bottle.

"I don't know." Morgan used the towel to dry her forehead. "I'm still trying to understand what is going on."

"A father who's a candidate for president and most likely the winner of the next election and a grandfather who sits on the Supreme Court. Sounds like a power play I'd be willing to join."

"Would you really?" Morgan whispered. She asked it of herself, not Allie. "I used to imagine my real parents. Of course, I knew my mother, but not my father. He died—" She stopped. "He wasn't there so I could remember. After my mother died and I was on the streets I used to imagine them alive and sitting in wonderful houses, filled with books, him traveling the world as some big-shot diplomat. Everywhere he went he'd look for me. Little did I know most of it was true." She paused and checked Allie's reaction to a story about herself. She didn't often tell people her thoughts and feelings. "Not the part where he was looking for me. He didn't even know I existed, but he *was* a big-shot diplomat and he did travel the world."

Morgan sat silent for a long moment. "I wonder what happens when he really finds me?"

She meant *if* he finds her. And if she's alive. He should have waited a few days, even hours before making his announcement. It might not have been necessary. She and Jack still had to get to FBI headquarters. Jack hadn't mentioned anything in the last day or two about their trip, but she knew somehow there was trouble ahead of them, and this time it wouldn't be as easy to get away as stealing a helicopter and flying into the hills.

CHAPTER 12

Benjamin Franklin's exploits with the kite and a key is a story every school child knows. Jack thanked him as he crossed Main Street and walked into the red brick building housing the Clay County Public Library. He liked the place. It smelled of lemon oil and knowledge, but also had what he sought—computer access to the Internet. Jack chose a seat along the side, careful to place himself where he wouldn't be seen by people entering or leaving and where he could research the information he needed.

The computer could pull information from thousands of miles away to this small library, a place where the entire population of the town was in the low three digits.

It had taken him some time to convince Morgan to stay at the camp where he knew she was being protected while he drove into town with Jan. Agent Burton had accompanied them and Jack left the two to return without him. Jack knew Jan couldn't be in better hands. He afforded himself a smile as he thought of them. Then his demeanor changed to all business as he concentrated on the screen.

He found the Korean newspapers with ease. The ring Jan had kept in the safety deposit box of the town's only bank was in the breast pocket of Jack's jacket, zipped closed so he wouldn't lose it. He'd recognized the crest on it immediately. The president of Korea, Morgan had said. He hadn't really believed her when she said it, but he did now. But more than the ring was the paper it had been wrapped in—a torn newspaper. The story in it tripped one of Jack's memory cells. He recognized something about it.

Accessing archived files, he searched under the name of President Ji-Moon Chang. Jack had to go back thirteen years to find the original paper. He read through it quickly, then sent several pages to the printer. He had it, the real reason someone wanted Morgan dead. It was time to get her and get out.

Jack logged out of the Korean area, returning to the library's home page. Then he went into the settings and changed the properties to remove any reference he'd made to the areas he'd visited. Spending another ten minutes, he went to nine sites that had no interest to him before leaving. If anyone came after him, they wouldn't find the history of his visits to the Korean papers, but to investments in mutual funds, chocolate companies, graphics design and books on fixing a dishwasher.

Moving to the copy machine, he made copies of the newspaper and the other papers Jan had concealed. Then, leaving the library, he returned to the camp. Jack didn't go straight to Morgan's room, but stopped at the camp store. It was only open several hours a day. The campers were in practice sessions and the store was deserted. Hanging on the walls were T-shirts with the camp logo, faces of famous gymnasts, the insignia of the Olympic Games. There were also hats, socks, headbands and wrists bands, leotards, jackets, every form of paraphernalia a gymnast would need.

Jack bought two padded envelopes and left. Sitting down at a deserted table outside the cafeteria, he addressed both of the envelopes to the same person—Forrest Washington. The first had his name and address only, while the second had name and address and a code that meant no one would open that envelope except Forrest Washington himself.

Jack packaged them up, put the ring and papers inside and pulled the sealing strip free, closing the contents of one inside the other. Stamp machines were near the store for people who wanted to send letters and postcards home to their families. He inserted coins, taking more than he thought was the required amount of postage, and affixed it to the top envelope.

The mail truck sat in front of the office when he got there. The uniformed mailman slung a closed canvas bag into the truck as Jack approached.

"Can I get this in today's mail?" Jack asked with a friendly smile.

"Sure can," the man said. He took the envelope and eyed the stamps. Then he dropped it in a plastic container that was nearly full. "You have a good day." He climbed into the driver's seat and pulled away.

If anything happened to them now, Washington would know who had done it and why. Jack watched until the white truck was out of view before heading for Morgan's room. Allie was on the phone when he got there. From the one-sided conversation she must have been talking to her agent.

"Another week at the most," she was saying. "Jan really needs my help." Her long hair swung about her shoulders as if a camera was photographing its swing for some shampoo commercial.

"Where's Morgan?" he asked.

Allie pointed toward the balcony. "Out there," she mouthed, putting a hand over the phone's mouthpiece.

He went in the direction Allie pointed. Jack's heart beat in anticipation. Each time he thought of Morgan, his blood pressure increased. He knew she hated the confinement of this room, but the consequences outside it were worse. Jan had life-size photos of the Olympic winning team on the walls of the office and in several different gyms. Most of the campers might be too young to remember the Seoul Olympics and not recognize Morgan right away, but it only took one to put her features to the face on the poster, especially if Morgan showed anything like the skills she performed twelve years ago.

Jack stepped onto the balcony and stopped the moment he saw the gun pointed at his chest.

"What a pleasant surprise, Mr. Temple." An oriental man spoke without an accent. He had his arm around Morgan's neck. Her chin was forced upward so she couldn't move her head. A strip of duct tape covered her mouth and her hands were behind her back, presumably wrapped in the same unforgiving substance. "It is a pleasure to meet you again."

"Sorry I can't return the sentiment, but we have never been friends."

"That is because you insist upon having morals."

"And you work for the highest bidder. Who is it this time?" Jack refused to supply him with any names although he had plenty that came to mind. Since he'd read the paper Morgan had flown home with twelve years ago and seen the ring, he knew the factions in Korea vying for this information were on both sides of the political arena. It could be any of several people.

"No names, Mr. Temple. I must respect my clientele." He spoke like a lawyer defending the rights of a client. His smile showed even, white teeth that could double for a toothpaste ad. But regardless of the smile, his clients were thugs. They might dress in fine clothes and have impeccable manners, but they represented the ruthless in society.

Richard Chung had been born in Korea to a Korean mother and English father. Although educated in England, he scorned his father's heritage. Returning to Korea he took his mother's name and joined the army. He went into intelligence and eventually found himself part of a network that denied its own existence.

"Let her go, Chung." Jack glanced at Morgan. Her face was pale and she looked scared and helpless.

"I can't let her go, Jack. I came all this way to find her. Discovering you makes it doubly rewarding."

Jack wanted to smash the oily smile on Richard Chung's face, but he was holding Morgan. Allie was still on the phone in the next room, unaware that death lay only a few steps away. If she hung up and joined them, Chung would have no reason to keep her alive. And Jan's concern about her school and the campers who were here would be done no service by having someone killed on the site. The first thing he needed to do was get them off this balcony and away from the camp.

"Chung, these people have nothing to do with what you think Morgan or I know. Why don't we go somewhere and talk?"

"I was thinking that."

Jack took a step forward. Chung raised the gun and he stopped. He could hear Allie continuing her conversation, but she was out of his range of vision.

"Take off the jacket," Chung ordered in a low voice. Jack knew he wouldn't get to keep the gun concealed under the lightweight jacket. Chung hadn't survived this long by making mistakes. He raised his hands. "Slowly," Chung cautioned, raising his arm a bit and letting Jack see Morgan wince in pain. "Any suspicious move on your part and I'll drop her where she stands." Jack and Chung had tangled before and he didn't doubt for a minute the truth of the man's words.

Jack pushed the left sleeve down his arm and pulled it free. The holster under his arm showed the gun he carried. Chung's eyes went to the holster and Jack pushed the tiny button to silence the walkie-talkie in his pocket. The two FBI agents would receive a signal and know there was a problem in progress.

Jack slipped the jacket totally off and lowered it to the floor so the pocketed communication device did not thud against the treated wooden floor.

"The gun now," Chung said. "Two fingers, no more."

Jack released the snap closure with one finger and lifted the heavy revolver out of its holster using only his thumb and forefinger.

"On the table." Chung waved his own gun at the large umbrella-covered patio table that sat near the corner of the balcony. Jack laid the gun on it. "Back away," he said. Jack did. "Turn around."

Chung had been known to shoot people in the back. He wasn't concerned about the campers, but Jack didn't think he wanted to call attention to himself by firing a gun in these surroundings. He was a man who liked to escape unnoticed, undetected, alone, without a clue left behind. Allie was in the room only steps away. He had to know she was there. Jack could hear her on the phone. He surely could too. Her call seemed to be ending. In seconds she'd hang up and step through the open door.

"I do not kid you, Mr. Temple," Chung said in a voice so

menacing Jack knew he meant business. "Turn around." Jack had to do something quickly. He hoped the two FBI agents were closing in, but he couldn't wait for them to arrive.

"If you think I have a backup you're wrong." Usually Jack would have a second gun, a backup revolver, planted somewhere else on his person. He didn't keep it in the same place all the time, but when he embarked on this journey he didn't know he'd need one. When Sam had brought him the holster gun, he hadn't requested a backup and Sam probably assumed he already had one. But there was something Sam had given him and he was going to have to use it now.

Morgan was in the way. Jack wished she weren't, but the way Chung held her he had no clear way to get to him without going through her. Slowly he began to turn. Chung had to expect him to do something, try something. The two of them had encountered each other before and always on opposite sides of the crisis. Scorewise, Jack held the upper hand. Chung would want to even the boards.

A quarter way through the turn Jack reversed direction, dropping to the floor, rolling over and coming around to face Chung with a gun in his hand. He fired the pulse gun at his enemy. The blast issued from the gun with a strong kick, and hit Chung in the right shoulder, knocking him backward. He released Morgan and she fell to her knees. Burton was on him in an instant, handcuffing the inert body. Jack rushed to Morgan.

The main thrust knocked Chung cold while the reverberation ricocheted into Morgan. She was groggy and incoherent as Jack lifted her.

"What . . . was . . . that?" she asked as her eyes rolled back in her head. Jack carried her into the bedroom and laid her on the bed.

"What happened?" Allie cried. She was heading toward the door when Jack stepped across the threshold.

"She'll be fine," he answered. "She just needs a little sleep."

"You know I told her we should have gone to bed early last night, but would she? Nooo." Allie exaggerated the word as she continued, heedless of the danger they had all been in moments ago.

Jack laid her down, his heart thumping so loudly in his chest he was surprised Allie didn't comment on it. He smoothed Morgan's hair away from her face. She looked so defenseless. Her face was still pale and her breath shallow. Jack needed to wake her up.

"Get me some ammonia," he nearly ordered Allie. She didn't question his motives, but ran into the hall and came back with a first-aid kit. She remembered Jan kept them everywhere for accidents and emergencies. Jack found the vial. It was enmeshed in a knitted fabric to prevent cuts. He broke it and waved it under Morgan's nose.

"What's wrong with her?" Allie asked again. This time there was concern in her voice.

Jack had never been so scared in his life. Chung had no idea how much power he held over Jack with his arm around Morgan's neck. Jack would have done anything Chung had asked him. When he stepped onto the balcony and found him holding Morgan hostage, Jack was more concerned about her safety than the gun that was pointed at him.

At that moment he knew he was in love with her.

"Hart Lewiston, have you completely lost your mind?" Carla turned angrily and glared at him. She had been pacing the floor, clenching and unclenching her hands, since Hart got back to the hotel room. This was routine for Carla when she felt helpless, when things got out of her control. He knew her reaction would be volatile over his decision to go public with the news of Morgan Kirkwood's relationship to himself, but he hadn't expected her explosion to go on this long. She was like a Fourth of July starburst that kept exploding. "Have you looked at the polls?" she continued. "Do you have any idea what your standing is now that you've gone on national television and told the nation you have an illegitimate daughter?"

"Black daughter, Carla. Let's not forget the point of contention. I have an illegitimate black daughter. And she's older than our marriage. When she was born her mother didn't tell me and I didn't know you. So none of this smears you."

"You're wrong. All of it smears me. We're a team, Hart,

or at least we're supposed to be. Yet you do this without my consent.''

"Carla, as I have said for the last three days, I had no choice in the matter.''

"It wouldn't have made a difference, would it Hart? If you had a choice, you'd have done the same thing.''

Hart combed his hair back with both hands. He was tired of fighting with his wife and fighting with his campaign manager, and his head felt like it had a pressure cooker inside it. It seemed as if he were fighting with everyone. "Carla, she is my child.''

"Stop calling her a child," Carla snapped. "She's a thirty-year-old woman.''

Hart sighed. He wanted this to end. He'd try reason one more time. "Carla, would you want me to turn my back if you were the woman I got pregnant and only found out we had a daughter now?''

Carla faced him squarely, lowered her chin and looked at him over the rim of glasses she only wore in the privacy of their home. "That would *never* be us, Hart.''

A few days ago Hart would have sworn he'd seen every mood his wife had, knew her completely, how she would react in any situation, but she'd surprised him with her dislike of the current situation. Carla had once worked for the Children's Relief Organization. She'd traveled the world over, even to many third-world countries, on behalf of children. To think that this child, his child, could cause such an explosive reaction in her was beyond his belief.

"Carla, we'll weather this." Hart took her hand, but fell short of pulling her to him. "The polls will return to favor us. They have in the past. The country will recover from the shock and we'll win this election.''

"What planet are you living on?" She pulled her hand free. "You go on television before we have time to find out what this person or persons want and"—she paused, swallowing—"make an announcement that has such far-reaching implications.'' She spread her hands. "What were we supposed to do? What were we supposed to say?''

"It was painfully obvious to the national television audience,

Carla, that you didn't stand with me. You weren't even at the press conference. And the press noticed.''

She turned away from him.

"If anything lowered the polls it was the fact that we didn't present a united front. More time on the evening news went to the fact that you didn't attend the announcement than the fact of the daughter.''

"So this is my fault.''

"Carla, I'm not trying to lay blame anywhere. I'm trying to understand what it is that has you so upset.''

"You can't figure it out.''

"No, Carla, I can't. If this has to do with you being the First Lady, we haven't lost yet.'' Hart walked up behind her. There was a time when she would have turned into his arms. "I'm sure Morgan Kirkwood will not cost me the election. Trust me, you'll have your chance.''

Hart placed his hands on her shoulders and pulled her back. Then he leaned his chin on her shoulder and slipped his arms around her. "We'll make it, Carla. As long as we're together.''

The six of them sat around one of the coaches' dining tables looking as if they were about to leave for a funeral. Only Jim Burton and Jack seemed to have appetites. Allie ate only a few spoonfuls of her grapefruit, excusing herself, saying she had to make up for all the fattening foods Jan had made her eat over the last few days. Jan said she had to do tumbling later and she was too old to do it on a full stomach. Jim Burton challenged her remark, saying she wasn't too old for anything. He completed his full breakfast and was drinking a large glass of orange juice. Next to Jack's empty plate were two sugar packets with the torn-off tops stuffed inside, indicating the number of cups of coffee he'd consumed.

Morgan had eaten half a bowl of cereal and drunk half a cup of coffee. The buffet bar was stocked with yogurt, oatmeal, healthy foods, if that was a person's preference. It also had bagels, sausage and eggs to order for the coaches only and an assortment of fruits, individual or mixed as a salad. Yesterday had scared more than the wits out of her and apparently her appetite went with it.

She'd been sitting on the balcony trying to read, angry with Jack for forcing her to stay behind. She hadn't gone very far into the book. If someone had asked her the title she would be hard-pressed to remember anything about it. Even the color of the jacket escaped her. She'd heard nothing, not the creak of a step, the tread of a shoe or the movement of the air about her. She was completely focused on being outwitted and that had allowed Chung to walk right into the place where she hid. He could have killed her and no one would have known anything, but at the moment he slipped his hand over her mouth and pulled her into a position where she couldn't move, she heard Jack's voice in the room. He froze, holding her, listening intently to the few words Jack spoke to Allie before stepping onto the balcony. Then he nearly relaxed. Morgan felt the change in him, surprise, rigidity and total calm. It was as if he had really come for Jack and she was only the pawn he used to get to his real mark.

"Don't you think you should stay a little longer?" Jan's voice broke into her thought.

"We've already overstayed our welcome," Jack answered. "We got what we came for. After yesterday's incident it's best if we don't put you or your school in any other danger."

"Well I'll have the kitchen make sure you have food to take with you." Jan got up and hugged Morgan. "I don't want you to go," she whispered. Then she released her and walked away. Morgan felt the emotion in her and matched it with something she wasn't used to feeling.

"I gotta go too, hon," Allie said. "Jan's got me teaching a class in the big floor gym. It's the furthest one from here. I'd better get going." Allie stood and went to Jack. He stood up. "Take care of her."

"I will."

Allie hugged him. "I'm holding you to that," Allie said in a voice meant only for Jack, but Morgan heard it. Turning back to her, Allie hugged her too. "I don't want you to go."

"We'll be fine, Allie," she told her. "It's only ninety miles. Once we get there we'll have the full protection of the FBI."

Morgan smiled even though she felt like crying. It took a great effort to keep her voice from shaking. She had corrected her previous lie that they were going to Washington. The FBI was closer and it seemed to make Jan feel better to know they only had to go ninety miles to reach safety.

"And I'll never see you again."

"Of course you will. Where did you get an idea like that?"

Morgan glanced at Jack, then at Jim and Max. She wondered if one of them had said anything to her about what happened after Morgan got to the FBI. She hadn't. She didn't want to think about it herself. All three men shook their heads to her silent question.

"I'll call you when all of this is over."

"Promise me," Allie insisted. This morning she was wearing a white leotard with black stockings. She had a long jacket over it with the camp logo on the breast pocket. "Promise me."

"I promise."

"You know Jan and I will always be there. We made a pact."

Tears gathered in her eyes then. "Yes, Allie, we made a pact. Just keep that cell phone number and soon I'll reach out and touch you." She saw the serious look in Allie's eyes. "I promise."

She hugged her again and stepped back. Going toward the screened door, Agents Burton and Tilden joined her, all of them leaving at the same time.

She sat back down. Jack played idly with the sugar packet. "More coffee?" she asked. He shook his head.

"It's going to be hard on you all."

Morgan didn't want to talk about this. She wanted to run away. She wanted to go to the beam gym, the only other place she'd been allowed to go and only under the cover of darkness when the campers had retired to their cabins and all the counselors had accounted for their charges. She wanted the padded prison, for that prison gave her what she'd never had and always wanted. It gave her Jack, who was there to check on her. It gave her Allie and Jan, her friends, regardless of their background or circumstances. It gave her safety and hope.

She stopped at the thought of it. Hope. That was what she'd wanted, what she'd reached for all her life and only been allowed to glimpse for short periods of time. This was her haven, her safety net, her sanctuary, and she wanted to stay.

"We're going to have to leave soon." Jack spoke as if he could read her mind. He might be reading her face. She was used to controlling her features, but she hadn't tried a moment ago. Her thoughts were probably evident on her face. And Jack was an expert in reading her wishes.

"What about the ring?" He hadn't told her much yesterday. The bank seemed unimportant after Chung had tried to kill them.

"It wasn't just the ring. It was the paper it was wrapped in and the other papers in the envelope."

"The printing was in Korean," Morgan remembered.

"There was writing on the back of the clipping."

"I never figured out what it meant."

"You could read it?" Jack's eyebrow went up.

She shook her head. "They never had a course in Korean anywhere near St. Charles. I would have enrolled. I took conversational Chinese, but it was only offered for one semester before the professor left to return to New York. The symbols, while similar, are not the same."

"I know. I read Korean."

"You do!"

"Yes, I do," Jack replied. "It's rusty but I can get by in a pinch."

Why should she be surprised? He flew helicopters, had a pulse gun, could move quieter than an air bubble, and understood terrorists. Why should reading an Oriental language be anything other than standard operating procedure?

"What did the paper say?"

"How much do you know about Korean politics?"

Morgan shrugged. "Not much. I know there is a North and South Korea. The north is communist and the south is democratic. The government structure of the south is much the same as ours. After the Korean War in the '50s they set up a republican form of government. I think the one they are operating under now is the Fifth Republic. I can't remember why they have numbers to their republics. I believe they changed when presidents had the constitution rewritten. They have a president as the leader and a prime minister who functions much like a vice president. There is one legislative body called the National Assembly.

"You know more than most history majors."

"What does this have to do with the ring and the papers?"

"The ring holds the crest of a very old Korean family. Dynasty generations. The stories surrounding it vary from it being lost many years ago to being safely stored in the presidential palace."

"Then it does belong to the president?"

"It's actually the property of his wife. The ring comes down through her family, not his."

Morgan picked up the sugar packet, twin to the one Jack toyed with. "How did it come to be in a prison?"

"I can only speculate. At the time you were in Korea, the president was Ji-Moon Chang. His son, Pak, is currently running for the office his father once held. His opposition naturally wants to find something that will keep him from winning. And you have it."

Morgan stopped fidgeting with the sugar packet and stared at Jack.

"The gist of the message on the paper names Pak Chang as having an affair with the daughter of his father's prime minister. It says he is the father of her illegitimate child. The scandal following the rumor drove the prime minister to commit suicide. In Korea, scandal causes a major loss of face. When it involves a high-ranking family it can bring shame to everyone associated with the family. In the United States an illegitimate child would cause only a few heads to turn."

Morgan felt as if a knife had been plunged into her heart. Her body went still. Jack noticed. She'd nearly forgotten about Hart Lewiston and his declaration only a couple of days ago. She was the illegitimate daughter of a presidential candidate.

"I didn't mean—"

"It's all right," she stopped him. "I know what you meant. I understand the sociology and mores of foreign countries are different from the culture we live in. Here a child out of wedlock means little in the way of keeping a man from advancing in his career." She thought of Hart. His standings weren't as high as they had been a few days ago, but he would pull through. His kind always did. "In Korea it is a major dishonor. Since Pak Chang comes from a family that traces its roots back to the dynasties of Korean aristocracy, the dishonor would be major to that family and enough to dislodge him as a viable candidate. He'd be lucky if they didn't tar and feather him in a public square. At that he'd get off light. Only a few years ago, he'd have had to kill himself to restore honor to his family."

"The child isn't the all of it," Jack continued. "The newspaper recounted the story of a man who came forward and stated he was the father of the child. He subsequently married the mother. This quieted the rumors about the relationship of Pak and Youn-Jung, the prime minister's daughter."

"This paper proves Pak Chang is the father?"

"No, it proves the man who said he was the father, was not."

CHAPTER 13

Jan's hug made Morgan feel as if her friend held her in a hammerlock. She squeezed so tightly Morgan felt her ribs would be bruised. "I'm scared, Morgan," she whispered, relaxing her grip.

Morgan took a deep breath. "The two agents will still be here. Jack promised me. You'll be perfectly safe."

"Morgan," she stretched her name out, squeezing her arms again. "I'm not scared for me. It's you."

"We're going ninety miles away, not to the moon. I'll call you when we get there."

"Morgan, Allie and I are serious." Jan lowered her voice. "That guy yesterday scared years off my life. And Jack and Max wouldn't be arguing if this weren't something serious."

James Burton stood between Jack and Max Tilden several steps away. Morgan glanced at them. They were disagreeing over something. Morgan couldn't hear what they were saying. Their voices were too low for her to hear, but it looked as if Max and Jim were on one side of an issue and Jack stood alone on the other. Morgan took a step toward them when Allie ran up.

"Morgan, I was afraid I'd missed you. I just wanted to say good-bye again." She hugged her again and stepped back. "Don't forget to call us."

"I won't."

The three women approached the three men. "What's going on?" Morgan asked. They all stopped talking at once.

"We were discussing the route and had a difference of opinion," Jim Burton said.

"It appeared to be more than disagreement over a route," Jan said. "This is mountainous territory. We don't have a lot of routes. You either take the interstate or you go the back road, not roads, there is only one other way and I don't recommend it. It's ninety miles on I-79. Otherwise you go up to Millstone and take old route 33 to 19. All that does is make the trip longer."

Jack opened the door of the dark green Lexus sport utility vehicle that had been secured for their trip. Morgan didn't know how or where the vehicle came from. She also didn't know what happened to the van they had arrived in. Jack told her a vehicle would be secured and it stood in front of the camp office, physically present. He commanded and his wishes were made real. The vehicle had enough supplies for a week in a Colombian jungle, not on an interstate highway in the United States. There was a first-aid kit fit for a surgeon and a virtual arsenal of weapons Morgan refused to mention.

She turned to her friends, exchanging hugs one more time and again promising to call the moment they got to the FBI in Clarksburg. Climbing into the passenger seat, she pulled the arm rests down and Jack closed the door. Morgan wanted to open the window but the engine needed to be on for the controls to work. She smiled, watching Jack saying good-bye as her friends hugged him too. She could tell both Allie and Jan were whispering things in his ear. She assumed Jan was extracting promises from him to make sure Morgan called the moment they arrived and Allie was giving orders that he take care of her.

Jim and Max didn't look happy, but they didn't have the blank stares they usually assumed either. Jack shook hands with them before getting in beside her. Morgan waved as they drove away. She lowered the window and craned her neck, keeping them in view as long as possible.

Her heart was happy. For the first time in her life, she was leaving somewhere and not feeling as if she were escaping, running away and leaving behind people who wanted her gone. Jan and Allie clearly wanted her to stay. They were concerned about her.

Friends, she thought. And a warm feeling washed over her.

Ninety miles, an hour and a half to freedom. Morgan thought of old movie titles. *Thirty Seconds Over Tokyo, Thirty-Six Hours of Hell, The Eighty-First Blow, Eight Million Ways to Die, Thousand Mile Escort* and the song *A Hundred Miles of Bad Road*. She sat next to Jack. Their van had been comfortable, but its replacement was sheer comfort.

Morgan wondered what Jan and Allie had said to Jack, but more she wanted to know why Max Tilden and James Burton had had an argument with him. Max and Jim had been exemplary in their protection. Maybe they were concerned about them leaving. They could have waited for the FBI to come and get them, although she knew Jack would never have sat still for that. Maybe they thought there was more that could happen.

Morgan tried to hold onto the glow that had accompanied her exit, but eventually her mind went back to the story Jack was telling her before Jan had brought the basket of food from the cafeteria kitchen and interrupted them sitting at the coaches' table. She wanted to understand the rest of the story. Jack left Clay and drove along the Elk River. He entered the interstate at exit 40 six miles south of Servia.

When they appeared to be heading north, she turned the radio off. Jack had tuned it to a country station. She knew he did it for her.

"Jack, you were telling me about Pak Chang before we left." Morgan shifted in her seat, bringing his profile into view. His face was almost patrician, a straight nose, his cheekbones angular and hard, his chin strong, and she could she the shadow of a dimple in his left cheek. She'd never noticed it before. It was so faint it looked as if he'd tried to rub it away, like a child, viewing the dimple as an imperfection, would try to get rid of it.

"You said the man who claimed to be the father of the prime minister's daughter's child could not have been telling the truth when he claimed he was.'' She waited for him to continue.

"His name was Robert Rhee, educated, but from a poor family. The paper states there are medical records proving the man had a very severe case of the measles at age thirteen. As a result he was left sterile and could not possibly have fathered a child.''

"That takes us back to Pak.''

"It does," Jack confirmed. "And Pak Chang is running for president of South Korea.''

"The paper only says that Pak is the father. It's not a medical report. Not proof.'' Morgan had never seen a Korean medical report, but she was sure they didn't look anything like the newspaper and the writing on it.

"Proof isn't necessary in this instance. The scandal would be enough to kill his chances of winning. The opposition would demand the truth. Pak received the ring from his mother and it was inside a prison. I'm sure there is someone just waiting to authenticate that. I don't know whose handwriting is on that paper, but it states the man who claimed to be the father of the child swears Pak gave the ring to his wife. Someone else knew that, someone at the prison. Rhee was in that prison too. He died there. It would be made public. There's probably more. This is only a piece, but it's not the crucial piece. Once they get it, however, Pak would have no choice but to pull out of the race. His family would be disgraced.''

"What about the child and the mother? Where are they?''

"I don't know. But for their sakes I hope it's someplace safe.''

Morgan and Jack lapsed into silence. The countryside rolled by them in a blur of blue sky and green mountains. The road ahead was a bright black ribbon that disappeared around and through the majesty of the Appalachians. Morgan wished she could turn the clock back to twelve years ago. She wouldn't have let them take Hart Lewiston so fast, rush her into the other car and speed away so quickly that she forgot she'd stuffed the ring and papers in her pocket. When she changed clothes in the car to get back into her uniform she discovered the ring. She slipped it on her finger to give it a place to be and pushed the papers into her gym bag with her other clothes.

Her life wouldn't have been this different. She didn't know what it would have been, but she wouldn't be here now running for her life and putting Jack's in as much danger. He wouldn't be here either, she thought, and it saddened her. They wouldn't have been reunited. They would never have fought over his plan. He wouldn't be here to save her life and they never would have made love. A sudden piercing in her stomach went to her core and she nearly cried out. Jack glanced at her, but she waved him off with an "I'm all right."

Morgan wondered what was in store for them. If she were watching those movies on television it would be one adventure after another. The strong hero saves the fair maiden who is more of a hindrance than a help, but all ends well with a screen kiss, even if they are dirty and bleeding. The audience cheers and everyone goes home happy having lived through the experience vicariously.

Morgan wondered if she would be as lucky as the screen characters. This was real life. She'd survived trauma that should have sent her over the edge, but Jack had been there. Jack was with her still and he'd saved her life just twenty-four hours ago. They only had one and a half hours to go. She prayed the trip would be uneventful.

"What happens now?" she asked as they sped along. "I mean . . . what happens to that guy at the camp yesterday?"

"Richard Chung will be put away for a long time. The number of outstanding warrants against him on this continent and others will have international police departments fighting over the right to house him for decades."

"Did you find anything out from him? Who is after us?"

Jack shook his head. "He's a master at not talking. Short of torturing him I don't think we could get anything out of him."

Morgan knew they got him off the campsite as soon as possible. The police weren't called because Jack didn't want any of the campers to know. He and Max took him into town and alerted the authorities after him.

"Do you think it's someone working for Pak Chang?"

"It could be. Chung is a high-priced assassin. Whoever hired him would be paid well."

Morgan thought that over. She'd thought her life on the street, dealing with druggies and thieves, was bad. It was nothing compared to having to run from unknown killers. Assassins. She never thought the word would enter her daily vocabulary, but she had to be aware of them now. They were after her and she didn't really understand why.

"What about Max and Jim?" she asked. "Your discussion was long and it appeared strong language was being exchanged. What happened?"

"Hart Lewiston. His announcement of you as his daughter means you're entitled to FBI protection. Max and Jim received orders that they should keep you there until your agents could arrive from Washington to protect you."

"And you said?"

"There wasn't time. If Chung found us, then others would too. We're heading for the FBI in Clarksburg. Until then I'm your protection."

"And that satisfied them?"

"It appeared to."

Morgan would have bet it didn't.

There were more parks in Washington, D.C. than anyone ever thought existed in the ten-mile-square tract of land allotted to house the capital of the United States. They were small, some only the size of a city block, others as large as several acres. Rock Creek Park, which ran through the city from the Watergate complex into Maryland, was the most known. Second was Lafayette Square across Pennsylvania Avenue directly in front of the White House. Lady Bird Johnson had brought it to public notice with her beautification project in the late '60s.

The park he walked in was a lovely treed-acreage between the Washington Monument and White House called the Ellipse. A huge circular road cut through the park and was always fully populated with late model cars, Jeeps, vans and pickup trucks bringing tourists to visit one of the major wonders of the nation's capital.

The man he sought walked toward him, unhurried, as if he were leisurely enjoying a warm day in the area and concerned with nothing more than the sweet fragrance of the air.

He bowed to the man who would have been wearing a kimono in his home of rock gardens, sliding doors and sparse amounts of furniture. On the street he was dressed in black slacks and a white, open-collared shirt. His purpose might have been to appear as a businessman enjoying the city's offerings, but even without the kimono, he looked as if he were wearing it. Together they fell into step.

"Have you located her?" he asked.

He was glad to respond affirmatively. "She's in West Virginia."

"The man with her?"

"He's calling himself Jack Temple. We've known him under many names, most notably as Case." The man used no last name.

The Korean smiled. "We will meet with Mr. Case again."

"The plan to capture them is taking place as we speak."

"As we speak?"

"It's going down now," the man explained, careful to keep his distaste for the man out of his voice.

Higher peaks of the Blue Ridge Mountains could be found further to the east as the landscape and jurisdiction changed from the state of West Virginia into the Commonwealth of Virginia. The area Jack drove through was hilly and green, and it filled the air with the summer scent of grass and flowers. It should be calming. Morgan wasn't calmed. Too much had happened in the past several days. She was keyed up, wound tight like the skin of a drum and ready to play her toneless song.

"What are you doing?" Morgan cried as she gripped the door and the armrest. Jack suddenly left the road and veered off onto shoulder, then the gravel, dirt and grass. Part of the guardrail was missing and Jack took the opportunity to leave the paved road.

"It's ninety miles. For us it will be longer. There's no way Chung was working alone."

"You can't know that."

"Yes, I can. I know him. He covers his bases. He'd have a backup plan. The roads leading out of Clay could be watched in some way, or booby-trapped. They've tried helicopters before. This time they could be dressed as cops or truck drivers, postal workers, anything."

The SUV bumped and she clutched the door frame tighter to stay seated. Pulling her seat belt tighter, she anchored herself to the chair. Jack headed directly toward the mountains. Living in Washington, D.C., and then in the flatlands of the Midwest, Morgan would have thought of secondary roads that took her through the small towns of America, but she would never challenge the hills, take her vehicle off-road to an untried track. This was the stuff of commercials, Hollywood stunt drivers and fools. She knew they didn't fit into the first two categories, but circumstance had driven them to the third.

Holding on, Morgan watched the grass that replaced the black-topped surface. This could be a mistake, but she didn't think she'd bring that up right now. Hopefully Jack had thought of it. He swung the four-wheel drive vehicle around a hill, cutting them off from the main road and the road from them, hidden from civilization and help if they needed it. They were alone, out here in the hills. They had a tank of gas and ninety miles to cover.

"You've been quiet a while," Jack said. His eyes didn't leave the path in front of them.

Morgan glanced through the window at her side. "I was thinking."

"About what?" he asked.

"Life, society, sociology, group dynamics, that sort of thing."

"Heavy stuff," he replied.

Morgan laughed and turned in her seat. "It's not that heavy really. It comes closer to our society, our sociology, than the world at large."

"Don't leave me in suspense."

The vehicle bumped over rocks and stones, through mud and grass as Jack propelled it forward.

"A while ago there was a rock star. Someone extremely famous, but I don't remember his name."

"Obviously not a country-western star." He grinned at her quickly before returning his concentration to driving.

"It grows on you," Morgan explained. She smiled at the banter. She didn't often hear it from Jack. He was serious, always on point, looking for the sinister, the life-threatening.

"Don't let me waylay your thoughts. What was it about society at large?"

"Apparently this guy had a house in a relatively small town," she continued. "Often he was plagued by overzealous fans, people coming by at all hours of the day and night to gawk, breaking off fixtures to take away as souvenirs, flowerpots, anything that wasn't nailed down. They would show up in the middle of the night or first thing in the morning haunting him. For privacy he had a twelve-foot fence erected. I don't know what kind, but you couldn't see through it. The vandalism continued and he was always calling the police. It got so bad that the police asked him to replace the fence with something they could see through."

Jack thought about what she said for a long moment. Then he said, "You're saying our fence is those mountains behind us. We're out here alone. Vandalism must be dealt with and we have no police to call. They can't see us and they won't come to rescue us if we need them?"

"Exactly."

Forrest Washington reached across Brian Ashleigh's messy desk and lifted the remote control. He pointed it at the television built into the wall of Ashleigh's darkly paneled office and turned the machine off. The film of Hart Lewiston revealing he had a daughter had just completed. The news media was still wrenching stories out of it. Speculation on what would happen and why he'd chosen this time to break the story were debated by anchors and news-magazines alike. Washington thought it was giving Hart greater leverage than his opponent. In the back of his mind he wondered if Lewiston had used the information for this exact purpose. His performance before the cameras was practiced, choreographed, orchestrated. He appeared sincere, stunned and genuinely interested in discovering where his daughter was. He said nothing about her being in hiding or being instrumental in helping him escape from a Korean jail. Washington knew he was ignorant of that.

"You've always known she was his daughter?" He asked a question, but there was no question in his voice. "I wondered what the reason was for you and Clarence Christopher to attend a meeting about a twelve-year-old case that involved someone as small as Morgan Kirkwood."

Ashleigh sat quietly at his desk, his fingers linked together as if in prayer. His eyes were piercing, though. Nothing godly about them.

"When she first came to our attention we didn't know."

"We?" Ashleigh didn't volunteer anything. "You and Christopher?" The nod was slight, almost not there.

"She was naturally investigated when her name came to us. It was ironic that her parentage showed the name of the very man we wanted her to rescue."

"Her grandfather is a Supreme Court judge. Her father is very probably the next president of the United States, and you let her find out about it on network television."

"Forrest, it wasn't our place to tell either one of them. We did what we could to keep her protected after she came back. We had no precedent or authority to do so. When Hart announced his candidacy, then she became legitimately protectable."

"But no one told her."

He shook his head. "We'd already dispatched people when her call came into the FBI and Jack walked into the middle of it."

"How did Hart find out?"

"Apparently someone sent him a package with the information in it. All the details added up for him and he believes he's the girl's father. Of course, we know it to be true."

"Jack and Morgan are in West Virginia. They're heading

for the FBI there. I'm leaving this afternoon to meet them. What do we do about letting Hart know where his daughter is and what danger she's in?''

''We tell Lewiston nothing.'' His voice was commanding.

''He has a right to know.''

Ashleigh sighed. ''I know he does and he will, but we want her safe first.''

Washington understood what he meant. Morgan Kirkwood was bait. They were looking for something and she was the key to their finding it. Washington had a report on his desk that explained some of it. Since he'd talked to Jack he'd paid special attention to the climate in South Korea. Tensions were hot there and rising day by day. Rumors abounded about Pak Chang and his association with Youn-Jung Kim, who later had a child. The rumor mill claimed he was the father. Public opinion was split over the issue. His followers hadn't completely lost faith in him yet. The only thing holding them off was the woman and child. No one had yet found them, but that was only a matter of time. Then he'd have nothing to save him.

Forrest knew that to be true. The proof was in his office. Jack had sent it to him. The ring and papers arrived this morning and he'd put a full team to work analyzing everything from the date of the paper to the handwriting on it. The ring was authentic. The paper too. They were still checking on the writing, but he should have a report sometime later this afternoon.

The note Jack sent with the package told him if it was at all possible, he should find Youn-Jung Kim and her child and get them to safety. He was sure they were in danger. Washington immediately sent word to a Korean operative to find her and get her to safety. That message would have gone to Jack if he were still in the part of the world he'd lived and operated in for the past twelve years.

Youn-Jung Kim wasn't the only one in danger. Jack was too. Somehow Jack and Morgan were the linchpin holding all these forces in place. Both were in danger and Washington was sure neither knew how much.

He needed to get to Jack.

To warn him.

* * *

The terrain was uneven. Jack could do nothing about reducing the bounce of the vehicle. Each time he tried to avoid a rocky surface, he ran into another one. Morgan had relaxed her hold on the chair arm, but she hadn't let go of it. He noticed she kept looking nervously into the mirror on her side or up into the sky. Jack should have warned her that he was going to take a different route. Springing it on her cold seemed to have brought the danger back to her. Being with her friends was good for her. She connected with them, felt safe. It would have been good if they could have stayed there, but after Jack read the papers she had, he had to get her more protection than he could provide and for a much longer time.

He'd told her they got nothing out of Chung. That was only partly true. They had gotten nothing from Chung, but they found his car. Inside it was a Korean newspaper running a story on the election and current scandal going on in Korea. It didn't tell them much. Jack didn't know if Chung was working to destroy the papers and return the ring so there would be no question, or if his allegiance was to the side that wanted Chang to lose the election.

They couldn't force the mother and child to submit to blood tests. The public would stand against either side trying to do that. If the child's mother hadn't come forward in twelve years, she wasn't likely to without a really good reason.

Jack glanced at Morgan. He was going to lose her. Each bumpy section of the nonexistent road took his future and her further away from him. At the end of this road was witness protection for her and oblivion for him. He'd broken his rule with her. He'd fallen in love and he didn't know how he would survive after he turned her over to Jacob Winston.

The idea of running occurred to him. They could disappear, skip the country, assume new identities and start over, but he rejected the idea. Morgan would have agreed, but it was no life. He'd lived that way for a large part of his life, using assumed names and surviving on his own. He didn't want that life and he didn't want to live that way with Morgan. He wanted something normal; stereotypically-televisionish was his description of what he wanted. Working, probably teaching at a university, coming home to a family and children each night was ideal. With Morgan it would be perfect. But that was not to be.

"Jack," Morgan's voice held restrained panic. He glanced at her. She was looking in the mirror on her side of the SUV. Jack glanced into his. He saw them. Behind them were three vehicles, all heading toward them, bouncing over the same uneven terrain as their own vehicle did. Jack knew they weren't mountain climbers or weekend explorers out to conquer the hills before returning to their own televised lives. Their motivations were more devious.

Jack pressed the accelerator harder. The Lexus shot forward, bumping over a hill and leaving the ground for a split second before it crashed to the earth. Morgan gasped but did not scream. Quickly he scanned the area ahead of them. They needed a vantage point, a place where they could dig in and be safe against the trucks coming behind them. Jack didn't see any place that fit his requirement. Ahead of them was a high mountain. It was too far away to afford them the protection he needed.

"What can I do?" Morgan asked.

"Nothing," he snapped, stronger than he intended. He knew she'd want to do something.

She looked in the mirror again. "They're gaining on us. We're not going to be able to outrun them."

"Just sit tight."

"What about all this stuff?"

Behind them the cabin was full of equipment, sleeping bags, camping equipment and a few resources she didn't know about.

"I could open the back door and start tossing it out. Maybe they would hit one of them and they'd lose control."

"Stay where you are," he said. The Lexus pitched at that point and Morgan gripped the seat arms. "Pull your seat belt as tight as you can stand it. Shoulder harness too." Jack pulled his own. Behind them a column of trucks had formed a line one behind the other. Jack grinned as he glanced at them. This may be just what he'd hoped for.

Rounding the curve, he disappeared from the group pursuing him. He'd hoped for a place to hide, trees high enough to camouflage their direction, but nothing presented itself to his liking. He looked at the hill. "It might work," he muttered.

"What?" Morgan shouted. "What might work?"

He headed straight on, toward a narrow crop with small hills on either side. Behind him he saw the three trucks. Jack eased his foot off the accelerator, slowing the SUV.

"Jack, talk to me," Morgan commanded. "You're slowing down."

"There's no place to hide. I want to get them close enough to us to cause an accident," he said. Morgan didn't question Jack's decision. She glanced over her shoulder and through the window to the mirror, sometimes holding her breath, but she trusted him. Jack took his hand off the steering wheel long enough to squeeze the hand she gripped the armrest with. It was cold with fear. She looked at it for a moment, then at him. Trust shown in her eyes. Jack returned his hand to the steering wheel and his attention to the ground.

The three trucks were close enough now for him to determine the make, model and color of each one. He wove side to side in a cat-and-mouse attempt, playing on the psychology that they would think he was trying to get away from them.

When they were a third of the way between the two hills, Jack headed to the right. Immediately one of the trucks behind him took to that side, climbing higher than he did in an attempt to cut him off. A second truck took the other hill.

"Good," he whispered to himself. They did exactly what he expected them to. If this trick worked he'd take out the three of them in one tragic swoop. Jack eased back on the accelerator, swinging the sporty van from side to side. Each of the trucks on the hillsides went higher and lower as he did while the one behind him got closer. He was betting it all. Either this worked or he and Morgan would be in the hands of the people they'd been running from since they left St. Charles. He glanced at Morgan. She was beautiful. Her skin was tight and she clenched her teeth, but Jack thought she'd never looked better. He wanted to run his hands down her cheek, touch her, reassure her everything would be fine. He couldn't. He didn't know that, and Morgan would only appreciate knowing the truth. He didn't have to tell her what was about to happen. She already knew.

The two hills on either side were mirrors of each other. Their steepness rose at the same angle. Several yards more, Jack thought. He looked behind them. The four vehicles could be a convoy. Formed, three crossed and one behind, they traveled at the same pace. The ground ahead of him was flat for several hundred yards. The hills would rise steeper, then fall away. It had to be *now*.

Jack waited. He watched the truck behind him. It got closer. He could see the man in the driver's seat. He wasn't Korean or any extraction of Oriental heritage. He could have been from any European country or from any state in the United States. His features were taut and determined. He drove with concentration and purpose. Jack's eyes made contact with his in the rearview mirror. They held for a second, then Jack floored the accelerator and took off.

On cue, each of the trucks behind him did the same. The incline on the side of the twin hills grew steeper by a sharp degree. Both trucks began to slide downward into the path of the oncoming truck that pursued Jack with unbridled abandon. The truck on the right hill hit a rock and started a roll. It fell onto the flat ground just as the one on the left came to a stop. The impact of the two swung them around in a weird dance that was joined by the third truck crashing into the first two and jumping into the air in a ballet that fell short of completely clearing the pileup. The three of them slid together like Siamese triplets trying to turn in separate directions.

They came to a crashing halt of tangled metal, their noise magnified by the valley between the hills.

"Yes!" Morgan whooped, looking backwards. "You did it." She reached for him, but the trappings of her tight seat belt and harness kept her in place.

Jack bumped along the nearly flat ground. Several yards ahead it ended in a turn. Swinging the vehicle around, he came to an abrupt stop. Ahead of them sat a military helicopter. Jack recognized the heavily armored McDonnell Douglas AH-64 Apache. This gunship had less speed and range than its successor, a Russian Mil Mi-24 Hind used in the Afghan war of the 1980s, but the sophisticated navigation, ECM, and fire-control systems on board more than made up for the lack of speed. In

any case Jack was trapped. He couldn't outrun it. It stared at
them like a fierce animal, big, green, its rotors silent, its gun
pointing straight at them.

"Why the hell didn't you tell me, Clarence?" Hart Lewiston
slapped the week-old newspaper on the desk of the FBI Director. "Someone tried to kill her."

"The newspaper doesn't say that." The paper said there was
a gas leak and a neighbor investigating the smell had been
killed in the explosion.

"It doesn't have to. You and I know what newspapers don't
say. Her house blew up and someone was killed. She hasn't
been seen since. Where is she, Clarence?"

"Hart, we're trying to find her. We've been on this since
the incident occurred."

"You knew, didn't you, Clarence? When I walked in here
two days ago spilling my guts about a child I didn't know
existed, you already knew."

Clarence took the seat behind his desk. "Sit down, Hart."
He said it quietly. The man in front of him was angry and
might get angrier. Clarence decided to tell him the truth. He
was her father. He deserved to know.

Hart hesitated, but took a seat in front of the desk. He looked
at Clarence with an unobstructed view.

"Morgan has been under limited surveillance for twelve
years, since she returned from the Olympics in Korea. We
offered her witness protection. She refused it."

"Witness protection. Why?"

"Morgan was a gymnast and she was on the Olympic team.
She had a legitimate reason to go to Korea."

"Why should that matter?"

"We had a man in a Korean prison with information in his
head. We needed to get him out."

Hart came out of the chair so fast he nearly toppled it over.
"I don't believe it. Are you saying that girl"—he pointed at
the newspaper—"that nineteen-year-old was the person who
got me out of jail."

Clarence looked up at the towering senator. "Not entirely,

but without her you would have died there. When she agreed to do it, no one knew either of you were related."

Hart sat down. He nearly collapsed into the chair as though his leg muscles had stopped functioning. "When did you find out?"

"A few days ago." He didn't know before that, but Ashleigh had.

"You should have told me."

"I wasn't her mother. If she chose not to tell you and Morgan didn't tell you, it wasn't my place."

It was a weak answer, but it was the truth.

"Where is she now?"

"West Virginia. She should be at FBI headquarters in less than an hour."

"I want to go there."

Fear manifested itself immediately in the coldness that gripped her, shooting through her body like pure heroin injected into several veins at once. Morgan's hand shot out and grasped Jack's arm. Breath caught in her throat, preventing her from screaming. A cold finger slid down her spine, its coldness so stark her entire body shuddered. She blinked at the huge green monster, expecting it to open fire, cutting them down in the weakly protected van.

"Get out of the vehicle," a voice boomed through some kind of address system, metallic, authoritative, decisive, imposing. It vibrated through her like a cold Chicago wind. "Hands in the air."

"What do we do?" Morgan asked, not taking her eyes off the two men in the helicopter.

"Comply," Jack said. He opened the door and raised his hands. "Morgan, do exactly what they say." She heard the warning in his voice.

She opened her door, raising her hands in the same fashion as Jack. As soon as she was outside the helicopter door opened. A man in fatigues stepped out, pointing a rifle at them. The man was a green giant, dressed in the same colors as the helicopter. His dark skin blended into the surroundings, but the rifle remained brilliantly black, the sun glinting off its barrel.

"Who are you?" Morgan tried to keep the quaver out of her voice.

"I ask the questions." His voice was gut deep. It barreled through Morgan, enforcing her fear. "Move away from the van." He jerked the gun to the side.

Morgan stepped in the direction he indicated. She glanced through the door at Jack. He moved one step also.

"You!"

Morgan jumped as he shouted at her and shoved the gun. She felt more than saw Jack move. The giant swung the gun toward Jack. He stopped.

The big man pulled a pair of handcuffs out and threw them on the ground between Jack and Morgan.

"Pick them up," he snarled at her.

Morgan looked at them as if a snake wiggled there.

"Pick them up." This time he spoke quietly and slowly, enunciating each word as if she spoke a foreign language. Morgan stepped in front of the van and picked up the silver shackles. "Put them on him." He indicated Jack.

Morgan looked at Jack. She stared into Jack's eyes. He nodded slightly. She walked toward him, her eyes never leaving his as she put the handcuffs on his arms.

"It'll be all right," he whispered.

"Move away from him," the giant ordered.

Morgan stepped back and turned around. She stood directly in front of Jack. The giant threw another set of cuffs at her feet. "Those are for you. Put them on." His snarl grated like blackboard chalk.

The look Morgan gave him could melt stone. Obviously he was harder than stone. Morgan reached down and lifted the dusty shackles. She stared at the green giant as she braceletted her hands together.

"Now, get in." He waved the gun toward the opposite side of the helicopter. They both moved. "Not you." They both stopped, but he indicated Jack.

"Where are you taking us?" Morgan asked.

"To hell. Now do as I say or I'll take a dead body back. It means nothing to me one way or the other."

"Morgan." Jack's voice held a warning. "Do as he says."

She responded to Jack's comments and walked toward the silent bird. The man sitting in the pilot's seat trained his gun on her, a small hand pistol. He opened the door as she approached and stepped out. The back doors were already open. Morgan stepped on the skid, but couldn't get into the aircraft with her hands banded. The pilot hauled her into the seat and slid the door closed. Jack was seated next to her, but the giant additionally cuffed his leg to the bolted seat. Morgan immediately knew these two understood each other. Had they met before? Jack had known the man at the camp who tried to kill her. Did he know this man too? Or was he known by his reputation? In any case he was taking no chance that Jack would do something abruptly. The door next to him slammed closed, making Morgan clench her teeth.

Above her the rotors started to turn. The noise grew to a roar. Morgan thought quickly. She had to do something. They couldn't capture them both. Jack had sent the ring and papers to Washington. They no longer had them. So there was no longer any reason to keep either of them alive. If one of them got away, the other could buy time. Jack could do nothing. He was tied to the seat in which he sat. It was left to her. Her heart thundered at the plan hatching in her brain. She'd never expected anything like this. She would have to leave Jack. It was the only way they could survive.

Quickly she looked at their killers. They had placed earphones over their ears. Morgan turned to Jack. "I'm leaving," she mouthed, not speaking out loud.

Jack frowned, but made no move. Morgan wasn't sure he understood her, but she couldn't explain. The helicopter lifted off the ground. The green giant had stored his rifle. He had a handgun holstered on his right. It was out of sight. The pilot's gun was also stored. Both his hands worked the stick in front of him. Morgan stole a glance at Jack. His eyebrows rose as if to question her motives.

She couldn't explain. Every second counted. There was no time to tell him that with both of them, their captors had checkmate. They could play her against him, threaten him to her to tell them what they wanted to know. Jack might be strong and able to cope with what they could do to her, although she doubted it. He played the strong, silent type, but she knew underneath he'd cave as surely as she would in the face of a threat to him.

One of them had to get away if the other was to be protected. These men were killers. She didn't need a course in anti-terrorism to tell her that. As soon as they found out neither of them had what they wanted, at least one of them would be expendable. Morgan couldn't take the chance that it might be Jack.

The helicopter continued to rise. They must be twelve feet off the ground. She had to do it now. The rise was swift. Another eight feet and she'd be trapped.

Whipping her head around, she turned to Jack. "I love you," she shouted over the rotor noise. In movements as fast as lightning, she grabbed the door lock with her shackled hands, pulled it open and flipped herself, head first, through the opening.

With hands sure from years of practice she grabbed the skid support. Grit and dirt from the ground replaced the chalk for a surer grip. Without thinking, she swung her weight from one skid to the other, getting away from the open door and a possible bullet. She hung there a second before letting go and dropping to the ground. Her training, which would have her pounding her feet onto the hard-packed surface, deserted her as the survival instinct in her made her bend her knees and quickly fall into a roll, removing the vibrating impact that would go up her shin muscles through her knees and into her hips.

Around her, debris circled in the maelstrom created by the beating rotor blades. Small stones, twigs and grass hit her from all sides. She was directly under the bird, out of eyesight, but in the open. She needed a hiding place where the helicopter couldn't land. The van was too far away. If she went for it, she'd be an easy target for the guns she was quite familiar with. The bird moved, obviously searching for her. Morgan ducked behind a bush. It began to descend.

A shot rang out. Morgan jumped. Her head snapped around.

The sound didn't come from above, but from in front of her. Again she heard it along with the accompanying thunk of it hitting something. It had to be someone from the three trucks that had pursued them, but why?

The helicopter rose higher and took off amid an array of gunfire. Why were they shooting at the helicopter, she wondered? Weren't they in this together? Working for the same side? Morgan didn't wait to find out. The SUV was her only chance. Jack had left the keys in the ignition. She thanked him for his thinking.

Darting out from her hiding place, she raced for the van. She didn't know how far the other guys were and she didn't want to meet them face to face. Jumping over twigs, bushes and rocks, Morgan catapulted herself into the driver's seat, used both hands to turn the key, and took off in the direction where the menacing helicopter had sat. Acceleration slammed the passenger door closed. Morgan checked the rearview mirror and the sky. She had enemies in both places. She was pretty sure the trucks were useless, so her immediate danger would be the sky above her. She cursed the vehicle for its lack of a sunroof. She could see nothing.

They could probably see her. She drove blindly. Jack might have known how to get to Clarksburg over the hills, but he hadn't shared the knowledge with her.

Morgan strained to see the sky, hear the faint panting of disturbed air. She heard nothing. Where were they? Where were they taking Jack? Would they hurt him? A knot rose in her stomach as hard and immovable as the stretch of stone surfaces in front of her.

Morgan willed herself to slow the van down. Her heart pumped fast and her foot seemed to ride the accelerator at the same breakneck pace. Jerking her foot away, the van lurched in an attempt to rapidly reduce the RPMs. Something hard flew out from under the seat and hit her foot. She didn't have time to look down. Maybe it was Jack's gun. She hadn't seen the green giant search him, but while she got in the helicopter she couldn't see what was happening to Jack. She'd been searched.

So if Jack had taken his gun out of the holster and left it, that was what hit her foot. Morgan felt a little more comfortable knowing she had something to protect herself with if one of the enemies came back.

She stopped the van under two large trees. Their branches entwined over her head, forming a canopy and a hiding place for her. Looking down, she found what had hit her foot. It was small and black, but it wasn't a gun. It was a phone. Morgan grabbed it, accepting the technology, glad Jack had seen fit to get another one, forgetting the cell phone could be traced. She needed help and this was her lifeline.

Morgan squeezed the instrument to her breast, closing her eyes and praying silently. What was the name of the guy Jack trusted, she wondered, trying to remember what he'd said his name was. Nothing came to mind. She had to call someone. Quickly she dialed the only person she knew who could help her.

Jacob Winston.

CHAPTER 14

Clarence Christopher swept the door to Jacob's office open and came inside. He was followed by Hart Lewiston.

"Is that her?" Hart asked.

Jacob nodded. He'd had his secretary call Christopher the moment he discovered Morgan was on the phone.

"Where are you, Morgan?" Jacob spoke into the air.

"I don't know. I'm in the hills. Jack left the main road shortly after we got on the highway from Clay to Clarksburg, West Virginia." Her voice came over the speaker phone as clear as if she were in the next room.

"Clarksburg?" Hart said. "What's she doing there?"

"Who's that?" Morgan asked.

"Morgan, this is . . ." he hesitated. Jacob saw him swallow. "Hart Lewiston," he finished. Jacob wondered if he found it difficult to say he was her father. Accordingly, there was silence on the other end of the phone. Obviously father and daughter weren't on comfortable terms with each other. Suddenly he thought of his daughter, Krysta, and felt a pang of understanding wash through him.

"I jumped out of the helicopter but they took Jack."

"Are you all right?" Hart asked.

"I'm fine, but I'm afraid of what they might do to Jack. I need to know where they took him."

"You said they have a military helicopter," Jacob replied.

"He could be anywhere. Can you tell me anything more about the helicopter?"

"Only that it was painted like the camouflage clothing and it's different than the one Jack stole and flew away in Indiana."

"What!" Hart exploded.

Morgan ignored him and went on. "I don't think they took him too far away. They were sitting silently in a ravine, as if they knew we were coming. It looks like someone had a plan. Are there any old cabins, abandoned mines, ski trails, anywhere you could set a helicopter down without it being noticed?"

Jacob consulted the computer on his desk. The screen was recessed into the desk so no huge contraption with its myriad of wires marred the aesthetics of the surface. He had a command center at his fingertips. He looked up at Clarence, then pressed a button on the phone that put Morgan on hold. "Jenny, get Morris Lovel in here, now," he ordered his secretary and went back to Morgan. "We're getting help." Jacob didn't often speak to his secretary like that. He knew Jenny didn't take his commands personally. She'd been with him for years and they understood each other.

"Hurry," she replied. Jacob could hear the anxiety in her voice.

While they waited the intermittent seconds for Lovel to arrive, they heard strange metallic sounds over the phone line.

"What is that noise?" Hart asked.

"I'm taking off the handcuffs." They heard several more taps of metal. "They're off.

"Remind me to ask you where you learned to do that," Hart said.

Meanwhile Jacob sat down and opened the topography program Lovel would need. The short man with a crew cut and bow tie came in. His shirt was starched stiff, white and tucked in the waist of his pressed jeans.

"Lovel, find me a place between Clay and Clarksburg, West Virginia, in the mountains where you'd have shelter and be able to set a bird on the ground without notice."

The thirty-something wizard slid into Jacob's chair. His fingers hesitated slightly over the keys until he got a feel for them, then they moved like lightning. He found several locations.

"Morgan, we've got five places. He could be at any of them or four hundred miles away in Kentucky, Tennessee, or the parking lot outside my door."

"I know it's a long shot, but I feel they didn't do that. They're still looking for me. They won't go that far away. The helicopter was just sitting here waiting for us, as if it knew Jack would take this route. It had to have a base. I assume they would return to it."

"Maybe you can help us with a better location of where you are," Jacob said.

Lovel opened several screens while Jacob talked. He watched the topography change and quadrants zoom in for greater detail.

"Morgan, what are you planning to do?" Hart Lewiston spoke with tension in his voice.

"I'm going to find him."

"You can't," Hart shouted. "This is not your job. You're not equipped to do this. You could be killed."

She didn't speak for a second. "I believe my past experience makes me qualified," Morgan shot back.

"Morgan, I have to agree with Hart," Jacob said. "We can get you out of there and find Jack."

"There isn't time," she shouted. Jacob remembered the determined child in the films he'd seen. No matter how many times she fell or made a mistake in her routine, she'd get up and do it again and again. She was exactly the kind of person Jacob would have wanted on his team when he worked for the Chicago Police Department.

"Jacob." Her voice contained a little less fire, but the determination was evident. "Jack put his life on the line to save mine. I'm not leaving here without trying to find him. Both you and Hart should understand that. I'm his only chance."

Her comments seemed to hit Hart as solidly as a missile. Color drained from his face, leaving it sallow and pale before it filled with color. Clarence put his hand on Lewiston's shoulder and the presidential candidate looked at him. "I'm afraid for her," he whispered.

"I understand," Clarence replied. "We'll get her out," he assured him.

Jacob looked at Lovel. "Too dense," he said. "We need more to find her."

"What was that?" Morgan asked.

"Give us some details, Morgan. Is there a lot going on where you are? Mountain climbers, hikers, campers?"

"We left the highway about ten miles in." Lovel moved the mouse to a point on the screen. "We drove for about half an hour before the first group of trucks showed up."

"First," Hart repeated. Lovel triangulated.

"How fast were you going?"

"About thirty miles an hour. We had to keep going around trees and bushes."

Lovel made an adjustment.

"What happened then?" Jacob tried to keep control. He could only imagine how he'd feel if Krysta were alone with people trying to kill her. There was no way of getting Hart out of the office. Jacob knew they wouldn't be able to drag him out either, even though the man was torturing himself with every word he heard.

"Then the trucks started to chase us." She related the details of the accident and the helicopter and how she'd jumped to the ground. "That's all except for the gunfire."

"Explain that," Jacob said, cutting Hart off, who was sitting forward in his chair.

"It came from the ground and was directed at the helicopter. I don't know who it could have been and I didn't stick around to find out. Was Jack working with someone else?"

Jacob looked at Clarence. He shrugged.

"We don't know, Morgan, but it's possible. I'll give Forrest Washington a call."

"That's his name," she said. "I tried to remember what Jack had said, but the only name I could remember was yours."

"I've got something," Lovel whispered.

"It's all right. We're on it," Jacob tried to reassure her. "We've got something."

"What?"

"I'm going to put Morris Lovel on. He can explain it."

"I can see you, ma'am," he began.

"You can?"

"As long as you keep the cell phone on, I'll be able to track your position." He paused. "As for a place you can put a helicopter, there's an old mine about ten miles north of you. The mine is closed, dangerous and posted with signs and a fence to keep out curiosity seekers. It would be ideal as a hideout."

"All right, I'm on my way." The sound of the engine starting zoomed into the room. "I have to end this call. If you can find me, so can the bad guys."

She didn't immediately sever the call and Jacob left the line open.

"Hart," she said. He looked up. "We'll talk later. I promise."

"I'll be waiting," Hart said, but the connection had already been cut.

Jack opened his eyes. Absolute darkness. He could see nothing but inky blackness. His head hurt from the fists that had pounded against it in an attempt to get him to talk. He felt the dried blood caked on his face. The darkness was disorienting and cold. Jack's hands and ankles were shackled. From the feel of shards in his back, he was lying on the ground. The residue of coal hung in the stale air. This had to be a mine, defunct, dangerous and out of the way. Despite his discomfort he wondered about Morgan. Had she reached safety? Maybe she would return to the camp and get Burton and Tilden to help her. Or she could call the CIA and let Washington know. He refused to think of her with a broken leg or arm lying somewhere hurt. Or the men who shot at them finding her.

He needed to get out of here. The next time his captors weren't going to be as physical. They tried to beat information out of him, for the sheer pleasure of the fight. That hadn't worked. When they were sure he knew nothing, that Morgan was the one with the answers, they'd thrown him into the mine shaft, assuming the fall would kill him. If it didn't, he'd die there from his injuries or from rats and small animals eating away at his flesh.

Jack sat up, holding his head. He thought of Morgan again

and her migraine medication. His head needed more than her gentle pills could help. Blind stabs of light ricocheted in his brain and behind his eyelids. He waited a moment for the pain to subside. The fall hadn't killed him, though the way he felt he almost wished it had. Every bone in his body protested. His muscles screamed and his head felt as if it were being detached from his body by force.

A moment later he tried to think of something other than the pain. He had to get the cuffs off. He could work without his hands, but with his ankles tied together there was no way he could avoid the death in store for him. And that he wanted to do more than nurse his headache. He needed something round, like a screwdriver or a handcuff key. He wasn't likely to find either in this dark mine. And at this point he didn't know which way was either up or out. But going somewhere other than where he was expected to be was desirable. Jack felt around him. He was sure there were no tools left from the times when the mine was a working enterprise. He found only dust, dirt and rock. Then Jack thought of nails. There would still be nails. If he could find one small enough, it would work. He felt for the wall. The metal bracelets clinked on his arms. Knowing he couldn't stand in complete darkness without falling, he held onto the rough and crumbling wall as he got to his feet.

Working his way along the wall, he found one of the support beams. Nails were used to hold them together, to mount brackets to hang lamps. Jack felt along the wood. A splinter nicked his finger and he snatched it away. Then, going back, he carefully edged his way along until he found the place where the lamp would have hung. The bracket was still there. He let out a sigh of relief.

Working with both hands, he slowly loosened the fixture. The nails were most probably rusted. He hoped so. That meant layers of metal would be gone or easily removed, making it fit into the hole, and Jack would be able to get the shackles from his arms and legs. Jack gritted his teeth as he worked. For a closed mine, the fixture had been securely attached, and it took all his strength to get it to loosen. With a little more work the bottom support pulled free. Jack was careful to keep the nails from falling to the floor. He found three nails and carefully slipped two of them into the front pocket of his jeans. The nails in the top of the fixture he left for some future handcuffed prisoner.

Sitting down, he kept the beam to his back and tried the nail in the middle of the handcuff that tied his feet to within six inches of each other. It was too large to fit into the slot, but he felt shavings fall into his hands. Pulling it out, he rubbed it against the coarse fabric of his jeans, using the seam at the side of his leg, and hoped this would dislodge the rust and leave him with something small enough to fit into the slot.

It took several attempts. Jack's fingers burned from the generated heat and his leg felt numb at the spot where he'd rubbed it, but finally his legs were free. His hands required less work, as if working on his legs had taught him what he needed to know for his hands.

Scrambling to his feet, he kept contact with the beam. Listening, he tried to figure out which way would lead to the surface and light. He froze, instinctively crouching in place, hearing sound coming from behind him. He saw no light and wondered if some animal had crawled into the cave.

Jack waited several moments. He heard nothing further. He had to move soon. He didn't know how long he'd been in the cave or how long it would be before his captors decided to confirm his death. If there was a way out, it had to be in the direction he'd heard the noise. Waiting a moment longer, he listened for another movement. What happened to the animal? Had it come in and decided to retreat?

Jack move forward cautiously. Beam by beam, he made his way over uneven ground. The incline went up, reinforcing his belief that this was the way out.

Then he heard it again, the quick scurrying of something small and fast. He stopped.

"Jack." He heard the tentative whisper. "Jack, is that you?" His heart thudded to a stop, then beat fast enough to drown out the sound of an on-coming train.

"Morgan."

* * *

Who moved first wasn't important. Morgan found Jack as their two forms ran into each other in the darkness. They fell into the coal dust on the mine floor. She didn't think she'd really find him, but he was here, in her arms, holding her, kissing her. She hugged him, arched toward him, sealing her mouth to his as if she'd never been kissed before. He was solid, warm and alive. Tears gathered behind her closed eyes. Her hands raced over him, confirming that he was here, checking, every part as if he were a newborn and she needed to count his ten fingers and ten toes.

"I was afraid you were dead," she said on a heavy breath when they separated.

Morgan had been afraid they'd kill him. When she'd broken contact with Jacob's office she'd thought it was a futile attempt. She didn't think fate would allow her to find him in this vast wilderness or that he would be alive when she did. Fate had never been her friend, but tonight fate was with her. And Jack was in her arms.

"We've got to get out of here," she whispered. "They're not far away."

They scrambled to their feet and Jack asked, "Which way?"

Morgan held his hand, refusing to break contact. She led them back the way she had come. She had a flashlight and used it to retrace her steps until they could see the cave's opening. Then she doused the light in case the men from the house returned.

"It's dark," Jack said.

"Yeah. I had to wait hours before I could get in here. They kept going in and out of the house. I saw them bring you out and throw you in the mine. I nearly screamed." Morgan looked at him in the semi-darkness. "You look terrible," she said. Her hand went toward his face, but he flinched and she stopped. "It must hurt."

"It does," he agreed.

"The van is this way." She pointed to the right. The small structure which used to house a guard when this was an operating mine was lighted. Jack had been battered in there.

Morgan arrived in time to see two men carrying him from the structure to the mine. It had been daylight then and activity in and out of the small house was constant. Finally when darkness fell she went in to get Jack.

Crouching close to the ground, Morgan circled away from the house. The ground had been cleared when the mine was worked, but Mother Nature had returned to claim her land. The trees and bushes were thick and hard as if she had indignantly set up a barrier against future poachers. Yet Morgan went directly through it.

They traveled in silence for almost a mile, the meager flashlight their only source of illumination. Morgan refused to think of any natural enemies like snakes and bears. She didn't even know if they were indigenous to this part of the country. She was a city girl. She'd never lived in the country. Traveling through mountains, camping out, even girl scouting was something she had never done. But tonight she'd earned her merit badge. She'd gone in and brought Jack out. Not quite in a gun-toting blaze of glory, but she'd accomplished her goal. Her hand tightened in Jack's.

The SUV was hidden in a grove of trees that acted as a natural barrier. Morgan had enhanced it with branches that in the night hid the vehicle totally. When they reached it Jack asked, "How did you find me?"

"I called Jacob. He got somebody named Morris Lovel to help me."

"I don't understand."

"I don't either, but because of the phone, Morris could find me and find other structures or vehicles in the area. We narrowed the possibilities down to this one and he gave me some directions to get here." She paused, thanking God Morris had been right. She shuddered to think what they would have done to Jack if this had been the wrong location.

Morgan climbed into the driver's seat. "We can't go far in the dark, but I'd feel better if we put a little distance between us and them." She hooked her thumb over her shoulder.

"They have a helicopter and a Jeep. They can find us if we use the lights. It's better to stay put until daylight."

"The highway is only five miles away." She pointed in the

direction Morris had told her. "If we can't leave here, you should get some rest." She reached behind the console between them and pulled out a first-aid kit, then got out of the van and walked around to Jack's side. "Let me clean the blood off your face."

Jack got out and sat on a nearby tree that had died and fallen to the ground. Part of it hung over a small body of water, forming a low bridge. The water wasn't a charted lake or stream, only a body that formed after a recent rain. Many of them developed because of the high water content and the trees that liked to pull the moisture close to them.

Morgan opened the kit, and without even a moon in the sky for light, she poured water from a bottle onto a cloth. Carefully, she pressed it against his skin. The water was cold but Jack's skin was hot. The blood softened until it colored the cloth in huge red splotches. Mechanically, she worked, refusing to allow her mind to think that this was Jack, this was the man she'd fallen in love with, the one whom she might have lost tonight if she'd chosen the wrong direction.

Jack grabbed her hands. "It's all right," he said as if he could read her mind. "We'll get out of this."

Morgan went back to cleaning his swollen face. When she finished, she emptied the remaining water from the bottle and slipped their trash into a plastic bag.

"Leave me now." Panic sliced through her at the thought of him leaving before she realized he needed to be alone.

Going to the van, she replaced the first-aid kit and dropped the plastic bag in the back of the van. Morgan stood there fidgeting with the bag, the blankets, camping gear, waiting, trying not to think of the possible outcomes this day could have had, but they crowded in on her like huge dogs backing her in a corner, forcing her to face them, stare them down. Her heart thudded as fear threatened to overwhelm her.

Jack came up behind her. She could feel him, his warmth seeped into her and the weight of their situation pushed her shoulders down.

"I was never so afraid in my life," he said, "as I was when you went out that helicopter door."

Morgan worked her neck muscles in an attempt to swallow. Emotion at his words was no match for the note in his voice.

He cared about her. Tears clouded her eyes. She closed them. Morgan hadn't cried in years, but she couldn't stop herself. Scalding hot rivers flowed from her eyes and rained down her cheeks. Her shoulders shook. Jack turned around.

He'd washed up in the small lake. His hair was wet and he wore no shirt.

"It's all right," he assured her. "We're safe."

"Jack," her voice broke. "This is all my fault. You would be safe if it weren't for me. You could be in Montana looking at your mountains, enjoying the life you want. I'm sorry."

Jack pulled her into his arms. "Being on that mountain isn't going to mean anything if I didn't do everything I could to get you out of this."

"I'm not your responsibility." Morgan burrowed into his arms. She breathed in his scent, mingled with coal dust, sweat and rubbing alcohol. He was warm. She felt his heart beating under her ear, a strong, steady, slightly elevated tempo.

"You've been my responsibility since my off-handed comment landed you in this situation. We're going to get out of this."

He lifted her face, wiping her tears aside with his thumbs, then, cradling her face between his hands, he kissed her with such tenderness, Morgan thought she would die. His lips brushed over hers as his arms circled her. He didn't crush her to him, but held her gently as if she were fragile and needed careful handling. Morgan thought the only thing holding her together was Jack's arms. If he released her she'd scatter into molecules, microscopic, invisible, floating into the atmosphere, never to be reconstituted, never to be seen again. Jack's mouth teased hers, his tongue swept lightly over her inner lip. She groaned with the emotion that flowed in her bloodstream.

She wanted to press her body into his, show him how much she loved him, show him that in all the years they had been separated her love remained intact, shining, bright and hopeful. She wanted him inside her, his body joined with hers, his life completing hers. Morgan leaned into him, forgetting his swollen skin. Her arms raised and her body pressed into his as the kiss changed. His mouth grew more passionate, carrying her into the storm that built around them until it was raging, warring with her feelings and her need of him.

Somewhere in her consciousness she knew this was not the time or the place, but she forced her mind away from that thought and let her hands smooth over Jack's heated skin. He felt great, hot to the touch, and his mouth was doing things to hers that sent signals to other parts of her body. Her hands couldn't stop moving, just as her mouth couldn't stop caressing his. Morgan felt her feet leave the ground as Jack lifted her. Only slightly mindful of his sore face, she deepened the kiss, waving her head from side to side as she kissed him over the good places of his face. Her legs wound around him as strong arms supported her. Morgan felt the groans in her throat join with those in Jack's.

"I need you, Jack," she moaned, unmindful if she spoke aloud.

"You're driving me insane," he said, his voice laced with emotion. Setting her down on the available space in the back of the van, Jack pushed her back, following her onto the floor of the SUV between sleeping bags, food supplies and guns.

Morgan's hands went to the snap on his jeans and pulled it free. She unzipped them, keeping her eyes on his face. She could see the pleasure of her hands written on his features and she skimmed them across his body. Back and forth she continued the effort until his hands grabbed hers and stopped the action.

His hands weren't hurting her, but she could feel the effort it took for him to hold back, control himself. Morgan didn't want control, not tonight. She wanted the rules suspended, forgotten. Above them was a brilliant sky. Around them the forest primeval. They were Adam and Eve before the fall. Alone, together, in love. This might be their last night in Eden. Tomorrow . . . she wouldn't think about tomorrow. Instead, she ran her hands up Jack's chest, circled his nipples with her flattened palms.

In seconds they were dragging each other out of their clothes. When they were naked, he stopped and looked at her. Morgan didn't feel the need to cover herself. She wanted him to look at her. She wanted to stand and dance and walk and let him view her from all angles.

He touched her shoulders, his rough hands lighting fires wherever they went. When he kissed her again, Morgan raised her arms and swung them around his neck. His hands came to her breasts. The shock of pleasure that raced through her pierced to her core. Her head fell back and guttural sounds came from her throat, primitive cries, mournful moans that told him what he was doing with his hands and his mouth was pleasing. More than pleasing, it was sinful. And she wanted more.

Every inch of her ached for his touch, craved the tease of his fingers. Morgan moved closer to him, hampered by the confines of the small space. Jack reached into one of the containers over her head and came back with a foil square. Morgan smiled when she saw it. Taking it from him, she broke the seal. A slight hissing noise accompanied the tear as she opened it. Reaching between them, Jack gripped the van's floor as she touched him.

"Hurry," he said, his voice dark and strained.

Morgan slipped the protection over him. For a moment she smoothed her hands over his hair-roughened legs. She felt the muscles contract where she touched. Jack's face told her he was in agony, but the agony was from the pleasure she gave him. She knew how much her touch pleased him and she continued.

She kissed his shoulders, working her hands around his body, and her mouth across his torso, feeling the subtle changes in him as rapture enclosed them in a cocoon of fiery need. Hooking her fingers about his neck, she pulled him down as she lay back, giving him access to her body.

"I love you," she whispered as Jack entered her. Morgan couldn't hold back the throaty groan of pleasure that accompanied his penetration. She felt as if it were their first time, although she was familiar with him. The sensations running through her were different, as if her blood and adrenaline had coupled with TNT to cause an imminent explosion.

Morgan lost all sense of time and place when Jack moved inside her. They were alone. The world didn't exist outside their surroundings. She loved Jack and wanted him to know it. She gave herself, all of herself, all she had to give flowed through her and into him.

Jack cupped her hips and she raised them, giving him greater access. She felt him totally inside her as huge waves of love caught her in their glory and lifted her to a sea of sensation that prior to this she had not known, would not have believed was possible.

With Jack she knew everything was possible.

Anything was possible.

"Hart Lewiston tries to regain some of the ground he's lost in a recent trip to Atlanta, Georgia." The television announcer droned on with the lead story. Carla Lewiston curled up in her hotel bed and pulled the covers up to her neck. She watched her image on the screen standing next to Hart, smiling for the cameras and looking out over the crowd as Hart spoke into the microphone.

He looked tired, aged, she thought. In a matter of weeks he'd gone from a strong, robust man to someone she hardly recognized. They'd been married for twenty-three years, had traveled together, done everything with the same goal in mind, yet on the screen, emerging through the electronic wizardry of some long-dead inventor, was a man she hardly knew. When had that changed? Where had she been when Hart had become intent on family? They'd never wanted children. They hadn't discussed children when they got married. It was to be just the two of them. They didn't need children to complement their lives. They had their careers. Their lives were full, busy, satisfying, but she never thought she was too busy for Hart, or he for her. Yet they were different. She knew no one could ever completely know another human being, but she thought she and Hart came as close as any two people ever would to accomplishing that. But he'd proved her wrong.

The news story on Hart ended, replaced by Hart's *daughter.* Carla felt her anger rise. She frowned at the child, the nineteen-year-old Olympic hopeful. Didn't they have any current footage, she wondered? This twelve-year-old film of her at the Seoul Olympics was getting tired. She wasn't a nineteen-year-old any longer. She wasn't America's sweetheart vying for her place in the light. Her place had come and gone, but Hart saw fit to thrust her back onto center stage.

Carla sat forward, staring at the screen and the girl on it. Was she the trump card? This child was America. She represented us to the world. The international posters Carla had seen so often as the Director of the Children's Relief Program flashed into her mind. Germany was represented by a blonde woman with pig tails and a printed dress over which she wore a white apron. The Japanese wore kimonos. Carla knew the world thought of the United States as represented by a cowboy, complete with chaps and boots, wrangling a steer to the ground or of some jeans-clad young man with a two-day beard. But that image had been replaced in the international mind by this child, Morgan Kirkwood, astride her chosen steer, a gymnastics beam.

She stood poised on it, her uniform, not jeans, but a white leotard with the stars and stripes on her right arm. The front of the torso held huge slashes of red and blue. She was perfect, young, golden, her hair in a ponytail that bobbed with each movement. Her arms extended as if in a dancer's pose and her eyes, the eyes of innocence, the face of vulnerability, epitomized all that was good and right in America. A poster child for patriotism, Carla thought. Was that it? Was that why Hart had seen fit to suddenly pull her into the picture?

Carla shook her head and fell back against the plushness of the pillows in the suite's king-sized bed. He didn't need her. His ratings in the polls were miles ahead of his competition. All he needed to do was wait out the time. But he'd chosen to do something stupid and now he was trying to backpedal.

And she had to stand beside him, her smile carefully in place, and help.

Jack bolted upright. Stiff muscles protested his sleeping in the cramped space. Forgetting his discomfort, he checked over his shoulder, searching. He was covered with one of the sleeping bags. Morgan would have put it there. When he fell asleep he was covered only by her radiance and the afterglow of a love that blanketed them under a bubble of warmth.

Yet where was she? "Morgan," he called, already knowing she wouldn't answer. Listening for a moment, his suspicions were confirmed. "Damn!" Jack cursed. She was gone. His heartbeat escalated. She wouldn't be far. She couldn't have risked her life to save his only to leave him during the night. And especially after the night they had just shared. But she knew better than to go off alone. Or she should, he corrected. They were too close to the mine and its inhabitants, ready to kill them, for her to go off on her own.

Discarding the sooty clothes from yesterday, he grabbed a clean shirt and jeans and shrugged into them. As soon as he pushed his feet into running shoes, he weighed the most obvious direction she might have headed. Then he remembered the small body of water where she'd cleaned his face. It wasn't far, only a few steps. He went toward it with the speed of an agile cat.

Jack stopped short when he saw her. It was barely dawn. The air was still cool. Dew wafted off the water like a celestial mist. She swam in the dark pool, gliding through the liquid like a water nymph. Her hair, loose and darkened by the wetness, floated on the surface of her shoulders. Jack remembered it falling over his hands last night, thick and soft like dark velvet. His body tightened, reacting to hers with all the remembered love of a few hours ago and a lifetime of forevers.

She swam away from him, her head above water, her arms coming together in front of her and pushing the water away, slicing a path which she pulled into, only to repeat the action. He heard her humming one of the country music tunes she liked as if she had no cares in the world. Her body was nude, hidden by the concealing water, teasing him as parts of her surfaced while others went under. He saw her naked legs, her breasts, the soft curve of her hips peeking in and out of the mist. Jack stood rooted to the spot, unable to move or call to her, unable to do anything but watch her dance for his eyes only.

He'd never seen anyone swim like her. He swam with purpose, laps up and back, methodically, rhythmically, his only goal to get from one side of the pool to the other and repeat the action. Morgan swam without purpose, with a grace and elegance that made her one with the medium in which she'd immersed herself. Jack was caught up in her motion, watching with awe as something invisible but tangible took hold of his heart and squeezed it. He could only stare. He couldn't move, couldn't call to her. He only wanted to stand in this virgin land and watch her gentle ballet as misty ghosts banked off the surface. Ethereal and cloudlike, Jack felt as if they were alone in the world. This was their private Garden of Eden and Morgan was his Eve. The setting was perfect, the surface clouds ushering in the morning and Morgan warm and naked in his arms.

He was about to go to her and make his thoughts reality when she called to him, "Hey." She turned, facing him, treading water in her steamy setting. "You should come in. It's a little cold at first, but you get used to it."

Jack was lost. She disarmed him. She'd always done it, but he'd been able to control it in the past. When she was only a figment of his dreams, he could keep it at bay. With her this close, he couldn't. He wanted to get into the water. He wanted to scoop her into his arms and let the formless water buoy them. He wanted to join her in the erotic ballet, slide into her with the sloshing comfort of the liquid about them and make love until neither of them had a brain between them.

Jack looked away. Suddenly he was uncomfortable. It had nothing to do with Morgan, more with himself. He knew better than to get involved. He also knew he had no choice.

"It's time to get dressed," he said, trying to cover his discomfort, replacing an idyllic life together with images that talked of a future the two of them would never have. "We've got to get out of here."

Jack turned and headed back to the van. He couldn't watch as she came out of the water, ascending the sea like some golden-brown mermaid sacrificing her fins for legs to walk the earth and love a man. Jack couldn't be that man. As much as he wanted it, craved it so badly he thought sometimes his heart would burst, as much as he wanted to give up everything for her, it was not to be. He didn't need Jacob Winston to read him the riot act. He didn't need Forrest Washington to explain the rules of engagement. Neither of them could tell him anything he hadn't already said to himself, but neither of them had held

Morgan in their arms and listened to her soft, breathy sound as she made love.

"What is it with you?" Morgan asked, coming up behind him as he stood in the van's open door.

Grabbing his arm, she spun him around to face her. Hands on hips, she looked like a predatory lion ready to do battle. He said nothing. She appeared to grow angrier.

God, he thought, why did she have to be so beautiful? Her wet hair was slicked back off her face. It fell in spiked tendrils on her shoulders. Droplets of water soaked the ends, absorbing into her shirt as if it were a napkin. She wore no makeup. Her skin was tight and healthy, her nose and cheeks shiny. Ribbons of darkness skated across her midriff, proving she'd pulled the T-shirt over her head while her body was still wet. Jack gripped the door to keep from grabbing her and pulling her into his arms, smelling the freshness of the water on her skin and the cleanliness of her hair.

"You know what your problem is, Jack?" Morgan went on. She gave him no time to answer. "You stand back when love tries to touch you. You're a strong man and you think love will make you weak, vulnerable. It won't. It'll make you human. You've been out here saving the world for a long time. A lone ranger, needing no one, wanting no one. Is that the way you want it?" She paused, taking a breath. "To live your life having sex but not making love, touching but not feeling, meeting people but never taking the time to know them? If so, then we're much too different and life for us will never be a success."

"It's a moot point, Morgan. When we get to Washington, *if* they don't kill us first, you're out of my life."

She stepped back as if he'd hit her.

"Wherever I stand on love, back, forward or in between, is useless to discuss. So let's keep our minds on the problem at hand."

She stared at him for a long moment. Jack watched her facial muscles twitch as she tried to keep them in place. She wanted to cry. She was going to cry.

"Is that what we were doing last night, Jack? Keeping our minds on the problem at hand?" Not waiting for an answer, she stalked away. He moved around the van to where she could not see him before letting out the breath he'd been holding.

Standing back when love tried to touch him. It was part of his I.D. as surely as his name was. She'd taught it to him, although she didn't know it. It was a hard lesson, one he thought he'd learned well. He vowed never to get involved again, never let a woman get into his blood. When he let his feelings become involved he'd immediately walk away. He'd been good at it too. It had become his nature, but not now.

She had touched him, reached into his soul and held him in place, refusing to allow him to walk away. She'd worked her way into his heart and anchored herself there. His father had once told him he'd know he was in love when a woman was in his blood. Morgan had taken up that station and there was nothing he could do about it. He was in love with her, but he had to let her think he could walk away without a backward glance. She would surely be wrenched away from him as soon as they set foot in the FBI. He couldn't afford to let her know how he would suffer when she was gone. Let her hate him. It was better for them both.

He could never hate her.

CHAPTER 15

The silence inside the van was palpable. Morgan didn't understand what had happened. One minute they were making love and the next Jack was telling her to get lost.

She sat stiffly next to her door as far away from him as the tiny space allowed. Desperately her mind sought a solution to their dilemma. Jack was in love with her. She was sure of it, she told herself. He'd never said it. Between them stood her predicament. They could have no life together. If she didn't accept the government's protection she surely would be caught one day. If she wanted to live, she had to look at it rationally, the way Jack had. This had to end. They couldn't run forever. Either they would be caught and killed or they'd make it to Clarksburg and she'd enter the witness protection program. Jack would resume his life in the CIA or retreat to his Montana paradise. In either case, it would be without her.

Tears misted in her eyes, but she swallowed them down. There was no time for emotion now. She should be checking for vehicles following them or helicopters poised to shoot from the sky, but she was too caught up in—

It hit her then. Helicopters. There were two of them. Not two helicopters, but two different people shooting.

When the helicopter had taken off with Jack in it and she jumped to the ground, shots had helped her escape, shots that came from the ground. She wondered if Jack remembered.

Morgan almost turned in her seat. She had become used to talking to him, planning with him. She felt gagged by her own anger.

Jack hadn't said a word since he climbed into the driver's seat. His swollen face made his profile grotesque. His features were tight, his hands powerful, gripping the steering wheel as the SUV mowed down bushes and small trees, making its own road through the dense greenery.

Morgan glanced behind her, through the window at the back of the van. The sleeping bag she'd pulled over them in the early morning lay like a crumpled reminder of what she would lose only a few miles down this imaginary road. She'd never think of a van again without being reminded of Jack lying there, making love to her.

She woke before Jack had. Darkness shrouded the night. The crickets and cicadas had ended their song. All about her was quiet. Nothing moved to break the stillness, except for Jack's easy breathing. It was that very quiet that had awakened her.

The pond drew her like a siren's song drew a sailor. She went there and entered the water, swimming until she saw Jack watching her. His face was hard, set in the stony semi-darkness, as if he'd made some irrevocable decision.

And indeed he had.

"Jack." Morgan couldn't be quiet a moment longer. He glanced at her, his face still set. "I'm not going to bring up the lake."

She saw his jaw muscles tighten and it gave her a secret pleasure to know he was upset by his own decision.

"Last night—" She stopped. That wasn't what she meant to say. "Yesterday, in the helicopter." Her words were staggered, even though she tried to control them. "I only got away because of—"

"The other shots," he finished her sentence.

"You heard them?" she asked in surprise. Why was she surprised? Jack saw everything. He'd been trained to observe. Even the tiniest details didn't get past him. She wondered about his life. She wanted to know every detail of his life, his future.

They were only fifty miles, maybe less, from their destination. Time had eluded her. She'd spent twelve years trying not to think of him and only a couple of weeks thinking of nothing else.

"Any idea who they are?"

"I thought they were together until they started shooting. Why do you think . . ." She didn't know how to finish.

"There are two of them."

Morgan shuddered. She didn't really want her thoughts confirmed.

"Why?"

"I haven't a clue. You've made some powerful enemies."

"Do you think both of the candidates have people looking for those papers?"

"It's possible. The information is valuable to both sides. The men in the cabin knew about the ring and the papers. They wanted them. I assumed they were working for one of the groups in Korea campaigning for president, but I don't know which side. They would answer none of my questions."

Morgan slumped back against the upholstery. Then she heard it. The beat of the air. The unmistakable sound of helicopter rotors.

"They've found us," she shouted, her body instantly arrested with fear. She leaned forward, staring into the sky, trying to find out which direction they were coming from. She also wondered who they were. She'd feared only one side of the Koreans, but why not both? The papers could help and hurt either side.

Morgan racked her mind trying to think of something to do. Back in St. Charles she'd been in control. She knew everything about the area, the places to hide, dead-ends, roadblocks. It was her turf. Here she was lost. They had no road, only what they carved out of the forest. Jack banked hard on the steering wheel, taking the van into a ravine, and abruptly braked. She was slung forward and thrown back into her seat. She closed her eyes for a moment listening for the distant sound. The trees hung over each other here and the Lexus was hidden from the sky.

Morgan held her breath until she confirmed the sound was receding. The helicopter was going in the opposite direction from the one they were traveling. She glanced at the odometer. Since they left the highway more than twenty-four hours ago, they'd only traveled thirty miles. Sixty miles of prime forest sat between them and their goal.

"Jack, we have to return to the main road." She spoke logically. Emotions, which rioted through her, were absent from her voice. "At this rate it will take us days to get to Clarksburg, even if you're sure of the direction."

"I've come to that conclusion myself. If we were here alone and safe, it would be the best route, but with two different factions trying to find us, we need to find the fastest method."

"Why don't we just call your friend at the CIA and ask them to pick us up?"

"I thought of that, but . . ." he trailed off.

"But what?"

Jack didn't answer. He stared straight ahead looking at nothing.

"There's something not quite right. I can't put my finger on it. My gut tells me we've got to do this alone."

His instincts must have paid off in the past. He didn't say it, but she heard it nevertheless.

"Do you know who is chasing us? I mean both groups?"

"Only one. I don't know who's behind the second one."

Morgan thought again about her enemies. She could think of no one, at least no one that had a face. She had taken the papers from Korea along with Hart—her father. She got him out of the jail, but had only been seen by the one guard. Yet he had aided her. Had he told the others who she was? It had been years. Look at where Hart was today. Look at the politics of Korea. That guard could have bought himself a higher station with that piece of information. It could be the reason the Koreans had her in their sights now. They could also have killed the man with as much compassion as they held for her.

But that only accounted for one group of assassins. Had he played both sides of the field and sold his information to them both? She didn't know, but it was the only thing that made sense.

Jack's movement caught her attention. He leaned forward and looked up. He could see nothing through the trees. Only the slight craning of his head told her he was listening. She strained. No sound. The helicopter was gone.

But not for long.

They would circle and circle, expanding their circumference until they spotted the SUV and the two inhabitants.

Jack started the engine. He pulled out of the trees and through the narrow ravine. Now they were out in the open. Only a few trees helped to keep them shaded. Jack drove with breakneck speed. Morgan gripped the seat arms and often ducked oncoming trees. He was tense and she could see him check the skies and listen for sound as he propelled the van ever closer to the road they had left a day and a night ago.

When they saw it, a strip of black shining in the sun, they were above it. Jack didn't start downward, but continued parallel, forever checking the sky, until the road and the mountains met. He slipped back through a rail-less section and onto the blacktop. Cars, vans and trucks flirted with his SUV as they passed on their way to distant destinations.

CLARKSBURG - 40, the sign said. Forty miles. "We're almost there," Morgan breathed.

Jack nodded.

Morgan checked the rear windows. There were several cars behind them. No one looked menacing, but she knew better than to believe the innocence of appearance. Jack too checked the mirrors frequently. Five miles later Morgan relaxed a little.

Big mistake.

"Tighten your seat belt," Jack said needlessly. Since their first encounter with the road and all its surprises Morgan had worn her seatbelt just short of tight enough to slow her circulation.

"What's wrong?"

"They're back," he said, not differentiating between who "they" were. Were "they" the supporters of the Korean president? Were "they" the opposition to his election? Could "they" be someone altogether different?

Morgan's head whipped back and forth looking for something, anything. She didn't know what she expected to see.

"I don't see anything."

"Right," Jack agreed. "There is no longer any traffic on either side of the roadway."

Morgan checked the south side of the road. In both directions she saw nothing but the vast, beautiful landscape that should win some kind of highway award. On the north side, again the only vehicle cleaving the wind was the Lexus SUV in which she and Jack traveled.

"Where do you think they are? Should we get off the road?"

"We're going in."

Jack's voice made her look at him. It was cold, hard, determined. His face, even the swollen side, took on the chiseled effect of granite. Whatever was about to happen it was going to happen here.

"I want you to get down on the floor in the back."

"No!"

"Don't argue with me," he shouted. "This time they'll stop at nothing. Now get down."

Morgan moved then. She skirted around behind his chair. He couldn't see her, but she had picked the best place. She was wedged between his seat and a huge metal crate. There was a strap on the wall that Jack had installed. She didn't ask about it, but he felt her using it to strap herself to the reinforced wall.

The van was suddenly jolted as a barrage of bullets churned up the dirt and pavement. Along with it came the sound of helicopter blades beating the air. Jack was glad Morgan was behind him. He didn't need the distraction of trying to make sure she was all right while he dodged bullets.

It was the Apache. Jack was tired of the aircraft tracking them. More than tired, he thought. It loomed in the sky in the path of the SUV like a green bug ready to sting. And this time it had reinforcements. Bullets burst from the onboard guns. Jack ducked, but kept on the straight and narrow. He expected a pellet to hit the windshield, burst the glass and invade the cabin. He wore a bulletproof vest so he was protected from ordinary bullets and if the shooter aimed for his chest. Morgan hadn't protested when he'd insisted she wear one too.

Behind him the trucks were back. Two of them rode within the painted lanes and one used the shoulder. Jack knew this group was with the helicopter. It still bothered him that the others had shot at them. It had given Morgan the cover she needed to get away, but they weren't with these guys. Having two sets of killers out there was disorienting. He needed to deal with these now.

Jack was not without surprises. He'd given Burton and Tilden instructions on what he wanted in the SUV and they had delivered. He wouldn't mind having them around to back him up.

The helicopter hung lower. It was coming in for another bullet run. Jack saw the gunwales begin to turn. He wouldn't wait for another burst. He'd let them feel his sting. Flipping open the specially installed panel on the console that separated the two front seats, Jack hit the red button. On both sides of the van panels opened. Each held a rocket. The navigational system activated, targeting the flying aircraft. Jack hit the green button once and one of the missiles fired. He felt the drag on the van as it took off. It pulled the van to the left, spinning it across the road, out of control. Jack gripped the steering wheel so tightly he thought he'd pull the heavy plastic circle off the column. He tried to fight the ricocheting effect that threw the van back and forth across the double lanes as if some magnet attracted the metal body on one side of the road then the other in a zigzagging, crisscrossing pattern.

Before he regained control, he saw his missile clip its target. "Damn," Jack cursed. It hadn't been a direct hit, but it set the helicopter into a gyro spin. The bird spun around as much out of control as the van. The pilot worked feverishly to keep the bird in the air. It lost altitude. The van careened toward it, three thousand pounds of forged metal at seventy miles an hour. Collision was imminent. Behind them the three trucks brought up the rear, pinning them in like cellar rats.

Jack swerved hard. The helicopter sat down sideways on the pavement, its bulk dropping fast in a test that was never part of any performance evaluation of the bird's air-worthiness. Jack turned the steering wheel while practically standing on the brakes. He could see the gray-white smoke from the tires, smell the burning rubber as friction between the pavement and the tires disagreed in heated proportions.

The van spun completely around, coming to a stop three feet from contact. The Apache was behind him. Its guns were out of position, pointing at the median that divided the highway.

One rotor was bent askew in an angle that had it touching the ground like a balancing rod. The bird was down and out.

The trucks bore down on them. They had a minute perhaps before they got there. Jack switched from brake to accelerator. The SUV lurched forward.

"Jack, what's happening?" Morgan asked.

"Stay put," he ordered, forgetting that Morgan was even in the van. "We're going to play chicken." He muttered the last to himself.

He hadn't done this in years, but he was banking on human nature and the instinct for self-preservation in his enemies. Jack pressed the accelerator harder, increasing his speed. The three trucks in front of him came toward him at a speed equal to his own. Jack stared at them, rushing down the center of the two lanes. If one of them didn't chicken out and swerve the vehicle right or left, they'd have a head-on collision.

He didn't think about anything beyond the speed. The air whistled outside the van. The sound was high and whining as if he was hurting it as he cut through it. Fifty feet, he estimated. This was usually where the average driver peeled off. These were not average drivers.

Forty feet.

Thirty feet.

Still they came forward. Jack held his position. He selected another button on the panel and poised his finger over it.

"Jack." He felt Morgan look around his seat, trying to see through the front windshield.

"Get back," he shouted, pressing the button and letting go a barrage of gunfire that struck the ground in front of the processional.

Twenty feet.

The middle truck driver caved. Pulling his steering wheel to the left, he forced the truck next to him off the road. The two of them collided. The sound of metal mangling was loud as the two vehicles pitched through the guardrail and skidded down the side of the mountain.

Jack didn't brake. He continued traveling south, the opposite direction of the one he wanted to go. Checking his mirror, he saw the final truck swinging around and giving chase. Jack hit the brakes. The resulting squeal of tires and defiance of the laws governing bodies in motion had the Lexus spinning in circles. Plastic boxes, sleeping bags and supplies spilled about the inner space. For a moment he thought of Morgan. Had anything hit her in his attempt? He couldn't look back. He couldn't take his hands off the steering wheel to reach for her.

The truck bore down on him. Chicken wouldn't work this time. This time skill and luck would determine the victor. Jack was a good driver. He'd driven over sand, mud, through mosquito-ridden swamps, on the speedways of the world's top sports arenas and through the traffic of major highways. This fight wouldn't be won by the better driver, but by the one with the best wits and the most luck. Jack was determined to stand in that winner's circle.

Only a hundred yards separated them. He could see someone hang out the window and take a shot. Jack flinched to the side. The bullet struck the windshield. It shattered. His hand instinctively came up to protect his face. The sudden burst of wind took his breath.

Loose papers flew about the small cabin. Unidentified debris scuttled about the floor. A styrofoam cup struck his foot, but he ignored it. What he couldn't ignore was Morgan's voice. "That's it," she shouted.

Jack heard her moving.

"What are you doing?"

Morgan didn't answer. Several seconds went by. She scrambled toward the back of the van. He didn't know what she was doing. He glanced toward the rearview mirror, only to discover it had fallen to the floor when the glass shattered. More bullets chipped the ground in front of the van. He swerved left and right. Morgan would be thrown against the walls if she didn't hit one of the containers that he'd packed food and supplies in. Jack repeated the spray of bullets. They crossed the front of the approaching vehicle level with the lights. Bulbs burst in small explosions. The truck crunched over the glass, although Jack could not hear it. It continued its suicide run straight for him.

The deafening sound of gunfire came from behind him. A tire blew and the on-coming truck defied gravity as it jumped in the air. Morgan knelt in the open column of space, a rifle at her shoulder. Jack pulled to the left. The truck completed its arc on the right. It bounced, leaping into the air like a metallic ballet dancer yet to learn the graceful steps of the dance. Rubber tires came off at odd angles, bouncing and rolling across the highway. Metal bumpers were ripped away as the truck continued its odd streak along the roadway. Tripping over its own feet, it caught a fender piece that had broken loose. The truck flipped on its side, its weight carrying it completely over. Skidding along, creating a sparkle of fire-blue streaks as metal and roadway fought for dominance, the truck moved onward toward Jack and Morgan.

"Get down," he shouted to Morgan. "It's going to be close." Morgan dashed behind his seat and held on. He felt her hands at his waist as she gripped the sides of his chair.

Jack turned the steering wheel as hard as he could. The truck rushed in a straight line directly across the highway. "Here's where the luck comes in," he murmured. The truck headed on an irrevocable angle that would cross paths with their own. He prayed there was time to get out of the way.

There wasn't.

The truck, coming like a rampaging bull, clipped the back of the van. It started a weird spin. Jack heard the sound of metal striking pavement and knew the silver bumper had been yanked free of its moldings. Jack pumped the brakes, bringing the vehicle to a stop in time to see the huge hunk of tangled metal hit the guardrail where it came to a full and complete stop.

For a while everything was silent, the mangled truck engine's ticking the only sound. Morgan's head came up level with his.

"Is it over?" she asked.

He nodded. "It's over."

Morgan let out a sigh and launched herself into his arms. Oh, God, she felt good. Jack released his seat belt and drew her to him. *I love you,* he wanted to say. *I'll love you forever.* But all he said was, "It's over, sweetheart. It's over."

"Not quite," a deep voice contradicted him.

The FBI building in Clarksburg, West Virginia, is a modern structure built in 1993. It stands as a many-windowed white building. The director of this facility doesn't have the protection of the United States and its borders as one of his priorities. He isn't concerned with the enforcement of the law, only keeping track of its paperwork. Clarksburg is a huge computer facility, housing the fingerprint division for the vast resources of law enforcement.

On the third floor, in a corner conference room of dark paneling that looked as if it were polished only moments ago, two men entered the room, joining two others who'd been together far too often in the past weeks. Jacob Winston and Clarence Christopher shook hands with Forrest Washington and Brian Ashleigh before taking seats at one end of a long conference table. A speaker phone sat on the table between them.

"Has there been anything further?" Brian asked.

"Not since Morgan Kirkwood called yesterday," Jacob answered. He knew Forrest was concerned about Jack. "We don't know if she found Jack or not."

She found him. Jacob knew it. He didn't say it out loud. He didn't want to get anyone's hopes up. Yet he was sure Morgan had found Jack. The more he learned about her, talked to her, saw her in the films, the more he liked this woman. She reminded him of two other strong women. The first was his wife, Marianne, whom he worshiped and who he knew was patient and resourceful. The other was Brooke Richards, a former member of his special group of protected people. She'd endured five years of the worst kind of existence. Jacob had watched Brooke being the brave, courageous standard bearer while her own life died, but she didn't give up. She fought with everything she had to save her child and her love for her husband.

Morgan was a lot like them. She hadn't said anything to make him think it, but Jacob knew she wanted to find Jack for more reasons than because he'd saved her life or that he was in trouble because of her. She was in love with him. It was on the films. The way she looked at him twelve years ago. The way he went to her with those roses crushed to her breast. Marianne had noticed it, just as Krysta had seen the ring.

If she hadn't called in, she'd found him and then there would be other things on her mind that took priority over telephone calls to him.

Clarence had authorized a search and there were people out looking for them this minute. They would report in as soon as they found anything.

All they could do now was wait.

The door opened and all eyes turned to look up. A man in a white cook's uniform wheeled a cart in with coffee and food on it. Silently he laid the service out on a low credenza. No one said a word while he worked. He finished and left the room as silently as he'd entered it. The door clicked closed.

The telephone rang.

The unmistakable cock of a handgun sounded close to Morgan's ear. She gasped as she moved back in Jack's arms. He didn't let her go completely.

"Hello again." The green giant was back. Only this time he was wearing blood on his face and arms. His smile of bright white teeth was menacing enough to send a cold finger down her spine. "I underestimated you before, Ms. Kirkwood. Rest assured I won't do it again."

Morgan understood him exactly. She'd played her one and only trump card at their last encounter. This time he'd shackle her too.

Or kill her.

"Separate," he ordered them. "And keep your hands where I can see them."

Morgan raised her hands and moved back. The seat belt Jack had released snapped up. Jack's hands came up too.

"Now, out of the van." He moved around to the front, pointing the gun at Morgan through the windowless frame. "You even think of doing something smart and she gets it."

Jack stepped out.

"Over there." He pointed with one finger to a place away from the van while keeping the gun level and straight on target. Jack moved to the appointed spot.

"Who are you?" Morgan repeated her question from the first time she'd seen him.

"You don't learn, do you?" His face screwed into a dark frown. "I ask the questions. Out of the van."

Morgan started to turn toward the passenger door.

"This way," he said. "That door."

Morgan climbed over the console. It was awkward getting into the driver's seat. She lost her balance. Her leg fell onto the console. Bullets came out the front of the van and cut the giant across the legs. The giant screamed in pain.

Jack moved as he went down. He grabbed the gun from his hand and checked for others. Morgan jumped down from the driver's seat and joined him.

"Good thinking," he said. The man on the ground writhed with pain. Blood covered his legs, soaking into the fabric of his fatigues. The big man had tears running down his face.

Morgan got the first-aid kit from the truck. "I'm going to look at your legs," she told him. "But first . . ." She pulled out the set of handcuffs he'd forced her to shackle herself with and cuffed his hands behind him. Then she cut his pants legs and looked at the places the bullets had cut. He had two wounds in each leg. "You're lucky," she told him. "Apparently the bullets didn't hit anything vital. You'll be well when they strap you in the electric chair."

As she bandaged his legs, the sound came again. She and Jack looked at the sky at the same time.

"I thought the helicopter crashed."

"It did," he said. Jack looked behind them at the crippled Apache sitting on the road a quarter of a mile away.

"I hear another one."

"Let's get out of here." Morgan jumped up and started for the van. Jack grabbed her arm and stopped her. "What?"

Jack let out a whoop that would rival a victory yell.

"Jack!" Morgan pulled at his arm. They had to get away. Why was he hesitating? They were standing out in the open. Jack put his arm around her and pointed to the approaching bird.

"Look," he said, laughing. "The cavalry's arrived."

Jim Burton landed the black helicopter with the FBI decal on the side thirty feet from where Jack and Morgan stood. The green giant, still lying on the ground where he'd fallen, squeezed his eyes shut and pulled his body up and away from the churning debris caused by the aircraft's rotors. Morgan shaded her eyes until the blades slowed. With both hands she pushed wisps of hair back. The smile on her face at the approaching savior must have been as wide as an ocean. She was just as glad to see him as she'd been to find Jack alive last night. Relief threaded through her with the force of Niagara Falls.

"How'd you find us?" Jack asked as the roar of wind died down to normal.

"I got here as fast as I could after the phone call."

"Phone call?"

"I hoped Jacob would still be monitoring the line," Morgan explained. "While you were busy swerving all over the highway, the phone skittered across the floor. That's when I released the belt and lunged for it. I hit the redial button and then got the rifle."

"We got a call to get in the air," Burton picked up the story. "And speaking of calls, there's a really angry man on the headset who wants to talk to you, Jack."

Jack smiled and started for the helicopter.

"There was a roadblock in front of and behind you," Burton continued. "We've got them. The locals should be here any minute."

"Hey, I'm lying here. Bleeding." The green giant spoke like a wayward child being ignored.

"You're lucky you're not lying there dead," Morgan stated with more bravado than she felt. She hadn't thought when she pressed that button. Jack was outside and the green giant had a gun. She was trapped. *They* were trapped with nowhere to go. This time he wouldn't give them time to escape and he'd told her he'd treat her with the same care and consideration he'd given Jack. It was push that button or die.

Morgan's eyes were closed when the bullets began to fly. If they hit him in the chest or some vital part of his body, she didn't know what she'd feel, but she had to take the chance. And she was glad she'd only wounded him, even though he would not have given her the same consideration.

She checked his legs from her position out of his reach. The bandages were soaked with blood, but he'd be fine. He wouldn't die.

''What happened here?'' Burton asked.

''They chased us. Three trucks and the skybird. He was in the chopper.'' She indicated the man lying on the ground and then related the entire ordeal for Burton, ending with Jack's comment on the cavalry's arrival.

''Who are you working for?'' Burton asked the man.

''Yo mama,'' he snarled.

At that moment they heard the sirens. Coming toward them was a six-pack of police cars.

''Great,'' Morgan said, glancing down. ''We can turn you over to them.''

Blue and red lights on the car's crossbar cycled back and forth, like colored strobes. Sirens blared as if they were horn testers out for a final run before horns were forever banned. Morgan covered her ears.

''How are Allie and Jan?''

Burton's face suddenly turned soft. ''Out of their minds with worry.''

Morgan knew how he felt about Jan. She hoped her friend would give him a chance. Morgan liked him. He seemed a really good guy, like Jack.

''You didn't call,'' Burton was saying when she brought her attention back to him. ''I practically had to tie Jan up to get in the chopper without her. I promised I'd let her know immediately when I found you.''

They both looked at Jack. He was obviously trying to get a word in. Morgan could see his mouth say the word ''but'' as if he were stuck in a rerun. The cars, their sirens winding down, came to a stop a few feet behind the van. Uniformed officers, guns drawn and ready, rushed to them.

Jim Burton held up his identification badge. The officers acknowledged it. ''Everything all right here?'' A tall man with graying hair and the build of an ex-football player spoke.

''There's a helicopter up there.'' Morgan pointed to a place behind Jack. ''He came out of it.'' The green giant smirked at her. ''There were also three trucks. Two of them went over the side. The other is there.''

The officers listened to her and the obvious leader dispersed men to check out the places Morgan mentioned.

She glanced at Jack. He had his arm over his head as he leaned on the windshield of the helicopter. But *he* was talking. He'd managed to get a word in and probably taken over the conversation, she thought.

The officers moved around her. Like a well-oiled machine they split into teams and went to work taking care of the wounded or the trucks. A car with two officers sped around them and headed for the downed helicopter around the bend. The other officers knew what to do. They appeared to be locking down everything, making sure there was no danger from explosions or surprise attacks.

The tinkling sound of a cell phone went off. Burton pulled a unit from his pocket and the ringing became louder. He spoke in short, cryptic phrases. Without a good-bye or a word to her, he pressed a button and replaced the phone in his pocket. Then he went to the tall officer in charge and spoke quickly.

Coming back to her, he indicated she should follow him. Morgan had to walk fast to keep up with him. They joined Jack, who ended his phone call as they approached. Burton helped her into the bird without a word. Jack and Burton got in the front seats. Climbing into the back, Morgan remembered the last time she got aboard a helicopter. Her heart beat a little faster even though she didn't expect to have to dive out of this one. She sat behind Jack, nervous, unsure of what was about to happen.

Morgan felt as if she were being rushed. Most of her life she had controlled her own destiny. She'd been her own champion of causes, responsible for herself, making her own decisions. Now, as this bird lifted her off the ground, she felt as if she'd been inside some game. For twelve years she'd been running around in circles, back and forth through the same maze of tunnels, going nowhere.

And now the sign read, "Game Over."

She'd lost.

CHAPTER 16

The FBI's Criminal Justice and Information Services—Fingerprint Identification Division Complex was a multimillion-dollar construction project. The complete complex sat on 986 acres within the city of Clarksburg. Total employment at the facility exceeded 3,600 people.

The whitewashed, three-story building flurried out in an array of connected facilities. It had no helicopter pad. The chopper set down at the edge of a parking lot that had been cordoned off. A car sat on the other side of the orange and white barrier. Two men got out as soon as Burton turned the engine off and the whine of the blades started to fade.

Jack and Burton got out. She sat where she was, her throat dry, her legs feeling as heavy as lead pillars. Two men walked toward them. The taller one was lanky with dark hair. He didn't squint even though the sun shone directly in his face. He moved with an air of confidence that spoke of quiet control. The second man was shorter. His body was squarely cut, square shoulders leading to a thick but not fat waistline. Morgan had the impression that he was solid from the skin all the way through.

Jack smiled and shook hands with the shorter man. Then they hugged in that awkward I-am-a-man-and-men-don't-hug manner. Morgan knew this had to be Forrest Washington. She remembered his name now. Jack then shook hands with the other man. They said something to each other, but Morgan couldn't hear what it was. She still sat in her seat.

She stared through the glass in front of her, unseeing, unmoving, afraid of what was to happen. She'd been running for what seemed like years, but her journey ended here. It was over. She'd get out and walk into that bright, white building and her life would never be hers again.

Briefly, she thought of Hart Lewiston. Her father. She'd never get to know him. She hadn't decided if she even wanted to know him, but the decision wouldn't be hers. Even as president he couldn't protect her from a bullet.

And Jack.

She did move when she thought of Jack. He was still talking to Forrest Washington. Morgan reached for the door and pushed it open. Outside it stood the other man, the tall one. He had clear blue eyes that were trusting. Morgan found it hard to look away from him. His presence spoke of safety and care. She actually thought he cared about her. A stranger cared about her safety.

"I'm Jacob Winston," he said. "Director of the—"

"You don't have to introduce yourself." She'd never met him in person, but she knew who he was. Once she thought of him as her savior. Today he appeared as her jailer, kind eyes or not.

"Neither do you." His mouth curved into something less than a smile. "I've seen films and photos of you."

Morgan dropped her eyes. Everyone had seen those films.

She'd done the deed, performed for the world and no one would ever let her live it down. They saw it as pride. She could tell that even Jacob Winston, honcho of the witness protection program, thought of her as a national hero. While all she remembered was risking her life, nearly losing her life for—

She stopped. For her father. She'd saved the man who fathered her, who said he didn't know about her, but claimed her for some unknown reason.

"I was very young in those films," she said.

"And very brave," he finished.

He helped her out of the aircraft. The white letters F-B-I

caught her attention as she stepped onto the blacktop. She looked at the man Jack was talking to, then up at Jacob.

"Forrest Washington?"

Jacob nodded at her question. The two men stopped talking and Forrest looked at her.

"I'm glad you're safe," he said.

Morgan reached out and shook hands with him. He was only a couple of inches taller than she was, and for all his bulk his hands were surprisingly soft and gentle. Not like Jack's, which were rough and calloused. Washington's skin was a darker brown than her own, but where her underlying pigment was yellow, his was red. He wore a mustache and his brown eyes were serious and concerned.

"Why don't we go inside," he said. Instead of walking the short distance, a car was there and they all piled into it. The ride was only seconds long, then they went into the white building and were led to a conference room on the third floor. Waiting for them were two men. One of them, a man in his fifties she estimated, had a shock of white hair and ruddy complexion. It made him stand out against the dark wood paneling. Morgan recognized him. She'd seen him a few times years ago. He was introduced to her as Clarence Christopher, director of the FBI. The other man was Brian Ashleigh, director of the CIA. He had the kind of face that was hard to put an age to. Morgan assumed, due to his position, that he was probably a contemporary of the FBI director. His eyes were light brown, and his blond hair was graying in streaks and balding on the crown of his head.

Morgan was dutifully impressed but didn't say anything. She wondered why they were here and for her. She assumed Jacob would accompany her back to Washington and from there she'd be sent to her new home with a new identity. Then she remembered Hart Lewiston and her relationship to him. Were they here because her father would probably be the next president?

She shook hands with them both and sat down. Jack set a cup of coffee in front of her and took the seat next to hers. Morgan wanted to take his hand. She needed something to hold onto, but she only watched as Jack tore a sugar packet open and dumped the contents into his own cup of hot liquid. Then as usual, Jack stuffed the top he'd torn into the bottom and dropped them on the polished table. Morgan lifted her cup and sipped. She was suddenly extremely hungry.

She tried to concentrate on food. When was the last time she ate? What time was it? But she couldn't. She could only think that there were too many people in this room. Maybe it had to do with Hart Lewiston. He was political and the top men in the agencies were here to stay on his good side. If he were elected president they would work for him. It wouldn't hurt to make sure his daughter received their attention.

She stole another glance at Jack.

"Jacob." She sought out the only man, other than Jack, she could put her trust in. The silence had gone on too long. "What happens to me now?"

Her question garnered more quiet and looks passed between the men in the room. Morgan's ears turned red hot. She took Jack's hand under the table.

"We hadn't planned to get into any details," Jacob said. "You and Jack have been through a lot. You're probably hungry and tired."

"I want to know," she said before he could go on.

"That is not an easy question, Ms. Kirkwood," the white-haired director of the FBI answered. "Your father . . . complicates things."

"My father?"

"Hart Lewiston."

"I know who you mean. What does he have to do with this?"

"It's not like we can put the daughter of the next president in the program."

Anger flashed through Morgan. It was irrational. She didn't want to go into the program. It would mean leaving Jack. She wanted to be with him. She wanted to spend her life with him. Yet that survival instinct inside her had been loosened. She wanted to live. She'd been dead all these years and she didn't want her life to return to that existence. Going into the program would close a cell door on her, return her to the place she did not want to be. Yet the words in her heart broke forth of their own volition.

"I don't believe the decision is his."

Jack woke up in a safe house in northern Virginia. He'd been asleep for almost twelve hours and his head ached from too much sleep. It had felt good to lie on a soft pillow, pale green sheets that smelled like flowers and a soft comforter that made him yearn for Morgan. Jack had spent a lot of his life in places where beds weren't an option and other places where the ground was preferable. His assignments didn't often call for scented sheets and mattresses.

He wasn't sure if he didn't want one of those places now. As long as he could keep Morgan with him. Yesterday Jacob had ended the meeting shortly after it began. Morgan was in no condition to endure a long meeting, he'd said. He'd been partially right. Jack and Morgan both needed to rest. Now that they were in protective custody they could afford to wait another twenty-four hours to straighten out the details. Jack wanted the reprieve. Another day with Morgan. He wanted another night with her too, but by the time they'd flown to Washington and then been transported to this place, Morgan had been worn out. She'd never admit it, but she looked tired and he felt it.

Morgan was in the next room. He wondered if she was awake. Leaving the bed, he pulled on clean pants. Clothes had been sent to him. The sizes were perfect and the clothes were stiff with newness. Asking where they came from would be useless. He just pulled them on.

Outside, the lawn was long. The property, dotted with weeping willow trees that swayed in the soft breeze, was huge. He could see a paddock in the distance. The smell of horses wafted on the air with the scent of freshly cut grass.

Jack poked his head around the door adjoining his room to Morgan's. He'd left her there after their arrival. He'd wanted to stay with her, hold her, but they needed sleep more than they needed each other. She'd fallen asleep as soon as she got out of the shower. Jack had retired to his room and done the same.

Morgan sat in the middle of the bed, her knees up, her hands hugging them, her face turned toward the windows. The room was modern, complemented with furniture that was low and had straight lines. One wall was all windows. Morgan had opened the curtains and light filtered in. After sleeping in caves and vans covered with branches, he understood her insistence that they leave the curtains open last night.

She wore a pink nightgown. Her hair was pushed back from her face, reminding Jack of the morning he'd seen her swimming in the mountain lake. She appeared to be watching the horses.

"Hi," he said. He approached the bed.

"Hi," she answered. She didn't smile. She'd been deep in thought. "Did you sleep well?"

"No," he told her. She smiled then and he knew she understood his meaning. They'd been together constantly for the past few weeks. Sleeping without her had only happened because he was exhausted. If he'd stayed with her neither of them would have slept and they both knew it.

Jack sat on the covers. She reached for him. He came closer to her, immediately taking the soft hand, noticing the cuts and bruises that marred her arm, souvenirs of their ordeal. The marks would fade in time, but the sight of them cut through his gut like a rusty knife.

Morgan leaned forward. Her arms went around him. Jack folded her into his embrace and squeezed her close. She smelled of the soap and shampoo she'd used the night before. Jack inhaled deeply. She was warm and soft and he wanted nothing more than to hold onto her forever.

"Do you know anything?" she asked softly.

"Nothing that you don't know." He kissed her neck. "Only that Hart Lewiston is pulling out all the stops to find out where you are." Morgan pulled back and looked at Jack. "How do you feel about him?"

"I haven't really had time to think much about him." She looked confused. "There is so much to think about. He's a senator. He's going to be president. He's from a different life. And I'm a grown woman. It might have been different if I were twelve and on the streets. Then I'd have given anything for a warm bed.'' She smoothed her hand over the pink sheets. ''Now, I could only be a liability to him and . . .''

''And you?'' Jack prompted.

She frowned in an expression that said she had many problems and none with a solution. Hart Lewiston was only one of them. Jack understood. He had his own unsolvable complications.

''He's going to be the next president,'' Jack continued. ''His announcement about you caused a dip in the polls, but he'll recover. His father is a Supreme Court judge. He's popular, a national hero.'' Jack tipped her face up to look into her eyes. ''That makes you a very important person.''

''I don't feel very important,'' she said. ''Just scared.''

Jack was scared too. He didn't know if she could see it in his eyes, but he didn't try to disguise it this time. He wanted her to see him, see into his soul and know everything he thought and felt. He pulled her forward and kissed her. He couldn't not kiss her. He was scared of being without her again. Terrified. He knew what it was like to carry around a love so heavy that it was painful to push it aside and do other things, and he knew what it was like to run out of time. They were nearly out of it.

Emotion streaked through him like a lightning rod and he kissed her deeply. He held her close, feeling her softness, imprinting her lines on him, slipping his hands over the satiny feel of her nightgown, rubbing the backs of his hands over her breasts, swallowing the soft breath of surprise that escaped her throat when his touch reached one of her erogenous zones.

Jack felt himself grow hard. He wanted her. Centuries must have passed since he'd last held her. And this could be the final time. He knew he shouldn't. He knew it wasn't fair to either of them. They should talk, but he couldn't help himself. Pushing her down among all the pink folds of the bedcovers, he kissed her shoulders, her collarbone, listened for her short intake of breath that had become familiar when they made love. He loved her, would always love her. He kissed her again, long and deep, his hands buried deep in the richness of her hair. He couldn't believe the way she made him feel. Did other people feel like this? How could he ever have thought he was alive before he met her? How was he to survive without her with him? She wasn't his other half. With them there were no halves, no quarters, no parts at all. With them there was only a whole. Together they were one solitary unit, one entity, one intensely burning flame that burst into being whenever they came together, one single form of energy, packed densely as if the bonding between them was now and forever.

Moving one tiny scrap of fabric no wider than half an inch, Jack kissed the skin he uncovered. He repeated the action on her other shoulder. Morgan's arms slipped down Jack's. He felt her fingers trail over his skin. Jack pulled her up and released the straps from the prison of her arms. The gown pooled at her waist, baring her breasts. Jack groaned when he saw the clear, smooth skin that covered her from neck to waist.

Lowering his head he kissed one puckered nipple and was rewarded by her catch of breath and the arms that clutched his head, holding him to her. Her nipple pebbled in his mouth. He listened to her pleasure-moans, the sound driving him on.

She was so smooth, so soft. He wanted to know every inch of her, touch her, taste her. He wanted to learn her secrets, explore her caverns, and, once learned, return for a second pass. He wanted to make that pass every day, include it in his daily routine, look forward to waking in the morning and finding her with him.

Jack eased back and slipped the gown down legs as long as Pennsylvania Avenue. He felt himself pressing harder against the denim of his jeans with each inch of leg exposed under the pink covering. He wanted to be inside her.

Pulling the zipper on his own pants, he rid himself of them and joined her on the bed.

"I don't think I'm going to be able to live without you," he whispered in her ear. His hands slipped under her, taking her hips and lifting her up to meet his entry. He closed his eyes, clenching his teeth, clamping down on the pleasure that ran through him as he pushed himself into her. Waves of pleasure splashed through him as he filled her, going deeper and deeper with each thrust, driving himself into her until he thought he would explode. Morgan moaned his name in his ear. She kissed him, kissed him all over, holding him with her hands

and then her legs. She circled him with those unending legs.
Jack had to have died and gone to heaven.

Jack nearly shouted. He couldn't hold on. He couldn't hold
anything back. He let her know through his body that he loved
her, with each thrust that he worshiped her, with each kiss that
as much as he might try, he could never forget her. He'd wasted
so much time, precious time. They'd spent a lifetime apart and
they'd lived a lifetime in the past two weeks.

Jack knew he was going to die here, today, in a moment.
Morgan was finally going to kill him. He couldn't stop himself.
He no longer had the strength. Morgan had him clutched to
her and he never wanted her to let go. He felt his release. The
wave building in him, overwhelming him with the force of
pleasure so strong that it would drive him to death. He willingly
went, followed Morgan, jumped with her, rode with her, carried
her. He was power and she was powerful.

Flipping over, Jack traded places with her. She took control
immediately, although neither of them really had any. They
were spurred on by forces beyond the two of them, beyond
explanation. Magic, voodoo, poltergeist, Jack didn't know and
didn't care. He only knew that it happened with Morgan. She
was the catalyst, the fireworks display, the woman of his
dreams, the woman he wanted to marry.

He buried his face in her shoulder, muffling her name, as
their bodies joined and rejoined. He burned for her and the
burning consumed them, seared them into one bright, white-
hot light. Morgan collapsed on his chest. His breathing was
raspy, labored, hard. He dragged air into his lungs as a wave
of pure sensation tore through him. His arms tightened around
Morgan. He repeated her name over and over, whispering it in
her ear, running his hands over her lithe body, over her incredi-
bly long legs and over hips that were made for the contour of
his palms.

He didn't know if he could ever describe what she did to
him, how she made him feel or even if they could repeat this
impossibly wonderful love that happened between them. He
knew without a doubt that he loved her, that he'd given her
everything he had to give.

Even his headache was gone.

* * *

The horses fascinated her. Morgan had never seen a horse up close. She never knew she liked them. She'd seen the mounted police in Central Park in New York. And she'd seen horses pulling hansom cabs during a short trip to Chicago, but none of those horses were as beautiful as the ones running on the other side of the track. Morgan propped her arms on the slatted fence and watched. They moved with sureness, confidence, defying gravity as they danced in the morning sun.

"Do you ride?"

Morgan turned toward the voice. Jacob Winston stood next to her at the fence. She hadn't heard him approach. Her concentration had been on the horses.

"I've never been on a horse," she told him.

"Would you like to go for a ride?"

"I don't think so." She shook her head.

"You can go anytime you wish. Just let them know." He glanced toward the stables.

"I will," Morgan smiled, knowing she wouldn't. "I want to thank you."

"For what?"

He put his foot on the bottom rung of the fence. Morgan turned back to watch the majesty as horse and rider played with the wind and the sun in the distant field.

"For getting me out of that room yesterday."

He smiled. Morgan liked him. She'd liked his voice on the other end of the phone and the way he hadn't argued with her when she called and told him she needed information. He sounded concerned for her safety then and she knew now that he did care about her. Why, she didn't understand. They didn't know each other, yet he didn't look at her as if she'd gotten herself into this predicament and he had to get her out. She glanced at the ring on his third finger. He was married. His wife must be a very lucky woman.

"You needed time. Running for your life is hard work." She laughed then, realizing she hadn't laughed in weeks. "The Clarksburg location receives requests for more than fifty thousand fingerprint matches per day. It was built for that purpose, but it's not set up for meetings that needed the kind of security yours would.''

"Are we about to have that meeting now?"

"Not out here. I came to give you a message."

"A message?"

Morgan's hands tightened on the fence although she didn't know why. Jacob told her immediately.

"Hart Lewiston wants to see you."

"I can't." She bowed her head, leaning it on the rough splintered wood.

"There's a strong possibility that when you leave here you'll be going into permanent protective custody. It might be your only chance to talk to him."

"I'm not ready."

Morgan had seen Hart's face on television. He'd looked at her from every newspaper from Missouri to Washington, D.C. She'd heard his voice, knew his smile. She'd watched him speak, knew the way he stood for the camera with his wife holding onto his arm and smiling. She knew everything about him, yet he was a stranger.

Morgan had carried him, scooped him up and put him in a kangaroo pouch, and like a trapeze artist, flown through the air. Yet she wasn't prepared to face him.

How was she supposed to act? What did a grown woman say when she met her father for the first time? Should she joke? Should she be humble? Aggressive? Angry? Should she tell him she didn't need him after her mother died and she didn't need him now? She was used to surviving on her own. She could tell him she was onto his scheme, that she understood his motives. That she knew he only wanted to use her as a pawn in the Hart Lewiston political election machine.

"Just start with hello and see where it takes you," Jacob brought her back to the present.

"You must be a father." She looked up at him.

He took a position at the fence like hers and smiled and looked into space for a moment. "My daughter is three."

"She's very lucky."

"*I'm* the lucky one. I can't imagine life without her."

Morgan saw where he was going. "It's different with you.

You've been with your daughter all her life. You two have a history together. It might only be three years old, but for her it's her whole life. Hart and I . . ." She faced him, spreading her hands. "We have nothing."

"You have something, Morgan." He stared into her eyes, giving her the chance to remember.

"I saved his life," she said.

"You could have died getting him out of there," Jacob reminded her. "He knows that."

The metropolitan area around Washington, D.C., which included this secluded Virginia landscape, was usually bathed in humidity at this time of the year. Fortunately they were enjoying a brief period where the air was warm and breathable. Yet the doors to the house were closed and the air conditioning was running. Jacob stood with his back to the room.

The library of the safe house faced the paddock fences where he had left Morgan. She no longer stood at the fence. She'd stayed there a while watching the horses as she had been doing when he found her. Then she walked toward the stables. He waited for her to come back into his line of vision. He assumed she'd changed her mind about riding.

She was safe here. Everyone on this property had been hand-picked. Even the stable hands had security clearance.

"Is this what you brought me down here for?" Jacob turned as Forrest Washington came into the room. Jack entered on his heels.

"Jacob, I'm glad you're here," Jack said.

Washington was carrying a single sheet of paper. Jacob glanced through the window. Morgan came out of the stables. He recognized the agent holding the reins of two horses. One was a gentle mare. The hand helped her into the saddle and climbed on his own animal. Together they left in a slow walk.

Washington handed him the paper. Jacob read it and handed it back.

"You're not surprised?" Washington asked.

"I knew."

"It's why I came home," Jack said.

Washington turned and stared at him. "You came home to resign?"

Jack nodded.

"Well what stopped you?" Forrest Washington was not prone to frequent anger, but Jacob recognized it now.

"I met Jacob for lunch. Then . . ." He stopped. "I got side-tracked," he ended weakly.

"I think you need a vacation. Take some time to yourself," Washington began. "The past few months have been a nightmare. Then to come home and run into this."

"I don't need a vacation," Jack shouted. For a moment the room was quiet. No one said anything. Jack turned away from them. A moment later he turned back. "I want out, Forrest. I'm going into witness protection with Morgan."

He sat back in the chair, his hands steepled in front of him. He stared through the small triangle the hands created. The appearance was calm, but his slanted eyes told him differently. It had been minutes since he said anything. He appeared to concentrate on the walls. They were covered with silk prints of flaming dragons and ugly dogs. The stones in the flooring were colored, tan and brown with a few red ones. At least he wasn't sitting on loose stones. He didn't know which room he preferred more. Then he thought he'd rather be outside than in any of these rooms. They were too . . . too much. If they were bright, they were too bright. If they were dark, they were too dark. Too small. Too crowded or too sparse. Nothing was done in moderation, only extremes.

"All of them?" the other man asked, but he already knew the answer.

"Those that are still alive are in the hands of the FBI."

"I suppose I don't have to say how disappointed I am." The statement was spoken with a calmness he was known for. He could sit peacefully or he could flare into a raging dragon. In either mood his eyes were piercing. This time he looked a little different, however. This time it was personal. He was involved in this one more than any of the others. How, was the question. Nevertheless there was no question that all the facts weren't known. No one would put so much effort into finding one woman and now a man. "What do you plan to do to rectify this situation?"

Facing the older man, he swallowed hard. All he had was bad news. "At the moment we don't know where they've taken Ms. Kirkwood. She was at the FBI headquarters in West Virginia, but she's been moved. My guess is to a safe house, but it could be anywhere."

The other man shot up from his chair so fast it slid across the room and hit the wall behind him. "Find them," he shouted. "I will have no further delays or excuses. I want her and I want him. I want them dead and those papers in my hands."

He spread his hands, palms out, so the contrast of light and dark could clearly be seen. Compared with his own, the other man's hands were small, stubby, his fingernails short. He was proud of telling people how long the lines were. He would have a long life and live well. He proved he could live well by his surroundings.

Looks, however, were deceiving. The room was appointed with expensive pieces, dynasty items that had been transported all the way around the world to get here. Even people who had no idea of the worth of Oriental furniture could tell from the weight and high gloss of the room that it was populated with many American dollars. Regardless of the international exchange rates, nothing diminished the flash of the green. Yet all the money in the world couldn't wash the dirt off this man's hands.

"Come back again without completing this job"—he leaned forward, his fingers bearing his weight as he leaned on the desk—"and we'll use your blood to paint the rest of the stones in this floor."

He stood up and turned to leave. As he reached for the door panel, it opened. Three men stepped inside. One in front and two flanking the leader.

"FBI," he said.

"How do I look?" Morgan checked her image in the mirror for the tenth time in the last half hour. She'd changed clothes four times. She had on a black strapless gown with a white sash around the waist. "Cleavage," she said. She put her hands up. "Too much cleavage." She couldn't wear this. It was way too sexy.

She grabbed the zipper and pulled it down.

"Morgan, what are you doing?" Jack asked.

"I can't wear this. It shows too much . . ." She spread her hands. The dress slipped to the floor.

"Not as much as you're showing now."

She looked at herself. She wore a one-piece bustier, thigh-high stockings and three-inch heels. Everything she had on was fire engine red. She didn't know whose idea it was to buy this underwear. She hadn't ordered any of it, but she had had some like this before she blew her house up in St. Charles.

Jack picked up one of the other dresses. He held it by the rhinestone straps. Red. It had a fitted bodice and a skirt that billowed out at the bottom. It felt like liquid gold against her legs.

"Hart Lewiston is outwitting the press and his campaign people to make this little dinner. He'll be here in ten minutes. If you don't get dressed we are going to be conspicuously absent from dinner."

Jack had fire in his eyes when she looked at him. She felt the sting of desire in her belly. Jack approached her and for a moment they stared into each other's eyes. He had on a black tuxedo. He looked devastating. For a moment Morgan considered staying in the room. She would much rather make love with Jack than go through the ordeal of making small talk with a famous stranger.

Jack went down on one knee. He held the dress for her. Morgan stepped into it. Jack started raising it, dragging the fabric up her legs. Before he got to the tops of her thighs, the place where the stockings ended and she began, he leaned forward and kissed her skin. Morgan shuddered, grabbing his shoulders as sensation ran through her, threatening to buckle her knees. Jack pulled back and continued to cover her skin as fabric grew from the floor until he was standing upright and she was threading her arms through the jeweled straps.

"I'm scared." Why had she agreed to this? Jacob and Jack

had convinced her to meet Hart. It wouldn't kill her, they had said. "He wants to meet you," Jack had said. "And you want to meet him too. He's the family you always wanted."

Morgan was too afraid. It was going to be a disaster. There was no reason for her to meet Hart Lewiston. Why wasn't he out campaigning? He needed to regain the points he'd lost in the polls, not fly in here to meet a thirty-one-year-old daughter he'd never actually seen.

"You look fine," Jack said as he zipped her in and turned her around. He was calm while her heart was racing to the beat of a drum. "You look beautiful, with your hair up like that." He touched hair she'd curled and styled and pulled up into a mane on the top of her head. One micro-braid hung down the side of her face to her chin. "You looked like this when you came into your house, wearing that black dress and high heels."

"Jack, I don't want to do this."

He folded her in his arms. "Sure you do," he whispered. "If you don't, you'll wonder for the rest of your life what he was like. You'll kick yourself for a missed opportunity."

"I know what he's like."

Jack was shaking his head as she spoke. "You know his television image, his political views, his public service. You don't know the man."

Morgan leaned back. "He could be a terrible person in private."

"You'll want to know that too," Jack reassured her.

Morgan kissed him on the cheek. She put her arms around his neck and held on for a while. Jack knew what to say. That was one of the things Morgan loved about him.

"Ready?" he asked, pushing her back.

"Give me a minute." She went to the dresser. "Someone bought this jewelry. The least I can do is wear it." She put a pair of red teardrop earrings through her pierced ears, and their length danced along her jaw. Jack took the matching necklace, made of a gold chain with a red teardrop stone at the end, from Morgan and fastened it about her neck.

She picked up a tissue and turned to him, wiping her lipstick from his cheek.

"Ready," she said. Together they left the room. The corridor was wide and Morgan slipped her arm through his as they reached the top of the stairs. She looked down. What was this evening going to be like? she wondered.

She and Jack started down. Jack stopped halfway to the bottom. "There's something I want you to remember for the rest of the evening. Whenever you're afraid or at a loss for something to say."

Morgan tightened her grip on his arm. She looked up at him. "What is it?" she asked.

He leaned toward her. "Red is your color," he whispered close to her lips. "And I'll be thinking about getting my hands on the tops of those stockings every time I look at you."

There was more security here than he'd seen in any place on the campaign trail. Hart had no doubt that everyone from the chopper pilot to the maid that opened the door for them had the highest security clearance. He was used to security. Campaigning these days meant taking your life in your hands. There were plenty of crazies out there looking to be the next James Earl Ray or Sirhan Sirhan.

The helicopter ride had been short, no more than thirty minutes, although his watch had been removed before he boarded the craft and he and Carla had been blindfolded. He didn't know where they actually were. It was disorienting not being able to see. For a moment it had taken him back to his ordeal in Korea where part of his torture was to be blindfolded and beaten. He probably would have had a more troublesome time of it, except that Carla had complained the entire way about the absurdity of such a device. He'd never seen her so agitated. She'd insisted on accompanying him, although he'd told her he could do this alone. Still she persisted. Hart admired his wife. He knew she felt uncertain, confused, out of control. He felt the same, but he couldn't let that stop him. When those papers arrived a week ago, he was stunned. It brought his love for Rose Kirkwood back to him.

Hart had been surprised by the fire of it. He thought he was over her. He loved Carla. She was his wife of twenty-three years, but he never forgot Rose, and they'd made a daughter.

How could he not want to see her, talk to her, make her part of his life? But Carla's life was connected to his, and if he brought Morgan into it, he would have to have his wife's consent.

She'd sat rigidly during the ride here, but now she appeared to relax. Her face wasn't as pale as it had been. Hart knew she didn't like to fly. They'd arrived in a helicopter, a flight quite different from an airplane. Maybe now that she was back on the ground she would have more command of herself.

They went into a large drawing room. The walls were a muted blue. The furniture was dark and heavy and the chandelier that lit the room was huge and bright. Hart was reminded of the White House. A uniformed waiter, complete with white gloves and silver tray, brought him a drink he hadn't ordered. Hart tasted the orange juice and ginger ale concoction. He didn't drink often and liked the juice drink more than alcohol. It was exactly as he liked it. He had no doubt Carla's was also to her liking.

"Ms. Kirkwood will be in shortly," the waiter said and left them alone. Hart took a sip of his drink and looked at the huge painting of the Jefferson Memorial over the dark fireplace.

"Any idea where—" Carla began, but stopped when the door clicked. They both turned at the sound. The door opened and Morgan came inside. She walked directly toward them. Hart didn't know who he expected to see. He had the image of a nineteen-year-old, wearing a leotard and poised on a narrow beam. The woman who crossed the carpet with a tight smile wasn't nineteen and she wasn't wearing a leotard. His knees went weak and he set the glass down on the mantel where he stood.

After so many years he thought it was impossible. He never expected to see her again, but Rose Kirkwood, the image of Rose Kirkwood, floated in front of him and then stopped. He swallowed, knowing if he tried to speak at that moment his voice would only croak. He stared at her. She was as tall as Carla. Her skin was clear and smooth and he noticed her cheeks were tinged with an undercoat of blush that wasn't makeup, but some heightened sense of nerves. He felt it too.

"You look like your mother," he said.

* * *

Morgan didn't know what to say. So she said nothing. She stood looking at her father. He thought she looked like her mother, but seeing him was like seeing herself. She wondered why other women looked in the mirror as they grew older and saw the reflection of their parents, either more of their mother than they wanted or more of their father than they ever thought possible. Morgan saw her mother's eyes and her smile. People told her that when she was a child. She'd been able to see them ever since she was a young girl. She did have her mother's eyes and her mouth. Looking at the man across the room from her, she knew everything else about her appearance came from him.

Yet when he looked at her he saw her mother. Did he want to see her mother in her? She was brown, but the undercoat of yellow was directly derived from him.

She smiled at his statement, not contradicting him.

"Hello," she said, offering her hand to Carla. "I'm Morgan Kirkwood. You're Carla Lewiston." Carla accepted her hand. Her fingers were cold as they closed around hers. "I thought we might want to talk for a few minutes alone."

Carla looked stately. Her clothes said she was ready to carry out the duties of the First Lady with as much pomp and circumstance as any of the past First Ladies. Her sequined gown was royal blue with hidden slit pockets. One of Carla's hands disappeared in that pocket. The other hand held a matching purse. She played nervously with the short strap.

Morgan sat down on one of the sofas in front of the fireplace. Hart and Carla faced her. She noticed Carla take his hand as if she needed the solid protection of his presence. Morgan couldn't believe she appeared so calm. Inside her stomach was boiling. Jack had offered to stand with her, but this was something she needed to do alone.

Neither of them spoke and the silence stretched. "I'm a little nervous," she finally said. "I never expected to find my father alive or that it could be you. I thought . . ." she hesitated. "I thought you might want to have everything confirmed."

"Confirmed?" Carla spoke for the first time.

"Blood tests," Morgan suggested.

"We don't have to talk about that now," Hart said. "Tell me about you."

Morgan didn't want to talk about herself. Her story wasn't especially pretty. She hadn't grown up taking dance classes or being one of the cheerleaders in school. It was natural that he'd want to know about her, but it wasn't a story she wanted to tell. She was surprised he didn't already know everything there was to know.

She gave him the abridged version of her life, leaving out all the bad, only telling him that her mother died and she was adopted and went on to join the gymnastics team. The way she told the story you'd never know she lived on the streets, scavenging food and watching her best friend bleed to death. She wore an expensive dress, her hair was curled and her makeup flawless. She looked like someone living the American Dream, but Morgan lived the American Nightmare and it hadn't ended yet.

Dinner was better than she expected it to be, mostly due to Jack. Morgan was placed at the head of the table in the small dining room. Hart was on her right and Carla Lewiston on her left, and the rest of the table had Jack next to Carla, then Jacob Winston. On Hart's side of the table sat Clarence Christopher and Forrest Washington. Brian Ashleigh sat directly across from her at the other end of the table.

Hart spoke softly and asked her questions about her past. Morgan did her best to answer them as truthfully as she could. She steered the conversation toward him as often as she could, asking him about his life after he returned from Korea, although neither of them mentioned their common association to the Far Eastern country. Jack kept Carla busy in a conversation that didn't give her the chance to direct uncomfortable looks at Morgan. Morgan supposed it was natural for Carla to distrust and dislike her spouse's child, especially when she didn't know about her, but Morgan didn't like the looks she got any more than she'd enjoy dental surgery.

Morgan couldn't remember what they ate. She thought there was a lobster bisque, and her plate had a souffle on it when they moved from the table, but she had no memory of eating anything.

Back in the drawing room with a cup of flavored coffee in her hand, she stood next to the window with Jack.

"How's it going?"

"I'm not sure. I feel like a piece of sculpture. Hart plays the art lover who wants to examine every curve and obtain detailed explanations for each inch of the stone, while his wife hates art and wonders what the big deal is."

Jack laughed quietly. "I'll try to keep her away from you."

"Thank you, Jack, but like Eliza Doolittle, I think it's time she had her way with me."

Morgan smiled, set her cup down and turned toward Mrs. Hart Lewiston. Jack caught her arm and kissed her cheek. "Don't be too hard on her. She is the next First Lady."

He released her and Morgan walked across the room. Carla sat on a sofa and Morgan saw her stiffen as she approached. She smiled, hoping to make her relax. She'd been talking to Forrest Washington, who excused himself as she approached.

"Would you like more coffee?" Morgan asked. The older woman shook her head. Morgan took the seat next to her. "You'll make a wonderful First Lady," she said.

"If Hart is elected." She glanced at her husband, who was talking to Jack.

"I think he'll get elected."

"His announcement regarding you didn't help him."

She'd opened the door. Morgan knew this was the heart of her hostility. She resented her position being threatened by Hart telling the world she was his daughter.

Morgan leaned closer to her so no one around them could hear what she had to say.

"Mrs. Lewiston." She addressed her formally, knowing they weren't friends, and Morgan knew they wouldn't have the chance to become friends. "I am not here to threaten your position or to suddenly insinuate myself into Hart's life." Carla Lewiston looked at her with interest and question in her eyes. "I'm afraid there are things I cannot tell you. They involve most of the men in this room." Carla looked about. "They are not here because of candidate Hart Lewiston. When you leave here tonight you will never see me again."

Morgan waited for a sign. She expected relief in the woman's eyes, but she got nothing but stony silence.

"Why are they here?" she finally asked.

"I can't tell you." She paused and surveyed the room. "What I can tell you"—she stopped and looked back at Carla—"is that within a few days I'll be gone. Hart won't be able to find me. No one will." A pang of pain crushed her heart as she looked at Jack. "So you don't need to worry. Without my presence, the media will find something else to use as a torch. I'll fade into the woodwork. Your life will go on exactly as you planned it."

At that point Morgan placed her hand on Carla's. It was still cold. She smiled briefly and left the woman sitting alone. She wanted to go to her room. She wanted all these people out of here. She wanted to be alone with her thoughts, without the need to hold her head up, or smile, or conceal her real thoughts. She needed some time and space.

Jack caught her eye and she knew he understood. He came to her. He leaned close to her ear. "Remember what I said about red."

Morgan burst into laughter. She knew Jack had done it on purpose. He'd taken the fuel from her, making her laugh so she wouldn't cry.

"What's going on over there?" Morgan asked. Jack glanced back at the senator and the director of the FBI. "Your father," he said succinctly, making her freeze. "He wants to know what the FBI is doing to catch the people trying to kill you and how long you'll be sequestered in this house."

"Did they tell him?"

"Apparently not."

"I thought he understood his trip here was for this time only. That there would be nothing more."

"That might have been the original plan, but he's met you now."

"Maybe it's time I put an end to this."

"Want some help?"

She shook her head. Approaching the small group, they stopped talking and each took a step back. "I'd like to talk to

Hart, if you don't mind." Each man nodded as she looked at him. "Why don't we go for a walk?"

Morgan took his arm and led him toward the french doors. She opened them and they left the room behind. Morgan felt the sets of eyes trained on her. She led Hart away from the house. The sun set later during summer months. It was getting dark, but it was still light enough to see. The air was clear and brushed her naked shoulders. She stopped at the paddock fence.

"This is where Jacob convinced me to see you." She looked over the empty paddock. The horses were all in the stables.

"You didn't want to see me?"

She looked away. "Not at first. It's been a long time. I've lived my whole life without a father. It's too late for you to become one now."

"It's not too late for us to get to know each other."

"I think it is."

"Why?"

"You've read about me in the papers," she stated.

He nodded.

"Then you should know that tonight is it. Tomorrow you go back to your life and I . . . I continue with mine."

"It doesn't have to be that way. There must be something that can be done."

"They're doing it."

"We can hire an investigator."

"No—"

"Find out who is—"

"No," she shouted. "You're not listening to me. Everything that can be done is being done." She gripped the splintering fence and calmed her voice. "If there was a way, Jack would have found it."

"Jack?"

The single word was a volume in itself. Everything she felt about Jack was asked in the one word.

"Yes, Jack." She looked him straight in the eyes. A lump gathered in her throat. She swallowed it down. "I'll be leaving him too."

Suddenly he looked tired. Morgan had a thousand questions and no time to get answers. He probably had a thousand more for her. She called him her father, sometimes thought of him as her father, but there was nothing to bond them. She had a great love for her mother. When she thought of Rose Kirkwood, a feeling ran through her. She couldn't explain it. It was warm and bright and made her feel good. When she thought of Hart . . . when she looked at him, she had none of those feelings. He was a stranger.

She didn't know what he saw when he looked at her. Now that they had met, he could go back to his campaign and forget her. They had no tie, no connection, no love lost or found. They were two strangers who had a nice dinner. She had never been one to share childhood stories. Hers weren't the campfire variety and she thought they would make him feel bad if she told him the unvarnished truth. It was best for them to separate.

"I've done most of the talking tonight. Is there anything you want to ask me?" Hart asked.

"I'd like you to tell me about my mother."

CHAPTER 17

Clarence Christopher listened intently to the voice in his ear. He'd been waiting all through dinner for this call. Each time a waiter came in to serve another course he'd hoped to be called to the phone, but it hadn't happened. The entire evening had gone and nothing, but he smiled now.

"Are you sure you've got them all?" he asked.

"Fine," he said a moment later. "Make sure the report is on my desk in the morning."

He replaced the receiver. Jacob stood next to him.

"I take it they got them?" he asked.

"All of them," he said. "According to Carver, they are singing like birds. Where are Morgan and Jack?"

"Outside with the Lewistons. I guess this means they won't be needing my services."

"I think not. We have to be sure, but with what we have on them and what they tried to do, I'm sure their government will be willing to accept anything we present to keep the scandal off the front pages."

Jacob nodded. "It would be awful to discover that the presidential candidate was trying to kill the daughter of an American icon."

Clarence nodded. He heard the chopper blades as the helicopter returning Senator Lewiston and his wife took off.

"Why don't you deliver the good news to the happy couple," Clarence said to Jacob. "I'll let Ashleigh know."

Jack slipped his arm around Morgan as they walked back toward the house. The chopper carrying Hart and Carla Lewiston back to Andrews Air Force Base, where they would enter their limousine for the trip back into D.C., was overhead. The sound of the blades beating the air became fainter and fainter. Likewise the cars with Jacob, Forrest and Brian had also left for their return to the city. They were alone except for the staff. Morgan leaned into him and he tightened his arm around her.

"How did you like him?"

"I don't know," she said. "If we had time I suppose I could get used to the idea, but . . ." She left the sentence trailing. They didn't have enough time. She was scheduled to leave tomorrow for the program. He wouldn't see her again after tonight. She didn't even know it yet. Jack put off telling her until after Hart could get here and go.

He'd watched the two of them when the rotors started to turn. Carla had already entered the aircraft. Father and daughter faced each other awkwardly. Neither knew what to do. Jack put his hand on Morgan's back and pushed her. She hugged Hart like a stilted doll. He squeezed her and closed his eyes. Jack thought he genuinely would miss her.

They both would.

Inside, Morgan excused herself and went to her room.

"Before you go," Jack stopped her. "I have some news for you."

"I hope it's good news."

"It is."

She waited for him to say something.

"Well," she said. "Tell me."

Jack smiled. "I told Jacob I was going into the program with you."

A smile the size of the entire Commonwealth of Virginia spread across her face.

"But . . ." he trailed off.

"But?"

''But they caught the Koreans tonight. You won't be going into the program.''

Morgan opened her mouth, but nothing came out. Tears welled in her eyes and spilled down her cheeks. ''Are you sure, Jack?''

''I'm sure.''

''Are you really sure?''

He pulled her in his arms. ''On my honor.'' Jack didn't know it would make her cry. He knew she was happy, but her tears hurt him. He didn't ask her to stop or push her away. He held her until she stopped.

She stepped back when her emotions were under control. ''I'd better go wash my face,'' she said.

''All right, Red.''

She laughed through the tears and started for the stairs.

Jack started his nightly routine of making sure everything was secure. He checked the outside perimeter, contacting each of the stationed agents, making sure everything was secure. Then he'd go through all the downstairs rooms, looking for anything out of place, unlocked or unsecured. His hand was on the doorknob of the drawing room when the microphone in his ear activated.

''Jack, someone's just come over the fence on the south wall.''

''How many?''

''Three, but I think there are more.''

''Take care of them. I'm going to secure Morgan.''

He took the steps three at a time. Without knocking, he burst through the door of Morgan's room. She was in front of the mirror, pulling her hair down. She'd changed from the red dress and wore a white robe. She shifted when he opened the door.

''What's wrong?''

''Don't leave this room,'' he said and pulled the door closed.

He went back down the stairs, speaking into the mike as he went. ''Where are they now?''

''There are six of them and they're heading for the house. They've spread out.''

''Any around the back?''

''The back is secure.''

"Take them down," Jack ordered. "All other areas report."

"Caldwell, secure."

"Markum, secure."

"Greene, secure."

One by one they reported in. The only place it appeared they had penetrated was along the south wall. Jack headed around in that direction. Gunfire startled him. He hit the dirt, keeping his head down. Short bursts broke the silence. Jack crawled toward the sound. He pulled infrared glasses from a pocket near his gun and put them on. The world took on a red glow, and only the hot spots moved in the surreal world. With his gun in his hand, he chambered a shell and started toward the gunfire.

"Damn," he cursed after moving only a few feet. The helicopter was back. And it was landing. What was Lewiston doing here? He didn't need him too. He was a hanging target up there. Then the light came on and shone directly on the target. Jack smiled. "Thank you, Hart." He was showing them where the assailants were.

"They're retreating," he heard one of the agents say.

"Don't let them get away," Jack replied. They'd been chasing him too long. He wanted to know who they were and what they wanted.

The helicopter continued to follow the retreating men, keeping its light trained on them. Jack saw a hot spot through his glasses. The person extended his arm, aiming for the chopper. Lying on his stomach, Jack gripped his handgun with both hands, aimed and pulled the trigger. He heard the short scream of pain as the bullet found its mark. Jack had aimed for his shoulder. He wanted him alive. He wanted to look this one in the eye and make him tell the complete and utter truth.

He wanted to know who was really masterminding this operation. With everyone dead they would only be buying time until another assault could be planned or she went into the program. Jack wanted to prevent that if he could.

Another short burst of gunfire stopped his movement.

"This is Chandler. I've got two of them."

"Are they alive?" Jack shot back.

"Yes."

"Rayfield, two dead in front of me."

"Tomlison, report."

"This is Tomlison. I'm outside the fence. I got two coming over."

"I've got one down, but not secure by the west wall." Jack had to shout over the sound of the landing chopper.

"Neville here. I'm behind him, Jack." In seconds Jack saw the man he'd shot raising his good hand. Neville was on him, handcuffing him.

"Taylor?" The only female on the detail hadn't reported.

"I'm outside a truck about five hundred feet north of the front gate." Her voice was distinctive, low and purring as if she could roll all the letters in the alphabet. "There are two men inside. I could use some backup."

"Innis," her partner identified himself. "I'm on my way."

Jack got up off the ground. "Bring them in," he ordered. "Greene, make sure Mr. Lewiston and his wife are safe."

"On my way," Greene replied.

Morgan pulled a shirt over her head and grabbed her jeans. She wasn't staying here. She heard gunfire outside. Where was Jack? He was heading for it. He could get killed. She tried to put her jeans on while running. She tripped and hopped, all the while pulling at the stubborn pants. When she got them on, she slipped her sockless feet into sneakers. She took no time to tie the laces.

She heard more gunfire and then the helicopter. *What now?* she thought. If she never heard another helicopter it would be too soon. Yanking the door inward, she rushed into the hall. As she turned toward the front stairs a man stepped in front of her. Her heart lurched into her throat. He pointed a black gun at her.

"That's far enough," he said. He was dressed entirely in black. This one was only as tall as she was, but he was burly enough to knock the air out of her with only a swat.

Morgan stopped on the balls of her feet. She rocked back, feeling as if he'd pushed her.

"Who are you?" she asked, fear so evident in her voice she could hardly speak.

"Who I am is unimportant."

"What do you want?"

"More than you've got," he replied, reminding her of the green giant. "Now do what I say and we'll both be happy. That way." He indicated an area behind her. Morgan took a couple of steps backward. She didn't want to take her eyes off the gun. She didn't know this house. It was supposed to be safe. How did this man get up here? He wasn't part of the staff. She'd met all of them.

She had to turn so she didn't trip. Morgan knew if she did, he would use the gun as a club and she had no desire to be pistol-whipped. The walls had portraits on them. At the far end was a doorway that led to the back stairs. There was nothing between her and the door she could use. And this man had a gun pointed at her heart. She could do many things, but outrunning a bullet wasn't one of them.

Morgan opened the door and started down the stairs. His hand grabbed her shoulder. "Not so fast." She felt the cold steel through the T-shirt as he poked the gun in her back. Slowly she walked down the stairs. They ended up in the kitchen. Morgan hoped there would be someone there to help her, like Jack. She was disappointed. The room was empty.

Food and dishes in various stages of cleanup were spread about the room. The center island would have been huge in a normal kitchen but it fit this one. Above it was a massive wrought iron frame. Only a few of the gleaming copper pots hung from it. The rest were on the counter, the table and the sink. Morgan wondered where the kitchen help was. She hadn't heard any shots in the house, but there were other ways of killing people without bullets. She hoped they were all right.

"Through the door," he commanded.

Where was anybody? This place had a normal staff of ten, not including the gardeners. Tonight, with the dinner and Hart Lewiston in attendance, there was a complement of people at the house. She heard another burst of gunfire and jumped. She couldn't help glancing over her shoulder at the door to the front of the house.

"Don't look for help," the menacing voice said. "And if you think Jack Temple will come to your rescue, believe me when I tell you he's probably dead now."

Jack. Dead. Her heart sank, stopped, then lurched. She turned and pierced him with her eyes. "Jack is not dead," she spoke as if to a young child she was angry with.

"You hope," he said with as much venom as she had.

A door opened in the front of the house. Footsteps and voices reached her. The square man was distracted a second. He looked toward the door. Morgan didn't think. This was going to be her only chance to get help. She took two running steps and grabbed the frame hanging from the ceiling. Swinging across the array of pots on the counter, her feet scattered them as she arced to the other side. Hitting the floor she let go of the frame and pivoted to face her killer. He was raising the gun. Morgan went down and grasped the legs of the butcher block counter. She heaved it up. The bullet struck it, pitching shards of wood. She'd wonder later how she lifted the heavy table. The footsteps increased.

"Jack," she called. "He's got a gun."

Morgan didn't wait for Jack or for the gunman to come around the upturned table. Using it as cover, she rushed for the back door. She was out of it, slamming it behind her, before he could get to her. Going sideways on the porch, she took the banister in a solid jump instead of the steps. She spent several seconds hiding in the bushes expecting him to follow her. She heard no steps on the porch and no gunshots.

Leaving her hiding place, she made sure she didn't ruffle any branches or make any noise. She inched her way back to the porch. Silently peeking through the slats in the banister, she held her breath, expecting to see feet, prepared to quickly return to her hiding place. The porch was clear.

What was happening? She wanted to know. Grabbing the bottom support post, she heaved herself up to floor level. She could hear what sounded like fighting in the kitchen. She tiptoed toward the door, making sure she made no noise. She got close to the door when it suddenly burst open, slapping against the wall as it extended past the hinge design. Morgan jumped back, pressing herself against the wall. A man hit the porch hard on his back. He tried to get up, faltered, tried again, and finally passed out.

Morgan let out an audible breath. Jack came out on the porch. His stance was ready for battle. He must have been fighting with the refrigerator-sized man.

"Jack," she said when she could speak.

He whipped around. For a moment he stared at her. In two steps he had her in his arms. She breathed hard against him.

"Are you all right?"

"I'm fine," she said, her voice cracking. She tightened her arms around him. "I'm fine."

Morgan massaged her temples. She was tired and her head throbbed with pain. She hoped this signal wouldn't turn into one of her migraines, but it would be a miracle if it didn't. The night had been long, filled with the burning lights of police cars. Hart and Carla had returned.

Four men, including the one who'd held her at gunpoint, had sat on the rose and beige sofa as tight-lipped as statues. Hart looked pale as a sheet while Carla's face was blood red and her chin trembled.

Finally they were gone. Police cars lit up the night like a holiday procession heading down the driveway. Morgan and Jack stepped back in the door and went to the drawing room where Hart and Carla Lewiston remained.

"Thank God it's over," Morgan said.

"Not quite," Jack contradicted, causing her to look at him.

"What do you mean?"

He pulled the sliding doors closed and walked further into the room.

"Would you like to explain the rest . . . Mrs. Lewiston?"

Carla gasped at the sound of her name. So did Morgan. What did Carla Lewiston have to do with this?

"Are you out of your mind?" Hart took a step forward.

"I—I have no idea what you're talking about," Carla offered. The blood that had been so near the surface of Carla Lewiston's face drained to make her look like a Dracula victim.

Jack looked extremely comfortable in his role. "There's a

strange thing that's happened in the United States," he said. "A few years ago, terrorists started picking off candidates." He paced about the room. "Uncle Sam couldn't let that happen, not in a civilized country like this one." He stopped and faced her squarely. "So he instituted safeguards. Tonight was planned with extreme care. Everyone here, everyone with any reason to be here, was carefully screened. Many of them have worked this detail for years. Their loyalty is unquestionable. The house was swept more than once." He didn't bother to explain what swept meant. Morgan was sure Carla knew. "No one knew the location. Not you and not the senator."

"Jack, what are you accusing my wife of doing? She knows nothing about what happened here tonight."

"Doesn't she?" Jack glanced at Hart. Morgan was stunned. "Tell him!" Jack challenged Mrs. Hart Lewiston.

"Tell him what?" she asked. "Those men tried to kill us. And we don't have to stand here and be accused of being accomplices." She looked Jack up and down, giving him the same stare she'd give a scorpion.

"Where's your purse, Mrs. Lewiston?" Jack seemed to change directions.

"Jack, that's enough." Hart walked toward him. "If you're accusing my wife of something, come out with it."

He looked at Carla. "Last chance," he said.

"I have nothing to say."

"Morgan, would you open the door?" Jack addressed her. She did what he asked and the Lewistons' helicopter operator came in carrying a blue evening bag covered with sequins.

"Give me that." Carla lunged for the bag. Jack snapped it out of the man's hand.

"Thank you," Jack said to the pilot who left the room and closed the door behind him.

Quickly he opened the purse and reached inside. He pulled out a small device that looked like a portable phone. "This is what you used to send a signal to the men waiting on the ground. You brought them here and you sent them a signal to let them know you and the senator were in the air. Safely away from here. They could then come in and execute *your* plan."

"Carla, do you know what he's talking about?"

"No!" she assured him. "He's obviously making this up. Why, I don't know. Maybe he's responsible for the things that have happened to Ms. Kirkwood. Nothing really happened to her until he came into her life. Maybe he's working for the Koreans and trying to shift the blame."

Morgan thought she had a good argument. Jack could be working for anyone, but she knew better. The one piece of knowledge she had over anything Carla Lewiston knew was that Jack had held her in his arms.

"The Koreans have been caught, Mrs. Lewiston. Tonight before the FBI director left he received a phone call giving him the details of an FBI operation. The Koreans were picked up while you were having your souffle." He paused a moment. "It disturbed me to think that there were two separate groups trying to kill Ms. Kirkwood. Initially, we thought it was one until we tried to get to Clarksburg and found one group shooting at the other."

"How could I possibly do anything in Clarksburg?" she addressed Jack.

"We took down two helicopters. It took a while to trace them, but we discovered one of them was from Korea. The U.S. had sold it at an auction, but it ended up in Korean hands. The other helicopter, however, was attached to the Children's Relief Program."

Carla looked as white as a ghost. "Is this true, Carla?" Hart asked.

"Of course it isn't true," she denied.

"Then how do you explain this device?" Hart asked, taking it from Jack.

"It was planted, Hart. You've got to believe me. I've never seen it before."

"While the police were conducting their initial investigation in here, there was a crew outside, and they went over this little black box." Jack took it back from Hart. "The signal went to the truck that Taylor found outside the perimeter. One other thing they found was a complete set of fingerprints." He turned and faced Carla Lewiston. "Guess whose they are?"

"Carla?" Hart said.

She looked at him. "Oh, stop it," she said, venom dripping

from each word. "This is all your fault. We were doing fine. The election was a shoo-in." She paused. "But you had to destroy it because of her." She pointed at Morgan, who tried to remain still but stepped back as surely as if Carla Lewiston had sent a lightning bolt her way. "Hart, we had everything. We were this close." She used her thumb and forefinger to show a space only an inch wide. "Now look at us. We'll be lucky if we carry our home state. Winning is out of the question. The most we can hope for is a respectable loss."

"For that, Carla? For power?" Hart walked in front of her. "For the chance to be the First Lady you would *kill?*"

"It was my right!" she shouted. "I worked for it, following you around, taking jobs that were political because we were a power to be reckoned with. You think I liked working for those children? You think I liked getting in the dirt and having my shoes wet and grimy so a camera could take a picture that would further your career? We were a team, Hart. We wanted the same thing."

"No, Carla. I want to be president. I worked for it too, but I would never kill for it."

Hart glanced at Morgan. He came to where she stood next to Jack. "I'm sorry, Morgan. I didn't know. Carla and I have lived together for twenty-three years. I've known her for almost thirty. I would have sworn she was incapable of anything like this. I'm just so—" His voice cracked.

Morgan's heart broke for him. His world had ended. She flung herself into his arms almost before she knew what she was doing.

At that moment he became her father. She became his daughter.

"Is that sweet," Carla said, her words dripping with venom. "Father and daughter."

Morgan moved out of Hart's embrace and turned around.

"Well you haven't had the last word yet." Carla put her hand in her sequined pocket and pulled out a small gun.

Morgan gasped.

"Carla," Jack said. "That will solve nothing."

"Why didn't you stay invisible?" She ignored Jack, addressing her comments to Morgan. "You'd been in Missouri for all these years. Why didn't you stay there and leave us alone?"

"Carla, you don't want to do this," Hart said.

His voice seemed to make her remember him.

"And *you*," she spit the word. "You wouldn't listen to reason. We could have contained this. There was no reason for you to go public with the knowledge that you'd fathered a child." She took a deep breath. "How do you think I felt? Everyone whispering behind our backs. Wherever we went people stopped talking when we came in the room. And the polls. Do you want to talk about the polls?"

"Carla, this is temporary. We'll pull it off. Put the gun down."

Jack had been taking slow steps toward Carla, but she saw him and pointed the gun in his direction. "If you want a vent somewhere in the middle of your chest, take another step." Jack stood still.

"Carla, what do you want?" Morgan asked.

"I want you gone," she smiled. "I want to turn the clock back. Since I can't do that I'll settle for—"

"Carla," Hart interrupted her. "It's not worth it. You'll never get away with it."

"What a dramatic line," she said.

"He's right, Carla," Jack commented. "If the men outside that door don't kill you, you'll spend the rest of your life in jail."

"Put the gun down, Carla," Hart pleaded. "We can talk this over, the way we've talked over everything."

"We never talked *her* over," Carla shouted. Morgan had never seen anyone look at her with such hatred in her eyes. "When it came to her, it was just the two of you. I was left out." She lowered her voice. "Well I won't be left out anymore."

Morgan saw her aim. She was going to shoot her. Jack moved. Carla shifted her aim.

"No," Morgan cried and jumped in front of him as Carla pulled the trigger.

* * *

"Jack, let her go," the ambulance driver said. "We can't help her if you don't let her go."

Hart Lewiston pried Jack's fingers loose and the ambulance driver took her from him. There was so much blood. Jack couldn't remember seeing so much blood. How much did the body hold? How much had she lost? Was she alive? Would she die?

Jack watched as paramedics placed her on a gurney. One set up an IV drip. Jack's vision was too blurred to see what was in the plastic bag. Another medic mopped the blood from her shoulder. He applied something to the area and then they were wheeling her away. Jack took a step to go with her. Hart stopped him, applying pressure to his arm.

Jack turned away, his insides shaking. He walked behind the white-clad medicine men. Hart was by his side. Outside the red and blue lights of police cars and ambulances filled the yard for the second time that evening.

When Morgan jumped in front of him, Jack felt as if his entire life was over. Hart moved at the same time, subduing his wife, taking the gun from her and restraining her in the fierce fight she put up to get free. The room was suddenly filled with agents. Maids, butlers, cooks, gardeners, poured into the room. Hart sketched the details of what had happened while Jack held Morgan, whispering to her, brushing her hair back from her face. He didn't know who called the police or how long he held Morgan. They were there and she was being worked on.

Outside, the red and blue lights threw garish colors on the trees and bushes in front of him. Jack grabbed the leaf-laden branch of a bush near the front door with both hands as they lifted the white-sheeted gurney into the ambulance.

Hart remained with him. Jack felt numb on the outside but inside he felt as if a hot knife was cutting through him. His hands curved over the branches and he held on as if he could pull the bush from the ground roots and all.

He was in love with her. And she might die if she wasn't dead already. He couldn't turn around to see. Didn't want to face the reality that she might be gone, that he'd never told her and might not get the chance again.

He felt Hart move next to him and he looked sideways. The older man pushed both hands in his pants pockets. Jack had seen them shaking.

"Is she—" He couldn't finish the sentence. He didn't want to know the answer.

"We don't know," Hart said. "She's going to be fine, Jack. She's going to be fine."

Jack could tell by his voice he didn't know for sure. The medics told him nothing. She could be critical. Why had she done it? Why had she jumped in front of a bullet to save him? Didn't she know he'd rather take it than have her hurt?

He loved her.

He couldn't lose her.

Not now.

Jack had paced the tiny strip of floor before a single window in Virginia General Hospital for the past five hours. Hart slept awkwardly on a sofa inside Morgan's private room. FBI agents hovered outside the door, tired and longing for sleep. Morgan, swathed in white bandages across her left shoulder, breathed shallowly under starched sheets. She looked small and pale.

Sitting down in a chair near the bed, Jack took her hand and held it. It was warm and limp. In the subdued light he checked her fingernails for any sign that something might be wrong. They were pink and healthy looking. He let out a breath.

Hart shifted and Jack glanced at him. Jack had suggested that Hart return to the house and get some sleep, but he refused. He'd spent hours at the police station before coming to the hospital. Since his arrival in the early hours of the morning, he'd been like a beaten man.

His life was so altered by only a few hours. He had no idea when he woke yesterday morning that the day would end with his wife in jail and his daughter in a hospital. What this would do to his campaign was another story.

Morgan had been in and out of surgery. The doctor assured him she'd come through it fine and she would heal. She'd been lucky, he'd told him. Like Hart, Jack refused to leave her side.

He wanted to be there when she woke up. He wanted to tell her how much he loved her.

"Jack," Morgan said in a dry voice. Instantly he was on his feet, still holding her hand. He brought it to his chest where his heart beat so fast he thought it would burst. "Are you all right?"

He wanted to laugh. The sheer release of letting the pent-up tension go should do him good, but he didn't.

"How do you feel?"

"My shoulder hurts. And my throat is dry."

He poured her a cup of water and helped her up to drink it through the angled straw. "The anesthetic makes your throat dry."

"And the bullet?"

She remembered, he thought. "The doctor says you'll be fine."

"I guess my Olympic days are really over now." She tried to laugh, but ended with her face seized by pain and her hand reaching toward her shoulder.

"Let me call the nurse to give you something." Jack picked up the call button.

"No," Morgan said. "I want to stay awake for a while."

Jack took the hand she held up to stop him.

"What happened to Carla?"

Jack looked over at Hart. He was still asleep on the sofa. "She was arrested. You were right about there being two separate groups tracking us. The Koreans were behind one, but Carla was behind the other attempts on your life. She found out you were Hart's daughter and thought you were a threat to him and the presidency. She needed to get you out of the way." He looked at Hart again. "He really loved her."

Morgan peered at him. "She loved him too. Only a great love could make her do what she tried to do."

"You don't forgive her, do you? She tried to kill you."

"No," Morgan said. "I don't forgive her, but I do understand."

Jack looked at her. Her words seemed to have another meaning. She wasn't talking about Carla and Hart. She meant them.

"Morgan, I love you." He looked down at her, but she'd fallen asleep.

CHAPTER 18

"Did you say you loved me?" It was the first thing Morgan had said when she had awakened six weeks ago in the Virginia hospital. Jack had been by her bedside as he'd been when she woke the first time.

He'd gotten up from the chair he'd been sitting in and stood near the head of the bed. "I do love you," he nodded.

Morgan went to throw her arms around him, only to be reminded of the pain in her shoulder. She flopped back against the pillows.

"How long have you known?" she asked.

"Twelve years."

Morgan's eyes must have opened as wide as saucers. "You mean when we were in——"

He took her hand, interrupting her. "Yes, when we were in Korea. I gave what I felt about you other names. I told myself it was nothing special. That I could live without you. I told myself it wasn't love, yet the moment I found out you were in trouble I couldn't stay away."

The room was semi-dark. Sunrise painted the sky shades of gold and orange. Hart no longer slept on the sofa. Jack's voice was low and reverent, as if the two of them needed to whisper.

"You have to get well," Jack said. "The moment you're out of here we're getting married. Twelve years is a long enough engagement."

Morgan's recovery was nothing short of miraculous after that. She was happy. She didn't think she could ever be happier, but each day brought another surprise. The newspapers broke the story of her attempted murder by Carla Lewiston and Carla's subsequent arrest. Reporters descended on the hospital like Baptists at a revival. Jack and a battalion of private nurses kept everyone away from her, but the papers and television news stepped up programs of them, pulling out everything they had in their archives about her and Hart. Hart was constantly on the screen, and, strangely, his ratings in the polls went up.

Allie and Jan showed up the day after the story broke. Some of Morgan's other Olympic teammates sent flowers or fruit baskets. Get well cards poured in by the thousands, mostly from strangers. Jack got a kick out of teasing her about all the "friends" she had.

Days later her room looked like a florist's shop. The day she was released she took a phone call from the Olympic Committee. They asked her to officially open the games in St. Louis if she were well enough.

Morgan thought she'd die from happiness. She chose to do her physical therapy at Jan's camp, under the direction of her taskmaster friend and former team member. Leaving the hospital, she and Jack returned with Jan and Allie to West Virginia.

Only two weeks from the opening ceremony Morgan stood in the beam gym. The runway looked longer than she remembered it. The place was full of campers at different stages of exercise. Morgan had almost no pain from the gunshot wound. Her daily exercise routine helped her gain strength and muscle definition. She was nearly back to her normal self.

She concentrated on the beam. Freeing her mind of all thoughts, she looked only at her goal. Raising up on her tiptoes, she started the run. Picking up speed as she went, her arms pumping the air around her, she saw the springboard. With the precision of a broad jumper, she leapt into the air and came down on the springboard. Into the air she went, higher than she thought she'd ever done. She tumbled, her body completing a full revolution in the air and her feet coming down on the four-inch beam as if it were as wide as a diving board. She stood up straight, her arms extended. Then she did a one-hand cartwheel, turned and walked the length of the beam to her starting point. Concentrating again, she ran the short distance and reached for the sky. She did a full layout with a twist and landed on the soft padded floor without a hitch. Her arms went up and she smiled.

She smiled often these days and for no apparent reason. She'd think of Jack and a smile would break out on her face no matter where she was or what she was doing.

Jack and Morgan hadn't been separated since she was released from the hospital, but he'd gone to Montana last week. She missed him more than she thought possible. Working out with Jan, getting ready for a short performance in the Olympics, helped keep her mind off his absence. Her nights were the worst. She missed having his arms around her, making love with him, but she did have a few moments to give to Allie, who'd seized the opportunity to play wedding planner. She was planning Morgan and Jack's wedding.

Jan was in the back of the gym when she turned around. "Great!" Jan shouted. "You're ready."

"I think I'll try it again with the torch," Morgan said as she picked it up and came toward Jan. She was to light the torch at the opening, the Olympics' official notice to the world that the modern games were to begin.

"That's enough for today," Jan said. "We'll practice with the torch tomorrow. I'm sure you'll do the routine perfectly. Right now I believe there's someone waiting for you with a torch of his own."

Water sliced over Jack's head and down his back. Morgan's arms circled his neck and he kissed her. He knew she often ended her workout sessions with a long relaxing bath. Today she chose a hot shower and he thanked her for it. He'd been gone a week. It felt like a year. He was impatient. He needed her, wanted her, wanted to be inside her as fast as he could.

His body screamed for hers. He'd never known that before, never realized he could be so driven to one woman. She brought out the animal in him, and the lamb. He wanted to ram himself into her folds and he wanted to slide into her with all the tenderness he could muster.

The water sprayed them, creating a mist. Steam clouded the stall. He held her, taking her mouth, running his soapy hands over the curves of her slick-smooth body. She groaned in his mouth and he took the sound, his body aroused and growing harder with each drop of water that ran down his skin.

"I missed you," he said, only releasing her mouth long enough to reposition it. Her lips were soft, wonderful. His mouth was rough. His body was holding back, but his mouth drank everything she gave, and he craved more. Forcing her head back, his tongue swept into her mouth, taking possession, like a man who knew the exact moment of his death was near, like a man who wanted to savor, possess, fulfill, prolong the pleasure for just a second more, keep the blood pumping in his chest for just another moment so he could love just a moment more.

Water rained over them, spattering to the sides. It could have sounded like thunder, but the beat of his heart would have drowned it out.

He lifted Morgan, feeling her tingling breasts move up his chest as her legs wrapped around him. He pushed her against the wet, warm tile of the shower and entered her with the slowness of a man walking through knee-deep water. He felt her convulse as the first anticipated wave of pleasure shot through her. It shot through him like a quiet undertow, unsuspecting, sudden. Where there had been strength and sure-footing, he was fighting the shifting sand. Jack wanted to shout. Waves of pleasure shot through him and he filled her with slow, easy strokes.

Her arms wrapped around his neck as she gave him complete control of her. Jack didn't think she'd ever done that in her entire life. She couldn't move. He imprisoned her against the wet wall, their bodies as slick as the tile. He felt powerful and wonderful that she trusted him as she trusted no other.

Their bodies joined and rejoined as water poured between them. Her breasts were heavy and pouting each time they touched him, teasing him, giving him pleasure and taking it away, making him beg for it as the two of them held onto each other and the heat coming off their bodies threatened to boil the water at his feet, converting the sprays to steam as it came from the showerhead.

Jack kissed her again, his body lost to him, seemingly with a mind of its own. He moaned a low, animal sound, losing all control and moving faster and faster, pleasure, aching, longing pleasure, sensual, ragged, hot pleasure rioting through him, urging him on, making him feel as if the two of them would burn in a tsunami of fire that overtook them with a force neither could stop or deny.

Suddenly Morgan screamed, or was that his voice? They collapsed. He held her in place as the real world seemed to refocus. The water struck his body in needlepoints. His breath was audible, mingled with Morgan's. She slid down the wall, her legs, one at a time, brushing down his like the smooth liquid that drained through the shower floor. Jack didn't understand why he and Morgan still had substance, why they didn't dissolve and melt into the water and disappear too.

Neither of them had the strength to do anything. Their bones had turned to rubber and even simple things like turning off the water was denied them. Jack and Morgan remained there until their hearts returned to earth and marrow returned to their bones.

"You're incredible," Jack said.

"We're incredible," she said and turned the shower off.

This is where it had all started, Morgan thought. And it was a fitting place to end. She stood poised to begin her run. The arena just outside of St. Louis, Missouri, was packed to capacity with spectators. Sixty thousand people watched, cheering, waiting, anticipating the moment when she would light the flame signaling the beginning of the Olympic Games they'd waited four years to see.

Excitement as tangible as fine netting electrified the air. Morgan lifted the torch higher. The flame smelled of sulfur. Spotlights swept across her. She wore a white body suit with splashes of blue and red. The lights turned the white background a rainbow of colors.

Morgan looked ahead at her goal. She was going to do the part of the beam routine that had won her a gold medal at the Korean games, modified somewhat for the lighted torch. She looked up. Jack Temple stood at the end of her run. He was in nearly the same place he'd been twelve years ago when her concentration focused only on him. She smiled and started her run toward a future that was bright and filled with love.

Toward Jack.

EPILOGUE

". . . that you will faithfully execute the office of the President of the United States . . ."

January 20th. The day was cold. The wind blew from the Potomac River up Pennsylvania Avenue to the steps of the Capitol. Morgan turned her coat collar up closer about her neck. Jack's arm pulled her into his side, offering her a bit of his warmth. She looked up and smiled. Tears swam in her eyes. She was happier than anyone deserved to be.

Her grandfather and father stood in front of her. She had Jack and she had them—a family. Allie and Jan stood in the front row facing them.

She and Jack had gone to Montana when everything was finally over. There they'd been besieged by phone calls from other team members concerned about her. With Jack's help, her teammates had joined Hart's campaign. Morgan's heart swelled to discover how many friends she really had.

Hart won the election, not by the huge majority he'd hoped for, but by a hangnail, as one reporter put it. Yet a win was a win. Morgan knew even if it were by a tenth of a point, it counted. Supreme Court Justice Angus Lewiston administered the oath of office to his son while she and Jack joined thousands of people who looked on. Even if he only eked by in the electoral college, he had four years to prove his worth. Morgan had no doubt he would succeed.

It was a proud day.

Carla Lewiston had been indicted on charges of attempted murder, conspiracy, kidnapping and a long list of other charges Morgan couldn't remember. She'd wanted to be the First Lady. Little did she know that without her attempts to cover everything up, to keep the public from discovering the family skeleton, everything would have worked out as she wanted it. Morgan felt sorry for her. She had so much, but she wanted so much more.

"I, Hart Lewiston, do solemnly swear that I will faithfully execute the office of President of the United States, and I will to the best of my ability, preserve, protect, and defend the Constitution of the United States."

Jack tightened his arm around her as Hart spoke the oath. Morgan's heart was in her eyes when she met Jack's gaze. It wasn't so far from the alleys of Southeast to the steps of this famous landmark, but Morgan never dreamed she'd make the trip.

Or that the man of her dreams would be standing by her side when she did.

Dear Reader,

I hope you enjoyed spending time with Morgan Kirkwood and Jack Temple. I enjoy crafting stories and nothing pleases me more than a good romantic suspense. When Morgan Kirkwood and Jack Temple popped into my head the fighting had already started. *More Than Gold* showed me Morgan's dream. It seems simple to most of us who have a loving family, but for her the dream meant *More Than Gold*. Her triumph over the odds had me singing too.

As the Olympics begin this month, I hope you will enjoy them more knowing that the athletes go through years of painful preparation for their moment to shine.

I receive many letters from the women and men who read my books. Thank you for your generous comments and words of encouragement. I love reading your letters as much as I enjoy writing the books.

If you'd like to hear more about *More Than Gold,* other books I've written or upcoming releases, please send a business size, self-addressed, stamped envelope to me at the following address:

Shirley Hailstock
P.O. Box 513
Plainsboro, NJ 08536

You can visit my Web page at the following address -
http://www.geocities.com/Paris/Bistro/6812

Sincerely yours,

Shirley Hailstock

Coming in November from Arabesque Books . . .

__SECRET DESIRE by Gwynne Forster
1-58314-124-3   **$5.99US/$7.99CAN**
Victims of a harrowing robbery, widow Kate Middleton and her young son are rescued by police captain Luke Hickson. Neither of them expect, much less welcome, an instant spark of attraction. But when trouble strikes again, Kate realizes the only place she feels safe is in Luke's embrace. . . .

__SHATTERED ILLUSIONS by Candice Poarch
1-58314-122-7   **$5.99US/$7.99CAN**
When a hurricane damages fiercely independent Delcia Adams's island campground, she must hire Carter Matthews to help her rebuild. The more she lets him help, the more she discovers that the handsome stranger is a man of dangerous secrets . . . and irresistible fire.

__BETRAYED BY LOVE by Francine Craft
1-58314-163-4   **$5.99US/$7.99CAN**
All Maura Blackwell wants is money to save her grandfather's life and all her former flame Joshua Pyne wants is a child of his own. When the two strike a bargain to wed, neither of them expect an undeniable love—or the inexplicable urge to turn their make-believe marriage into the real thing.

__A FORGOTTEN LOVE by Courtni Wright
1-58314-123-5   **$5.99US/$7.99CAN**
As the administrator of a major ER, Dr. Joni Forest faced down personal and professional turmoil to make the unit respected. Now, the ER's former head, Dr. Don Rivers, is back, challenging her leadership—and reigniting the simmering desire between them. Now, the couple must come to terms with unresolved pain and career pressures in order to claim true love. . . .

Call toll free **1-888-345-BOOK** to order by phone or use this coupon to order by mail. *ALL BOOKS AVAILABLE NOVEMBER 1, 2000.*

Name_____

Address _____

City _____ State _____ Zip _____

Please send me the books I have checked above.

I am enclosing $_____

Plus postage and handling* $_____

Sales tax (in NY, TN, and DC) $_____

Total amount enclosed $_____

*Add $2.50 for the first book and $.50 for each additional book.
Send check or money order (no cash or CODs) to: **Arabesque Books, Dept. C.O., 850 Third Avenue, 16th Floor, New York, NY 10022**
Prices and numbers subject to change without notice. All orders subject to availability.
Visit our website at **www.arabesquebooks.com**.